before i go

before i go

riley weston

CAMPFIRE
PRESS

LOS ANGELES, CA

Campfire Press
15030 Ventura Blvd. Suite 706
Sherman Oaks, California 91403
Visit our website at www.campfirepress.com

First Hardcover Edition: September 2006

ISBN 10: 0-9779543-2-3
ISBN 13: 978-0-9779543-2-2

Library of Congress Cataloging-in-Publication Data

Weston, Riley.
    Before I Go: a novel / Riley Weston. – 1st ed.
        p. cm.
    ISBN: 0-9779543-2-3
    1. Women – Fiction. 2. Young Adult – Fiction. 3. Ice Skating – Fiction.
4. Mothers – Fiction. 5. Olympic Ice Skating – Fiction. 6. Love Story – Fiction
7. Title - Fiction

2006926391

10   9   8   7   6   5   4   3   2   1

Printed in the United States of America

BOOK DESIGN BY DOTTI ALBERTINE

For my Uncle Bobby
who continually shows me
the truest example
of faith and fortitude

CHAPTER 1

There were enough shavings on the ice for one hundred snow cones or more. But Madison Henry was oblivious.

Any other normal six-year-old girl would have fantasized about the color and taste of those snow cones. If the color was a deep red, she knew it would taste like the sweetest of strawberries, blue would taste like the summer blueberries you pick at the end of July and rainbow would be the best ever. Not green, for that would mean lime and most children would rather eat stale dog food.

Plenty of snow cones were outside on that very hot and sticky Fourth of July afternoon. It was the kind of day that just might end in a thunder and lightening storm. Children and adults of all ages lined the small main street waiting for the parade to come around the corner. Some carried jackets or umbrellas, and others were shirtless, willing to risk the weather god's wrath.

But Madison was inside the only ice arena in Willow Point, California, where the temperature always remained a constant forty-seven degrees.

It had always been like this. From the very beginning of her life, Madison Elizabeth Henry was destined to skate. And not the kind of skating where a mother dressed her child up in a cute little outfit for the lame public skating session on Sunday afternoons. This was different; and Madison and her mom, Annie, were very aware of that.

Her mother had introduced her to the ice when she was barely walking on her own. Even now, Madison loved to hear the story over and over, as if for the first time. How when she was three, as soon as her mother laced up her skates, Madison grabbed her mother's hands, and looked seriously into her face. "This is what I'm going to be when I grow up. A skater."

Her mother laughed deeply, throwing her head back as far as she could. "You haven't even stood on the ice yet!"

Madison smiled and replied seriously, "I don't need to, Mommy. This is going to be my life. For all of my life. I just know it."

Annie Henry stopped laughing and stared at her daughter, a faint smile on her lips. "Let's see if we can get you to stand on the ice first. Then we'll see about that shining Olympic career of yours. Deal?"

"Okay. Deal."

Nothing had touched the ice yet. Not a hole, nick or crevice was anywhere to be seen. Madison remembered looking at it up close for the first time. A big cube, she thought. Her own personal ice cube.

Annie walked Madison to the edge of the ice, holding on to her as tightly as she could without scaring her daughter. She watched like only an anxious mother could as Madison faltered slightly. Annie loosened her grasp of Madison's hand, one finger after another. Madison put one skate timidly on the ice and looked around the empty, spacious rink with determination. Madison's other skate gradually touched the ice. Within seconds, as the story went, Madison was skating completely on her own. Annie skated a few feet behind her, just in case she was needed, all the time praying she wouldn't be. When it was time for dinner, Annie had to literally pull a crying Madison off the ice with the promise of returning the very next day.

At the end of each day, Annie had to promise, again and again, they'd return the following morning. Every new day segued into the next three years.

Madison stood in the center of the ice, hands on her hips, her skate purposefully nicking hard on the ice. She glanced off to the side where her coach stood uncompromisingly rigid. "Well?"

"Do it again!" a woman's voice yelled.

"But I did it like more than twenty times already!"

"Well, then I guess it wasn't good for like more than twenty times." The woman looked at Madison sternly, trying desperately not to crack a smile. "Come on, Maddie. You can do better. I know you can. Now. Go back to your first position and try it again."

Madison rolled her eyes and skated a few feet back from where she stood before. She began skating, slowly at first, and then picked up speed, turning a corner.

"Head up, Maddie."

Madison lifted her head high. She switched her feet around effortlessly and skated backward.

"Arms!"

"I know!" Madison raised her arms to a beautiful position.

"Get ready...okay...now!"

Madison suddenly threw herself into the air; her arms snuggled tightly against her body. She made two complete circles in the air before landing almost perfectly on her right foot, her left leg extended gracefully behind. She stopped herself with the front tip of her skate and looked up with big brown eyes. There was what seemed to Madison, the longest pause of her young life. Then she heard those three little words ring in her ears.

"Do it again." The voice offered no explanation or understanding. Madison didn't fight or question it. She simply skated back to her beginning position.

"Feel the music, Madison."

"But there isn't any."

"Well, pretend that there is, okay?"

Madison repeated the first few movements. Just as she was supposed to jump, she spun out of it and stopped herself.

"What's going on? You can do this."

Madison shrugged her shoulders ever so slightly. "I'm tired, I guess."

"You wanna stop?"

Madison stared down at her skates and remembered when she got them. Her mother had bought them for her barely a year ago. They were so white she almost didn't want to wear them. And stiff. God, they were stiff. They hurt her ankles and shins so much after wearing them the first few times, she soaked in the tub for an hour each night. Now the skates were so worn, the wrinkles in the leather were filled with specks of dirt up and down the skates.

Maddie looked up. "I'm okay. I don't want to stop." She skated a few feet away and slowly turned back. With all the courage she could muster, she asked the inevitable. "Am I gonna miss the parade?"

The coach moved her sweater up from around her slender wrist and glanced down at her watch. She looked at Madison with a small smile that was unapologetic. "Yeah." She pulled her sweater back down, covering the reminder of time gone by. "Let's try it again."

Madison resumed her starting position. She took the deepest breath a six-year-old could and skated. She skated faster and faster. As she rounded the far corner, she flipped her direction backward.

"And...now!"

Madison heard the voice ricochet through the rink and she flew through the air. The move was polished and extraordinary. She landed with a huge smile covering the better part of her tiny face.

"That's it! See? That's what the judges will be looking for. You understand now what I've been saying?"

"Yeah, yeah. I know. I understand." Madison's eyes lit up. She stopped in front of her coach. "Can I go now?"

The coach smiled to her star skater. "Yeah. You can go."

Madison skated as fast as she could off the ice. Her rear-end hit the bench with a thud so loud, it was destined to bring a colorful bruise. She removed her skates with unbelievable speed and threw them on the rubber flooring beneath the bench.

"Just be careful."

Madison grabbed her shoes and jumped up. "Yep."

"Watch out for the—"

"...cars! I know, Mom!" Madison was out of her sight.

Annie Henry smiled to herself and skated toward the rink opening, like she had so many times before. She moved to the huge pile of skating gear Madison had once again left behind. She gathered skates, socks, leg warmers, gloves and sweatshirts and tossed them into the large, threadbare duffel bag. She smiled, remembering how her daughter looked in the morning. How they both looked when they arrived outside the rink at five-thirty in the morning. It was usually still dark out and the sun had yet to warm the town. They piled on layers and layers of clothes. Even in the summertime. Sweaters, turtlenecks, mittens, and scarves sometimes, too, if it was really chilly. But, it never failed, she thought. Within the first ten minutes, Madison had stripped down to the bare necessities, leaving the familiar pile for Annie to gather at the end of their practice.

Madison ran out the front door of the old rink. The sun shone directly into her face, making her eyes and nose scrunch up at the bright yellow light. Immediately, she heard the sounds of an off-beat band marching down the street. Up ahead, people had already started to follow the parade.

The townspeople always did this at parades. They marched along behind the last drummer in the band, as if to include themselves in the procession. As if it was their right. They all gathered near the Town Square, in front of Mr. Trundle's grocery store. The band continued to play old-time songs that some of the people actually danced to. There were clowns making weird things out of balloons, and games and food booths were set up everywhere you looked.

Madison took off in a dead run. *Maybe this will be the year*, she thought. Maybe she'd catch the last bit of the parade. It wasn't that she didn't enjoy the events that continued on throughout the day. She just wanted to see the actual parade this time. Like all the other children. But as Madison neared the end of the street, her heart sank and her feet came to a halt. She watched as the tail end of the parade disappeared around the bend. She had missed it once again. Her face caught up with her heart and feet, and slowly fell to severe disappointment. She glanced back toward the rink and saw Annie there, waiting for her to return. Madison gave Annie a look that only a devastated child can give a mother.

Annie shrugged with a 'what can you do?' kind of face. And really, what could she do? The Junior Championship Competition was in two weeks. They needed to practice. They didn't need to watch a parade.

A lonely clown across the street caught Madison's attention. He sat down on a beat-up bench and pulled off his red nose. Madison watched him curiously as he took off his rainbow wig and white gloves. Her eyes wandered over to one lonely yellow balloon floating next to the fatigued clown. It was like the reject balloon none of the other kids wanted. It was dirty and there was hardly any air left in it, causing it to float at her eye level. But, it didn't matter. To Madison, it was the greatest thing she'd ever seen.

Madison ran as fast as she could across the street. Her hand was outstretched ready to grab the balloon. But as her hand clasped the ratty string hanging down, another small hand grabbed it too, just above hers. Madison looked up and faced her enemy. In front of her stood an adorable seven-year-old boy. They stared at one another, neither one ready to loosen their grip on the string. Neither one ready to lose.

Madison smiled quickly to the boy. She knew how to play the game. "What's your name?"

The boy replied with attitude. "I'm Jackson Wellington III."

Madison looked him over. He was dressed rather well for a parade. Behind Jackson stood a maid in uniform waiting patiently. Madison's eyes met Jackson's. "Well, *Jack*...What do you think you're doing?"

"What am I doing?"

"Are you deaf? I said, what are you doing as in—what are you doing with my balloon?"

Jackson smiled slightly. He had met his match and he knew it. "What makes this *your* balloon?"

Both Jack and Madison looked at the clown now practically undressed. The clown looked at both of the kids. It was obvious he wanted no part of this and quickly walked away.

"Listen, the thing is, I've missed this parade every year and all I want is this stupid balloon. I'm, like, an *ice skater*. A real one. So, I'm sure, *now*, you understand. So...bye bye." Madison tried to take the balloon from Jack's hand, totally convinced her speech had worked.

But Jack didn't let go of the string and he stopped her as she tried to walk away. "The thing is...what was your name?"

Madison, in total disbelief, turned back to Jack. "Madison Henry. And there are no fancy-schmancy numbers after my name, by the way."

Jackson nodded. "See, the thing is, Madison, I never get to see the parade either. My father works a lot and never remembers to come home on time. All *I* want is the stupid balloon."

They had a major face off. Neither one budged.

Annie drove up next to them and rolled the window down, yelling out to Madison. "Come on, Mad. We've got balloons at the house. Give the balloon to the nice boy."

Without breaking her intense eye contact with Jack, she answered Annie. "It's not the same, Mom."

"Come on, Mad," Annie said reproachfully.

Madison put on her most sincere face; the face that got you that fourth cookie when you were only allowed two. With more determination than ever, she spoke to Jack, "Okay. Here's the deal," Madison paused dramatically, "I'll be your *best* friend if you give me the balloon."

Jack looked directly into Madison's eyes. There was a connection there that most adults would never know in their lifetime and Madison and Jackson had it. Right then and right there.

"You don't have to be my best friend. You can have it for nothing." Jackson slowly let go of the balloon and walked away.

Madison frowned slightly. This wasn't part of her plan. "Hey! Jackson with the numbers!"

Jack slowly turned around to her.

"Just so you know. I meant that. The best friend part. And I always keep my promise. Just so you know."

Jack smiled at Madison. "Yeah. Sure."

Madison watched Jack walk over to the maid and then walk away. She smiled and jumped in Annie's car, balloon in hand.

She had won.

∽ Chapter 2 ∽

Being eleven wasn't the same as it had been when Annie was eleven. And she knew it. Every night, a story appeared on the news about another child, *a child*, doing something horrible to others, or something horrible being done to them. Annie knew she worried too much about Madison. But Maddie was her daughter, *her life*. She couldn't, or wouldn't, fathom anything ever happening to her. So, when Madison had asked about a sleepover with Jack a few weeks before, Annie had thought long and hard. Sure, they'd done it many other nights. And nothing had ever happened. But, things were changing. They were bigger now. Maybe older was a more accurate word. Okay...so more sexually aware of their growing body parts is *really* what she was thinking. Annie didn't usually go to her husband for advice. Or, better put, an opinion. But this time, she did.

David was laughing to the point of hysteria by the time she got to her concerns with the imminent sleepover.

"David. This isn't funny. They are getting to an age where they're...well, they are more aware of their bodies, that's what."

The thought of anything remotely sexual going on between the children was enough to send David into another round of uncontrollable laughter. He could hardly speak. "Aware of their bodies? *Sexually?* Annie, really. Maddie's ten years old and, for the record, doesn't have a body. Jack's what? Eleven? You've got to be kidding me."

Annie took immediate offense. She didn't like to be laughed at. *Especially* by her husband. *Especially* when she could have made this decision on her own, like usual. "All I'm saying is, at what point do we stop allowing overnight visits? When they're fifteen? Sixteen? When Maddie asks to go on...on birth control?

David gasped for air. He looked over at his wife's face and knew the expression. He should after more than nineteen years of marriage. He calmed himself down and sighed. "Come here." He waved Annie over to him. Slowly and somewhat reluctantly, she moved to the bed and lay down next to him. David put his arm around her and squeezed her shoulder. "Listen. Maddie has *one* friend. That's it, Ann. Besides you and me, he's all she's got."

Annie looked straight ahead. Her voice was barely above a whisper. "She's all I've got too, David."

David could have taken this personally, but he knew it was true. Madison was the most important thing in Annie's life. Maybe the only thing. He lowered his chin to her head and kissed the top of it. Not knowing how long it would be before his opinion was asked again, David paused. These moments didn't come often and he loved being next to his wife. "How about this? How about the sleepover is a go this time around. Then, we'll just, sort of...reevaluate from this point on. How's that sound?"

Annie thought about the proposition. She waited a few

moments before looking up into David's eyes. She kissed him gently on the lips. "Deal." As David moved in for another, possibly more passionate kiss, Annie jumped off the bed. She quickly moved to the closed bedroom door and opened it slightly. "I'm going to tell Maddie it's okay." With a quick smile, she was out the door, leaving David alone. Again.

∞∞∞∞∞∞∞∞

David would never ever forget the day. The day he met Annie. The day his life changed forever. He could recall every single detail like it was yesterday. It was a ridiculously cold day. Colder than it had been in years. David had no choice but to help his father when the ice rink two towns away called in with an emergency. He still remembered walking out of his house and suddenly stopping, for the wind was so bitter and haunting, he could not move his feet. His father was already in the idling truck, yelling for him to move it along.

Everybody in town was calling his father that week. David had had plans that specific day. Big plans, he had told his father. Any fib, white lie or outright completely made-up story would do. Anything, as long as he didn't have to help his dad. He was twenty years old and not a kid anymore. He had an image to protect. Well, not really, but it sounded good when he tried arguing his way out of the trip. But as his luck would go, David's father dragged him along, clearly not buying any of his outlandish fables. It happened every few months, helping his Dad, and always in the hundred degree heat or the icy cold winters. David was still small enough to shimmy through the crawl spaces above the ceiling to fix whatever part of the air conditioning or heating unit needed it. So on that day,

David and his father were off to the ice rink to fix the air conditioning. In the *winter*. This was not going to be an ordinary day.

She was alone, sitting on the bottom bleacher. She wore work-out clothes and had ice skates on her feet. The second they entered the rink, David saw her. She was the most beautiful girl he had ever seen. The problem was, he didn't just think it. He said it. Out loud. Loud enough for Annie Bergdon to turn and look in David Henry's direction.

She stared at David for what seemed like forever to him. Then slowly, the smallest of smiles emerged on her face. That was the very second David fell in love.

CHAPTER 3

Madison and Jack laid side by side in his bright orange pup tent, their heads sticking out of the narrow opening. It might have seemed weird to anyone else, for the two of them to be having a sleepover. Not to them.

Both of them propped themselves up with pillows shoved underneath their chins. A large duffel bag sat just outside the tent, closest to Madison. Off to the other side was a worn, old cardboard box. Jack and Madison looked up at the star-filled sky. The moon was full and bright, lighting up small sections of Jack's extensive backyard.

Madison finally broke the silence. "Is your dad going to send you to that boarding school?"

"Nope."

"How come? I thought he was definitely going to make you go."

Jackson frowned. "You trying to get rid of me or something?"

Madison laughed out loud. "Not yet." She blew off the question. "I just thought you'd never be able to change his mind. He had that stupid brochure all filled out and everything." Madison changed her voice to that of a stuffy older man. "Jackson Wellington III. He'd be a wonderful candidate for your oh-so-sucky school." Madison looked over to Jackson. "What'd you say to him anyway?"

Jack avoided her look and shrugged. "Nothing."

Madison stared at Jack. She wanted an answer. They had been friends for over four years and she knew when Jack wasn't telling her something. It had been the cause of far too many arguments and disagreements in the past. She nudged him. "Tell me what you said."

"It doesn't matter. It's stupid. Now *you're* being stupid for asking so many stupid questions."

Madison still stared. Only her eyebrows rose, ever so slightly. She was not about to budge.

"What? What do you want me to say?"

Madison propped herself up higher on her elbows. "Jackson Wellington. You tell me right now what you said to your father. You know I hate when you do this. You make such a stinking big deal out of everything when you finally say it out loud, it is so—"

"Okay, already!" Jack thought for a moment, clearly searching for the right words. If it hadn't been so dark in the tent, Madison might have noticed Jack's face redden slightly. "I...uh...I just told him that I couldn't go, you know, because um...because of you."

"Oh." Madison sunk her chin down a few inches into her pillow and resumed her focus outside the tent. Suddenly, Madison's eyes popped open wider and she jumped back up. "*Me?* Why? Why'd you use me as your reason?"

Jack shrugged nonchalantly and tried his best to blow it off. "I don't know what the heck you're getting all crazy for.

I just told him, you know, it'd be way too hard to break in another best friend." Almost afraid of what he had just admitted, Jack covered immediately. He rolled over onto his back and looked up in a cocky way. "It's hard being the rich and talented Jackson Wellington III. No one wants to be friends with someone like me. You know?"

Madison laughed. "Yeah. I know." Madison rolled onto her back, too.

They sat in silence for a moment. Both looked up to the sky and watched the moon slowly change in front of them.

This time, Jack broke the silence. "Where's your watch?"

Madison looked around the tent. Both of them sat up and searched, barely fitting in the small space.

Jackson found it first. "Almost one o'clock. Are you ready?"

"Sure." Madison's eyes sparkled. With a straight face she added, "Obviously being rich and talented makes you a wuss who can't stay up with the athletically brilliant and extremely cute people. I understand." Madison giggled her way out of the sleeping bag. "Don't even try to think of a comeback for that. I'm too good and you'd just embarrass yourself." Madison stood up, hands placed coyly on her hips.

Jack jumped out of his sleeping bag. "You're just lucky I like you sometimes." He carefully picked up the box by Madison and carried it about ten feet from their tent.

Madison followed close behind him. "I told you not to try a comeback, Jackson. You suck at it."

Jackson placed the box next to a huge hole that had already been dug in the ground.

"Think your father is going to kill us when he sees the hole?"

Jack smiled a devilish grin. "My plan is that he won't ever find out. I mean, by the time we dig it up, I don't know. He might even be dead or something."

Madison frowned and hit Jackson lightly on the head. "That's a horrible thing to say, Jack. Take it back."

"What? I'm just saying..." Jack shrugged.

"Take it back anyway."

"Fine. I take it back, okay?" Jack carefully lowered the box into the dirt. He started to close the top of the box and stopped with a confused look on his face. He looked up to Madison standing over him. "Wait. Why are we doing this again?"

"Cause then when we're, you know, older and stuff, we can dig up the treasure box and remember being best friends."

Jackson thought about this for a second. "Why are we calling it a treasure box?"

Madison looked at Jack with a disgusted look on her face. "Honestly, Jack. You scare me. Just put the box in the hole."

"Right. Okay. Here it goes." Jack securely fastened the first two flaps on top of the box. Then he methodically folded down the other two. He took a handful of dirt and threw it over the cardboard.

"Wait!" Madison stopped Jack's hand from throwing more dirt.

"What."

"I forgot something."

Jack rolled his eyes. He pushed the dirt away and removed the box. He talked to himself as he lifted the box out of the ground. "So much for waiting 'til we're old."

Madison yelled back from a few feet away. "I heard that, butthead." Madison searched frantically through her duffel bag.

Jack watched with half anger, half amusement as Madison turned her bag upside down, spilling out all of the contents.

"Unbelievable." Jack shook his head.

Her face lit up and she grabbed a small item from the bottom of her pile. She ran back to Jack and slowly opened her hand. In her palm sat what was left of the gross yellow balloon from the parade four years earlier. Most of the string had disappeared and what was left was frayed and dirty.

Jackson could not believe it. "You kept this?"

"It's the balloon you gave me."

"I know what it is. I just, I don't know. I can't believe you kept it all this time."

"Well, I did. I mean, obviously, since there it is."

Jack was totally blown away. Only one other thing he'd ever given anyone had had an impact on him. Right before his mother died, Jackson made a card. It wasn't the prettiest, or even the best-colored. But he made that get-well card for his mom. His mother had cried, not because she was so sick, but because, she told Jackson, it was the prettiest, best card she had ever gotten. When she died, Jackson put the card in the casket with her, right before she was buried. Now it seemed Jackson had done something else that mattered.

Madison knelt down next to Jackson, their faces cheek to cheek. She stole a quick look at Jack and then back to the balloon in her hand.

"Are you gonna put it in there or not?"

"Yeah." Madison smiled ever so slightly.

Jack opened the box and looked inside. He smiled at Madison and reached his hand out to her. Madison extended her small hand to Jack and he took it in his. For the briefest of moments, they stayed just like that, their hands woven together by a crummy, dirty old balloon. Jack finally took the balloon from her and carefully placed it on top of the other items. He closed the box and gently dropped it back down into the hole.

Jack tried to break the weird moment with Madison. "You forget anything else?"

Madison gave Jack one of her special nasty faces. "No, ya dweeb." She threw dirt on the box with Jack. "Except, the *red* balloon."

Jack frowned slightly. "What red balloon? I didn't give you a red balloon."

Madison hid her smile behind her long, wavy, sandy-colored hair. "I didn't say *you* gave it to me, did I?"

Jackson stopped throwing dirt in the hole. He turned to Madison angrily. "What? You were gonna put some other dumb balloon in *our* box? I thought the whole reason we did this was because it was about *us*. Not somebody else who gave you a balloon."

Madison continued covering the box. "Just checking."

"*Checking?* Checking what?"

Madison smiled at Jack. "Checking to make sure this is as important to you as it is to me. That's what."

"Well, what does the red balloon have to do with anything?"

"Nothing. There is no red balloon. I was making sure you'd take this very seriously, I guess. Take our friendship seriously. Because, if someone else had given me a balloon and I kept it all this time, well, it would mean someone else meant as much to me as you did and I would hope that would make you jealous."

Jackson stared at Madison, completely dumbfounded. "I swear to God, you are the craziest person I know and all I hope is when we do open this box someday, I understand half of the stuff you say."

Madison smiled. "I bet when the box is opened...I bet you understand everything about me, Jackson Wellington."

Jackson shook his head at Madison. "Can I please finish covering the box now?"

She nodded, "Uh-huh."

Jack finally broke his gaze and threw dirt on top of the box and around each side. He mumbled to himself as the dirt slowly hid the cardboard. "Jeez. A year later and we're still here covering the damn box."

Madison watched him. Not helping.

"Do you mind?"

Madison tried not to laugh out loud. "No."

"I could use some help with this."

"I'm sure you could." Madison took only a handful of dirt and let the small amount in her hands gently sift through each of her fingers. Clearly, she was no help.

"You know, Miss-you-think-you-know-everything. How exactly are you going to remember where we hide this thing? I mean, I have a big back yard. We're never going to find it, you know."

Madison threw another small finger-full of dirt on the top of the box. "I'll remember where it is."

The box was totally covered. Jack leaned to his left and carefully grabbed a square of grass to cover the dirt. He placed the grass over the box and pushed it down in line with the lawn. "That's it. Done. No thanks to you."

Madison stood up and mimicked him. "No thanks to you." Jackson pressed the piece of grass in a little harder, making sure the seams couldn't be seen. Madison looked up at the night sky filled with stars. "By the way, I saw all your girlfriends."

Satisfied with the way the grass looked, Jackson stood up. "What girlfriends? I don't have any girlfriends."

Madison shook what little dirt she had on her hands off. "Yes, you do too. I saw them. From the soccer game last week." She walked a few steps away from Jack. "It's actually sad. They look so stupid yelling to you." Madison threw her hip to the side in a flirtatious way. She raised her voice and reenacted the scene for Jack. "Jackson!" Madison started laughing as she imitated the girls. "He always waves at *me*!" She switched her hip to the other side and put on a different voice. "No, he does not. He is *totally* waving at me."

Jack stared at Madison. His glare slowly moved into an evil grin. He didn't say a word, only grinned.

Madison shuffled uncomfortably in her shoes. "What?"

"Nothing."

"Then what're you doing? What's the face for?"

Jackson pointed to his face. "This face?" He let his hand drop down to his side. "I think that face means, well...you're about to get it."

Jack leaped toward her in one quick move.

Madison, thinking even faster than Jack could move, shrieked and ran backward, away from him.

He chased her around the huge yard, both of them running as fast as they could, barely avoiding one another. Just as Jack was about to pounce on Madison, she switched direction and he slipped on the dew-covered grass.

Madison laughed out loud and continued her quest. She danced around, screaming in a high-pitched girly voice, waving her arms wildly. "Jackson! Wave to me! Over here! I'm the one you want, aren't I? Jack-*son*!"

Jack bent over, his hands on his knees, and tried to catch his breath. He looked at Madison carrying on like a crazed idiot and he couldn't help but laugh at her.

CHAPTER 4

A soccer ball flew across Jack's perfectly manicured back yard. A teenage girl's voice shrieked loudly, followed by laughter. "You couldn't catch me if you tried! Ass!" Madison ran across the yard and kicked the ball again. She continually looked over her shoulder, making sure she wasn't close to the enemy.

Six years later, Madison had barely changed. At sixteen, she wasn't the most popular, or the most beautiful, or most...*anything*. Well, except most competent on the ice, but they unfortunately didn't really have a classification like that in high school. On a good day, she was your average girl next door. On a bad one, just next door. It never fazed her though. She'd been on the outside looking in for so long, she was hardly aware that groups like "most popular" and "most beautiful" even existed. But hardly didn't mean totally. She saw those girls at school. The ones who had their names on the "most" lists. She watched them out of the corner of her eye and when they walked by her without even a glance in her direction, Madison was reminded. She was reminded that she would never be one of them. But that was okay…it had to be. So, she was a little different. She never really had a growth spurt to speak of. Annie, to this day, blamed it on her vegetarianism. Like eating major amounts of green leafy things was a *bad* thing.

"You're never going to have the energy you need to compete if you don't eat something that isn't green!" Annie never stopped. What kind of mother would give the option of McDonald's or Burger King on a daily basis? The kind of mother that Annie was. The kind that wanted her daughter to be an Olympic champion.

Through the years and even now, Madison refused to change. She was a vegetarian. She didn't care that she was only 4'11" and 93 pounds. She wasn't trying to be Miss America.

Thank God for her one friend. Jack. Still Jack. At seventeen, he was beyond popular and beautiful, and on every 'most' list out there. Unlike Madison, he did have a growth spurt. It was one that had pretty much gone unnoticed by Madison. But not unnoticed by every normal teenage girl in school. Jack was part of each group, each clique. Every one knew him, every one liked him. Without any kind of an attitude to go with his overwhelming popularity, he was the one everyone wanted to be near. And Jack? He only wanted to be near Madison.

Jack flew out of nowhere and tackled Madison to the ground, hard. They landed in a tangled heap. He lay on top of Madison, refusing to move. Immediately, they exploded in a fit of laughter. "Told you!"

Madison tried to push him off her. He wouldn't budge. "Told me what? You didn't tell me shit!"

Jackson looked deeply at Madison. His head moved slowly down to hers.

Madison frowned slightly as his face moved closer and closer to hers. *What the hell is he doing?*

Then he moved his hand to her cheek, as if he was going to caress it. Then, in an instant, Jack flicked the end of Madison's nose. Hard.

"Ouch!"

Jack smiled and did a push-up over Madison.

She rubbed her nose repeatedly. "What'd you do that for?"

He pushed himself all the way up and stood over her, looking down at her, still flat on her back. "I did it, you *midget*, to get the ball." He ran for the still soccer ball a few feet away.

Madison sat up angrily. "Totally cheating, by the way. You can't just…"

But it didn't matter. Jack was running with the ball, kicking it back and forth between his feet. This was what Madison came to know as Jack's show-off time. She watched him closely. Jackson had turned out to be an exceptional soccer player. He'd been on the varsity team since he was a freshman. It was because of him the entire town showed up for every home game.

Madison got up and leisurely walked over to Jack. She watched him kick the ball into the air and continually bounce it off his knees or feet. "Understand something. I *let* you have the ball. And why? Because *you*, my friend, are a rotten loser. You didn't steal it away from me like you want to think you did. And, by the way? Your trick was lame."

Jack bounced the ball all over. He smiled. "It was not lame."

Madison moved closer and closer to him in a non-threatening way. "Please! Throwing me down on the ground and flicking my fragile perky nose? What kind of defense was that? I'll tell you. It was lame, fairly queer, even. Unless, of course, you think it might work when you play Westville. I'm sure the boys will love that pansy ass move."

Jack bounced the ball high in the air and gave himself a commentary. "This is it. For the record. Jackson Wellington III is going to break the all-time record, ladies and gentlemen." Jackson was too busy with his moves to see the evil smirk that crossed Madison's face.

She watched and waited. With perfect timing, as the ball was coming back down to Jackson's knee, and before Jackson knew what hit him, Madison intercepted and kicked the ball away from him.

"Maddie! You made me lose the record!"

Madison kicked the ball playfully. "As if you even *had* a record." She skillfully moved the soccer ball between her feet. After the past ten years hanging out with Jackson, she'd become a rather good soccer player too, thanks to his private coaching. She kicked the ball a few more times and then stopped, her left foot resting on top of the ball. She listened to the sounds around them. "So when do you play Westville?"

"Two days. Why? You coming?"

"Yeah. I'm pretty sure I am." Madison held up her hand, signaling Jack to be quiet. She didn't move her foot from the soccer ball.

Jackson frowned at her. "If you think I'm falling for that, I'm not, you know."

Madison, her focus not on Jackson, answered. "What are you mumbling about?"

"I said I'm not falling for that stupid trick again. The one where you pretend to be doing something spiritual and I think you're not paying attention, so I come toward you and try to steal the ball. Then you proceed to embarrass the crap out of me and right before I kick it…"

"Shh. Will you shut up for a sec?"

Madison concentrated. She looked around the yard slowly. Then, "Five, four, three, two…"

A horn beeped twice in the near distance.

Madison smiled. "God, I'm good. Mom's here."

Jack walked in Madison's direction while talking. "How do you know I don't have a record? I might have a record and you might've just blown it for me."

She resumed kicking the ball between her feet slowly and faced Jackson with attitude. "Now what are you talking about? I swear you're worse than a girl, changing the damn subject all the time."

Jack stood in front of Madison. "I'm talking about the fact that you said I don't have a record. For, you know…for bouncing." He paused. He knew this sounded ridiculous. "Or whatever."

Madison continued moving the ball around. "Jack, you forget, I know everything about you and I know you don't have some retarded record for bouncing a stupid soccer ball."

The horn beeped two times again, but closer. And this time each of the beeps lasted a good amount of time. Madison looked over at the driveway and rolled her eyes. "I better go before my mother has a heart attack. See ya!" Madison kicked the ball over to Jack, standing only a few feet away. He stopped it with his foot and glanced at his watch. "I thought you didn't have to go until four?"

"Yeah, well, we have the rink early tonight. Annie is under the impression I need to be practicing more. Go figure."

"Madison! Let's go!" Madison and Jack both turned to the voice. Annie now stood in the driveway, hands on her hips. As much as she tried to look angry with her daughter, she simply couldn't. Not until they got in the rink, that is. Then, either one of them would admit, something changed. For both of them. It was no longer a mother-daughter relationship. Not on the ice. That time was designated for the coach and skater, and *only* coach and skater.

"Call me when you get home?" Jack kicked the ball around to himself, back and forth between his quick feet.

Madison walked backward to Annie. She raised her chin with attitude to Jack. "Maybe. I'll have to add you to my long list of friends though."

Jack smiled. It was almost too easy. "You still counting your imaginary friends?"

"I hate you."

Jack stopped kicking the ball abruptly. He gave her a mean look and started running toward her. Madison screamed playfully and ran away. "Bye!"

Jack watched her run to the car and yelled after her. "Call me!"

Madison moved around the car, still running. She stood on the side of the car and looked over the roof. She yelled as loud as she could to Jack. "I'll call you!" She hesitated, thinking of the best line. "I'll call you when you break your little bouncy ball record!" Madison slid down into the car.

Annie smiled to Jack and waved good bye. She moved into the driver's seat. "Have fun?"

"Yep. All thirty-seven minutes." Madison looked out the window.

Annie quickly backed the car out of the driveway. "I'm

sure you meant that as a rude and sarcastic response. But, I'll tell you what. I'm not listening." Annie stopped the car in the middle of Jack's street after she backed out.

Madison waited in silence. Annie didn't move. The car didn't move. Madison refused to look in her mother's direction. She did her normal eye roll, deep breath, and even went to the level of window tapping. Still nothing. Madison couldn't take it anymore. "What are you doing? Isn't this remotely dangerous? Stopping in the middle of the street?"

Annie looked straight ahead. She leaned forward, turned on the radio and began to whistle along to the song playing.

Madison was getting more and more aggravated. "Would you just go?" Nothing. Nada. Zip. "This is considered child endangerment, you know."

Annie took a quick break from whistling. "Not listening, remember?"

"Oh my God, Mom." Madison rolled her eyes, this time for real. "This is stupid, okay? Can we just *go*? Please?"

A car turned right onto Jack's street and drove directly at them. Madison began to get somewhat nervous. "Mom! Come on!" She stole a quick glance at Annie who was still whistling. As Madison looked back, the car that had been aimed directly at them, turned into a driveway. Annie had won again. "I'm sorry I was snotty, okay?"

Annie took a quick break from her own personal musical. "And?"

"Rude. Snotty and rude."

"And you're...?"

"M-*om*! I said sorry!"

Annie smiled at her victory. She loved it when Madison made the word "mom" into two syllables. She knew she in fact did win when that happened. She put the car in drive and stopped her off-key harmonies. "Now, let's try this again. You have a good day?"

Madison stared out the window. "It was okay."

"Homework?"

"Yeah, some." She watched kids play outside in their front yards, carefree. Swinging, running, playing. "Why do we have to go to the rink early today?"

Annie stopped the car at a red light. She knew Madison was in one of those moods. She knew the minute she got in the car. She had been waiting for this question. "Because it's the only time I could do it. I've got to work the late shift tonight at the hospital."

"Why? Are they changing your schedule?"

"No. I told Kathy I would switch this shift to help her out. If you recall, she has covered for me almost every time I've asked her to help." Annie shot a quick look toward Madison before moving her car through the now green light. "We've asked her a lot, Mad, before every competition."

"I know that. Isn't there another nurse you could ask?"

Annie thought it would have been nice if her daughter's response was a sympathetic, "*Gosh, Mom. What a long day you've had. You have worked so many hours. Then you drive all the way over to Jack's to pick me up when you could've told me I couldn't go. Then you drive us all the way to the rink, which, by the way, is a solid forty minutes, without traffic, mind you, and then you coach me and then...then Mom, you have to go to work all night long and take care of sick people.*" Annie wasn't finished. If she was going to make the daydream good, it needed a big whopper of an ending. Madison would finish it off by saying, "*You know something, Mom? You are incredible. Doing all that. Just for me to be able to skate.*" Then she would take a dramatic pause, Annie thought. "*I love you, Mom. You're the greatest.*" Whoops. Annie almost forgot the best part. "*And, Mom? Thank you.*" Annie looked over at Madison, like she knew something Madison didn't.

"What." Madison's face was scrunched up in disgust. She couldn't stand when Annie looked at her like that.

Annie smiled. Obviously, today wasn't the day Madison would say those words to her. "Nothing, honey." She could still hope for tomorrow. And hey. Madison's "What" was another two-syllable winner. All was good.

❦ CHAPTER 5 ❧

*S*chool was bad enough. But when it was rainy and dark outside, it was even worse. Madison couldn't stand being there. She didn't fit in with any of the cliques, she didn't have any girlfriends, and she wasn't doing as well as she used to in her classes. With one person to call a friend, it pretty much sucked, and somehow, it seemed to be getting even worse.

Jackson could have girlfriends, any number of them. He had a ton of guy friends. And he was doing fine in school. It wasn't as if Madison was jealous, really. It wasn't like she longed to have girly sleepovers and talk about schoolboy crushes. She didn't feel the need to sneak cigarettes or steal a bottle of liquor from the unlocked cabinet in her kitchen. She had no interest in exfoliating facials or watching marathon horror movies. She didn't care if she got a C instead of a B on an exam. She was going to be a skater; and skaters, last she heard, didn't need to excel in calculus. But there were days, like this one, where Madison did have those moments of longing to fit somewhere. With someone other than her mother.

Madison's head was deep inside her locker. She exchanged

a few books for others. She didn't notice someone standing behind the thin metal door, hiding, ready to attack. Madison removed her head and slammed the locker door shut, immediately jumping a foot and letting out an embarrassing scream.

Jack smiled. A few students looked over in their direction to see what the commotion was about. Seeing that Jack was behind whatever was going on, the inquiring looks turned into waves and hellos to him.

Madison shook her head at him. "Why do you do that? You know I hate when you do that to me."

"Do what?"

Madison tried her hardest to be angry. She even squinted her eyes and pursed her lips tightly. "You know what, ya moron! You feel the need to scare me in front of people who already don't like me and now, quite possibly, hate me."

"They don't *not* like you. They just don't know you." Jackson tried not to laugh at the already uptight Madison. "Actually, thinking about it? They probably wouldn't like you if they did get to know you."

Madison opened her mouth to say something and decided against it. She turned abruptly and walked away from Jack, still grinning from his joke.

"Maddie! Come on, I was kidding!"

Madison ignored him and continued speed-walking down the hallway to get as far away from him as possible.

Jack rolled his eyes. He knew her so well. He knew when he had gone too far and this was one of those times. Jack sprinted fast to catch up with Madison. There wasn't a second when someone wasn't calling out to him as he made his way closer to her. There were the numerous soccer buddies high-fiving him as he passed, cute girls in very tight shirts and even tighter jeans putting on smiles that meant way more than have a nice day. Jack knew he could be a politician, if for no other reason than the way he knew just the right response to give each individual. The soccer guys got a slap in the hand; the pretty girls got a wink and a flattering comment. He greeted the other kids with a wave and a smile, even if he had no idea what their names were.

There was no smile that could compete, though, with the one he wore when he talked to Madison. He closed in on her just before she entered her classroom. "Mad! Wait a sec."

Madison stopped in front of the doorway and turned reluctantly toward Jackson. She looked over at the large group of kids a few feet away from her. *They're the beautiful people*, she thought. Cheerleaders with perky boobs and hottie guys with raging hormones were all calling for Jack. Her Jack, her friend. Madison could not stop herself. "Uh-oh. Your tribe is calling you."

"Why do you call them that? They aren't a tribe."

"Okay. Your peeps are calling you. That better? How about your homeboys? Your crew?" Madison turned away for fear Jack would see her smiling.

A guy in the tribe/crew yelled for Jackson again. "Hey, dude! C'mere for a sec! You gotta see this!"

Madison couldn't help herself. She was on a roll. In a lowered voice, she tried to mimic the guy. But she ended up sounding like a testosterone-filled monkey with helium in its lungs. "Hey, dude! C'mere for a sec!"

Jackson laughed out loud. He turned to the guy and waved him off. "I'll see ya later! I gotta take care of something." He turned his attention back to Madison. "So, why didn't you call me back?"

"When was I supposed to call you back?"

"Oh, I don't know. Every night? In particular...like, maybe, last night? When I left you two messages?"

"I think that was supposed to be sarcastic." Madison smiled. "Not bad for a rich kid."

Jackson looked inside the empty classroom. "Why are we standing in the doorway? The first bell didn't even ring yet. We look stupid standing here."

"I'm used to it," Madison said under her breath.

Jack and Madison stepped away from the door. He casually leaned up against a row of lockers. "So, what *is* your excuse?"

"Sorry. I'm a loser."

"Will you shut up? You are not a loser. I hate when you say that."

"Well, then obviously you shouldn't ask me questions that invite that response."

Jackson shook his head a little and looked away. Madison leaned up against the lockers next to him. "I am a loser about this. By the time we got home I was so tired, I didn't even eat dinner. I couldn't keep my eyes open."

Jackson looked at her hard. "That...uh...that's the best excuse you could come up with?" He shrugged nonchalantly. "I dunno, Mad. You better watch out. I think you're losing your touch there."

Madison giggled. "You should've heard the one my imaginary friends got."

"And, she's back!" They both cracked up for a few seconds before they were interrupted. A cheerleader approached Jack without concern over Madison. "Hi, Jack."

Jack turned to Kelly with a polite smile. "Hey."

Madison tried not to look at her. But she couldn't help it. Kelly was beautiful, perfect in literally every way. She had long, gorgeous red hair and it wasn't out of a box either, which pissed Madison off even more. *If her flowing tresses had come from inside a box, well then, she wouldn't be the beautiful girl that she is.* Madison stole another look. She would still be that beautiful girl. *She's got the perfect everything to go with her little cheerleadery uniform, including what fills it out in all the right places.*

Kelly smiled angelically. "You played a really great game yesterday."

"Thanks."

Madison cringed. *The game yesterday afternoon. He played Westville.* She had asked him about it a few days ago. How could she have forgotten? Not only did she not show up like she promised, she hadn't even called him. She *was* a loser, after all. Madison looked over at Jack and Kelly. The three of them stood in a semi-circle, each extremely uncomfortable for their own individual reasons.

Kelly finally broke the awkward silence. "Well," as she flashed too many of her very white, very bleached teeth, "I should get going to class." She paused before she walked away and gave a polite smile to Madison. "It was nice to see you, Madeline." Then she gave a real smile to Jackson. "Maybe I'll see you this weekend."

It was said more as a statement than a question, Madison thought. She watched Kelly walk to her cheerleader friends waiting for her, in a group of course, a few feet away. She listened as they giggled loudly at Kelly joining them.

Jack kept his eyes focused on Madison. "So, Madeline..."

Madison shot him daggers with her eyes. "Oh, that's funny. Really, though. Ha-ha-freaking-ha."

"Come on. She didn't mean anything by it. So she said your name wrong. Big deal."

"She didn't say it *wrong*. She said the wrong *name*. It's totally different!" Madison stopped herself from getting any angrier. "For the record, I don't even care. I don't."

"Uh-huh. I can see you don't." Jackson smiled. "I think you might be a little jealous that I have pretty friends. Admit it."

Madison's mouth dropped open. She shook her head "no". A little too emphatically. "What?! Me? Jackson, you know what? You have said some stupid things in your lifetime, but honestly? That was like the dumbest thing that has ever come out of your big mouth and—"

The bell rang loudly in the hall, interrupting Madison for a second. "Besides, why would I ever be jealous of some stupid fake girl who sleeps with a tooth tray and dyes her hair? I mean, give me a break." Madison hoped her headshake and eye roll made an impact on her statement. Usually, it added the crowning moment in her arguments with her mother.

Jackson frowned slightly. "She dyes her hair? How do you know?"

She moved slowly toward her classroom, trying very hard to keep her chin up high. "I...uh...I don't know. But she probably does." Madison stopped near the door and looked up and down the halls. They had definitely cleared out. "Shouldn't you be going to class?"

"I guess you haven't heard." Jackson stepped in closer to Madison, as if to whisper something top secret. "See, when you're a star, you know, a game-winning athlete? The school makes certain, like, *allowances*, for your...your..." Jackson thought hard and quickly smiled. "Your greatness."

Madison laughed out loud. "Your greatness? Oh, God. That's classic." Her face became serious, almost sympathetic. She shrugged her little shoulders lightly. "About your game?

I'm sorry. I totally forgot. No other excuse. I just…"

"Mad, come on. It's me. Don't worry about it. Really." Jack meant it too. He was used to Madison missing games, events, things they sometimes had planned for weeks in advance. He understood, without question, skating always came first. He had to understand.

That only made Madison feel crappier. "Did you win?"

Jack beamed proudly. "Yeah."

"Yeah?"

He couldn't control himself and he jumped in front of Madison excitedly. "We're tied, right? There's like *ten seconds* left on the clock and guess who scores the winning goal?"

Madison looked at him, deadpan. "Had to be Zack Browning."

"That was *so* mean." Jack lost all of his animated excitement.

"Oh my God." Madison rolled her eyes. "Okay, here. Do it again. Who scored the winning goal, Jack?"

"I did," he answered quietly.

"You're kidding! No way!" Madison jumped up and down once, lamely.

"Very funny."

A second bell rang loudly throughout the school. Madison moved into the classroom slowly. "See? I'm funny. A loser *and* I'm funny. Do you even know how lucky you are to be my friend?

Jack smiled genuinely. "Yeah."

Madison waved from inside her classroom, already sitting at her desk, and then shooed him away.

∞ CHAPTER 6 ∞

*A*nnie slowly and quietly paced through their small, out-dated kitchen. Her bathrobe hung open loosely, showing an old T-shirt of David's on her toned body. Without turning on any lights, she walked to the counter and leaned her chest over it. She shoved her fingers through the blinds, spreading two of them apart and peered outside. She glanced back to the blinds as she heard part of one rip a little further and wondered how many times David had taped the broken plastic rod up top back together again. It was funny. They could obvi-ously afford another piece of plastic for the worn blinds. Better yet, they could afford new blinds. But the blinds were just the beginning. The easy part. What about the wallpaper from the eighties that was starting to fold down in the corners of the ceiling? And what about the cheesy linoleum floor in the kitchen that was not only down-right ugly, but was crack-ing at the seams? Then there was the paint that was chipping away in nearly every room. But all that mattered was Madison needed new skates. There were her costumes to think about and they weren't cheap. There was the rink rental, which was astronomical and Annie knew George already gave them a huge break. There were competition fees and music tracks and the choreographer and...

Annie stopped and closed her eyes. She inhaled the strong coffee that had almost finished brewing. This was her time of the day. This very short ten-minute span. She took a deep breath and opened her eyes. She grabbed the broken rod on the taped area and carefully turned it, opening the blinds wide. It was still pitch black outside. Annie reached for a mug from the cabinet and poured herself some coffee. She glanced down to the clock on the coffee machine and cringed at the numbers, reading 4:10 A.M. Annie gulped a long swig of steaming coffee from her cup. Her ten minutes were over.

Madison slept soundly in her bed, unaware her day was about to begin. And dreaming that it wasn't.

Annie pushed her door open slightly and stood in the doorway, sending in a dim light from the hallway. She watched Madison sleep for a minute before she woke her and wondered what her daughter was dreaming. Annie glanced around the room. The floor was covered with dirty clothes, mostly from skating. She gave up complaining about that years ago. For some odd reason, the skating clothes didn't bother her as much as the other ones. Posters of alternative rock bands and a few ice skaters covered the rapidly fading paint. And there were pictures of Madison and Jack everywhere else.

Annie tripped on a large duffel bag overflowing with skating apparel. She grabbed her toe in pain, trying not to wake up Madison just yet. She shook her head at the mess. Nothing worked. No threats of not going out with friends. Madison didn't have any. No taking away time with a boyfriend. No time for one anyway. Annie knew it really wasn't Madison's fault either. She didn't have a free minute for anything, nothing, except skating and school. And they both knew it. Annie looked down at Madison's clock and watched as her numbers clicked over to 4:13 A.M.

Madison slowly opened her eyes.

Annie moved toward her bed and sat on the edge. She rubbed Madison's arm gently, back and forth. She whispered in that soothing voice only a mother can have at 4:13 in the morning. "You awake?"

Madison's eyes closed slowly. "Yeah."

Annie continued touching her, trying to persuade some energy into her. "Sleep well?"

"Yeah." Madison rolled over on her side and stretched out her other arm for rubbing, knowing Annie would oblige.

"We have the rink at 5:15 this morning. Figure we could use the extra 15, okay?"

Madison's eyes reopened. Maybe not *wide-open*. More like squint-opened. "What time is it?" Before Annie could answer, Madison glanced at her clock. If she had any energy whatsoever, she would've sighed, deep and heavy. But she didn't have any extra energy to waste on a useless groan when she knew it wouldn't get her a few more minutes of sleep anyway. She pushed herself up in the bed and closed her eyes for one last quick second.

Annie put her coffee cup on the bedside table next to Madison's clock. She got off the bed and began picking objects up off the floor. She looked around for a place to put the collected items and finally gave up, tossing them off to the side. *What did it matter?*

Madison opened her tired eyes and remembered she was supposed to clean up her room last night. *Or was it the night before? It really doesn't matter,* she thought. She hoped, based on Annie's last toss to the side, that she was thinking the same thing. She reached over for Annie's cup, sipped some coffee and asked, "Did your mother get you up this early when you skated?"

Annie smelled a shirt and then shoved it into a drawer. She turned to Madison with a smile. "No, she didn't." She bent down and picked up books that had fallen out of a nearby backpack. "My mother couldn't take me to the rink this early. She had other kids to take care of and we had no extra money for me to skate as much as you do. I had to work at the rink just to skate sometimes and furthermore," Annie paused and looked at Madison seriously. "I wasn't as good as you." Annie noticed Madison drinking her coffee and thanked God she could change the subject. "One more drink and no more coffee, kiddo." Annie walked over to Madison and extended her hand to her.

Madison stole one last sip and reluctantly handed the mug over to Annie.

"I'll meet you in the kitchen. Five minutes, okay?" Annie gently tapped the wall twice on her way out, for effect. She wasn't sure it worked, but she couldn't stop herself from trying.

Madison smiled. Her real answer was, "No, Mom, it's not okay. It fucking sucks. It bites the big ass of life. I don't want to get up at four o'clock in the damn morning when even the roosters are still sleeping. I don't want to be freezing for thirteen minutes in the forty-seven degree rink." But she knew she'd never say that. And she knew she would be fine once they got warmed up. She'd wake up. She always did. Then slowly, Madison moved her warm, down comforter off her body and swung her tired legs out of bed.

CHAPTER 7

Two blades cut deep into the glassy ice. The sound mesmerized Madison as she skated around the rink at a fast pace. Right foot over left. One after the other. The rink was empty, minus Madison and Annie, and there was silence instead of music. Just the sound of her skates making their own song.

Annie stood in place on the ice, her eyes never leaving Madison. It didn't matter that she wasn't doing anything specific. This was warm-up time. A good coach knows the tiniest things in a routine can ruin a champion, or create one. She watched Madison begin to move with a little more enthusiasm and patted herself on the back for how she eased her into the morning workouts. They both knew Madison was not what you'd call a morning person. Annie moved herself toward the center of the rink, circling around Madison in every direction. She wore skates too, so she could follow Madison around with ease. She tried not to think back to the time when she was the one to watch and her coach skated around her, surveying her every move, probably with the same attentive eye. "Keep your back straight."

Madison didn't look in Annie's direction as she answered her. "It is."

Annie turned her body around, following Madison. "I'm looking right at you and I'm telling you, it's not straight, Mad."

Madison continued skating around the edge of the ice. She picked up a little more speed. Still avoiding Annie's eyes, she responded curtly. "Maybe your head is crooked."

Annie ignored her. She was used to this interaction with her daughter and she knew when to let a certain issue go. That had been a hard lesson to learn but had come in extremely handy since Madison turned sixteen months ago. "Flip it back."

Madison immediately followed the order given and turned herself around so she was skating backward. She brought herself to Annie, circling around and around her. She folded her arms in front of her to keep her body warm.

Whatever sign of life Annie had witnessed a few moments earlier was clearly gone from the picture now in front of her. It was going to be one of those days, again.

Madison was not skating with any energy. "My legs hurt."

Annie had heard this one many times. This last statement had gotten Madison out of a few too many recent practices. Annie looked away from her daughter for the first time since they started. "You probably didn't stretch enough."

Madison slowed down even more. "Yes I did."

"If you did stretch enough, your legs wouldn't hurt, Mad." Moments like these she hated to be the coach. She noticed Madison's shoulders hunched up high, her hands on her opposite arms, still trying to get warm. "Get your shoulders down."

Madison angrily released her arms and flung them down at her sides. "Where do you think I should I put them? You're the coach. Tell me."

"Madison, enough."

Madison switched to skating forward and stopped abruptly near Annie. "What? I didn't do anything. All I did was tell you my legs hurt. All I did was be honest. Now I can't even tell you how I'm feeling? Is that it?"

"Don't give me that shit." Annie pushed away the sharp pain pulsating at a perfect beat through her head. She tried not to think about how long this morning could be.

"What shit are you looking for, then?"

Annie looked up at this girl in front of her. This vile, inconsiderate, rude monster she must call her daughter for legal and ethical reasons. In the calmest voice she could muster, she mumbled, "You wanna screw off, go ahead. Have a good practice." With that, Annie skated off the ice. She knew from past experience this worked. Usually. Except, it was silent this time as she neared the edge. She tried to inconspicuously slow her movements down, waiting for Madison to call her back. Just as Annie thought her plan backfired, she heard it.

"God! You don't have to get all huffy and walk out on me. My legs hurt! I just didn't know what you were talking about. I don't think other coaches leave their skaters in the middle of a slight disagreement. You don't have to get all pissy."

Annie stood there, off the ice, and stared at Madison. There were times when she gave in, nicely, to get what she needed from her daughter. Then there were times, and not often did this happen, that she needed to scare the living crap out of Madison. Today just happened to be one of those crap days. "You don't know what I'm talking about? I'll make it really clear for you, okay?" Annie skated back onto the ice, and angrily approached Madison standing in the middle. "What the hell I'm talking about is…you have a competition coming up in two weeks and your goddamn back is slouchy! Your shoulders are hunched over! You're too cold to release your hands away from your chest and skate appropriately! And you're telling me your legs hurt!" Annie stood menacingly in front of Madison. The rink echoed her already loud and harsh voice. "Now, I don't know about you, but I sure as hell am not getting up before the crack of freaking dawn every day to have your back goddamn slouchy two weeks before you skate in your biggest competition ever!"

After Annie yelled like that, it was the silence Madison hated the most. She knew when she had overstepped the boundary, crossed the line, whatever. It was never easy to figure out how to handle their relationship after this kind of episode, as Madison liked to refer to it. She stole a quick glance at Annie who refused to look at her. Then, with the straightest face ever, Madison responded. "So, are you saying my back is like, *slouchy*?"

Annie continued staring ahead, silently cursing Madison's outrageousness. But soon, a small smile crossed her face. Without looking at Madison directly, she replied, "You gonna skate sometime this morning?" With that, she allowed her eyes to move to Madison's.

Madison gave her a look that both understood completely. No words had to be spoken. No hugs were administered. Madison skated a few feet away, this time with a focused, newfound, very deliberate energy.

Annie smiled a secret smile all to herself. It worked. At

least, this time it did. She looked up to the control booth over the rink and yelled loudly. "We're ready, George!"

An older man's voice boomed through the rink's speakers. "Coming right up."

George Finner was the owner of the rink. Annie knew how blessed they were to have him around. She had thanked God for him so many times she began to feel guilty, as if her willpower had anything to do with the extremely short career he had as a pro-hockey player. George was forced to retire before his contract was up. It happened long before Madison was even born, but Annie still punished herself. George never lost his love for skating, after all those years. Annie found out the story over the many years there with Madison. George shrugged it off. He wasn't about to drown in pity, so he came back to his hometown and remodeled an old ice rink himself. Annie knew if it weren't for George, Madison wouldn't be a skater. He had watched her from the time she was three years old and prided himself on being a big part of her success. There wasn't a morning in the ten years of Madison's training that he wasn't there at the crack of dawn to open up the rink if needed. Or run the music for Annie, over and over again. Or some days, to just plain watch the miracle they both referred to as Madison Henry.

Madison skated around the rink a few times, throwing a small jump here and a quick spin there. Annie moved herself to the side of the rink, all the while still keeping an eye on Madison.

George's voice sounded through the rink. "Got you set up, Maddie. Whenever you're ready."

Madison gave a quick wave to the booth. She casually skated to the center of the ice and stopped. Then, without warning, something truly magical happened. Her hands, once stiff from the cold, were weightless and delicate. Her shoulders were straight and her back was no longer hunched over. Her right leg gracefully fell behind her left leg, the tip of her skate pointed into the ice. She stood beautifully erect, and lifted her chin high in the air. Then she took a deep breath and closed her eyes.

The music filled every empty air pocket in the entire rink. A few beats passed before Madison opened her eyes. When she did, there was nothing but sparkle, nothing but shine. No tired dark circles under her eyes. No attitude remained from the earlier disagreement. Not the smallest hint of anything negative. Then Madison slowly began to move her feet. To say she skated beautifully would be an insulting understatement. She was stunningly brilliant, flawless through each and every move she made.

Annie watched Madison skate the rink, arms in perfect position. As Madison set up to attempt a triple triple combination jump, Annie opened her mouth to yell something. Then quickly, she stopped herself and waited patiently. This was the one that gave Madison the most trouble. Annie knew this was what put the icing on the cake for the championship title. Her hands moved automatically into a prayer position, like they always did, whether in practice or competition.

Madison pulled her body high in the air, her feet crossed tightly at her ankles. She spun around quickly, three times in mid-air, once.

Please, Annie thought to herself. *Please let her do it.* Madison barely touched the ice after the first triple before throwing herself in the air once more. Again, three times she circled in mid-air. Madison completed the second triple jump without a hitch. Annie smiled and let out a huge yell before she could stop herself. "Yes! That's it!"

Madison smiled and talked back to Annie while skating. "Don't even do the happy dance."

୧୨ CHAPTER 8 ୧୨

*D*avid stood against the counter in the kitchen, the same spot Annie stood a few hours before. He held a half-full coffee mug in his left hand...the mug Madison gave him for Christmas a few years before. The newspaper was sprawled out wide in front of him, but he didn't necessarily read it. Instead, he leisurely skimmed through the pages, as if it were just something he had to do before his day began. It was a ritual all his own.

Annie entered, as usual, on a schedule. A tight schedule. She was tying the drawstring on her scrub pants as she inaudibly grunted, "Morning." She grabbed a loaf of organic wheat berry bread and pulled out two slices. David watched her, completely captivated, as she quickly moved to the toaster and threw the bread in, hitting the dial to light, and put the loaf of bread back where it came from, all in one graceful fluid movement. Annie didn't stand still for a second. She removed fresh eggs from the refrigerator and placed them carefully on the counter. Using her foot to keep the refrigerator door ajar, God forbid taking the time to reopen the refrigerator, she was back in the cold box grabbing the carton of orange juice, butter, and jelly. Just like that.

David couldn't help but be entertained by her. "How'd she do this morning?"

Annie barely looked over at David as he sipped his coffee. She frowned slightly with a quick shake of her head. She grabbed a bowl and cracked the eggs open, letting only the white portion slowly drop into it. "I've never understood how you can drink that."

David didn't take offense. He couldn't with Annie. He knew she meant well and he knew she was horribly over-worked and chronically exhausted. He loved her anyway, in spite of her moderate crankiness. And, just maybe, because of it. He glanced down to the cup still stuck in his hand. "Drink what? Coffee?"

"It's not coffee, David." She grabbed a frying pan from the lower cabinet and threw a chunk of butter in the middle. She put the stove on medium and allowed the butter to start melting. "I turned the pot off at four-fifteen this morning. It's what? Eight? Doesn't it taste like cold thick mud water?" Annie popped up the toast and threw it on a plate. She poured the egg whites into the hot frying pan. She didn't miss a beat.

David shrugged it off. "Maybe I like your cold muddy-water coffee." He put his cup down on the counter and slowly approached Annie. "Maybe it reminds me of you." As David reached out to brush a fallen piece of hair away from Annie's face, she switched direction without warning.

"Have you seen the spatula? It's not here." She threw open another drawer and furiously ripped through it. "No!" Annie noticed the eggs bubbling up in the pan. "They're gonna get ruined. She won't eat them if they're overcooked. Damn it!"

David turned around and took the spatula in question out of the drying dish rack. He calmly handed it to Annie. "Here."

Annie quickly took it from David. "Thanks." With that, she turned her back to him and scrambled the eggs, a conversation with him apparently not part of her schedule that morning.

David went back to skimming through his paper and took a sip of his cold coffee.

They stood in silence for a few moments before Annie remembered David's original question. She didn't intentionally blow him off, but when she realized she had, the guilt was always strong. "Madison was...she was okay this morning. Just okay. I mean, I know it's because we're working harder, and it's so early in the morning, but still. We don't have a choice. And she knows that." Annie looked over her shoulder to guarantee Madison's absence for another second. "I had to threaten walking out on her. That's how just okay today really was. Pretty not okay."

"Did you talk to her about it? Maybe something is bothering her."

Annie turned the stove off and looked at David. "*I'm* the something that's bothering her. She'll tell you that. I'm the one who is making things horrible for her." Annie scraped the whites out of the pan and piled them onto a nearby plate. "I don't know what to do, David. She's missing beats. She's not paying attention to me or anything I say, even the smallest of things, and it could very likely turn into an argument that not only wastes our time but the money. Today, poor George had to sit in the booth and listen to us fight for at least ten minutes straight."

David moved a few steps closer to Annie. "Well, she's probably exhausted, you know?" He took the pan away from her and put it in the sink. "I mean, *you* are, aren't you?" He squirted detergent in the pan and turned on the water, letting it run until the pan was overflowing with soapsuds. "With the morning workouts and night workouts and school and homework, she is overwhelmed. I'm sure once you get through the competition, she'll get back to normal. She always does."

Annie stopped for the first time since she entered the kitchen minutes ago. "I'm not a terrible mother and a horrible coach? You think she'll be okay? Really?"

David smiled and put his arms around Annie's body. He kissed her forehead and reassured her like no one else could. "Yeah. I think."

Annie felt the warmth of David's body next to hers and moved her hands slowly up his back. They stood completely still, their bodies so close not even a single sheet of paper could fit between them. Annie allowed her eyes to close.

David's voice was barely a whisper. "What time do you have the rink tonight?"

"I think five." Suddenly, her eyes opened and she looked up at David. "Why?"

He looked down into Annie's face with a secret grin. "Well, I had an idea. I was thinking I haven't seen the new routine in a while. Maybe I'll come down with some hot chocolate for Maddie. It could be a nice break for her."

"Really...for Maddie, huh? And what about her brilliant coach?" Annie gave him the same secret grin back.

David hugged her even more tightly and spoke into her ear. "If you must know, I have something entirely different planned for her coach. Something private, sexy even..."

"Really..." Annie's voice trailed off quietly into David's chest. She let David kiss her on the neck, relaxing for just a second. She turned her head to the side and noticed the eggs on the plate. "Wait. Her eggs are getting cold."

David slowly made his way to her face and kissed her softly on the lips. "That's what microwaves were invented for. Cold eggs." David knew moments like this were rare and few for them and he was not about to let this window of time be closed just yet.

"I can go to Jack's game today, right?" Madison stood in the doorframe.

Window closed.

David and Annie separated their faces slightly and smiled to one another. David spoke quietly to Annie. "Hold that thought." David gave Annie's back one last rub and took a strong gulp of his cold muddy coffee.

Annie gave David a quick wink. She picked up the plate of now-chilly eggs and threw it in the microwave.

A few moments passed in complete silence. Madison stood motionless, eyebrows raised impatiently. "Hel-*lo*. I asked a question. Is anyone going to answer me?"

The microwave beeped loudly. Annie opened it, grabbed the plate and very matter-of-factly, answered Madison. "No. You cannot go to Jack's game. There's your answer."

"Why?"

"We've got the rink today at five. I told you this morning. All of three hours ago." Annie walked the plate of eggs over to the table and set it down. She moved back to a drawer and took out a fork. "Come eat your eggs."

Madison didn't move from the doorway. She crossed her arms over her chest in attractive teenage defiance. "You didn't tell me. You never said anything about the rink later. I would have remembered if you did."

"Madison! I told you, okay? Discussion is over. Come eat your breakfast." Annie tried to remain calm as she grabbed a glass and filled it with orange juice.

"Well, why can't we go earlier? Why does it have to be five?"

Annie walked the fork and glass of juice over to the table and set it down next to the plate of nuked eggs. "We can't go earlier because I have to work. That's why." *Think peace. Peace, love and harmony have, on occasion, miraculously cured cancer so why couldn't it cure my daughter's piss-ass attitude?*

David took a quick breath and tried to lighten the mood, knowing full well it probably wouldn't help one bit. He grabbed his paper and moved to the table while addressing Madison. "Morning, honey."

"Morning, Dad." Madison resumed her discussion with Annie. "I don't get it. Why can't you just get someone to work for you later on tonight so we can practice then instead? What's the big deal?"

Annie turned to Madison angrily, the last straw had just broken the camel's back. "The big deal is...I cannot simply change my damn schedule to accommodate Jack's soccer game, Madison! I already call in every favor imaginable at the hospital on a weekly basis so I can take time out of my job to coach you!" Annie tried to reduce her volume, but one look at Madison's pouty face and she couldn't comply. "Why is it you think I'm working so much lately, huh? Maybe I should fill you in. I am taking over as many shifts as I can without dropping dead so we have the money to rent the rink as much

as we need. And why is that? So that *you* can *skate!*" She took
a deep breath, aware of the nervous breakdown and heart pal-
pitations that would ensue if she didn't. "Now, do you really
want to argue that my sole purpose is to disrupt your social
life?"

Madison shrugged with attitude. "Maybe."

"God, Madison!" Annie turned away from her.

"Maybe you've forgotten," she said as she stepped closer
to Annie. "I don't have a social life. I have one friend, who
happens to have a game today that I'd like to go to. I don't
think I'm asking for a lot."

Annie stopped herself from turning this conversation into
an all-out verbal war which, as she knew better than anyone,
it could become, with a snap of her finger. "There's your
breakfast on the table. Please eat it so we can get you to
school before third period starts."

Madison glared at Annie. "I'm not hungry." She spun
around and exited before Annie could stop her.

She watched Madison until she was out of sight. Knowing
David's eyes were on her, she glanced over to him and quickly
looked away. "Don't say it."

David dug into Madison's plate of unpleasantly cold eggs.
Without waiting to swallow, words flew out of his full mouth.
"Did I say anything? I don't think I said anything."

"Maybe not, but you were about to."

"What would I have said?" David shoved more eggs into
his still stuffed mouth. "If I did, in fact, say something?"

Annie answered reluctantly. She hated it when he did this,
his backward psychology. She only fell for it when she was
ridiculously overtired. Like right now. "That she's still a kid.
That she's training hard. That she's tired..." She heard the
words she had just said out loud and thought for a second.

She glanced back to David and got his nonchalant shrug and sympathetic look. "Shit." She shook her head low and stretched her body on the counter with a groan that said 'my body hurts' and another that said, 'I know I screwed up,' and she turned to David. "I'll uh…I'm gonna go…" She pointed in the direction of Madison's exit, at a loss for words.

David smiled. He was used to their mother-daughter relationship. It usually started right about now. *Just before a competition.* "Just go talk to her, Ann."

"Yeah." Annie nodded her head and walked out.

Madison lay in her bed, the covers pulled up tightly under her neck. She always slept like that. No matter how hot it was. She had to be covered, protected, in a way. As soon as she heard the inevitable footsteps approaching, she flipped her body onto her side so Annie couldn't see her face. The minute Annie entered her room, the covers came up even higher.

Annie pushed her door open without knocking. She sauntered in and sat casually at the bottom of the bed. "Hey."

Madison thought for a few beats, staring at the wall. She hated these moments. Does she roll over and face her? Should she yell more? Talk, even? Maybe not say anything at all? Maybe she should make Annie sweat it out for a few more seconds? Before Madison continued arguing with her inner self, she found herself rolling over and facing Annie.

Annie tried to smile. "Sorry."

Madison loved this part. "Oh? Sorry for what?"

"Mad, come on. You know what."

Madison rolled herself back toward the wall, ignoring her. It was more fun when she made Annie work for it. She should have done it this way from the beginning.

"What do you want me to do? Spell it out for you?"

Madison smiled slightly at the wall. "Yeah."

Annie moved behind Madison and physically turned her over. Madison did nothing to help her. She lay on her back and stared at the ceiling, looking through her mother. Annie snuggled down next to her and put her arms around Madison's small body. They were silent for a few moments, looking above.

Annie slowly turned her head to Madison. "We're almost there, you know?"

"I know," Madison answered, still looking at the ceiling.

Annie's voice was soothing and sincere. "Tired?"

Madison continued staring upward, blankly. "A little."

Annie gently touched Madison's hair and pushed it away from the side of her face. "Wanna stay home today?"

Madison's eyes opened wide to face Annie's. She would do anything to stay in bed all day. "Can I?"

Annie grinned. She did it on purpose. She knew it would get her attention. "Nope." She jumped out of bed and gently hit Madison's leg. "But I'll give you five extra minutes, my friend."

"Okay. Honestly? Honestly that was the meanest thing you have ever done."

Annie moved to the door. "What can I say? I am the meanest mother ever. I do nothing for you and I lie and I yell at you every day..." Annie exited, still shouting things to Madison from down the hall. "What else? I never feed you breakfast, and if I do, it's never warm, always reheated and I never let you go anywhere, ever..."

Madison smiled as Annie's voice became a distant mumble. That was it. End of argument. End of discussion. There was going to be no soccer game today. Somehow, she'd have to find a way to tell Jackson she wouldn't be there and an even better way to make it up to him. Madison closed her eyes and quieted her thoughts for a moment. "Madison! Let's go!" She heard Annie yelling from the kitchen. Moment was gone.

Reluctantly, she opened her eyes and pushed back the comfortable warm covers. She threw her legs off the bed and stood up. Suddenly, she lost her balance and fell back down on the bed. Madison focused for a second and shook it off. It took a few more moments for the many stars buzzing around her head to come to a complete halt. She sluggishly stood up straight and stretched her arms up high, arching her back. She told herself it was just one of those times, when you get up too quickly and get dizzy. Oh, yeah. No breakfast today either which obviously didn't help. She released her stretch and moved to the mirror over her cluttered dresser, bringing her body in front of the glass to look at herself closely.

It was just one of those times.

CHAPTER 9

There was something about school cafeterias that made Madison want to projectile vomit. It had been that way since, well, since forever. If you weren't in a group, if you didn't have that clique thing happening, forget it. Lunchtime was an endless period of unimportant chatter.

Madison stood in the entrance, searching, praying for an unoccupied table, preferably one that would remain unoccupied over the course of the meal. Spotting one in a corner, she quickly moved through the large noisy room and got as far away as she could from any human contact. She threw her brown bag lunch down on the table and plopped the overstuffed backpack on the bench next to her. Without even peeking to see what was in her lunch, Madison immediately moved to the backpack and took out books, notebooks, and a pen. Lunchtime wasn't lunchtime for Madison. It was catch-up time. Homework time. Sometimes even nap time. She ignored the laughter and secret whispers shared by friends she'd never have and dropped her head deep into her books. There was simply not enough time in her day to make a friend, let alone friends. Not that any one of the girls would've been her friend anyway. She had realized long ago that teenagers can be brutal, especially when you're different.

Madison didn't enter the room unnoticed. She'd, of course, like to think she did. But, not so far away from her self-induced cave, Jackson watched her closely.

He sat at the table that was envied by all. Here sat the beautiful people. The popular ones. Today the soccer team guys watched the cheerleaders make their way around the cafeteria, filling every available section of empty wall with posters promoting the upcoming school dance. Jackson was elbowed hard but continued to stare in Madison's direction.

Tommy leaned into him and elbowed him again.

"What're you doing? I'm right here."

Tommy had been Jack's friend for years. Not the kind of friend you trust with your life, but certainly the kind of guy to hang out with once in a while. "Check it out." He pointed in the direction of Kelly, reaching up as high as she could to hang a poster.

Jackson obliged and glanced over. Kelly's very small skirt was just about to hike above that oh-so-important thigh-meets-butt underwear mark.

Tommy grinned. "Five bucks says she's thonging it."

Jackson shook his head with a smile.

Tommy frowned. "What?"

"Nothing. I didn't say anything."

"Dude. I just showed you probably the finest piece of ass you've seen ever. One that could so easily be yours and you shake your head no. What the hell is that?"

"It...it's nothing, man. I just don't, I don't think it's gonna...she's nice and all. But, you know..."

"I do know. I know you're an idiot. How about that?" Tommy laughed.

"Shut up." Jack didn't take him seriously. He blew it off and looked over at Madison, still by herself, studying away.

Tommy grabbed an unattended bag of lunch across from him. He looked inside and took out the sandwich. With a quick smell, he opened the wrapper and started eating it. He followed Jackson's eyes and saw Madison in the distance. With his mouth full of someone else's sandwich, Tommy shook his head at Jackson in disgust. "I don't get it."

"Get what?"

Tommy looked over at Madison and nodded his head in her direction. "Her. Over there. Is she the reason you won't be having a party in Kelly's pants? The skater chick who doesn't talk to anyone?"

"Madison."

"Right. Madison. You still hang out with her?"

Jackson shrugged uncomfortably. No one ever asked about his relationship with Madison except Tommy, as if on cue, every few months. Even if other people did ask, other people like Kelly, he still wouldn't know what to say. "Sometimes. Sometimes we hang out. She trains every day. She's going to the Olympics, you know. She's really good. Amazing, really. So...but yeah. I see her."

Tommy nodded knowingly. He grabbed cookies out of someone else's bag. "How?"

Jackson was hoping this conversation was over. Out of the corner of his eye, he watched as the cheerleaders made their way around the edge of the entire cafeteria. One by one, he watched as the students jumped off their benches excitedly, to make room for the girls they either wanted to be like or wanted to be getting down and dirty with. He watched as they got closer and closer to Madison.

Tommy nudged Jackson again, cookies now crumbling out of the corner of his mouth. "How, man?"

"How what?"

"How do you hang out with her?" There went someone else's milk off a tray.

Jackson shrugged without commitment. "I dunno. We just do."

Madison tried not to look as the cheerleading squad approached, armed with posters, markers and masking tape. She lowered her head down further into her book. Maybe if she pretended she didn't see them, they'd magically disappear.

"Like do you hang out, like, *naked*?"

Jackson turned to Tommy. "You wonder why you can't get a girlfriend that lasts more than a week? You're a freaking pig. I'll see ya later." Jackson got up and walked away.

"Um, excuse me?"

Madison looked up and saw Kelly. Cheerleader extraordinaire. She didn't say anything. She simply stared at her with a look that said 'drop dead please...I'm rather busy right now.'

Kelly put on her radiant, I-sat-under-the-dentist's-laser-whitening-gun-too-long smile, and repeated herself somehow without changing her delivery. "Um, excuse me?"

Madison raised her eyebrows ever so slightly. "Yes?"

"Hi. Can we use your bench to hang up some of these posters? They're for the school dance. Gotta spread the word, you know?"

Madison looked at her deadpan. "Yeah, of course you do. And I heard you're the best spreader. But do you need *this* specific bench? The one I'm sitting on?" *So what if they are going to call me a bitch. At least they'll call me something.*

Kelly looked at her squad for reinforcements. No one said a word. Who the heck said no to a cheerleader? "It shouldn't take us too long."

"Uh-huh." Madison hesitated, sealing her fate. "No. I'd rather not."

Jack watched carefully. He knew that face on Madison. He knew when she was about to say or do something she might possibly regret. He walked a little faster in her direction.

Kelly frowned down at Madison. No one told Kelly no. She was the captain of the varsity cheerleading squad. She had power. End of story. That is, until now. Kelly tried to laugh it off. Maybe this was Madison's humor. "I'm sorry. What did you say?"

Madison withdrew another book from her backpack while talking. "I said, 'I'd rather not.' Move, that is. I was up at four-thirteen this morning so I could skate before I came here to school. I'm tired. Really, very tired. I have two makeup exams this afternoon that I haven't even studied for and a paper due tomorrow, for which I haven't yet started to read the book it's based on. I have twenty-eight-and-a-half minutes left to do everything I just mentioned." Madison looked up at Kelly, without missing a beat. "So, if it's all the same, I'd rather not move right now."

"Here. Give 'em to me. I'll do it later." Jack smiled at Kelly and gently took the posters from her arms.

"That is so nice of you, Jackson. I'll just have to make it up to you."

Madison rolled her eyes and coughed loudly twice. Somehow it came out sounding like *wh-ore.*

Everyone's eyes turned to Madison. She looked up with the most innocent of faces and patted her chest gently. "Excuse me. Gotta cold."

Kelly put her hand on Jack's arm and held it there just a little too long. "Thanks again."

"Not a problem." Jackson waited until the cheerleaders were on to the next table before he sat down next to Madison. He carefully put the posters on the table.

Madison pretended to read from her book, ignoring him. "Why'd you do that?"

Madison didn't look at Jackson and proceeded to speak very quickly. "She called me Madeline that time. I don't like her. She's a whore. Whoops. Was that out loud?"

"Mad," Jack sighed, more to himself than to Madison. "You wonder why people don't ever talk to you or invite you anywhere?"

Still with her head buried in her book, she responded. "You talk to me and on occasion, though not often, you invite me places."

"You know what I mean, Mad."

Madison continued reading. "She's still a whore."

"Maybe. But that's not the point." Jackson had to look away so Madison wouldn't see him smile. God help him if Madison knew she won.

"I could've taken her, you know."

That was it. He had held it back for as long as he could. Jackson laughed out loud.

Madison finally looked up from her book with a grin and watched Jack shake his head at her. "Knew that one would get ya. You should've been here when I told Kelly-whore I heard she was a good spreader."

Jack's mouth dropped open. "You did not."

"One of my finest moments, I do believe." Madison hesitated and tried to think of the perfect way to tell Jack she screwed up his game later and before she could stop her mouth, it popped out. "Can't come today."

Jack nodded his head a little and gave Madison a much smaller smile than he just had. "Your mom's probably right, you know."

"No she's not even."

They both looked away from each other for a few uncomfortable seconds. Their eyes simultaneously glanced over to the posters being plastered everywhere.

"What time are your programs this weekend?"

"Check-in at nine. Short program Friday at eleven and long program on Saturday starts at three. Why are you asking? You can't come, right? You have a three o'clock game on Saturday."

"I know. I was just, you know...wondering. I...uh...I'll think about you."

Madison began to put her books in the backpack. "Really? Like right in the middle of the game? You'll stop and think of me? Or keep the play going and think of me?"

"Guess that depends on whether I'm about to score or not. You're not that important that I'll lose the game for you." Jackson handed Madison a book. "Yes, I'll think of you during the game, in the middle of a play, it won't matter. I'll stop the damn game. How's that?"

"That's good. I like it." Madison looked inside her untouched bag of lunch. "I'll be home around eleven o'clock. The victory party starts when I walk in the door."

"Oh, so you're planning on winning this thing."

"You bet your ass I am."

Jackson noticed the food Madison didn't eat. "I have a novel idea. How about you eat some lunch since this is what they call lunchtime."

"Not hungry. I gotta go see Mr. Juner about the make-up exam. You want it?"

Jackson shook his head no. "So, am I invited to your victory celebration?"

Madison stood up and threw her weighted-down backpack over her small frame. "When have you ever *not* been invited?"

"Just checking." Jackson stood up next to her.

Madison stared at the school dance posters sitting on the table. "You got some work to do."

"You gonna go?"

Madison cracked up. "To what. To that?" She pointed at the colorful posters badly decorated by none other than Kelly.

"Yeah, to that. What else?"

A small laugh could not be stopped. "That would mean I'd have to have friends, wouldn't it?" Madison took a few steps around Jack and looked around the room.

Jackson gave her a serious look. "You have one."

She turned to Jackson slowly. "What. What's that supposed to…you'd go to the dance with me?"

Jack shrugged his shoulders. He reached down to the table and picked up the posters. "All I'm saying is, if you wanted to go, and you don't get asked by anyone or whatever, then as your only friend, it's my duty to take you."

"Really. Well, what if one of your Barbie-like tribe followers asks you, then what?"

A semi-evil grin crossed Jackson's face. "Then, obviously, the deal's off." He laughed at Madison's expression. He got her good and he knew it.

"You are so *uninvited* to victory night." She walked away at a fast pace.

"Madison! Come on! I'm kidding!"

Without even turning her body around, Madison gave Jack the finger over her shoulder and continued walking out of the cafeteria.

"Oh! That was low!" Jack followed her for a few steps. But when he passed his table of friends, Tommy pulled him back into the group. "Dude! You totally missed the panty shot! We're talking G-string, dude!"

Jack smiled at Tommy and stole one more look in Madison's direction. At that same moment, she turned her head back to Jack with a smile.

And that's all Jack cared about. All that mattered was Madison smiling, and smiling only to him.

CHAPTER 10

*S*ix and seven-year-old skaters, all dressed in little blue matching outfits, performed a synchronized routine in the middle of the ice. Enormous banners hung along the side of the rink reading PACIFIC COAST CHAMPIONSHIPS. There was not an empty spot in the bleachers or any room to walk in the arena. The audience, consisting of men and women of all ages, tried not to laugh as one skater fell, creating a domino effect on the ice, sending all of the kids to the cold surface. A coach soon appeared and whisked the tearful culprit off the ice. The crowd clapped loudly as their screams of laughter echoed through the packed arena.

Off the rink, in their own individual spaces, coaches discussed last minute reminders and encouragement with their skaters. Some of them clearly wore the been there, done that look on their faces. Other girls had the look of fear and death in their eyes. Another skater broke down in tears and ran away from her coach and into her mother's waiting open arms.

The young skaters made their way off the ice. An announcer's voice rang loudly through the arena, introducing the first skater of the competition. The crowd gave polite applause as the girl slowly glided her way to the center of the rink.

Madison stood still in front of a long mirror, listening closely to the loud speaker in the room. Suddenly, her skirt was jerked roughly downward. Madison looked below at Annie, sitting on the floor. Annie yanked at it again. Harder.

"Ouch!"

"I am not hurting you, Mad. Give me a break, okay?"

David gave the cramped room a quick once-over, quietly walked over to a table against the far wall and sat on the edge. He carefully put down Madison's bag full of everything she might need. It was Annie's idea. *Anyone could live out of the bag, probably for days*, David thought. He peeked into the overstuffed duffel. Gatorade, three different kinds. "*Who knows what flavor Mad will be in the mood for?*" Annie had pointed that out to David a few too many times when he questioned her need for the variety. Seven different kinds of protein bars, some low carbohydrate, some high, some with chocolate, some yogurt-covered. "*Madison can't skate on an empty stomach, so these are perfect, depending on how she's feeling.*" Again, he shouldn't have bothered asking. There were numerous socks, tights, sweatshirts, sweatpants, T-shirts, underwear. You name it. It was in there. A second pair of skates? Of course. A back-up costume? Yep. Makeup? Shampoo? Deodorant? A variety of feminine protection? Check. She had that in the bag before Madison had even gotten her period. "*Bring it all*," Annie always said. A few times David even caught a glimpse of a back-up costume for the first back-up costume in the bottom of the bag. "*You never know when Madison might rip hers, you know? Or what if another skater has a similar dress on? Then what?"* David never argued with Annie when it had anything remotely to do with skating. She knew best when it came to that. He'd settle for carrying Annie's bag of tricks, supporting them both when needed, cheering Madison on, and driving them to the competitions. That was where his skating involvement ended. Except the bills. Always the bills.

Annie moved her legs underneath her body and knelt higher on the dirty carpet. She tugged and pulled at Madison's skirt again.

"What exactly are you trying to do, anyway?" Madison said.

"Your skirt is too short."

"It's fine, Mom."

"What did you do? Have Carol shorten it when I left you with her the other day? It was not this short when I was there, Madison. What the hell happened?"

"I dunno." Madison gave a loose shrug. So she had Carol hike it up an inch or two. *Big fat monkey balls. So what.*

Annie stopped pulling at the costume. "Answer me this. Do you want your butt to hang out in front of the judges? Huh? You want to pull off a perfect triple toe loop only to have your rear-end be the center of attention and not the jump you just nailed?"

"Hadn't thought about that." Madison paused with perfect Hollywood timing. "Maybe I do."

This was the place David interrupted, or at least, he attempted to. *It's all part of the competition*, he reminded himself. He hopped off the table with an all-too-fake smile. "Okay. How about we all take a deep breath. Ready? All together now." David inhaled deeply. By himself.

Madison and Annie stared at David with identical annoyed faces. *At least*, David thought, *at least they have something in common.* "Or not. No breathing deeply." He glanced from Annie to Madison. He knew when to take his cue. "Okay then. Good. I'm gonna go get us something to drink. How does that sound?"

Annie and Madison answered simultaneously, and in the same tone, "I'm not thirsty."

David heard them both. In stereo. He was smart enough to ignore them. Previous experience told him to. "A few Cokes maybe?" Without waiting for an answer, David passed by both of them and walked out the door.

Annie continued to let the hem out of Madison's skirt. She mumbled to herself in frustration as she carefully moved the small emergency scissors around each piece of thread.

Madison didn't take her eyes off of Annie through the mirror. While Annie's attention was conveniently on the costume, Madison slowly took little pieces of her hair and pulled them out of the clips they were in, now creating a loose wispy look. Didn't matter that Annie spent an hour trying to get each strand of hair tightly fastened within the clips.

"There's nothing else we can do about it now. I let it out as much as I could. Honestly, Mad!" Annie stood up, stretching her cramped legs. "Next time you want to shorten your skirt-" She stopped abruptly, mid-sentence.

Madison knew what was about to be said next. She tried to ignore it. "It's not too short, Mom. Really. It's fine. Thanks for fixing it."

Annie stared at Madison's head. "What the *hell* happened to your hair?"

"I dunno."

Annie tried to pull the long strands back up to the clips.

"What do you mean you don't know? Is that your answer of the day? You don't know how the skirt shrank two inches? You don't know how your hair got messed up? How does hair come out of the clips?"

"It just...fell."

"Madison, really. This looks ridiculous." Annie undid the clips and pulled Madison's hair back up into them. "You know I hate this. What happens when this stupid piece of hair gets in your face? Huh? Or...or what happens if it hits you in the eye while you're spinning? What then?"

Madison stood still while Annie redid her hair. "I guess, then...I would be blind."

Annie stopped and looked directly at Madison. She wasn't happy to say the least.

"What. I'm telling you what. You asked me 'what then?' I would be the one-eyed skater. I would go down in history. World-famous. Blinded...by a piece of wispy hair." It was all Madison could do not to laugh at herself.

Annie finally broke her eye contact and continued fixing Madison's hair. "Do you really love to piss me off that much?"

"Honestly?"

Annie stopped for a second, a clump of hair in her hands, and looked at Madison again. "Honestly. Do you?"

Madison's smile wasn't immediate. Rather a slow, mischievous grin. "Yeah."

David cautiously entered the dressing room, with a Coke in his hand. "You two almost ready? They're about two skaters away."

Madison and Annie met their gazes in the mirror. Annie broke the ice. "We're ready."

The three of them walked down the long corridor leading

to the waiting ice. Madison stopped briefly and adjusted her skate guard.

Annie stopped with her and waited. "Okay?" Her question, as Madison was painfully aware, wasn't just about the skate guard.

Madison looked up at Annie sincerely. Their connection was obvious to anyone standing within thirty feet of them. "Okay." Together they walked toward the rink entrance. Without missing a beat, Madison reached over to Annie and tightly took hold of her hand.

As they entered the arena, Madison clutched Annie's hand a little bit tighter. There was a very narrow opening to move through. David led the way to the edge of the ice and looked up at the overhead board. Madison's name was next. He stopped near the opening to the ice and allowed coach and skater to move up as close as possible.

Annie and Madison intently eyed the girl skating on the ice. Annie leaned down to Madison's ear and yelled over the music. "Victoria Jerkins. She's the one who beat us last year, remember?"

Madison nodded, her eyes glued to the skater. Does she remember? Of course she does! Wasn't she the one who had to bend over for the second place medal to be placed around her neck? But this wasn't a time to slap Annie with a nasty comeback, although many instantly came to her mind.

Victoria was graceful and beautiful on the ice, and off. She was born with legs that simply didn't end. Annie joked last year that she wore her butt on her shoulders. Madison looked at her again. *Now it appears she wears her ass on her head her legs are so long.* Madison tried not to think about it and shook it off. *Who cares how long her damn legs are.* Victoria landed another triple. Perfectly. *She's gotten even better,*

Madison thought. She heard through the grapevine Victoria had six triples and a quadruple jump in her routine. If she landed it, Maddie knew that no matter how good she was, Victoria's quad was going to put her on the top podium. Madison had landed a few quads recently, but the landings had been shaky at best. And Annie was the first one to say her quad was far from ready to be in her program.

Madison watched as Victoria landed a perfectly executed triple toe loop jump.

Annie and Madison exchanged a quick glance. Annie moved to her ear again, translating the look on Madison's face. "You're a close second to her after the short. You've improved more than anyone here. You know it and I know it. So what? She has a quad. You've got seven triples and they are all perfect, Mad."

Madison thought about all the hours skating in the cold, all the early mornings when the sun had yet to rise, all the late nights when other kids her age were having fun hanging out; all the endless practices, all the run-throughs, all the hard work. She thought about every tiny step she had made to get here. She *had* gotten better. Annie was right.

At that very moment, Victoria Jerkins fell hard on the ice. She didn't land her quadruple jump.

Annie and Madison exchanged an immediate calculating glance. They knew what each other was thinking. Annie looked at her for a moment before opening her mouth. "I know what you're thinking, but you don't need a quad. You don't, Madison. You need to land every triple."

Madison stopped her with a defiant nod. She took an extremely deep breath. "I can do it."

"Maybe but it's not necessary. She fell and that means only six triples and a deduction for the fall. You've got seven triples. We don't need it to win, Maddie. Really, get it out of your mind right now. It's too risky. You're not ready."

Madison glanced at Victoria, just finishing her routine. Her eyes stayed on the ice as Annie's words resonated in her head.

Annie's face remained calm. She studied Madison to make sure her daughter heard her loud and clear. No stunts. No chancy jumps. Not here. One competition away from Nationals. Almost to the Olympics. "Remember, keep your back—"

"Straight. I know."

Madison bent over and removed her guards from her skates. Annie reached out her hand and took them from her. Without stopping, her hand knowingly continued back and held the guards out to David standing behind her.

Over the loud speakers, the announcer boomed, "That was Victoria Jerkins. After this short word from our sponsors, here at the Pacific Coast Championships, up next, we have Madison Henry!"

Madison didn't pay attention to the crowd clapping enthusiastically. She didn't listen to her name echoing throughout the packed arena. She stretched down to her feet and straightened up, and suddenly fell into Annie, losing her balance. Annie's arm was the only thing that stopped her from falling flat on her face.

Annie frowned at Madison. "What was that?"

"I just...I stood up too quick."

"Did you eat the energy bar earlier?"

"Mom!"

"Okay, okay." Annie held up her hands in front of her body as if to stop herself from saying anything more.

David took a few steps in and kissed Madison on the cheek. "Go get 'em, Maddie-girl."

"Thanks, Daddy."

Out of nowhere, Jack approached behind Madison. She didn't have a clue.

Annie's face brightened noticeably when she observed Jack behind her skater. Jack had yet to miss a competition, in all the years he and Madison had been friends. And she knew how much it meant to Madison to have him there. Probably more than her daughter would ever admit.

Madison looked at Annie strangely. "What's wrong?"

"No. It uh, it's nothing." Annie regained her composure.

Without warning, Jackson leaned his head into the back of Madison. "No one uninvites me to a victory party."

A huge smile beamed across Madison's surprised face. She turned herself around to find Jack. "What are you doing here? What happened to your game?"

Jack shrugged and shook his head with a questioning look on his face. "Craziest thing. I had this like, flu thing this morning, you know? Really severe. Couldn't move, couldn't even sit up. So sick I couldn't play. But then, as soon as I called coach and told him I was out? And this is where it gets really weird...right after I hung up the phone, that very second...I was fine. Completely cured." Jack even went so far as to snap his fingers dramatically. "Just like that. So I got in my car and started driving. And somehow I ended up here."

Annie eyed Jackson closely. "Funny how those flu things come and go that mysteriously, huh?"

Madison looked at the ice. She knew she should be warming up right now. But there was something holding her back. Jackson? A few extra seconds to rest? She didn't give it any more examination. Whatever the reason, she was relieved to take the extra time. "So, if you felt so much better, so quickly, why not call your coach back and tell him you're feeling oh so much better, huh?"

Jackson rolled his eyes. "That would make me look like a big faker liar, now, wouldn't it? I can't help it if I'm a quick healer."

Madison opened her mouth to give Jack one of her infamous responses when she heard it.

The announcer roared over the speakers again. "Will the Hilton Skaters please clear the ice?" The school of young skaters gradually made their way off the ice, vying for as much time as possible to be noticed.

With a sincere look to Jack and a squeeze of his hand, Madison said, "Thank you."

Then without any hesitation, Madison turned to Annie. Their eyes locked instantly with a silent understanding only the two of them were privy to. They didn't break their intense contact as the announcer continued. "Up now, our last and final skater of the competition, Madison Henry!" There were various screams and yells from the fans. "Madison was in second place after the short program. She is definitely one of our Olympic hopefuls." Madison and Annie grinned as he took his dramatic pause. "Ladies and Gentlemen...Madison Henry!"

Annie grabbed Madison's arm just as she was about to step on the ice. "Don't do it. You don't need a quad. Okay?"

A small, but very serious smile crossed Madison's face. "Okay." Madison reassuringly patted her mother's hand and put one foot on the ice, then the other. That was when everything went silent in her mind. She was oblivious to the applause, shouts and roars of the fans so close to her. She didn't think about her skirt being too short or the hair she so desperately wanted to make wispy around her face. She didn't think about what Jack had to do to get there for her, just to watch her compete for four minutes. She didn't think about the time, money and energy spent on her life, her mother's life, every day.

She skated to the center of the ice and stopped, in a perfect position. All she heard was the music. Soon, without even telling herself it was time, her skates instinctively began to move. Her head lifted high in the air, almost as if she was a real princess with the right to have this attitude.

With every difficult move, the crowd's cheering reverberated throughout the rink.

David and Jack, as always, watched with extremely anxious faces.

Annie stood just a bit in front of them, watching every single move in her silent prayer and never cheering. She ran through every checklist in her mind. *Back straight, yes. Head high, got that too. Fingers and arms outstretched, she remembered. Skates pointed, yes, thank God.*

Madison skated faster and faster near the edge of the ice preparing for her second jump, a triple triple combination.

The crowd was silenced in preparation.

Annie waited patiently and watched as Madison pulled her body high into the air and counted the one, two, three complete rotations, and down. Then immediately, Madison threw her body into the air again three more times.

She landed solidly and her face glowed with excitement. Energy flew from her fingertips.

David and Jack shouted hysterically along with the crowd.

Annie's eyes sparkled quietly. Everything so far looked good but it was too early for celebrating. Only she knew the difficulty still awaiting Madison. She still had another half a program to complete and she knew anything could happen.

Madison went through the mandatory section of her program. Her required skating, as they called it. This wasn't the part that scared Annie. This was the stuff Madison had been doing since she was nine. Annie watched her champion. Quick footwork, graceful arm movements and then the arabesque that was so exquisite it brought cheers from the crowd as Madison continued down the long side of the ice.

Soon Madison was skating fast again, moving her skates quickly in and around each other. *Here it comes*, Annie thought. *Five jumps down, two more to go and we can call it a day. A victorious day.*

Madison once again pulled her body up in the air and completed a difficult triple axle with complete perfection. It was late in the program so there were extra points, Annie reminded herself. Her landing could be a little stronger, but they could work on that before Nationals. Annie finally allowed herself to smile, even if it was only a small one. *One more and we're good to go.*

Madison was nearing the end of her program, preparing for her final triple but something happened. Still feeling the pace of the music, Madison moved differently across the now choppy and nicked ice. Her skates began to move even faster.

Annie's face paled. *Oh God.*

David moved to Annie's side. "What's going on? This doesn't look like..." His voice trailed off.

All Annie could do was shake her head no, just once, without even making eye contact with David. *She can't try it. She has to be tired...exhausted from the routine.* Annie shook her head again slowly. Without looking at David still, she yelled to him. "She's adding a quad."

"What? Why would she do—?"

Annie's hand grabbed David's arm, stopping him mid-sentence. She was the only one who knew how close this was going to be. She knew. She could see Madison was losing energy. Rapidly. Annie would've been worried over the seventh triple. A quadruple jump was cause for complete panic.

Madison pushed her body to move faster. She was aware this jump could mean the title. She knew landing it would get her to the top riser on the podium and she knew if she screwed this up, it would be nobody's fault but her own. But if she could land it, she would be one of very few who have successfully landed a quad in competition. And it would seal her Olympic fate.

She fought the feeling that her legs were noodles underneath her. She fought the massive dizziness she had felt since she stopped spinning minutes ago and she quickly prepared for the jump of her life. With every ounce of energy she had left, she threw her body soaring into the air, higher than all the other jumps previously. So high the crowd gasped in concern. Madison had never jumped with such extraordinary power and she knew it. She persuaded herself silently in her head. *C'mon, body. One. Two. Three times around. Do it one more time. Four times around.*

And then, she landed...

Perfectly. She was on one leg, the other stretched out fully behind her. The tip of her skate pointing masterfully to the ice. It was then Madison realized she had never before successfully completed that jump in competition so late in her program. *Hell*, she thought, *I've never completed a quad in competition ever!* Within ten seconds, her music would stop. Madison created her own finish to the routine, which before one minute ago, had an entirely different ending. She spun furiously, her head tipped back, her left foot bent up perfectly behind her. Suddenly, her quad jump thoroughly sunk in. Barely holding her final pose, she screamed out loud in excitement. She skated at high speed around the ice with her arms automatically waving in the open air above her head.

She did it.

The crowd went insane. Stuffed animals of all shapes and sizes and flower bouquets of all varieties were thrown on the ice for her. Madison's grin covered her entire face as she blew kisses to the little girls screaming her name. Then she looked over to her family and her Jack and let out a huge yell of excitement.

David and Jack were jumping up and down in each other's arms. David reached his free arm to Annie's shoulder.

She looked up at David with a smile. But she remained just as reserved as she did when Madison was skating. She finally connected with Madison's eyes. Annie did what she always did. She held up her right thumb in front of her body, in a small gesture. Madison returned the thumbs-up, just the exact same way.

∽∽∽∽∽∽

Annie placed the huge cake on the table in front of Madison. She quickly walked back to the silverware drawer and took out a large cake knife. With her back turned to the table, she listened. The giggles coming from Madison's mouth were borderline hysterical and Annie smiled to herself. She loved that laugh and she didn't hear it nearly enough. She turned and stole a peek at her daughter, the Pacific Coast Ice Skating Champion. Madison still wore her first-place gold medal around her neck. Jackson tickled her every few seconds, sending Madison into yet another fit. Without realizing it, tears welled up in her eyes. *We have come a long way*, Annie thought. *A very long way.* Not wanting to try to explain the dampness in her eyes, she turned away from the happy table. Quickly wiping her face and getting control, she grabbed some glasses from a cabinet above the counter. Her actions did not go unnoticed by David. They never did.

"Need any help over there?" David stood and moved toward Annie. She shook her head no, but that didn't stop David from approaching. He stood behind Annie and wrapped his arms around her waist. He snuggled his head through her hair and found her ear and whispered. "I'm proud of you."

Annie didn't turn around to him. She grabbed another glass down from the shelf. "I didn't do anything. It was Madison."

"Well, from where I'm looking, Maddie has someone to not only coach her brilliantly but also has someone who drives her to and from the rink every day, sometimes twice a day. Someone who works her butt off six, sometimes seven days a week at a very stressful job so her daughter can skate, someone who bakes cakes for every small and large victory…"

Her voice tried to hide the crackle she knew was coming. "I ordered the cake from Costco."

When David spun her around, he saw her tears. He couldn't help but smile a little at this woman, his lovely wife, who was out-and-out pouting like a six-year-old. He heard Madison and Jack behind him completely unaware of any conversation going on but their own. He lifted his hands to Annie's face and gently dried her wet cheeks with his fingers. "You're cute."

"No, I'm not. It's stupid, me crying. I'm just...I don't know what I am. I'm happy."

"Ann. It's not stupid. It's natural to feel like this. You're exhausted. You've been working hard for so long now, right? And today, you won." David grinned wide. "You won *big*."

Annie smiled back and shook herself out of the funk. "We did win big, huh?"

"Yeah." David kissed her forehead and pulled her close to him, hugging her tightly. "So who really cares the cake isn't homemade? I mean, *I* was hoping for homemade, but that's okay. Store-bought processed batter is, you know, it's fine. It's good. And I guess you can't match Costco's icing."

Annie frowned slightly and bit by bit lifted her head up to David. Seeing David's mischievous face, Annie's whacked his butt hard with her hand. "You shit."

"Who's a shit?" Madison's ears, of course, picked up on the foul word.

Jackson snaked a taste of icing with his finger. "You know, I've heard spanking is said to have many a positive effect on troubled relationships."

Annie and David shook their heads at the two sitting at the table. Annie moved around David, grabbing two of the four glasses on the counter. She brought them over to the table and sat down. David grabbed the knife and the two remaining glasses and walked back to his chair.

Madison stuck her finger in the side of the cake and licked the icing off her finger. Annie saw Madison's impatience. "Could you wait a second? I've got the knife right here."

David handed Annie the knife and she cut the first piece.

"Do you have a back-up cake?" Madison read the writing on the cake over and over again. 'Nationals Here We Come!'

was written in beautiful cursive pink icing. She stuck another finger in the cake and swiped a long line of icing. This time, it went unseen by Annie.

"Why?"

"Cause this could've totally sucked if I didn't win. A champion cake for a big loser? That could've caused major pain and suffering and probably years of therapy."

Annie gently slid the piece of cake onto a plate and handed it to Madison. "But you did win."

Madison dug into her cake and grinned. "I know. With a *quad*."

Annie cut another slice and handed it to Jackson. She cut two more pieces and put them on plates while she talked. "I was thinking earlier about some things. We've got a few months before Nationals, right? And that doesn't give us a lot of time to...uh...to iron out a few minor problem areas." Annie handed David a plate.

David immediately picked up on Annie's evasiveness. "It doesn't give you extra time for any goofing off, but come on, Ann." David shot a smile to Madison. "She's great. What do you have to do? Everything's the same. And it'll be like today, right? Same routine, same costume?"

The piece of cake sat in front of Annie, untouched. She casually put her fork back down on the table. Now was as good a time as any. "Obviously the quad is out, but ah...actually, I thought we should think about changing the program a little."

This was news to Madison. She had worked on this routine for months and it was all in preparation for Nationals. Sure, when she went to the Olympics, they would alter her routine. They'd have to a little. But for Nationals? No one changes a routine when you've got a winner. And they had a winner. Madison abruptly stopped chewing with her mouth full of cake. "I don't want to change it."

David, clearly disturbed by what Annie was proposing, stopped eating the cake and looked at Annie. "What's wrong with the routine this way? She won today. Madison did. No one else is at home with the gold medal."

"I just think we can do slightly better." Annie lifted her fork from the table and dug into the cake in front of her. "That's all."

"Well, if you ask me, and obviously you should, since I'm the one skating...I don't want to change it. I think it's fine and I, for one, like the quad. I added it at the end which I know didn't really fit. But we can just find a better place to throw it."

Annie remembered they had a guest. Not that Jackson was a real one; he'd been more like family since the beginning. Still, this was going to be a fight to the finish and she wasn't about to start it now. "Why don't we talk about this later, okay?"

This was not the time to press this discussion and Madison knew it. She could tell by the look on her mother's face. Plus she was too excited to let Annie ruin her good mood. She wanted to enjoy the perfect white cake with white sugar icing from Costco, which secretly, she would take any day over her mother's.

After a few moments of silence, David smiled at Jackson. He always knew when to break the ice and now seemed like the perfect time. "So, Jack...aside from that baffling flu bug earlier, how's the soccer going?"

Jack was used to being around Annie and Madison when they got like this. He was not at all uncomfortable, and never had been. He had been in the middle of much more heated conversations than this one. And in some disturbed way, he welcomed it. It was like being a part of a real family and he'd take that anytime. Jack finished his cake off in one big bite. "It's pretty good. We've only lost one game so far this season. I've been scoring a lot and...and uh..."

All eyes moved to Jack, and Jack's eyes moved from one person to the next as he tried not to smile.

Madison looked at him strangely. "What's wrong with you? What's so funny?"

Jack shrugged and answered nonchalantly. "It's not funny, really. In the sense I have a joke or anything. It's just um...I found out today that the International Junior Soccer Team wants me to play...next summer."

"Are you serious? Oh my God!" Madison dropped her fork.

Annie smiled proudly. "Jack, that's great! Why didn't you say anything?"

"He just did." David laughed.

Madison hugged Jack excitedly from her chair and continued talking. "This is like, *huge* for you. It will totally get you noticed, obviously, and you'll get to travel all over the world!" Then Madison broke her embrace and looked into Jack's eyes. "Wait. What'd your dad say when you told him?"

It was clear Jack could have hugged Madison for hours longer by the look on his face. "I haven't exactly told him yet. He's been working on this big case and been kind of busy so I thought I'd..." Jack stopped himself and shook his head. "I'm not sure how he'll take the idea of me leaving for the whole summer. I mean, how long has he been planning on me working at the firm with him, you know? Might not be so pretty."

Annie smiled proudly. "How many weeks will you be gone?"

Madison's eyes shot to Jack. She hadn't thought of that. She had never really been without him.

Jack's glance moved from Madison to Annie. "Um, it's for the summer. The whole summer. I'll leave as soon as school is out and come back on Labor Day. I'll get to travel every-where…England, Spain…" He slowly allowed his eyes to read Madison's face. Immediately he noticed the change in her attitude. What had just been a happy face was now one full of confusion, and maybe a little sadness. He tried to break the awkward silence. "It's pretty cool, because Tommy was asked too, so I uh…I'll at least know one person." Another look to Madison.

As a matter of fact, all eyes were on Madison.

She quickly realized this and covered instantly. Madison resumed eating her cake and looked at Jack with a mouthful. "Well, you know what? It's great. Really great!" She purpose-fully swallowed a bite far too big for her mouth and put on a believable smile. "Because, my friend, tonight is victory night. For both of us."

David raised his drink. "There you go!"

Madison looked at Jack and smiled. "Don't even think you'll make the Wheaties box before I do. I've already called it."

There. She got through the disturbing moment. Too much cake and too many fake smiles, but she did it. And Jack had no idea how much him leaving for the summer shattered her inside.

CHAPTER 11

*M*adison and Annie waited at the front door of the rink, their breath floating like miniature clouds in the cold morning air. The sky above them was still dark, and the sun showed no signs of warm life yet. Madison's eyes closed as she stood motionless, resting her body against the old, brick building. Annie moved her feet side to side to keep warm. She knocked on the glass door again.

Seconds later, George appeared and unlocked the door, looking as tired as them.

"Morning, George." Annie turned to see Madison still standing against the building, eyes shut.

George put the keys back in his coat and stepped aside, giving Annie and Madison room to enter. "Ladies." He held the door wide open and gave Annie an understanding, sympathetic glance. His eyes then shifted back to a sleepy Madison. "Hey there, peanut."

Madison slowly opened her lids with much effort. "Hi, George." She stumbled in and walked by George.

As George's attention left Madison, his eyes hit Annie with a question. The same question asked many times before. "She okay?"

Annie knew what it meant. She had seen this exact same look on his weathered face too many times to count. "She's really tired."

George let the heavy door swing shut. "Price you pay, huh?" He locked the rink back up.

"Yeah." Annie motioned to the door. "Listen, I've got the choreographer coming—"

"Six A.M. I'm on it." He looked down at his wrist and looked at his watch. "We've got an hour and ten minutes. I'll make sure to let her in."

"Thanks, George."

Annie walked to the rink. Madison was sitting on the bottom bleacher. Her bag was at her feet and her skates sat on the floor below her. She stared blankly onto the ice.

Annie approached from the side and watched as Madison's eyes closed again. "What are you doing?"

Madison immediately opened her eyes and focused. "Nothing. Just sitting."

"You think you can get your skates on? We're wasting time here."

Madison, with considerable effort, reached down to one of her skates and put it on her left foot. Annie sat down next to her and looked out at the perfect ice. She quickly put her skates on.

"Mom?"

"Yeah." Annie grabbed Madison's right skate off the ground and handed it to her.

"I'm tired." She took a deep, calculated breath. "Really tired." She started lacing up her skates.

Seeing the energy Madison was wasting, Annie finished lacing up her skates for her. "Me too, baby." She stretched as she stood up and extended her hand to Madison still sitting on the bleacher. "C'mon. Up you go. We've got a lot of work to do." Annie pulled Madison up.

Madison removed her guards and threw them into the bag on the floor. *Just get through this practice,* she told herself. *Get through this and sleep during lunch. And Mr. Juner's class.*

Annie skated out on the ice with Madison skating unhurriedly behind her. She watched as Madison began circling lethargically around the outskirts of the rink and tried to remember what it was like for her when she was training so many years ago.

For Annie it had always been like a moderate chore. Not that she didn't love to skate, she did. But it wasn't as easy for her as it had been for Madison. She had to work hard at each and every move. Each and every practice, each and every competition. She thought about the recent competition and how Madison simply threw in a quadruple jump at the end of a four minute program! She could never have done that. Not physically or mentally. Not in a million years. A routine to a skater is like her Bible. You don't just throw in a jump like she did without rehearsing it, ever. Especially that difficult of a jump. And if you did, certainly the outcome wouldn't be successful. *Unless,* Annie mused, *unless you're Madison.*

"We gonna skate today or what?" Madison called from across the rink.

Annie turned her head in Madison's direction and smiled proudly.

"What's that look for?" Madison skated up close to Annie.

Annie shook her head. "Absolutely nothing."

Madison grinned as she skated around Annie, creating a bigger and bigger circle. "You're scaring me, Mom. I don't like you smiling for no reason. You can't start to lose it yet. We've got another few weeks before that's allowed, remember?"

"I remember."

CHAPTER 12

The security guard waved Annie down as she pulled into the hospital parking lot. Annie knew she was late, but she obviously couldn't go plowing through the gate, as much as she'd like to. And Steve had always been a big fan of Madison's. The least she could do was give him a quick hello. She rolled down her window and smiled politely. "Hey, Steve."

"Hey, there. Heard about the Pacific Coast skating thing. First place. That's something, huh?"

Annie glanced toward the hospital. "Yeah, it's uh, great. Listen, I'd love to talk more but I'm so la—"

"Didn't stop you to chat, Annie." Steve's face crinkled up slightly in embarrassment. "I stopped you because you were driving a little too fast for the hospital grounds. Told to give you a warning."

Annie felt the color rise up in her face. She was the one who was embarrassed. "Right. Sorry. I'm...you know, a little late."

Steve nodded in understanding. "Figured. But be careful. Wouldn't want anything to happen to you." With that gentlemanly warning, he tapped the door twice and backed away.

She knew she should be thankful, but at that moment, all that was going through her mind was that infinitesimal interaction just cost her forty-six vital seconds. She pulled into a parking spot and within a flash, she was running into the hospital, praying no one had observed the clock. That was all she needed, to be written up again for being tardy. She couldn't let that happen again until after Nationals.

Annie thankfully slipped in without being noticed. She quickly made her way into the nurse's lounge and grabbed a cup of much-needed strong, black coffee. As she exited, she grabbed a chart, making herself look like she'd been there for a while and that she was busy. If anyone did notice her hundred-yard dash, then no one here cared. Assuming she was in the clear, Annie took a quick breather. The halls were quiet, letting her rightfully assume the patients were taken care of. The only other noise was the steady beeping of a heart monitor coming from a nearby room.

Annie looked through the charts on the counter in front of her. Everyone had been seen within the past hour. It was a little odd that not one other nurse was visible, but it was always a welcome surprise. Annie savored those last few seconds before her shift started or on a special day like today, after her shift already started. That very limited amount of peace and quiet. It certainly didn't happen with Madison around and rarely happened while she was at work.

Work. How funny it was that she was a nurse. She remembered when she was little and was asked, as every child is, what she wanted to be when she grew up. It was always a skater. She knew it in her heart. But what consistently came out of her mouth was a doctor. She would sit back in her chair and marvel the thought. A doctor. She hated the sight of blood. Couldn't really stand sickness of any kind, and yet, there she was. Spouting out the word "doctor" as fast as can be. Maybe in the back of her mind, she just knew. Knew it wouldn't always be about skating. Knew that one day, something far more important would happen to her. Knew that she would, in fact, be able to see blood, deal with it, and maybe even learn to appreciate the ill. It took her years, but she did it. She smiled as she remembered getting her degree, and the entire weekend after, when she made David refer to her as Nurse Annie. A story, quite frankly, that had never been repeated through the years except to her one old friend.

Annie's head floated up from her daydream. She caught the back of a female doctor walking by her and instantly she knew. "Susan!"

The woman stopped and turned in Annie's direction. Once she saw the voice belonged to Annie, a warm smile replaced her slight frown. "Hey, you. I didn't even see you."

Annie walked around the counter to meet her halfway. "I was trying to play hooky for two more minutes. I can get a pretty good nap in two minutes, you know. How the heck are you? I miss you."

Annie and Susan moved to give each other a genuine hug. They had been good friends for over twenty years. Not the fake, once-a-year Christmas card friends, but the kind of friends that had seen each other through it all and still remained close, even without the time to spend chatting over coffee or shopping at the local mall.

They gently released each other and stepped back an inch. "Don't blame it on me. I'm just a damn doctor. You're the coach to the famous skater chick." Susan grinned.

Annie smiled back proudly. "Did you see her?"

"Did I *see* her? Did I *hear* is more appropriate. They had the television on under the counter. The one I'm not supposed to know about. I swear to God, the nurses had the volume up to ten. The poor sick people, is all I got to say." Susan shook her head in what would be considered a negative gesture, but it was obvious she did not have a real problem with it. "They had every television on the entire floor tuned in to you and Madison. The hospital rocked when she finished. Literally."

"It was unbelievable. You should have heard inside the rink. I've never heard anything so loud in my life, Sus. She was brilliant."

Susan's beeper went off. She checked the page and rolled her eyes. "Gotta go. Listen, when am I seeing you for coffee talk?"

Annie hesitated for a beat. "Probably not until after the Olympics. But I stopped you because I have a small favor."

"There are no small favors. So much for your lovey-dovey 'miss you, Susan' bullshit." Susan smiled. "What is it?"

"I...uh...do you have any time to look at Madison? I know you're booked through next year but, I think I can take advantage of our beautiful friendship, can't I?"

"Sure. Yeah, of course you can." Susan started walking away backward. "Is everything okay?"

"Oh yeah, she's great. It's just, with Nationals coming up, and all the extra practicing, she's been really tired. And because I am so damn smart, I thought maybe you could reinforce the importance of the vitamin intake and make sure she's not anemic. She obviously won't listen to me. I'm just the nurse, the coach and the mother."

"Call my office and tell them to fit you in whenever you can make it."

Annie grinned and raised her eyebrows, hopeful. "We can make it today."

Susan stopped walking and thought for a beat then she

shook her head no. "Jesus. I'm totally booked, Ann. Is today it?"

"This is the last time we'll have an entire half hour free. Please? Pretty please? Friend? Best friend?" Annie tried to look as sympathetic as possible and guiltily added, "Friend, oldest and only friend, who knows my deep dark secrets and would never tell a soul about my Nurse Annie weekend."

Susan broke out in hysterics. "That was one of the best damn stories you have ever told. You should've become a romance novelist." Susan couldn't stop laughing.

"Uh-huh. You say that while laughing. Don't think I would've made much money if my throbbing thigh and heaving chest story made you still laugh some twenty years later."

Susan calmed down and smiled a little. "You are really going to take advantage of our friendship, aren't you?"

"Oh, yeah. Absolutely."

Susan sighed and shook her head. She stole a quick look down at her watch on her wrist. "Okay. Here's the thing though. Can you make it by three?"

"Susan, thank you." Annie ran up to her and planted a wet kiss on her cheek.

"Trust me. You can pay back the favor with front row seats at the Olympics. In the meantime, I would like a turkey sandwich on rye, no mayo, a bag of chips of your choice, and lastly, I'd like a Slurpee."

Annie laughed out loud as Susan walked down the hall. "A Slurpee? What kind of request is that from a doctor? You know how bad they are for you?"

"A *cherry* Slurpee!" Susan gave Annie one last smile and walked away with a quick wave over her shoulder.

❦❦❦❦❦❦❦

Madison threw books and folders in her locker, took different ones out and shoved them in her backpack. She struggled trying to balance the bag on her knee as she zipped it up. She finally got the bag closed and threw it over her shoulders and in a quick move, shut her locker door. Jack was standing there, waiting for her to jump. Even a little. She didn't. A slight smile came to Madison's face. But one that was quite clearly a forced one. "Hey."

"You didn't jump. You always jump. It's like, the highlight of my days."

"Sorry." Madison then jumped up in the air and pretended to be frightened for half a second. "There. Was that any better?"

"Actually, yes it was. I feel much better now. I told you. I don't like disorder in my day. And me scaring you and you jumping? That, my friend, is an everyday joyful occurrence and by not participating in my fun, you disrupt my day." He smiled at Madison. "You're coming to the game today, right?"

"Yeah. I told you last night on the phone, and I told you again this morning. We were standing right here, by the way. I told you at lunch I was going. Again. Maybe you got hit too many times in the head with your soccer ball."

"You're very funny, you know that? I'm just making sure you aren't going to forget. Or blow me off again. These games...they're not dumb school games. These are for the International Jun—"

"Junior Soccer Team, Jackson. I know and I'm going. For the last time." Madison leaned up against the locker, trying to take the weight off her shoulders from the heavy backpack. She didn't apologize for her crankiness.

"So, uh...where're you gonna sit?"

Madison looked straight ahead, ignoring Jack's gaze. "I don't know. I haven't thought about it. I guess wherever your tribe isn't."

A bell rang loudly through the halls. Madison gently pushed Jack with her bag. "I'll...uh...I'll see you at the game, okay?" Madison walked around Jack and into a classroom nearby.

"Yeah. Okay." He watched Madison sit down at her desk and take out a book. He frowned slightly at Madison's weird behavior. That was only the first bell and considering they always hung out for another minute or so...was she blowing him off? Trying to ignore him? He racked his brain for a second, wondering if he might have said anything to upset her. Nope. Nothing. But it's something. Something isn't right. She looked thin. She'd always been on the skinny side, but now it looked a little more obvious. She looked paler than usual too. *Maybe she's just tired*, Jackson thought. *That's probably it.* It wasn't like she'd been in any kind of sunshine recently. And she was working out so hard. He finally broke his stare and walked down the hall toward his class. Ten steps later, a manicured hand touched his shoulder.

Kelly smiled flirtatiously and removed her hand. "I hope I didn't scare you."

"Uh, no. You didn't." Jack continued walking, hardly slowing down. He didn't want to deal with Kelly right now. He knew she had a thing for him. Everyone knew. She made that beyond clear. She was at every game, cheering him on. She sent notes in the classes they had together. The phone calls, the messages through their mutual friends, the emails, text messages, the freshly baked cookies! He got it. Enough said and overdone.

Kelly followed him closely. "So, you have a game here today, right? The International soccer game?"

"Yeah, we do." Jack tried to be as polite as possible without losing his patience. *Why can't Madison remember like Kelly?* Even she knew about the new games and how important they were to his future. *Be polite, have patience.*

"That's what I thought." Then she smiled. Again.

Patience gone. Before he could edit what was going through his head, Jack's mouth opened to words already spilling out. "Look, you have the game schedule, Kelly. I mean, you asked me to email it to you the day I got it. You've set up a new cheerleading squad to come cheer me on. Besides me and Tommy, no one else from our school is even on the team." He didn't mean for it to come out as hideous as it did. Before he could think up some kind of apology or explanation, Kelly saved him.

"Yeah, I know. I just, I wanted you to..." Kelly stopped talking and smiled at Jackson. "I'm sorry. I guess by trying to make small talk, I have completely embarrassed myself."

A pang of guilt slowly stopped Jackson and he looked at Kelly. *She's really pretty*, he thought. Not like the other bimbo-like cheerleaders. For a moment, he felt terrible for trying to blow her off. She didn't do anything wrong. Unless liking someone is cause for punishment.

"You didn't embarrass yourself. I didn't mean that to come out the way it did."

Kelly nervously looked away as the second bell echoed through the school. "Guess I should make this quick." She looked at Jack. "The reason I wanted to talk to you is uh...I was wondering about something. I don't know if you maybe have plans or not and I know it's kind of early to be asking, but I was thinking...maybe you'd want to go to the dance with me."

Jack didn't know what to say. This was so not what he was expecting to come out of Kelly's mouth. "I wasn't um...you know, that...that's really nice." *Could I stutter any more?* But, it's just that I kinda made plans already with someone. But thanks anyway." Jack glanced to his class. "I should go. Really though, thanks for asking me."

Kelly hid her disappointment with a smile and a nod. "Sure."

"I guess I'll see ya at the game." Jack walked away from Kelly and entered his class.

CHAPTER 13

"Great. Two-forty-five. We're gonna be late." Annie sped down the road, with side glances to Madison every few seconds. A light ahead turned yellow and she looked at the clock by the radio with a roll of her eyes. She turned the radio on a low volume and slowed the car down. If she expected to get some sort of a response out of Madison, she was wrong.

Madison stared out the passenger window wearing a very pissed-off face. Without a word or a gesture to Annie, she leaned in to the radio and hit it off.

Annie knew going to the doctor was going to be difficult. It always was. But this time she had forgotten one small thing. Jack's game. Madison had asked her about it over a week ago. Annie had promised her she could definitely go to this one. She knew Madison would not be happy about going to the doctor. But she hadn't prepared herself for the fit Madison threw when she saw Annie waiting outside of the school twenty minutes ago.

Annie stepped on the gas as soon as the light turned green. "This is the only time Susan could see you, Mad."

No response. Not even a blink of an eye. Shit, this was going to get ugly.

"And really, if you think about it, it's the only available time we have with Nationals coming up. Right? We don't have any extra time here to be playing around." Annie dreaded these moments. The one-sided conversations that had been known to last hours. Days even, depending on the situation and this one wasn't looking very promising. "Maddie?"

Madison turned into the window even more, literally squeezing herself into a concentrated ball. All Annie had contact with was the back of her head.

"You've got no right to be pissed at me." *Okay. So maybe she does*, Annie thought. But at least she'd get a response from that statement. Maybe some additional pestering would help hurry it up. "No right. *At all.*" Annie stole another look at her daughter's angry backside. Not even the slightest movement. She took a deep breath and decided it was obviously time for another approach. They were almost to the hospital and she'd be damned if Madison wasn't talking by the time they got there. "So, okay. Maybe...*maybe* you have a little right to be somewhat upset with me, but that's it. Just a little. Maybe." Then she waited for it to start. Any second now...it would happen.

There it was. Madison's voice.

It was quiet at first and she still didn't turn around to face her, but Annie would accept anything about now.

"I'm missing Jack's game." Each word was hit with unwavering anger.

Daggers. Sharp daggers, Annie thought. "I know. I'm really, really sorry about that. I know I told you that you could go. Totally my fault. But this appointment shouldn't take that long at all and then...I don't know. Then maybe..."

Madison turned furiously to Annie. "Then *what*? Then we

have the rink, don't we? So don't even act like I can go to the game after the fucking doctor, 'cause you know I can't. At least have the common courtesy of apologizing to me and acknowledging you're the one that screwed everything up. Again."

Not the kind of moment she was hoping for. Annie tried to keep things from overheating more than they already were. She couldn't stand when she heard language like that from Madison. At least, when she was serious. Then again, this was probably not the most appropriate time for discussing her foul potty mouth. *Might as well get it over with.* "You're right. You can't go to the game after the doctor. We do have the rink already booked." She turned her car into the hospital parking lot. "I *am* sorry that you're missing Jack's game. Just do me a favor. Don't be rude, okay? Susan is totally squeezing you in and I refuse to be embarrassed by your attitude." Annie barely stopped the car in front of the hospital entrance before Madison jumped out. "Wait a second. Just let me find a parking spot."

"I know where to go." Madison slammed the car door shut and walked away.

Annie watched her enter and mumbled to herself, "That went well."

⊂ଚ⊃ ⊂ଚ⊃ ⊂ଚ⊃ ⊂ଚ⊃ ⊂ଚ⊃ ⊂ଚ⊃

Madison sat on the examination table wearing her T-shirt, underwear and socks. By the look on her face, it was undeniably clear the situation between Annie and Madison had yet to be resolved. Madison stared at the floor and kept her back facing Annie.

Annie paced in front of the window. She knew this wasn't

the time to even take a crack at talking to Madison. If only she was five again. If only Annie could make it all better with a simple hug or a vanilla ice cream cone. If only.

If only Annie knew her daughter was thinking the exact same thing.

A knock on the door made them both snap out of their individual contemplations for a moment. Susan poked her head in before entering the exam room. "Just me." She quickly entered and shut the door behind her. She smiled politely and looked from Annie to Madison and back to Annie again. "Aside from what I believe to be a crappy mood day for both of you, you're all set."

"Except for the fact that I probably lost over two quarts of blood." Madison reached for her jeans with a hidden eye roll.

Annie turned apologetically to Susan. "She's not anemic?"

Susan shook her head no. "All clear."

"What about the dizzy spells? Remember I told you about her getting dizzy? Right before her free skate at the Pacific Coast Championships?"

Madison jumped off the table and pulled her jeans up over her narrow hips. She avoided looking at Annie when she talked. "There were never any dizzy spells. I was dizzy *one* time. For a split second. That isn't equivalent to dizzy *spells*."

Annie pursed her lips, and practically bit her own tongue. What she'd like to do to Madison right now would probably constitute child abuse in most states. And it definitely should not be performed in front of a state-licensed doctor. She looked at the back of Madison and shook her head for Susan's benefit only. "Even though she's not anemic, she should be taking vitamins, right? For general health and wellbeing?" Annie gave Susan an obvious look and an eyebrow raise to make her point. This was the reason she made Madison come in here. For reinforcement.

Susan caught on a little too late. "Oh. Yes. That's right. Vitamins are very important, Madison. You should be taking them every day." And when she glanced back to Annie who was still playing charades, Susan quickly added, "Even twice a day. Take your vitamins twice a day and that should help the...the sometimes dizzy spells." Catching herself, "Uh, *spell*."

Madison turned her head to Annie. "Could you be any more obvious?" Then she turned to Susan. "Can I go now?"

Susan stole a look at Annie. It's one thing to be the doctor. It's an entirely different thing to be the mediator and not a job Susan readily took on.

Annie shrugged her shoulders to Susan. She'd lost this little battle and there wasn't a thing she could do about it. She looked out the window and thought about the long night to come.

Susan touched Madison's shoulder as she walked her to the door. "It was good to see you. Good luck at Nationals. I hope you know we're all rooting for you."

"Thanks." And with that short word, Madison was out the door with a quick slam.

Only then did Annie turn around. She smiled politely to Susan. "Sorry about that."

Susan walked to the counter and dropped Madison's chart on it. "Not a problem. Goes with the territory."

"Does it? Do all the kids you examine have this nefarious attitude, out of the comforts of their own home? Because Susan, I don't know what to do." Annie moved to the table and leaned her upper body on it. "She's like this to me literally all the time. There doesn't have to be a reason. Today, there actually happened to be a pretty good for reason for her rancid behavior, but usually? Me cooking her breakfast can provoke it."

Susan shrugged. "She's a teenager, Annie."

"That's it? That's your big professional opinion? I know she's a teenager, Susan."

Susan looked at Annie with love and patience. "I'll give you some more of my professional opinion." Susan looked at the counter for a moment. She obviously didn't want to hurt Annie's feelings. "Here's the thing." Susan looked into Annie's eyes unswervingly. "She's training. Training hard, if I'm not mistaken. She's exhausted. Extremely exhausted. From what Madison tells me, her schoolwork hasn't suffered too much, which means she has to be drained from studying too. And she's skating how many hours a day, Annie? Four? Maybe five?"

Annie stood up straight and nodded. *At least five or six*, Annie thought. *And that's an easy day. And one that is very rare these days.*

"And she's also growing a little, finally. She should be tired with everything that's happening right now. Without the skating even entering into the equation. Give her a break. I'd be a cranky girl too."

"You're right. I know. It's just hard."

"I know." Susan held out her hand to Annie. "Come here."

Annie smiled and moved around the table. She took hold of Susan's hand and before she knew it, fell into her friend's arms for a moment of tranquility.

Susan walked Annie to the door as she talked. "Push the vitamins. Make sure she sleeps...and I mean more than five hours a night. And that goes the same for you. Make her a couple of milkshakes whenever possible. It'll make her smile and give her a little extra protein. Sound doable?"

Annie nodded. "Oh, yeah. I can handle milkshakes. Vitamins too, probably. I just can't handle everything else."

CHAPTER 14

$\mathcal{D}$avid sat on one of the lower sections of the bleachers, his favorite place to watch. He picked up his plastic white fork, dug it into the open container of Kung Pao chicken, and watched Madison skate through her new and improved routine. No music played over the speakers this time. The rink was silent except for the scrape of her skates against the clean ice and once every few seconds, Annie's voice. He looked down at the untouched containers from their favorite Chinese restaurant still in the bag beside him. How many nights had they done this? Too many to count. He glanced down at his watch. It was already past eight o'clock at night, and still, no dinner for either Madison or Annie. David knew he couldn't say a word about this. He couldn't help but wonder if Madison even ate lunch today or if Annie ate a snack on her break. He stopped asking about their days a long time ago, when skating became the only topic of discussion in their house. There was not enough time in the day to find out if Annie had any new patients or if Madison did well on her math test. It wasn't as if he didn't try. They truly didn't have time to do anything, talk about anything, unless it revolved around the rink. That's just the way it has to be, David pondered. At least, for now.

Madison skated without energy, without trying. She plainly just went through the motions, with no extra effort whatsoever. David understood this situation couldn't be good. At all.

Annie skated back and forth, her keen glare on her daughter. She knew this was by far the worst she'd seen Madison in weeks. Trying to remember her conversation with Susan, she relied on every bit of patience she had in her. She calmly yelled to Madison. "Remember to keep your head up."

Madison raised her head slightly and continued skating. Her hands were barely an inch away from her sides, when they were supposed to be extended outward, parallel with the ice.

Annie shook her head and glanced over to David with an added shrug. As always, David gave her that look. The one that said, 'It's okay. She'll get it together.' Clearly he was not going to comment out loud on the situation. Annie snapped her eyes to Madison skating. "C'mon, Maddie. Your back is hunched over. You're not going to be able to pull up enough for the triple."

Madison didn't respond, didn't even glance in Annie's direction. She skated around, gathering more speed. She prepared herself for her next jump, a triple toe loop. Using every bit of energy she had, knowing there was very little left, she pulled her body up. Suddenly, she popped out of it, only completing a single and then deliberately stopped skating. Her hands found her hips and she barely moved her blades on the ice. She bent over at the waist, out of breath.

Annie, on the other hand, was out of patience. "What the hell was that? For Christ's sake, Mad. That was supposed to be a triple, not a goddamn single! You know that!

Madison kept her eyes focused down on the ice, praying for the strength to finish this practice.

"Are you listening to me?" Annie's voice echoed through the rink.

Madison lifted her head slowly, as if it weighed fifty pounds, and looked over at Annie. "I'm listening."

"Well, what's going on? You're barely moving. You think this is going to get you to the Olympics? Skating like that? You were doing singles when you were six years old! What's wrong?"

Madison's words were hardly audible. "Nothing is wrong."

"Oh, really?" Annie shook her head in disgust. If that was her idea of an explanation, Annie had heard enough. "Take a break."

"I don't need a break."

Annie skated away as she yelled to Madison. "Well, I do." She stepped off the ice by David. "I'm gonna go talk to George about tomorrow's time."

David shrugged and quietly talked to Annie, keeping an eye out for Madison. "Maybe she's tired, Ann. Or hungry. I'm sure you both are. Maybe just give her a minute to eat a little something."

Annie stared a little too long at David. There were so many things that were on the tip of her tongue right now. So many things she could scream in David's face. Did he even think about the money that it cost them every night to rent out the rink for Madison? That each second Madison wasn't on the ice practicing, was money wasted? Right down the old stained toilet bolted down in the bathroom they all shared? That Nationals were less than two weeks away and their daughter was skating like she was six years old? That she was tired, too, and just as hungry? Annie finally took a profound breath, threw her guards on her skates and exited the rink, before she said something to her husband she knew she surely would regret later.

Madison watched Annie exit through the door and only then did she skate to the edge of the ice. She warily made her way to the bleachers and sat down by David. She peeked into the bag full of unopened Chinese food. "What'd you get?"

"What do you think? What do I always get you?"

Madison shrugged and glanced at David. "Stir-fry vegetables."

"Then what do you think is in there?" Then David saw it. A smile, albeit, a very small one, but nonetheless, a smile.

Madison dug into the bag and pulled out the biggest container.

David handed her a napkin. "I got the biggest size they had. Figured you'd be hungry tonight with all the training." David knew there was a very small opportunity for Madison to rest. Whether Annie was really talking to George or whether she was in the bathroom banging her head on the tiled wall, didn't matter. He knew either way, he had a very limited amount of time.

Madison opened the container and picked at the food with her fingers. "Thanks, Dad."

He hated to ask the next question. At least, when he asked Annie, the answer always turned into a long lecture from her. Mainly consisting of the responses: "*Of course I'm hanging in there. Somebody has to.*" "*What? I don't have time to worry if I'm okay. We have a competition coming up. I have to be okay.*" But Madison was a young girl. His little girl and he was entitled to ask her. And with her, he never got the lecture.

On the other hand, he was aware he usually didn't get the truth, either. "You hanging in there, Maddie-girl?"

Madison looked up to David, weary and lethargic. "Yeah. I'm good."

Okay, so he was right and she lied. He also knew it was the only answer he was going to get from her so it was pointless for him to press the subject any further. He shook his head at Madison eating with her fingers. "You want a fork for that?

"Nope."

And there it was again. At least David was pretty sure he just saw another movement with her mouth. Another smile. But as he looked at Madison a little more closely, he began to notice other things too. She looked thinner. By at least five or six pounds. And there were dark circles under her eyes that could be considered quite prominent. Most girls her age would be wearing makeup. *Maybe that's it*, he thinks. *Maybe all dads see this without the latest craze caked on their teenage daughter's faces.* He was thankful when Madison started up a conversation. Otherwise it would've become very apparent he was staring at her with a frown on his face.

"Hey," said Madison as she bit off the top of a stem of broccoli.

"Hey, what?"

"Are we going on vacation this summer?"

David laughed as Madison tried to chew the huge broccoli crown she had shoved in her mouth. "I don't know. We...uh...we haven't really talked about it yet. Why?"

"Cause we've never missed a year at the beach and no one has mentioned it. I was just wondering why."

David shifted uncomfortably on the hard surface below him. They hadn't had time to discuss how exactly to handle this. Now he was on the spot, not Annie. She would, of course, know just what to say to delay the answer. *How about there just simply had been no time to talk about it? Does that sound acceptable,* David wondered? *Should I maybe tell her the truth? That we cannot afford it this year? That I can't afford to hire someone to help me run my business?* Unless, of course, his daughter brought home the gold medal? "Guess it depends." It made no sense, his answer, and David knew it. But it fell out of his mouth before he could stop it. There was a wonderful silence for a few moments and David flashed a quick grin for his own benefit. He even went so far in his delusion as to pat his own back. *Look at me go. Not too shabby. I can handle intricate questions just like Annie can.*

"Depends on what?"

Crap. Okay, so he knew in his heart it was probably too good to be true. David thought as fast as he could. Of course, Madison wasn't going to accept a wishy-washy response. She wanted a plan. She wanted to know. He was not about to tell her there would be no trip this year. "I guess it depends on…well, the skating and things." *There we go. Good one,* he tried to convince himself. The 'and things' would help out later when they had to explain why they weren't going anywhere. *Final answer,* he did it.

"But we always take a week off from skating. I mean, no matter what. One week. At the beach. No skating." Madison grabbed a long slice of carrot and dangled it in her mouth. "Mom even said."

Oh, great. Well, then it's mom who will be breaking the ugly news for sure. So it wasn't the final answer. David tried to act cool. "She did, huh?"

"Well, maybe not really in so many words, but…I know that's what she meant."

David reached into the bag and pulled out another carton. It was worth a try, and Annie hadn't returned yet. He opened it up and put it down by Madison. "How about some carbs? I got the chow mein with vegetables, too. Some of those noodles will give you energy."

Madison was about to reach into the carton for some chow mein, with a fork even. But she heard the door to the rink close and knew her break was over.

Annie marched toward them with no expression to show what she was thinking. Or how much her head was killing her from banging it on the bathroom wall.

Madison handed her carton to David without a word and quickly jumped up off the bleacher.

David gave her a quick wink as she carefully moved to the ice. He closed up the cartons of food and put them back in the bag. He caught Annie's eye as she passed him and gave her a brief reassuring nod. And if he wasn't mistaken, he thought he got one in return.

David regarded Annie and Madison on the ice as they talked quietly in the center of the rink. They were quite a pair, the two of them. His girls. Even when they fought or disagreed, they had this kind of *sense* about each other. He had seen it so many times over the past few years, yet it never ceased to amaze him. He'd never experienced that kind of connection with anyone, much less one of his parents. But Annie and Madison had always had it. His mind wandered to how upset Madison would be if they had to tell her they couldn't go to the beach this year. But David knew Annie would find a way to make it better. Cheer her up. She always did. Annie had to deal with the brunt of the uncomfortable things that occurred within their little trio of a family. The events no parent wanted to deal with, Annie somehow did.

David caught Madison's eye and gave her a little wave. He laughed to himself as she gave a quick wave in return, and then, secretly behind Annie's back, Madison rolled her eyes. Did Madison ever consider all the things that Annie did do for her? Besides annoy her. Teenagers can be difficult and ones that spend so much time with their mother, well…they can be even worse. Only David knew the endless days Annie had. He thought of all the times he'd caught her secretly crying quietly downstairs in the middle of the night, and how often she had gone on literally no sleep for days just so she could make sure enough nurses owed her favors when competition time rolled around. All the things she had given up over the years so Madison could skate. As David leaned back on the bleachers, he hoped one day Madison would know those things too.

∽ CHAPTER 15 ∽

She loved these quiet times, when the rink was empty except for her. No one, not even Annie, was there to disturb her inner peace. She bent over her knees and methodically laced up her skates. There was never a need to rush during these special times either. No clock was ticking, no money was being wasted. George let her skate all alone whenever she wanted. There was hardly ever any free time. Maddie smiled to herself. *No wonder George offered it.* But once in a while, Annie had to work. Or run errands. Madison came back to her familiar place without the thought of pleasing anyone, most importantly, herself. She could be crazy. Or immature, even. She could slouch her back, or let her hands fall to her sides sloppily. She didn't even have to jump if she didn't want to. But she knew she would. She always did. Not to say she didn't thoroughly enjoy this time by herself. She did. But she knew she'd always be a skater. A champion, and champions never stop being champions. Even when they were all alone.

With both her laces securely double-knotted, Madison stood, stretched, and walked to the edge of the ice. She smiled when she noticed George had been there already, on his one day off, to make the ice beautiful for her. There wasn't a nick anywhere, as far as she could see.

She skated around the rink at a snail's pace and wondered what the kids from school did when they had free time. Some of them were on a sports team. Like Jackson. Maybe others belonged to a club, like drama, or debate or...well, she really didn't know what other clubs schools had to offer. Maybe some do nothing. Sit in front of the television watching...well, she didn't really know what was on television either. Come to think of it, she hadn't known what was on television for three years. Jackson made fun of her once for not knowing any of the top ten shows on the big networks. When she was through reaming him, he not only apologized profusely, but from that point on, began Tivoing episodes of all his favorite shows. That way, she could watch whenever she had a few minutes of freedom. Every week, there would be a new list on his Tivo for their "date nights"...even though those were few and far between.

Jackson. He always seemed to pop into her head, no matter what else might be occupying her at the time. Madison shrugged it off as she turned herself around and skated backward effortlessly. It wasn't brain surgery, and as a matter of fact, it was a logical answer. He was the only friend she had. The only real one she'd ever had. She had a girlfriend once when she was seven or eight. The play dates lasted three months until Madison decided it was a waste of her time. She sat Annie down one day and told her no more. She remembered how upset Annie was. Apparently, she had worked really hard at finding a friend for Madison to play with. A *girl* friend. Not that Annie had anything against Jack. She just thought it would be nice for Madison to have a female around besides her.

126

But Madison only wanted to play with Jackson. It had always been him. So really, who else could always be in the back of her mind? Or even the front of her mind? *Of course. Makes perfect sense.* Jack was her best friend. Always had been. *Always will be.*

Enough thinking. Madison moved her feet minimally faster. Then the skates proceeded to speed ahead, preparing her for a jump destined to bring her high into the air. She flipped back, forward and back again quickly. Her toe dug into the ice and she threw her body up. She completed three full circles and her blades found the ice once again. A perfect landing.

Her mind drifted to Jack again. She wondered what he was doing right now. She thought he had mentioned soccer practice. Maybe that's what he was doing. *Maybe Kelly was there watching Jack practice. Maybe he was already done with soccer and maybe he took Kelly-whore to get something to eat after he finished. He was always hungry after practice.*

Madison abruptly stopped skating. Why would she care what Jackson did or with whom? It was then she heard the voice that couldn't be mistaken for anyone else.

"You call that skating?"

Madison turned to the rink entrance and smiled at her unexpected visitor. She didn't move from her spot on the ice. "How'd you even get in here? George always locks me in when I'm here by myself."

Jackson grinned. "I have my ways." He took a few steps toward the ice, but still stood behind the ledge. "I know people."

"Uh-huh." Madison skated backward, making little figure eights. "*Kel-luh-ey.*" She wasn't expecting it to come out of her mouth as loudly as it did, or in that sarcastic tone.

Madison smiled to herself. *Yeah, right.* "Whoops. Did I say that out loud?"

"Uh, yeah. Yeah, you did, actually. Got a problem with Kelly?" Inside he couldn't help but smile and hope she did in fact have a problem with Kelly. A big, huge, jealous problem.

Madison innocently looked at the ice underneath her skates and continued moving. "I don't have any problem with her. I mean, if you like that kind of person. Your choice."

"I never said I liked her and, by the way, she isn't a bad person either, contrary to your belief."

"So, you *do* like her!"

Jackson stood up straight and moved one small step at a time, almost cautiously, toward the rink opening.

Right at that moment, Madison tripped on her skate. She prayed Jackson was looking in another direction, that he hadn't seen her after all. But when she casually glanced over to him, she knew instantly. He saw her fumble, falter, whatever. He saw. And now he could barely stand up he was laughing so hard. Madison waited for him to get over it, hands on her hips, struggling desperately to appear pissed off.

Jackson was still laughing as he spoke, "As I said before, and yes, I must repeat myself. You call *that* skating?"

"What'd you do, take an *ass* pill?" A good comeback was never far from her mind. Just to be sure, she added, "Boob." *Boob? Good, Maddie. Smart.*

"What did you say? Did I take an *ass* pill? And did you just call me a *boob*?"

Madison giggled with no attempt to quiet herself. She pushed off with one skate and deliberately moved back and forth in front of Jack, taunting him. "And what if you did hear that from me? What would you do about it?" She stopped briefly in front of Jackson. "You wouldn't do anything. You, Jackson Wellington, are a big wuss." Madison skated backward away from Jack, giggling more in sixty seconds than she had in months. She turned her back on him and skated the outskirts of the ice. But as she passed by Jackson, he popped out on the ice with hockey skates on his feet. Madison heard the skates. She turned and saw him approaching, and a quick scream of delight escaped her throat. She upped her speed and soared around the rink. The only problem was, Jack wasn't too bad a skater, thanks to her, and was soon very close behind. Madison squealed piercingly as he reached out to grab her shirt and knew it was no use. She allowed Jack to catch her. She was simply too tired to fight. And maybe, just maybe, she didn't mind being caught.

They were nearly out of breath, from both laughing and skating and slowed down to a relaxed pace, side by side.

"So, would that be considered a win?"

Madison looked at him with a smile and a frown. "A win? You wanna count that as a game? You that hard up to beat me at something?"

"No." They skated for a few moments in silence, but Jack couldn't resist. "I'm just saying it seems like a win to me."

Madison answered him in her most sarcastic tone. The one she usually reserved for special occasions with Annie. "Fine, Jackson. You won the game. Are you happy now? Can we move on from your pitiful life?"

In place of words, Jackson shook his shoulders back and forth and cracked his knuckles.

Madison watched him out of the corner of her eye. He was acting very strange. If she didn't know him as well as she did, she would think he was nervous about something. "You okay?"

"Fine." His eyes were straight ahead, avoiding Madison at all costs. "Why?"

She shrugged. "Well, for one because you are suddenly staring so hard at the ice, you look like your eyes are going to pop right out of their sockets. Two, because you're cracking your knuckles and doing that weird shaky thing with your shoulders. And you only do that before a game or when you have to deal with your father. And 'c', because—"

"You mean three."

"What?"

"You were giving me one, two and then you said 'c' and not *three*."

Madison stared at Jackson with a definite frown. Now she knew something was going on with him. "Okay. Three." She waited for a response from him to explain. Nothing. "And *three*, you're ignoring me." She waited again. Not a word from Jackson. She gave him a few more moments of deliberate stillness then complete and total frustration took over. Madison whacked Jack in the arm and grabbed his shirt, stopping him abruptly.

Jackson had no idea where her aggravation was coming from. Maybe he might have a little idea but there was no admitting it yet. "What?"

"*Me* what? You're the one that's acting all weird."

Madison thought this was the longest pause she had ever witnessed in her life. She watched as Jackson's mouth opened but nothing came out. Just when she thought a verbal utterance was approaching, his mouth shut tight. "Okay, now you're totally scaring me, Jackson."

Then he snapped out of it, like nothing at all had happened. He smiled at Madison, finally looking her in the eyes, and started skating again. "Come on. Skate with me."

She shrugged it off and chalked it up to just one of those unexplainable moments in life where a guy was just plain whacked out for some lame reason. She was aware of relationship issues. She'd seen a few episodes of *The O.C.*, and read a few *CosmoGirl* magazines while waiting at the dentist's office. Okay, so that was a year ago, but still. She watched Jack skate ahead of her and quickly followed him. They skated around the ice at a much slower rate than they did before.

Jack finally broke the ice. "How long you here for?"

"I'm not sure. Probably not too much longer. I've been here for a while already."

Then Jackson did his weird knuckle-cracking, shoulder-shaking thing. It once again did not go unnoticed by Madison.

"You here on Saturday?"

Madison smiled. She was there every day and Jack knew it. "Have I ever not been? Come on. You know the schedule."

"Day?"

Now he was starting to really freak her out. He was acting beyond peculiar. "Day as in Saturday during the day?"

Jack nodded yes.

She answered casually, trying to understand what was going on. Maybe it was a case of temporary lockjaw. Or maybe it was some disease, verbal dyslexia, that makes words come out inverted or simply not at all. "Uh, yeah. Saturday. During the day. I'm skating. Here."

Jackson was silent for a few moments. "Night?"

Madison smiled. "Okay. What's going on?"

"It's nothing. Really. It's just that Tommy? From the soccer team?

"I know who Tommy is, Jack. For like six years now."

"Well, he's having this... I don't know. Some party or whatever."

"Maybe I'm riding on the short bus today, but what exactly does Tommy's whatever party have to do with me?"

Jackson repeated his knuckle cracking and shoulder snapping. "It's got nothing to do with...well, I guess it has something to do with you. In a way."

"Jackson!" Madison abruptly stopped skating. "What the hell is wrong with you? If you're trying to ask me advice about I don't know, what's-her-name, whose name we both know I know, *don't*. Okay? Because I have no idea what to tell you to do or say to her! And really, I truthfully don't want to know about—"

Jackson stopped suddenly, which froze Madison in the middle of her sentence. He skated in front of Madison and, after what seemed like another outlandish amount of time, he looked into her eyes. "I thought maybe you'd want to go. To Tommy's party. With me."

Madison stared at Jack. *Did he just say what I think he did? No. Not possible.* And if it was possible, he probably didn't mean it in the way that she was thinking he might have.

"I figured you couldn't go. I thought I'd ask you anyway."

"Oh." Madison kicked herself. *Oh? What kind of answer is that?* "So, you what? You asked me because you feel bad for me? Or because you already knew I couldn't go anyway? Or that I don't really know anyone from school and time is beginning to run out for my chances to be nominated for prom princess? Or that I never go out and do anything fun?" *There. It's probably one of those reasons. Of course. Duh.*

"I asked you because...I wanted to. Because I wanted you to come with me."

After an extremely lengthy delay, "Oh" was the only thing that came out of Madison's mouth. Once again. "I'll ask my mom but, with Nationals coming up and everything...she's probably not going to allow any extracurricular activities." At least this time, she thought, she was able to put forth a small smile in Jack's direction. "But, uh...thanks anyway though. Maybe we could go somewhere, some other time?"

Jackson nodded, and returned her smile, although it was apparent he was slightly disappointed. "Yeah, maybe some other time." Jackson, in his nervousness, got his skates caught up in each other and hit the ice hard. Only his hands stopped him from lying flat on the frozen surface.

Madison couldn't help but smile a little bigger. "You call that skating?" She took off as fast as she could. Anything to distance themselves from the recent conversation.

Jack barely managed to get himself up and off the ice without falling again. His eyes stayed focused on Madison as she sped around the rink. He waited for her to pass by him and chased after her. Once again, Madison squealed with delight, lighting up Jack's face like nothing else in the world.

⌑⌑⌑⌑⌑⌑⌑

It wasn't that Madison and Annie fought all the time. Or as Annie liked to say, disagreed vehemently while having a heated discussion. It was just that they spent so much time being coach and skater, they sometimes forgot how to switch back into their roles as mother and daughter.

Except today.

Madison didn't plan on saying anything to Annie about Jack. What was there to say really? Nothing happened. No sexual moves were made, per se. He asked her to a dumb party. This, Madison concluded, meant absolutely nothing. He'd asked her to a lot of parties, lest she forget. All of which she couldn't go to for one reason or another. It wasn't like he tried to hold her hand or even remotely insinuated this was more than a good friend asking another good friend to hang out. But, somewhere during the day, something might have, just maybe, changed.

Jackson was obviously acting different. Or strange? Downright bizarre, even. As Madison walked out of the rink into the fading sunlight, she wondered how long he'd been acting like this. Could it be new just starting today? Or had it been going on for a long time and she just never let herself notice it before now? Or was she the one that was acting not so normal?

Annie pulled into the parking lot right on schedule. Madison stood in front of the door, kicking dirt around with her sneakers. Normally, Annie would beep, or even yell for her to move it a little faster. But today, Madison was smiling. At least she was pretty damn sure it was a smile. Yep, corners of her mouth seemed slightly turned up, and even a few of her pearly whites could be seen. *As small as it is*, Annie thought, *I'll take it. Good sign.* That would hopefully mean a nice dinner with no attitude, arguments or out-and-out fights. She returned the smile to Madison and waved to her from the car. She had no idea why Madison would stand there and kick dirt around but she was not about to be the one to take that smile away. She threw her bags that she had collected over the past few hours of errands into the back seat, making room for Madison. As Annie turned back around to the front, she witnessed the most peculiar thing. Jackson exited the rink. With hockey skates in his hands. Not that he hadn't ever done that before, skated with Madison on what she referred to as the 'free day.' But definitely not recently. *Yet here he is and he's looking at Madison and they're talking quietly.* Annie snapped her head away. She shouldn't be watching. Or should she? It was only Jackson. Obviously, it can't be anything important. *Can it?* If it's nothing, well then, sure she can look at them. She'd looked at them for years, right? So it was nothing new...right? She quickly tried to find a perfectly good reason to stare at her daughter and when she realized there was no legitimate one, she stared anyway.

Madison gradually made her way to the car and threw her bag in the backseat. She opened the front door and slid in without missing a beat. She fastened her seatbelt and waved goodbye to Jackson a few yards away. All the while, she said nothing to Annie.

Annie reversed the car and drove away. *There must be many ways to bring up potentially awkward conversations with your daughter*, she said to herself. She just didn't know of them.

Before she had time to think what was inside the *How to Deal With Your Angst-Ridden Teenage Daughter* books she'd seen numerous times in the book store windows, she heard it. Madison's voice. She dismissed the fact that there was no eye contact. Screw the eye contact. She wanted the crucial information. The heavy scoop. *Madison's thoughts.*

"Jackson asked me to a party."

Annie experimented with being as nonchalant as possible. *But oh my God! Jack asked Maddie out!!* "Really? Is he having the party?" Annie knew if he was the one throwing it, it could mean a courtesy invite. Jackson had always been Madison's friend. And always considerate. Of course he'd invite her, he always did. And maybe he was simply being thoughtful. He'd always been like that. Who was she to get all excited about nothing?

"Some guy from school is having it. Tommy. He's on the soccer team."

Annie pulled on to the main road and drove as slowly as she could in the far right lane. For a second, she contemplated faking engine trouble and throwing the hazards on. She wanted this talk of theirs to last as long as possible. *Did Jackson ask her **out** out? As in a **date**, out?* "So, when is it? Tommy's party?"

"Don't worry. I already told him I can't go. It's Saturday and we have practice all day and night."

Annie looked straight ahead. Nationals were a week and a half away. She was only too aware that Madison had absolutely no social life because of the skating. But she also knew this couldn't be the time to start having one. If Madison only knew how much it killed Annie inside. "Sorry."

"It's no big deal. He just asked me to a dumb party. He was probably just being polite."

And all Annie could do was nod her head yes.

⚭ CHAPTER 16 ⚭

Four-fifteen in the morning, Annie thought as she drank coffee in the near-dark kitchen. She convinced herself she had the
energy to keep doing this for less than a week. Just five more
days. She smiled to no one, a clear sign her sanity was on the
way out the door. What the hell was she thinking? If this
worked out, and Madison won...*when she won*...they were
headed for the Olympics. *The Olympics*! Who would've
thought? Well, she did. Always had, since the first day Maddie
was on skates. If either of them thought it was hard now, wait
until *those* practices started.

She couldn't help but lean her arms on the counter in front
of her for added support. She knew she took a chance of
falling asleep again by allowing her body this luxury. After all,
she'd done it before. But not today. Not with Nationals
around the corner.

Annie remembered the car ride home and the talk about
the party Madison wouldn't be going to and she tried not to
think about what else Madison was missing. She knew as well
as anyone these were some of the most important years of her

life. There was absolutely nothing normal about Madison's life. There were no sleepovers with girlfriends, except one time when Annie remembered insisting Madison have a girl-friend when she was eight. *Seven?* There had been no trips to the mall to drink iced frappuccinos and giggle at the cute boy behind the counter at Starbucks. There had been no first dates to the movies to see whatever action movie was just released or scream through a third sequel to a horror movie about to make over one hundred million dollars…let alone a date at all. There had been nights where Annie had literally cried her-self to sleep over it, the agony over what she was doing with Madison and whether it was right or wrong. Then there were the nights where sleep never came at all. Nights where David had to hold her close to him and tell her over and over that she was doing the best thing for Madison. That this was what Madison wanted. She would listen to him repeat himself, and nod her head in agreement. But when the alarm woke her at four-something in the morning, she'd wonder if she made the right choices all over again.

They had made a pact. If Madison started to feel that skat-ing was not something she wanted to do anymore, she would tell Annie immediately. She would simply say 'no more.' There would be no questions asked. No explanations needed. No argument. They would simply stop skating. But until that time, Annie would wait until the end of each competition to see the small but so crucial thumbs-up gesture from Madison that sig-nified something of great importance. Keep going.

Annie opened the door to Madison's bedroom and quietly entered. She hated waking her up at this ungodly hour. She was her mother and in a normal world, she would want her to sleep ten hours a night. But they both were too aware just how abnormal their life was. Annie watched Madison's breath move in and out of her body and reminded herself once again that Madison had always given her the thumbs-up. *Keep going.*

✧✧✧✧✧✧

As always, Annie stood in the center of the rink, skating the same three feet, back and forth, yelling directions to her student. The new routine was a tough call but one Annie felt sure they had to make. Okay, *she* felt they had to make. Her old routine was fine, fine for everything up to this point, this level. Madison didn't agree with her decision and was making the situation hideously tense. Even Annie agreed it was somewhat understandable. But this routine, something new, she felt was necessary to win. They needed a change. They needed to surprise the judges, shock them even.

And Madison had been fighting it all the way.

Annie watched as Madison's arms dropped sloppily to her sides and shook her head in disgust. "Arms! Where are your arms, Mad?"

Madison immediately lifted her arms straight out to her sides. Not gracefully but at least in the vicinity of being appropriate.

"Maddie, I can't yell these reminders out to you during Nationals. You know that. You have got to keep all of these little things in the front of your mind at all times." Annie looked closely at her daughter. She looked different and she couldn't quite put her finger on it. She shook her head again as Madison's chin dropped. "Chin up!" *What was it? Maybe Madison has lost a little weight.* Susan had said she dropped a couple of pounds, but she chalked it up to the absurd practices. Of course she'd lose some weight! Annie made a mental note to start upping her calories. But when she looked at Madison at a new angle, Annie decided the difference was more in her face. It was on the pale side. Annie shook it off. *Okay, so she's lost weight. The poor girl is skating morning and night. She barely sleeps and never has an appetite before any competition. Especially one of this magnitude. She hasn't been in the sunlight for weeks. Maybe months. Of course she's pale.* Then it crossed Annie's mind how bad she herself might be looking.

Madison was trying to keep up with the music to no avail. She skated faster but still missed her jump. She ignored the fact and replaced her triple double combination with an easier jump. She gracefully lowered her arms to her side, as if that would make it all okay, even unnoticed. Thinking quickly, she extended her left leg out behind her body and glided backward.

Annie stopped and simply stared at Madison. It wasn't necessarily an angry look she shot to Maddie or even an unhappy one. It was the one Madison dreaded the most. The disappointed face.

Madison regretted stealing a look at Annie while trying to make it through her routine. She knew she could instantly tell what her coach was feeling and she knew, from too many times before, she shouldn't know what Annie was feeling until she was completely done with her routine. Madison tried to push her body through the pain to finish.

"Point your toe. It looks like garbage."

Madison pointed her toe as hard as she could. As she came out of an extremely fast spin, she dug her foot into the ice and abruptly stopped skating. She could not bring herself to look at Annie and leaned her hands on her knees while trying to control the considerable amount stars buzzing around her head.

The music stopped echoing through the arena.

Annie realized there wasn't any more coaching she could do. Madison knew it all. She knew the routine, and she knew what she had to do. Annie looked down and gently kicked the ice with her skate a few times, hoping the words would come forth. She slowly looked up at the young girl in front of her and tried her damnedest to encourage and support. "We've got no more time here, kiddo. We're looking at less than a week. I know that you know this. But honestly? I'm at a loss. You know what is about to happen here for you. Don't give me crap that it's a new routine. It's been new for almost three months. You knew it within four weeks, Mad." Annie took her dramatic pause. She scrambled hysterically to think of something powerful. Something significant. Not that it had helped in similar situations before but she was ready to try anything at this point. Maybe if she repeated herself. Repetition was good. That had worked before. "We have five days." She held up her hand with her five fingers outstretched for effect. "That's it. Five. And then it's either Olympics or…"

Madison stood up straight. "I know."

"Well, then…what is it? Are you really forgetting the new routine? Are you nervous? Because that would be totally understandable if you were. Maybe if you talked about it. Out loud. To me, or…or Daddy, if you'd rather, or Jackson even. He gets nervous I'm sure with his soccer games and everything. If you voiced it, maybe you wouldn't be as nervous."

"I'm not nervous." She moved on the ice, almost touching Annie as she circled around her.

Okay, Annie thought. *This is not going to be easy.* "Maybe the new routine is too hard. Do you want to go back to the old one? At this point in time, I wouldn't care."

Madison only shook her head no.

"What then? What are we going to do?" Annie's voice

was desperate and she knew it. "I don't know how to help, Maddie. I don't know what to do. Tell me what I can do."

Madison calmly came to a halt. She looked at Annie and struggled to take a deep breath. Then a reassuring smile crossed her now-determined face. "I can do the new one. I'll be fine." She maneuvered her skates backward and moved away from Annie. "We'll be fine."

"You sure?" Then she saw it. Usually saved for after the long program of a competition, but much needed today, here in the rink. The thumbs-up in front of Madison's chest.

"I'm sure." Madison grinned. "Keep going."

Annie nodded and gave the return thumbs-up back to her daughter. "Keep going." Without removing her focus on Maddie, Annie yelled up to the booth. "Okay, George!"

Madison found her starting point and took her position. *I can do this,* she tried to convince herself. It was a repeated mantra she had gotten rather used to over the past few weeks. *I can do this.* The words echoed over and over in her head. Somehow she found humor in the horrible headaches that had been wreaking major havoc on her tiny body. *Probably from this nonstop chanting I'm constantly doing.*

The music poured loudly through the speakers again. Madison started moving, gracefully, perfectly. Annie watched every move with anticipation. What she saw in front of her was a champion. An Olympic champion. Madison skated more beautifully than she had in days...weeks...maybe ever. Madison pulled up for a triple toe loop and nailed it. Annie smiled. Her smile was so big that she had to cover her face with her hands. *That's it,* she thought. *That is it.*

There was no reason for Jack to still be at school. He wasn't waiting for a ride; he had his own car. His workout ended an hour before. Since he got on the International soccer team, he had been training in the school weight room three times a week. Sometimes his friends hung out with him, keeping him company. And once in a while the cheerleaders would find an obscure reason to be there too. They were also known to meet at Gertie's diner after games and workouts under the guise of eating. Most of the time, though, Gertie's was the place hookups happened and inevitably ended.

Even though it was chilly outside, it was still beautiful. Jack had no interest in hurrying home to an empty house, so he convinced Tommy to kick the soccer ball around on the field for a few extra minutes, even though the above-mentioned crowd was already waiting at Gertie's.

Tommy hung up his cell with one last kick of the ball to Jack. "I'm being summoned, dude." He yelled to Jackson as he walked away backward. "Sure you don't want to come? Kelly will be there!"

Madison wasn't sure Tommy noticed her walking toward them before or after the mention of Kelly's name, but she stopped in her tracks.

Neither Jack nor Tommy acknowledged her looming some fifteen feet away, and yet both were aware of her presence.

After a noticeable look in Madison's direction, Jack waved Tommy off. "I wanna practice some more."

"Hey, moron! You lifted for over an hour. We just had a scrimmage game. You won, okay? What are you practicing for?"

"The Wheaties box." Jackson shrugged and smiled. "See ya tomorrow." He turned quickly in Madison's direction, hoping she heard his comeback. He assumed from her grin, she did.

Jackson nervously looked away, facing the empty field and lone soccer ball. *Is she walking over here?* He kicked it back and forth between his feet. *Is she looking at me right now?* With his right foot, in one quick move, he lifted the ball smoothly in the air. *Does she know how hard it is to do this?* He bounced the ball on his head, over and over, high in the sky.

"They say that causes serious brain damage, you know."

Jack grabbed the ball with his hands and beamed. *She was looking at him.*

Madison stood on the edge of the field, waiting, watching.

He controlled the growing grin on his face before he turned to her and resumed kicking the ball, this time bouncing it on his knees.

Madison moved to the bleachers. She took a few steps up and then stood still. "Are you showing off? For me?"

Jack continued his quest for perfection. "I'm still trying to break my record. You ruined it years ago, remember?" Jack stole a quick look to make sure he was still being watched. "How'd you know I was here?"

"The same reason you know where I always am."

"Oh, yeah. Duh."

"It's either here or what's that place called? Gertrude's or something?

Jackson smiled. She knew the name. "Gertie's."

"Whatever. I didn't see your car there when we drove by, so I figured you were still here." Madison progressed up to the top of the bleachers, resting for a beat every few steps.

Jack kicked the ball up in the air with his foot and caught it in his hands. He walked toward the bleachers and dropped the soccer ball next to his equipment bag. He jogged up the benches two at a time until he reached Madison at the last step.

She was leaning over the top, facing the back. The sun was setting in perfect tones of pink and orange. Jack leaned over the railing in the same way, as the sun lost its energy for the day. "So, where you been?"

Madison looked at Jack sideways with a smile. A smile that clearly said *where else?*

"Yeah. Figured. Stupid question."

"Nay." Madison looked ahead. "Well, maybe." Then the infamous giggle.

Jackson pushed her slightly with his upper body. "You ready?"

"I think so. Ready as I'll ever be." She dropped her head and lowered her voice. "Look, I'm really sorry I haven't been around. I know I missed another game this week. I just kept hoping each day would get easier, we'd end sooner…" A small laugh escaped her. "Of course, today I was also hoping I wouldn't forget the new routine or fall on my butt coming out of a triple, or skate into the side of the rink but what can you do, huh? You can only hope for so much I guess."

There was a moment of silence as Jack tried to control what could potentially turn into a fit of laughter. "You fell into the boards?"

Madison looked directly at Jack. She tried her hardest to keep a straight face, but to no avail. "Smack. Right into the wall." Laughter overtook both of their young bodies.

"I don't mean to be rude or anything, but didn't you see it coming?"

Madison shook her head no. "Not until it was too late. I dunno what happened. I guess I just misjudged or something. I'm trying to think which was funnier. Me upside down against the boards or my mother's face at me upside down against the boards."

"I wish I could've seen you. Wait...are you okay?"

"Yeah, as if you care. Now that I've brought humor into your life from my pain and suffering. You could've asked me if I was okay like five minutes ago."

"You're right. I could've. I still wish I saw you crash."

Madison watched the sun lower itself in front of them. "I still wish I saw your game."

Her sincere statement surprised Jackson. Was she kidding? Was another dig about bimbo cheerleaders with all-too-white teeth about to surface? She was known for doing that, acting all serious and then throwing him a humdinger. He looked over at Madison. She was perfectly lit in the disappearing sunlight and her face revealed she was totally genuine about missing his game.

"Don't even apologize, Maddie. I know you're doing your thing. I would never want to screw that up for you or make you feel bad because of it."

"Yeah. I know you wouldn't. Besides the fact you would be like, the worst friend ever to come between me and that insignificant thing called the Olympic gold medal."

The sun sank into the ground rapidly. The sky was that flawless combination of day and night, dark blue and light pink. The moon started to stake its claim on what was to come.

Madison and Jack simultaneously looked at each other too long for people who were just friends and immediately snapped their heads away awkwardly.

Jack finally broke the deafening silence. "You never did answer my question."

"I fell into the boards. Cut me a little slack." Now it was her turn to nudge him slightly with her body. "What question?"

"What're you doing here?"

"I don't remember you asking that question," Madison coyly replied.

"And if I did?"

Madison shrugged. "If you did, which you *didn't*...I would've said I came to see you."

Jack's face reddened ever so slightly. "Yeah?"

"Yeah. Why? What's wrong with that?"

"No—nothing. It's just, you know, I'm uh...it's just nice you came. Really nice."

Madison finally turned, took a step down and sat on the bench beneath her feet. She leaned her upper body back on the bench above and stared at the sky over her. With each new blink, her lids closed more. "Will you be there? At Nationals?"

Jack's voice was barely audible. "I wouldn't be anywhere else." He stared down at Madison as she snuck in a catnap below the clouds. *Did she not hear him?* Jack wondered. She wasn't answering. No funny comeback. Not even a look in his direction. She was tired. *More than tired,* he thought. She had to be completely exhausted. And she came to hang out with him. He sat down on the same bench next to Madison. He took off his sweatshirt and rolled it into a makeshift pillow. Ever so gently he lifted her tiny frame up, away from the hard wood, and placed his sweatshirt under her.

Madison's eyes fluttered open for a split second and she grinned a thank you.

Jackson waited until her eyes closed again, and a concerned frown replaced his grin. "You doing okay?"

Her eyes remained shut as she responded meekly. "Yeah. Fine. Why?"

"No reason. Just looking out for my best friend, is all." *So many reasons but now is not the time.*

CHAPTER 17

Never had any of them seen anything like it. Not Annie in any of her past competitions a lifetime ago, not Jackson at any of his soccer games, even the State Championships, and most importantly, not Madison even in her grandest dreams. The arena was filled beyond its legal capacity, much to the local fire marshal's dismay, and no empty space was to be found. Almost every inch of wall space had been plastered with signs and posters of various sponsors. Most of the signs were enormous white banners announcing the NATIONALS. Television crews spent a week setting up their cameras at every angle in the arena, with one aimed at a huge Olympic flag strategically placed for one sole lens. So far today, reporters had stopped Madison on four different occasions for interviews and photos and she had not touched one skate to the ice.

Jackson and David nervously stood outside the skaters' changing area, both jittery like expectant fathers, neither one able to utter a word to the other. Only quick glances followed by even quicker nods passed the time.

A skater's dressing room never changes. It doesn't matter how much time goes by. There were always those few, insecure jealous girls who found it more important to watch other skaters prepare than to pay attention to themselves. There were the girls that would do anything to sabotage the yet-to-be-announced winner. They would say anything, do anything, just for the possibility of throwing the gold-medal-hopeful down a notch, or even two, if they were good. To each other's faces, they couldn't be more full of love. A kiss for each cheek when they saw one another, the recognized air kisses. They'd been known to add a pat-hug on the back if the skater placed. With the pat-hug, the arms never really encircled the back of the body. The hands? They just patted the skater's back. It was these same girls that pretended to listen to their coach, or even their mother, but had their eyes focused on the skater that beat them in a competition three years before. They wondered if her boobs looked too big for her outfit, or maybe it was her butt. Or they might think, hopefully, the girl had put on some weight, or God forbid, she'd lost weight. Was her outfit flashier? Was it more expensive? Was she prettier?

Will she win? Will she beat me?

It was this unavoidable time in the dressing room that Madison abhorred most of all. And it was the time when Madison most thanked God that Annie had been through all of this crap before. Annie prepared her for the worst of possibilities. She had been there, done that, as the saying goes. Because of that Madison had always remained on the outside of the air-kissing, pat-hug clique. *Big surprise.* One more clique Madison didn't belong to. But that certainly didn't mean she went unnoticed by them. She had already been touted as the one to beat and every skater and every coach in that dressing room knew it. Including Madison and Annie.

Madison sat perfectly still in a chair off to the side, away from the mirror, away from the other skaters. Her eyes were closed, her hands gently placed in her lap.

Annie stood over her and brushed her hair into a high ponytail. Annie's idea.

Madison decided to agree with her last night instead of entering into what could be a heated discussion. And frankly, she simply couldn't expend any extra energy on something that didn't matter in the long run. She had learned to pick and choose her fights, *discussions*, carefully and Annie did have some rather good points on the hair-style subject. Madison would never admit this to Annie, but her wispy hair did get in the way more than a few times in the past. When her hair wasn't sticking to her lip gloss, creating what probably looked like a nasty misplaced mustache, it was entwining itself into the self-imposed mandatory mascara clumped on her eyes. And yes, she of course ardently denied it when Annie asked her about it after.

Madison never opened her eyes when Annie did her hair. Especially when it was the ponytail. She could almost reverse her life back to when she was five, maybe six. When her hair was fixed like this for each practice session on the ice. Before either of them could imagine their future. Madison tried not to fall asleep as the brush went deeper into her scalp. She wondered if maybe Annie did imagine this moment, them headed to the Olympics. Maybe Annie imagined it from the very first session Madison had had on the ice. There had been too many nights in recent weeks for Madison to count where she thought about her future after the Olympics, after skating. It had never kept her awake like this before. Then again, things weren't the same for her and she knew it. It was nothing she could put her finger on exactly, but for the first time ever in her life, she contemplated the notion of no thumbs-up after her long program to Annie. It was just a fleeting thought. But, however momentary, it was there. She would never do it, not give Annie the thumbs-up, their secret sign to keep going. Even with the restless nights, long practices and recent body pains and aches...she was a skater. Destined for greatness.

Annie held the ponytail holder in her mouth. "Hold on. I'm going to make it really tight now, okay?"

"Not like Chinese tight though. I get bad headaches when you do that," Madison said peacefully, her eyes still shut.

Annie wrapped the elastic band around Madison's hair as tightly as she could without starting a discussion as to why she was going snug. Her daughter knew. She brushed the perfect ponytail and moved around to the front of Madison. "Too tight?"

Madison shook her head no, still refusing to open her eyes. When she did, she knew all too well the moment would be gone forever and she was not ready to wake up just yet.

Annie reached to Madison's hair near her cheekbones and started to pull at strands of hair around her face.

Madison's eyes popped open. She grabbed Annie's hand instantly and stopped her. "What're you doing?"

"I was making the wispy hair. How you like it."

Madison, not letting go of Annie's hand, squeezed it and smiled. "I like it like this. Just like this."

Four skaters stepped onto the ice and began to warm up. Madison was the last of them to take to the ice. As she began to run through some of her more difficult transitions, she noticed a television camera on her, the red light conspicuously blinking. She did a perfect double axel and continued skating. Annie's voice resonated in her mind. *"Don't look at them. They aren't even there. Ignore them. Don't listen to what they are saying. When you hear the announcer over the speakers, don't let either ear listen to his voice. Only hear your skates on the ice."*

Madison took a deep breath and picked up speed. She attempted a triple jump but didn't complete it. She popped out of it and shook it off. *Come on,* Madison thought to herself as she skated at very slow tempo around the rink. *Get it together. Forget that you're tired. Forget that your head is pounding. Forget all the stuff it took to get you here. It's about today. And today means the Olympics.*

Annie frowned at Madison's missed jump and repositioned herself closer to the edge of the ice. *What is she doing now?* Madison should be practicing her jumps and stretching out her legs and from what Annie could see, all she was doing was skating around like she was in a level-two group class. She walked a few steps back to Jack and David, sitting on the bottom bleacher, both looking far too anxious with the amount of time that remained before Madison skated. Annie handed them Madison's jacket and skate guards and heard her own voice full of tension. "I don't know what she's doing but it sure as shit isn't called warming up."

David and Jackson knew there was no response for Annie and even if they did have one, Annie really didn't want it.

They both exchanged apprehensive looks and their eyes moved back to Madison.

The announcer's voice broke the tension. "Skaters, please clear the ice."

David reassuringly said, "She'll be fine." It wasn't meant for anyone in particular, but said more in an attempt to convince himself.

Madison and the other three skaters made their way off. Coaches waited for their skaters to clear the ice and quickly moved them to their section. Madison was the last one to leave the ice. A group of young girls screamed out her name in unison, but Madison didn't even blink.

Annie said nothing to her. No scolding words. No reprimand. She simply offered her an already-opened, room-temperature bottled water.

Madison barely drank a sip and handed it back to Annie.

Annie couldn't give any her advice. It was too late for that. They both knew what today meant. They'd known it all their lives. Madison lifted her head to Annie. They simply looked at each other, and slowly their hands clasped tightly together. Annie smiled to Madison. "Still having fun?"

Madison gave her a nod. Not a big nod, but definitely a sincere one.

Annie nodded back to her. "We always said, whenever you want to stop...when it's not fun anymore..."

"Mom." Madison cut her off but not in a defiant or rude way.

Annie hesitated for a moment. "You never said to stop."

Madison tightened her grip on Annie's hands. "I don't want to." Madison lifted her right thumb in front of her chest and pointed it up to the roof.

Annie mimicked the gesture with a smile. "Okay then."

The announcer's voice broke through the rink loudly. "Good evening! And welcome back to the National Championships! There are four skaters remaining..."

Another even larger group of girls screamed out "Madison!" Madison didn't break her contact with Annie.

"Ladies and Gentlemen, the Pacific Coast Championship's Gold medalist and one of our Olympic hopefuls, Madison Henry! Madison is in first place after the short program performed on Friday evening."

The crowd went wild, screamed Madison's name, and gave her a standing ovation before she had one skate on the ice.

David and Jack jumped up from their seats, yelling and clapping rowdily. Never for a moment thinking about how silly they looked to others, grown men jumping and hollering.

Madison and Annie shared their clandestine words that were never spoken aloud. It was simply a look that always said it all. Annie squeezed her hands together one last time. "Okay?"

"Uh-huh."

"Deep breath."

Madison obeyed Annie's direction and inhaled deeply. She smiled slightly to Annie and turned away. It was to the ice she spoke now. "Okay."

Madison didn't falter as the crowd screamed even louder. She inhaled one more time, as deeply as she could. She knew the time had come. She had to move her feet and step onto the ice and for the next four minutes, skate like her life depended on it.

She glided with determination to the center of the rink, to her starting point. She took her position, her head down, arms gracefully crossed in front of her chest. It was in that space and time when she noticed one could hear a pin drop. There was not a sound from anyone, or anything. She knew she had a five-second pause before her music started and she counted the seconds down in her head. Five, four, three, two, one. Her music began to echo through the building. She lifted her head and she skated once again, knowing her sole purpose. Every one of her moves was beyond exceptional. Madison appeared to soar, like an angel would if eyes could see to the sky above.

Annie's face tensed up, knowing what was coming next in the program. It was the triple toe loop. Madison could do it. She always did. But Annie knew all too well the first and last jumps were the hardest.

Madison skated faster, turning her body backward, preparing for the triple jump. She lifted herself up high in the air. The move was effortless, as if she were weightless. *Boom*, Annie thought. *Perfect*. A huge smile brightened Madison's face as she completed yet another jump, a triple triple combination jump, beautifully. Her routine was positively flawless and she knew it.

Annie tried to remain calm. Anything could happen. Madison had a long way to go. The long programs took everything out of the skater. It sucked bodies dry of every bit of energy and then some. Annie could see it in Madison, the onset of her struggle. "Please, Maddie." Annie wasn't even aware that she spoke out loud. "Come on, Maddie. Hang in there. A few more minutes, baby."

Madison pulled out of her spin and hesitated for the slightest second, almost as if she didn't know what to do next.

Annie's mouth dropped open. "Not now. Not here."

Then, in perfect professionalism, Madison snapped out of it before anyone noticed that something was not quite right. She put her best face on for the judges as she skated by them.

Annie had always told her to just listen to the music and it would always carry her through the routine.

But this time, it's not working.

Madison let her own voice inside her head bring her to the finish line. *"This is it. One more jump. I can do one more lousy jump."* Her skates picked up the necessary momentum she needed to be able to skate into the last jump. *"Almost there."* Like her mother, she had no idea she was talking out loud.

Then she did it. She threw her body into her final jump. It was as if she flew around in slow motion. Once around, twice around, three times...she hit the ice and flew immediately back into the air, circling three more times. Her blades hit the ice, once and for all, in a perfect landing.

Nearly home. Fifteen second count down. Time to spin, don't stop...change position. Change again. And again.

The crowd broke into wild applause. Even the judges had to smile at the remarkable performance they had just witnessed.

Madison skated through the last of the required spins in the final seconds of her routine, thinking about the long soak in the tub, and the restful night of sleep. *Finally.*

Annie was smiling from the side. She quickly glanced up to David and Jack, which she normally never allowed herself to do.

David smiled at his wife, clearly thrilled and very proud. Annie turned back to Madison's finish with a huge smile on her face and shook her head in disbelief. *She did it. My girl is going to the Olympics.*

But then, before the crowd could give its congratulatory ovation, before Annie could hug her daughter, before Madison could stand on the top podium to accept the very deserved, first place gold medal, suddenly without any warning, Madison Henry collapsed in a heap on the ice.

The crowd gasped loudly. Every person in the building jumped to their feet. Muffled voices moved through the arena in every direction. "What happened?" "Is she okay?" "Oh my God!"

But Annie didn't hear any of them. She didn't hear Jackson screaming "Maddie! No!" She didn't even feel David's hand grasp her shoulder. She could think of only one thing.

Get to Maddie.

CHAPTER 18

Madison never minded hospitals before. She was not the kind of girl whose hair would stand on end at the mention of visiting a sick relative in a hospital. *Not that they really had any*, Madison thought. But she knew it was more because Annie had always worked in one. Madison accompanied her on far too many occasions when time didn't permit otherwise. Too many practices that went too long and there wasn't enough time to get Madison home before she had to start her shift. Madison didn't mind. She knew most of the nurses and even a few of the doctors. Maybe she was never afraid because she never really had to go visit any sick people. She was just there. Hanging out. Waiting to go home. Or back to the rink.

But this time was different. This time she minded hospitals. This time she wasn't there during the in between.

A few vases of flowers had been strategically placed around her room in an effort to brighten it up. Too many cards to count had been stacked on the dresser and night table by her bed. The first day she was there, Annie had gone crazy in the gift shop and bought them out of every different kind of flower they had. It was remotely embarrassing when anyone came to visit her and couldn't see Madison in the bed, let alone the room. She finally asked the nurses on-call later that evening to give the flowers away to those patients who might not have insane mothers like Annie.

Madison didn't remember what really happened on the ice. It was weird, surreal almost. Everything was fine, aside from being somewhat dizzy. But she'd been dizzy before. More so recently. And she had lost her appetite. Which was no different from the weeks leading up to any other competition. It was to be expected. But she vaguely remembered just wanting to sit down. It didn't matter that she wasn't done with her program. It didn't matter that she would be resting on the ice in front of thousands of people. She just wanted to stop. And before she knew it, everything in front of her had turned to a foggy blurred white. Almost like puffy clouds from the sky had fallen down to the ground. And there they were. Clouds were everywhere she looked. On the ice, in the arena, next to her and covering her. And all she wanted to do was lay down in the middle of them. So she did.

The next thing she knew she was in her hospital room. And that it resembled some kind of jungle thanks to Annie's gift shop flower purchases.

The television was on but the volume had been muted. Madison wore her own pajamas under the hospital bedcovers. She sat upright in the bed flipping through an already read *Star* magazine.

Annie entered the room and walked apprehensively to Madison. "Hey."

Madison's face filled with anticipation and anxiety all at once. She threw the magazine off the bed and clasped her hands together. She stared at Annie, waiting for some kind of clue of what her future might hold, knowing what Annie had to say would determine everything. The silence was too much to bear and Madison finally blurted out, "Well?"

"I...uh...I don't know how to say this, Madison." Annie continued her poker face.

Madison leaned her body forward as much as she could without rolling over in a somersault. "Mom! Come on! Don't do this to me. What did they say?"

Annie moved to her daughter with a saddened expression.

Madison eyed Annie's face and let her own fall into severe disappointment. "Oh." She couldn't look at her mother. She looked away as tears began to well up in her big brown eyes.

Annie calmly sat down on the bed and faced her girl. She took hold of Madison's hands, and kept her head down. Just as she noticed the first tear well up in Madison's eyes, Annie raised her chin up to meet her face. Then the strangest thing happened. A huge smile broke out across Annie's entire face. "We're going to the Olympics!!! They're letting you skate!"

Madison screeched out loud. The kind of scream you would hear in a scary movie. Then Madison heard her mother yelling with her. She jumped out from under the covers and tackled Annie, embracing her mother as tightly as she could. The hospital bed rocked like it was a trampoline, shifting up and down, back and forth.

"What'd they say? Like exactly. Word for word." Madison stopped jumping, out of breath. "Play by play."

Annie couldn't contain herself. She hadn't giggled like this since she was fifteen years old. "They said...okay. They said you have won enough competitions and have scored consistently high enough to qualify, most likely. All we have to do is get you out of here so you can skate for the Olympic

Committee just to prove to them you're okay, but, that's nothing! That's not going to be a problem! The Olympics!!! Maddie! We did it! You did it!"

Madison stared at her mother, completely speechless. She couldn't move a muscle. She was actually going to the Olympics. After all these years. After all the non-existent friendships and missed childhood, after all the crappy health food Annie had shoved down her throat, after all the long-ass hours on the ice, and the early mornings and the even later nights, after all that...She was going to the Olympics! Her voice was barely a whisper. "Oh my God."

Annie stopped jumping up and down and placed her hands on Madison's arms. "What? What 'oh my God'?"

Her voice was even and low. "I'm going to the Olympics?"

Annie feared her smile would never go away. To hell with the laugh lines! "You, Madison Henry, my daughter, my skater. *You are going to the Olympics.*"

Before either one of them could stop it, the screams resurfaced. Within seconds, Annie's coworker and friend entered the room. "I know it's a crazy thing, but there are some sick people in the building and it might be good if we try not to cause any more heart failures." Kathy stopped just before she exited and smiled at Madison. "Congratulations, Maddie."

Madison looked at Annie. "Wait a minute. So what do we do? I mean, now that we know? What happens now?"

"Well, obviously we gotta get you outta here. As fast as we can." Annie got off the bed and straightened out her clothes with the palms of her hands. "I'll go talk to Susan and see what she can do." Annie walked to the door and turned back to a still-stunned Madison. "Hey, kiddo?"

Madison turned to her mom with a smile.

"We did it."

"Yeah. We did." Madison flopped herself back down on the bed, her hands raised in victory above her head.

⊙⊙⊙⊙⊙⊙⊙⊙

"Annie, we haven't gotten all the test results back." This was the reason Susan hated to be the doctor to her friend's kids. For this exact reason pacing in front of her.

Annie impatiently moved back and forth in front of Susan's desk. "No, I know that. But, it's probably what you thought before, right? I mean, obviously it was a complete body breakdown, unbelievable exhaustion. That would make anyone crash and burn like Maddie did. Susan, you know she's been training so hard and she wasn't sleeping enough but now...Now we can make sure that we monitor everything more closely. And...and I'll take her out of school. I'll home-school her. She should be anyway. That way there's more time to train and sleep. I would think getting her back skating would only make her stronger. She needs to rebuild her strength. Don't you think?"

Susan opened her mouth to say something but before she could utter one syllable, Annie was talking again.

"She's been stuck in here for days being poked, pushed, prodded and pricked. And, Susan, come on, you know she looks so much better than she did. Doesn't she? She just needed to get caught up, you know, and rest a little. She was sleep and nutrient deprived. She was so stressed out." Annie stopped pacing and looked directly at her friend sitting behind her desk. She allowed herself a breath of air and fell into the brown leather chair behind her.

Susan looked down at Madison's closed folder on her

desk. In her heart, she wanted to think Annie was right. In her head, she had a gut sense it wasn't.

Annie leaned on her knees and decided a more soothing tone of voice might be more appropriate. Susan was the doctor and she wouldn't want anything to come between their friendship. "Sus, look at me."

Susan reluctantly met Annie's eyes.

"I'm a nurse. I know it's not the same as being a doctor like you. But I know illness. You know I do. I would never ask you to release her if I felt she was in any danger whatsoever. I'm her coach, I know, but I'm her mother first."

"You're going to drive me insane until I go ahead and sign the papers, right?"

Annie couldn't help but smirk just a little. Susan knew her all too well. "Oh, yeah." There was what seemed to Annie the longest few moments. Susan stared down at the folder reading Henry, Madison.

Susan patted the folder lightly a few times and then looked at Annie. "I'll sign the papers this afternoon."

Annie squealed louder than before. She catapulted herself out of the chair and flew around the desk to Susan. She lifted her friend out of her chair and squeezed her as hard as she could. "Thank you! Thank you! Thank you!"

Susan finally broke free from Annie. "Okay! I have to uphold a certain amount of professionalism around here." Susan tried not to smile as she straightened out her crisp white coat.

Annie ran to the door. "I'm gonna go get her ready to leave."

Susan yelled to Annie. "I want a signed photograph! And don't you forget it!" She watched as her good friend ran out with more excitement than she'd ever seen. Susan relaxed back down in her chair and reopened Madison's folder. She read, and reread, flipping through pages she could probably recite by heart. *And if it was my daughter on her way to the Olympics...? But it's not. It's someone else's daughter and I am her doctor. If nothing is wrong, then a few extra tests won't ever need to be divulged.*

⨏ CHAPTER 19 ⨏

*A*nnie was up at the crack of dawn. It didn't matter they weren't going to the rink until six. She couldn't sleep. She hadn't gotten much sleep since they found out about the Olympics. There was so much that needed to be done. But the first thing was getting Madison strong and healthy again. She had been reading, perhaps obsessively, about the positive effects of homeopathic remedies to boost the immune system. Every day since her discovery, she gave Madison another energy shake to try. And today was no different. Annie poured a greenish-gray milkshake concoction from the blender into a tall chilled glass and tried not to gag at the smell of it.

Madison walked into the kitchen dressed for skating practice. Her face contorted into something not so pretty when she got a glimpse of today's special shake edition. "What's in there?"

Annie didn't hear Madison coming down the hall. She quickly and discreetly hid a bottle that read "pure algae." She positioned herself nonchalantly in front of other mysterious ingredients she'd been adding to the blender. She handed the glass to Madison with a smile that was worn by Amway sales people trying to sell you the latest stain remover during your dinner hour. "Here. Try this one."

Madison reluctantly took the glass and looked at it closely. She lowered her nose into the top and sniffed. "What is *that*? That is not okay, whatever it is."

"Well, I can tell you this: I tried it and I think that it, uh, it's way better than yesterday's." Annie turned her back to Madison and inconspicuously put the bottles away. "Better than the day before too."

Madison's nose crinkled up to her forehead. "What's that smell?"

"Huh?" Annie took the blender apart and moved it to the sink. Anything to keep busy. Anything to avoid telling her daughter she'd been making her drink algae...and other things that might not go over all too well.

"Mom, really, what is it?"

Annie gave her a little frown that said, of course, "It's a milkshake."

"It's six o'clock in the morning." Madison handed the glass back to Annie. "I don't want a milkshake at six o'clock in the morning."

Annie refused to take it from her. She hit the water on and washed out the blender. "Drink it. It's good for you before practices. It gives you energy."

"The last four haven't given me any energy. The last four have given me dry heaves."

"That's 'cause I wasn't doing it right."

Madison couldn't help but smile. "And now you are?"

"Oh, yeah. Totally."

Madison sipped the shake. She couldn't blame Annie; a mother would always be a mother. And all she was trying to do was help her. But the shakes had to go. Madison took another drink. It sat in her mouth far too long. So long, she knew if she was to swallow it, chances were good she was going to vomit. Madison, with the liquid gunk still sitting in her mouth, asked, "Mom?"

Annie turned to Madison, her hands full of dish detergent.

"Why is it green?" A drip of shake sludge escaped her mouth and started moving down Madison's chin.

Annie looked back at the blender trying desperately to think of a believable answer and trying not to laugh in her daughter's face. "It's food coloring. I thought it would be fun. A colorful shake is always better than a plain one. Right?"

Madison's mouth curled up and she ran to the sink and spit it out. Okay, so she threw some gagging in there to make her point really clear. She didn't care that she was over-exaggerating. Just as long as Annie wouldn't be making any more frozen drinks for breakfast.

Annie stared at Madison and her dramatics. She got it. No more shakes for breakfast. She dried her hands on a towel and grabbed the car keys. "Ready to go?"

There was, of course, one last really loud, really obnoxious choke before Madison replied, "Yeah."

❦❦❦❦❦❦

Annie pulled her car into the loading passenger section and stopped. The parking lot was empty. She glanced at the clock and then at Madison. "Almost nine."

Madison was still dressed in her skating clothes, her beat-up skates thrown on her backpack on the floor of Annie's car. She slowly opened her eyes and reached down to the floor, and wondered how she was going to make it through her day.

She moved her skates off to the left of her feet and grabbed her backpack from underneath. She struggled just to lift the bag onto her lap.

"You okay?" Annie had witnessed this display of exhaustion.

Madison nodded yes through a huge yawn.

"'Kay. You've got your clothes to change into, right? For school?"

Madison patted her backpack. "Yep." *Like I even need to bother. What's the point when I'll be putting them back on again in a few hours?*

"If any teachers give you trouble, have them talk to Mr. Hildegard. He knows about your special hours. We could still start home-school to give you more time to—"

"No. I'm okay." Madison opened the door and threw her fatigued legs out of the comfort of the car. It took her a moment to stand. It was another moment Annie caught.

Annie watched Madison carefully. She was tired. That was still it. She'd make it a point to ask Susan about any other vitamins or even some herbs Madison could take for her low energy level. "See you later, okay?"

"Okay."

Annie leaned over the front seat to the passenger side. "Hey."

Madison bent her body with effort back into the car window.

"You looked really good this morning. Much better I think. Could you feel it?"

Madison nodded a simple yes.

"So, try to be the first one out the door after school so we can get back to the rink, okay?"

"Okay." Madison shut the door and made her way into the

school. She gave Annie a quick wave goodbye over her shoulder and told herself it was only fifteen more hours until bed.

It had been so long since Annie had laughed that hard. There was always a period within the work day that was slow. A time during which the patients napped or amused themselves with the many DIRECTV channels the hospital offered, and the nurses had completed all the necessary rounds for their shift. One of the nurses on duty somehow always found a way to pass her time at the hospital a little faster. Today it happened to be with a black market, foul-languaged chipmunk song she had found on the Internet.

As Alvin segued into his nasty chorus, simply not repeatable, Susan approached the nurse's station. She went unobserved by Annie and the other three nurses.

Susan couldn't help but overhear the distinct chipmunk voice singing very off-colored words. She vaguely smiled and looked up at Annie laughing and pondered if she had ever seen her laugh so hard in all the years they had been friends, and quickly answered her own question. *Never*. Since they met way too many years ago to remember. Annie had always been serious. Funny, sincere, and light-hearted, but always serious.

Annie felt someone watching her and, still hysterically laughing, glanced up from the computer. "Hey!"

Susan jumped slightly, not ready for the sudden attention on her.

Annie laughed even harder. "I'm sorry. I didn't mean to scare you." Annie's focus went back to the screen and she tapped Kathy on the back. "Go back and play it again. We gotta show Susan."

Susan struggled to get Annie's attention. "I'll uh, I'll hear it later."

"No, Sus, really. It'll only take a second. You have to hear this. Wait."

The nurses couldn't control themselves. It was like having a laughing fit on a Sunday morning in church. All because the jerk in front of you releases the most hideous earth-shattering fart, a fart that smells like a city sewer, and everyone, one by one, starts to giggle. Quietly at first. Then slowly, the giggling turns into downright, hardcore, out loud laughing.

Susan smiled politely and gently touched Annie's arm, trying to switch her attention away from R-rated Alvin. "Actually Annie, I need to talk to you."

Annie was borderline out of control. "Now?" She glanced at the computer. Alvin was back. "Oh! Here it is!" Annie looked at Susan again and for the first time noticed her face. "Now?"

Susan nodded with a sincere but small smile. "Yeah. Now would be good."

Annie started walking away with Susan. She turned after a few steps and yelled back to the nurses still crouched behind the counter. "Find that other one for Susan. I'll be right back." Annie tried to recall the lyrics to the song, and in doing so, she had herself cracking up all over again. Tears fell out of her eyes as she tried to pull herself together.

Susan opened the door to her office and they both entered. She moved to the edge of her desk and leaned against it, facing the leather chair. She extended her hand to Annie and motioned for her to sit.

Annie talked as she sat down. "I'm sorry." She did everything she could to gain some control. "Okay. Okay." She breathed in and out a few times. "Look, if this is about us watching those illegal cartoon things, I know we're supposed to be..." A small giggle escaped her lips. Annie shook her head no to herself and rubbed her hands over her cheeks. "Okay. No more. I'm done. Sorry."

Susan looked at Annie and took a deep breath.

Annie's face drastically and immediately changed. "This isn't about the nurses."

"I got some test results back from last week."

Annie sat up straight in the chair. "What tests? I thought we had gotten all of them back." Annie studied Susan's face. *She ordered more tests. After she released Maddie, she ordered more tests. The kind you don't ever want to know about.*

Susan dropped her head to the floor. She would have traded this day for anything in the world. She finally mustered up the courage to look Annie in her eyes. "Annie, this is the most difficult thing for me to..."

"Susan. What did they say? Did they say...she's okay, right?"

Susan tried to fight back her tears. This was not in the job description. Especially when it was your best friend's daughter.

Annie stood up and confronted her. "Susan? Madison's okay, right?"

"Annie." Susan leaned forward closer to Annie.

Without fully understanding why, Annie's eyes began to fill with tears. "Tell me...tell me she's okay. Tell me!"

Susan's voice cracked. She could barely speak and when she did, her eyes filled with tears identical to Annie's. "Madison has....it...it's cancer, Annie. Ewing's Sarcoma. Annie, she's been living with this for a while. The weird joint pains, swelling and muscles aches...we attributed it to her heavy training." All Susan could do was shake her head.

Annie spoke evenly, her voice controlled and rigid. "There must be a mistake. I know every mother and father must say that to you, but I'm telling you, Susan, I'm telling you there is some kind of mistake. Something must've gotten mixed up. The blood tests and the...the...they could have made a mistake, right?"

"I wish to God I could say it was a mistake."

Annie turned away from Susan and shook her head no. She felt the tears falling from her eyes and immediately stopped them. She faced Susan. "Ewing's Sarcoma? It's totally curable. She'll be fine. She will. I mean, she's strong. You know how strong she is and...and she...she's young. Oh God." Annie couldn't hold back her tears any longer. She covered her face with her hands.

Susan reached for a Kleenex and handed it to Annie. "I called Dr. Tanger for you. He's expecting your call. He's the best pediatric oncologist I know. He'll take the best care of her. I promise."

"I have to go now." Annie walked toward the door in a daze.

"Annie, wait." Susan reached for Annie's arm.

Tears fell down Annie's cheeks as she turned to Susan, and for once in her life, she was speechless.

"I am so sorry." Susan squeezed Annie's arm gently and lovingly.

Annie nodded her head and walked out the door. She continued walking in a trance, down the hall, right by the nurses' desk.

Kathy was the first one to notice her and frowned at the weird sight. Annie was a walking zombie. "Annie? Where're you going?" Kathy got out of her chair and walked a few paces behind Annie. "Hey. You okay? Ann?"

Annie continued forward without an acknowledgement of any kind. She could not stop. She had to get out of there as fast as she could.

Annie got into her car, her hands shaking, and shut the door, in complete shock. She tried to breathe, but her body wouldn't let her. Suddenly, a glare shot into the car and flashed in front of her eyes. Her eyes traveled down to the floor of the passenger side and she saw the blades on Madison's worn-out skates. Her arm stretched down for them and she lifted them gently onto her lap. Annie moved her fingers over the many grooves and worn lines dented into the skates. How long had Maddie even had these? And then the question hit her and she couldn't stop it from entering further into her mind. Will these be the last skates she ever has?

Annie looked up to the crystal blue sky through the front window, searching for some kind of explanation from someone that didn't answer her. Then she dropped her head forward on the steering wheel and sobbed.

⁂

How long she had been standing in the school parking lot she didn't know. She had no memory of driving her car all the way across town. She didn't recall anything, except exactly what Susan had told her hours and hours ago. She painfully remembered every single word of what was spoken in Susan's office. She must have stepped outside her car at some point, while waiting for Madison. Was she hot? Cold? Were her legs cramped from standing still for so long? She looked around at the other cars pulling up behind her, waiting for their children to come out of school. *Their healthy children.*

A loud bell rang throughout the school grounds, jolting

Annie out of her thoughts. She hadn't prepared what she was going to say to Madison. She hadn't even talked to David. If he had tried to call her, the hospital didn't have any idea where she was. She recognized the fact she should have called him right away. He should have been with her today. But Annie wanted to be alone. She had to be alone.

The doors swung open wide and the first one out was Madison. Annie looked at the sixteen-year-old girl running toward her. She couldn't be sick. She wasn't pale anymore. At least not like she was before. She had energy. Much more energy than last week and she was smiling. She was smiling just for Annie.

Annie put on the best smile she could and waved happily to Madison. "Hey. You're the first one out."

"You told me to be."

"Yeah, I did." Annie looked around the school at the kids piling out of the doors in clusters. "Where's Jack?"

Madison dropped her backpack on the ground, conserving as much energy as she could for the rink. A slight frown became visible on her face. "He's got a scrimmage game for the International team. They're doing it here too. I told you yesterday."

"Right. I knew that. I mean, I remember now that you're saying it." Annie looked at Madison, and without any warning, tears welled up in her eyes.

"Mom? What's wrong?"

Annie hesitated, not able to say anything. She reached out to Madison's face and touched her hair, pushing it away from her eyes. "You look so pretty today. You know that?"

Madison's frown deepened. This wasn't the kind of attention she was used to with Annie. "You've been dipping in the

Xanax again, haven't you? They're gonna fire you, Mom. I'm telling you right now. You're gonna be out of a job soon."

All Annie could do was smile.

Madison reached down for her backpack and hoisted it onto her shoulder. "Ready?"

"You know what?" Annie took the backpack off of Madison's shoulder and put it on hers. Her voice was quiet and subdued. Somehow she managed to keep her composure and continue smiling. "I think...I think that today is a day off." She didn't know what exactly would come out of her mouth. Suddenly, it was there. A decision. A day off from skating.

Madison glanced around behind her. This was obviously some kind of joke. Annie would never let her have a day off. Not now. They were too close. They had a lot of work to do. She said just this morning. She looked back to her mother apprehensively. "You're not serious, right? I mean, are you? Serious?"

"Yeah. I think it's a great day to go watch a scrimmage soccer game. Jack can even drive you home afterward. Just tell him to drive slow, okay?"

"Sure. Yeah. I promise." Madison was dumbfounded, and afraid to move.

"Go on. Get outta here before I change my mind."

Madison lifted herself up on her tiptoes and brought her face up to meet Annie's. She pulled Annie's face down the slightest bit and kissed Annie on the cheek, and then she leaned in to her ear and whispered to Annie. "You look pretty too, Mom."

Annie watched Madison run to the soccer field and waited until Madison found Jackson before she left. She knew

Madison must have told him she was staying because Jackson turned to Annie with Madison by his side and they both waved excitedly to her. Annie returned the wave, just as excited, and watched as far as she could in the distance, until she couldn't see her daughter anymore.

And then she watched some more.

CHAPTER 20

*D*avid cast his gaze out over the back yard. It wasn't much to speak of, he knew. It was all they could afford when they got married. God, they were so young. Annie especially. Funny. This was their starter house. The one to fix up, make some money on, and then move onward to a bigger and better place. Yet here they still were, so many years later. He thought back to his grand plans for the yard. An in-ground pool with a diving board over to the left, an English rose garden to the right. Even a gazebo was going to grace the back of the yard. That was his plan. As he stood outside in the chilly night air, he looked around at his square piece of property. A row of roses would bloom in the spring. Not quite a rose garden, but for most days, it was close enough. Off to the left, he'd had a hot tub installed. Above the ground, obviously, but it was still a fairly large unit that held water and that made it similar to the pool described in the brochure from Paul's Pools. A brochure that had disintegrated long ago. As for the gazebo, nothing ever went in its place. It had all been okay. Settling for something less than he imagined.

Because in the end, it all should've worked out the way they planned. The way they had hoped and dreamed and assumed it would.

Annie advanced closer to David, but stopped a few feet away. She touched the back of the patio chair with her hand. If she could feel something, something cold and smooth on her skin like the metal part of the chair, it must mean this wasn't just a bad dream. That must mean it was real, as much as she wished it wasn't.

Annie stared at David's backside, very aware he was refusing to look at her. She knew he heard what she was saying, at least on some level. But for that same reason, he couldn't look at Annie. For minutes, she opened her mouth and tried to say something, anything, but no sound dared to escape. Finally, and much to her surprise, words fell, slowly and matter-of-factly. "They need to do more tests to find out if the cancer has spread...so they'll know for sure." She took a few moments and reminded herself to breathe. "Also to find out what stage the cancer is in. Then Dr. Tanger can plan the appropriate treatment. He's apparently the best. Susan said he was. She would know who would be the best for us. For Madison. I've heard of him before too." Annie waited for David to turn around. To face her. To scream at her. Blame her. But he stood perfectly still, his back the only image in her eyesight. "I...uh...I have to tell her. We do. I think we shouldn't put it off. We'll get an appointment with Tanger and start planning things as soon as possible. I guess tonight when she comes home, we'll just..." Annie shook her head back and forth in disbelief.

"She looked so pretty today, David. She didn't look sick. Not at all. And you know what else? She was happy too. I don't remember seeing her like that. I know she's happy when she wins a competition, or she...I don't know, when she does well on a test, but today? There was no reason for her to be happy. She didn't sleep well last night, she had training all morning, had to go to school late again reminding everyone that she is special and yet there she was. Smiling. She was running as fast as she could to be the first one out the door."

Annie got more and more emotional as her words continued. And the harder she tried not to cry, the more her tears fell by the dozens. "Just like I had asked her to. 'Try to be the first one out the door,' I had said. She was only going back to the goddamn rink to do it all over again and she was smiling." Annie gasped for a quick breath. "What if they can't stop it, David? What if I can't make her all better this time?"

David's shoulders shook up and down uncontrollably. He covered his face with both of his hands and remembered the only other time in his life he had cried before tonight. The night his father died.

Annie went up behind him and circled her arms tightly around his waist.

David slowly turned his body around to Annie and they immediately melted into each other, holding one another up, wiping away each other's tears.

Without any warning, Madison stormed out of the house and ran on the patio. "Jack won! He even scored the winning..."

Annie and David abruptly pulled away from each other, startled. They turned to Madison with tear-streaked cheeks and at the same time, quickly put on the most fake smiles imaginable.

Madison frowned at them and took a few steps closer. "What's wrong?"

David tried to speak, but couldn't. Like Annie earlier,

nothing came out of his mouth. He looked at Annie with sympathy. He couldn't help her. Not this time. For once, he was glad it came down to Annie to step up and deal with the problem at hand.

Annie glanced at David for support and instantly knew by his face this was all up to her. She took a deep breath and smiled. "Jack scored the winning goal, huh?"

"Yeah. I said that already." Madison looked from one parent to the other. *Someone must have died. That's why they're outside crying.* "What is it? What's going on?"

Annie took a step away from David toward Madison. She kept her voice completely even. Not scared, not shaky. "We need to talk to you about...the uh...some tests you had. The results came back and they showed something that was...wasn't quite right."

"What does that mean? I have to go have more tests?"

David suddenly turned his back on Madison as his shoulders convulsed in ways not at all normal. Madison was smart enough to understand that her father was crying. And old enough to know he didn't want her to see him like that.

Annie had hoped for support. She had hoped this would be both of Madison's parents dealing with something every parent feared. A child's sickness. David never contributing to any family issue couldn't have come at a more inappropriate time. She shot a look at David's head that only she knew the meaning of.

"What? Am I sick or something?" Madison waited.

Annie walked over to Madison, hoping each step would bring forth the appropriate words.

"Mom? Will somebody say something?"

Annie tried with all her might to be strong. "You have this thing...a disease, Maddie. A cancer."

"What?" Madison fell backward and barely caught herself on the patio chair before continuing on to the ground.

Annie reached out to grab her arm and Madison angrily shook her off. She knew that might be a reaction. Madison could be so angry. Not at David, she knew. At her. "It's called Ewing's Sarcoma. The cancer. But, we can get you better, Maddie. It sounds bad, I know it must. And I know you are probably scared, but there are all kinds of treatments now and we'll figure out the best ones and we'll get through this, okay? Then...then we will get right back on track with everything."

Madison found the seat with her hand guiding her and fell bit by bit down into it. She looked around the yard that needed mowing, at the table that needed cleaning. It took more than a few moments for her to respond to Annie. *This is what people in shock must feel like. How could I not know I was so sick? Did I know? Did I ignore it? And if I did, how long have I had this cancer? How long has it been hiding out in my body?*

"Maddie?" Annie was kneeling at her feet.

Madison's words were quiet and small. "Are...are they totally sure? That's what it is?

Annie nodded the smallest of nods. "Yeah. But, like I said, it'll be fine. We just have to meet with a doctor..."

Madison interrupted Annie. "Susan?"

"Um, no. We have to see a specialist." Annie dragged a chair over and placed it next to Madison's. Without fully standing up, she rose to the chair and sat down.

She knew what kind of doctor. "A cancer doctor."

"Yeah. An oncologist."

Madison frowned even more at the mere mention of that name. *An oncologist.* She tried to hear it, to let it sink in. *What had just happened?* She was at the soccer game. *Jack scored. And now? How could things change like that? It's not fair.* She looked over to Annie, watching her mother still keeping up a good front. There was really only one question that needed to be asked. Only one thing that mattered above all else. "Can I keep skating?"

Annie answered without thought. "Of course! We'll have to get Dr. Tanger's permission...he's the doctor. We'll have to get his approval and everything but I honestly don't see why you couldn't skate when we're finished getting rid of this thing. Right? Probably would be really good for you to regain your strength. Maybe he might even tell us you should be skating now. While we're on the road to getting you healthy."

"What about the Olympics?"

Annie knew this was coming. "Again, we've just got to wait and see what the doctor says."

"But I'm supposed to skate for the committee in a—"

Annie stopped her daughter's voice with a touch of her hand on Madison's knee. "Mad, we need to talk to the doctor first."

Madison nodded, but the nod was clearly an unsure one. "Could they...?" She allowed her voice to trail off. She lowered her head and looked down at her body. "Maybe they uh...they made a mistake. It could happen, right? That happens all the time. We saw that on *20/20*, remember? It happens. It does." With the slightest tinge of hope, she quietly added, "Doesn't it?"

Annie had harnessed every bit of emotion and had done an admirable job. Until now. She gave Madison the most sincere smile she could and through her tears, "I don't think so. Not this time, Mad." Annie inhaled loudly and held her breath for as long as she could. She couldn't let herself go. Not now. Not in front of Madison. "We'll find out more after we talk to Dr. Tanger, okay? I'm sure he'll be able to answer all the questions you have." Annie shot a look to David's back. "*We* have." She waited for some reaction from Madison. Nothing. She just stared at her infected body.

After an extremely long pause, Madison asked the question Annie had dreaded more than the skating. "Can someone die? From this, I mean?"

"Well, yeah. Yes, *someone* could. But...but you won't. You hear me? You will not, Maddie. Okay? You know how I know this? Because you're strong. You have always been so strong. Remember all those times the different flus went around? Or the chicken pox? You never had more than a twenty-four-hour virus. You never even got the chicken pox. You have always been able to fight anything off and you will this time too. I know it, Mad. Something else you should remember: We have a great doctor, the best one, and I'll bet you, we probably caught this thing before it got..."

Madison, with tears in her eyes for the first time, looked Annie in the eyes.

Annie answered with the only answer a mother could give. Madison didn't want to hear any pep talk about chicken pox or flus. "It'll be all right, baby. I promise."

Madison nodded an okay to Annie, whether she believed the answer or not. In this instant, she had to believe her mother. She looked over to David, still standing with his back to both of them. Madison slowly got up out of her chair and walked toward him. "Dad?"

As hard as he tried not to cry, as hard as he tried to be strong like Annie, he found no way to stop his sobs. He dropped his head even lower. He couldn't even bear to hear Madison's voice. He couldn't bear the thought of someday never hearing it again.

"Daddy?" Madison touched his arm lightly.

He finally looked down at his daughter with his wet face. And he didn't say what he probably should have. But he did say exactly what he wanted to say. "I'm so sorry, Maddie-girl."

"I'm gonna be okay, right?"

David glanced over his shoulder to Annie. This was not a question either one of them could answer. Yet, he knew they had no choice but to say the same thing, as a team. For the time-being, believe it with all of their heart and soul. "You're gonna be fine, honey. Just like mom said. It's going to be okay." David reached underneath Madison's arms and picked her up like he did when she was little and hugged her close to his body. He tried to remember the last time he had picked his daughter up like that. *Was she nine? Maybe ten?*

At that moment, he vowed to himself to never forget picking her up and hugging her close to him that night.

CHAPTER 21

"The chemotherapy is not a pleasant experience, as I'm sure you've been told. In any case, I'd like to go over a few things you might or might not have heard. We have made much progress regarding chemotherapy treatment. But, sadly, there are still several side effects, ranging from bearable to severe and from a remote possibility to very probable."

Madison's eyes scanned the office as Dr. Tanger's voice dragged on. She absorbed most of what he was saying. She was getting restless. They had been listening to him rattle on for over forty minutes. She had counted the same few squares in the tan Berber carpet over one hundred times. She knew this was serious. But she also knew this pretty much was all preliminary mumbo-jumbo medical garbage. Annie would have told her anything that was truly important before they met with the doctor.

Annie glanced over to her daughter staring at the carpet and indiscreetly nudged her arm.

Madison looked up nonchalantly. She was listening. She

lifted her eyes up anyway to meet Dr. Tanger's, simply to appease Annie.

He was still talking, Tanger, looking back and forth between the three of them. "...Some of the side effects I was speaking of earlier could include nausea, or sometimes vomiting, bleeding in the urinary tract, mouth sores, discoloration of nails, hair loss, lung disease, heart disease..."

Madison interrupted Dr. Tanger. "So basically, what you're saying is, if the cancer doesn't kill me, the chemotherapy will, right?" As always, she was never far from a good comeback.

All eyes focused on her.

"What? It was a joke." Madison moved around in the oversized chair.

Annie and David were speechless.

Only Dr. Tanger found a way to respond to her. He smiled politely to Madison and fiddled with the open file on his desk. "And it was a good one. A good joke. Most people who come in here don't have a good humor about them. I, for one, think it's vital," and as if Madison didn't know what that meant, he added, "*extremely important*, during your treatment." Then Tanger opted to focus on Annie and David. "We'll treat the cancer with chemotherapy and then, if necessary, chemotherapy and radiation simultaneously. I do believe it's our best hope."

Best hope? Madison watched her parents both nod solemnly to Dr. Tanger. *Why are they agreeing to something that sounds so horrible?* Madison glanced to Dr. Tanger and then back to Annie. *Why do they look so devastated when Mom said I would be fine?*

"We'll obviously need to do further testing as soon as possible to find out what stage the cancer is in."

Madison had waited long enough. She was tired of the medical babbling and wanted to get to the point. This question was the reason she even agreed to come and talk to the doctor anyway. "Then I can go back to training? After you do those tests?"

Dr. Tanger frowned slightly and moved his center to Annie. She had told him that she had prepared her daughter. Extensively, she had said.

For a long minute, there was no sound but shuffling in the hallway outside.

Annie didn't need reminding she wasn't totally honest when she told Madison about her sickness. It wasn't that she lied to her daughter. But she wasn't about to be the one to destroy every dream she'd ever had either. Wasn't it her responsibility as Madison's mother to help keep her hopes up?

David broke the silence when he cleared his throat nervously. "Annie thought it would help her. You know, to...uh...to skate again as soon as she can."

Annie fumbled with her words tentatively. "I...um...I told Madison, if she felt up to it, and only if she did, it would probably or maybe it might be a good thing for her to do. Skate a little. You know, keep her strength up."

Madison suddenly felt like a caged animal. Maybe this was why they conveniently sat her in between them. So they could corner her. Destroy her. She turned to her mother accusatorily. "That's *not* what you said. You never said it like that. You said I could skate!" She looked over to David for support. "Didn't she, Dad? You were right there. You heard her."

Dr. Tanger intervened before David had to choose a side. His focus was on Annie and no one else. "Mrs. Henry." He glanced to Madison's file on his desk. "Your daughter is very ill."

"I'm aware of that, Doctor." Her voice was barely above a whisper.

"Well, clearly with what has just been said, I'm not sure you are. With the treatment plans we have just gone over…" Tanger shook his head. "I don't think Madison could, or better said, *should* be trying to skate. This is an extremely crucial time for her."

Madison leaned forward in her chair. She eyed Dr. Tanger and before she could stop herself, the words spit out of her mouth. "That *her* you keep referring to? It's *me*! I don't need for you to talk through my mother to tell me I'm sick, or that I can't skate, okay?"

Tanger had no time to apologize to Madison.

Madison stood and faced Annie, her arms defensively folded across her chest. She didn't yell. She had no energy left in her body to. "You said I could skate. You said all we had to do was come here and talk to the doctor and then I could go back to training. I have to skate for the Olympic committee, Mom."

Annie tried to remain calm. "I know. I know what I said and I'm sure we're all just not understanding each other clearly." Annie grasped for the smallest bit of hope. "Dr. Tanger? You mean she can't skate maybe right *now*, I know. But soon, when she's better? When the treatments have had time to take effect? Then we can just start off slowly, right?"

It was when Annie spoke those last few sentences that Dr. Tanger realized this girl, this diminutive sick girl in front of him, had no idea just how ill she was. Susan had warned him about Annie. She had gone into detail about Annie coaching Madison for the Olympics. He was aware Annie was a registered nurse. So how could she not have told her daughter what was happening? "Madison, would you mind stepping outside for just a moment? I'd like to speak to your parents alone."

"I'm not leaving. I want to hear and since it concerns me and my body, I think I have more than enough right to stay."

David touched Madison's arm lightly. "Madison. Just give us a few minutes."

She jerked her arm away defiantly. "I'm not going." She sat back down in the chair and waited for Tanger to continue.

There was an unpleasant pause. Dr. Tanger looked at Annie and David, and then finally, to Madison. His face changed as he gazed directly to her. At that moment, Madison knew there were more, many more details that had been conveniently omitted for her benefit. For her wellbeing. And these details, she knew, could not be good.

Madison looked to the one person who had always made it all right. The one who promised her she would be all right. And from where Madison sat now, the one who lied to her. "You said, Mom...you said it would be okay. You said I would be okay. On the patio. That's what you said."

Annie took a quick breath of air, knowing immediately it would not suffice for what she had to say. "I think that, if we do what Dr. Tanger says, follow the treatment he thinks is best, then maybe you can..."

Madison jumped out of her chair again, and this time there was no sweetness in her voice whatsoever. "Stop lying to me! Just tell me! Is it true? Is it true what he's saying? Am I so sick that I might not be able to skate?"

Annie couldn't bring herself to look at Madison.

"Madison, it's not that simple," Dr. Tanger said through the thick air.

She turned to him with the same anger she'd released on Annie and David. "Yes, it is. It *is* that simple." She paused with defiance. "Forget about the Olympics, okay?! Tell me right now! Will I be okay after the treatments?"

"I just don't know yet, Madison."

"You're a doctor! You're supposed to know! I don't get it. What is wrong with everyone? I'm the one that is supposedly sick. I'm the one who has to go through all these terrible freaking treatments and no one can tell me the truth?" Madison snapped her head back to Annie angrily and stormed out of the office.

David stood and addressed Dr. Tanger. "I uh...I'll go talk to her." He walked out without waiting for a response from either of them.

Annie listened to the door close behind her once again. Relieved it wasn't the same slam that shook the office as when Madison left seconds before.

Dr. Tanger casually closed Madison's folder on his desk and put it to the side.

Annie couldn't help but notice the many folders that had been stacked in a pile before Madison's was placed on the top. How many other children were sick? Were they as sick as her daughter? If they were, how did those parents tell their child? Or did they? A feeling of suffocation started to overwhelm her and she stood up. "I'll call your office to schedule the tests." Annie walked to the door. Tanger's voice stopped her as she was about to exit.

"I know you want to keep things positive around Madison. Keep her spirits high, her hopes up. I think that is a very good way of handling the situation. I do. So please do not misinterpret what I'm about to say to you, Mrs. Henry. You need to keep in mind, in addition to keeping things positive for Madison, you also need to prepare her for what may possibly be ahead."

Annie stared at the door in front of her. She released the door knob and turned to Dr. Tanger. "Prepare her for what may be ahead? You mean, what *you* think is ahead for her. Because I'll tell you right now, Dr. Tanger, I won't let her die! Do you understand me?" Annie choked back all the tears that sat on the edge of her eyelids. She turned back to the door in a swift move. *"I will not let her die."*

***

The biggest fight Annie ever had with her mother was when she was seventeen years old. Of course, looking back on it now, it seemed rather funny. Fights always do somehow, when enough time has gone by. She had taken a spare set of car keys, sneaked out of her house after her mother had fallen asleep, and taken her mother's old Nova out for a little test drive. So what if it happened to be two o'clock in the morning? And what difference did it make that Annie also had had a few martinis? What was the big deal if she was in the back seat of the car with the sheriff's only son when she was finally caught a few hours later?

Annie spent the next three months in her room. Every night after dinner, she was sentenced to a twelve-by-twelve box. A box with the ugliest floral print wallpaper ever known to man. The previous owners had even wallpapered the ceiling. The only thing Annie was allowed to do was skate. Every day. The days Annie had no interest in the rink, she thought about the alternative: Staying inside the house the whole day and night with her mother. Immediately, she found the rink a wonderful, exciting place to be. The funny part now that time had passed was she realized she didn't even really like Bobby Utterman. Nothing had even happened that night. She did remember dry heaving outside the car for at least twenty minutes while Bobby fooled with the car's AM radio. But if she hadn't had the martinis, stolen the car keys and gotten caught, she would never have met David that bitter, cold winter. She probably wouldn't have been at the rink every day like she was. Their paths might not have crossed like they did. There had always been a reason for everything that happened in her life.

Until now.

Annie opened the door to Madison's room as quietly as possible and took a step inside. Madison could be sleeping and Annie knew that would be a good thing for her. Maybe for Annie too. She was all-too-aware Madison probably didn't want to talk to her or even see her for that matter, but she knew she had to at least try.

Madison was curled up on her side, lying on the bed, her body facing away from the door.

Annie moved a step closer to the side of the bed and whispered. "Maddie?"

Madison didn't move a muscle. Not even the smallest flinch was seen.

She whispered so quietly, even if Madison was awake, she most likely wouldn't hear Annie.

"Madison?"

Without a hint of movement of any kind, Madison's voice was loud and clear through the tension. "Get out."

Annie closed her eyes for a moment. Apparently, Annie's gut instincts were right on the money. This was not going to be easy. Madison would make sure of it. "I need to talk to you. It won't take too long. I think it...it's really important we talk."

Madison refused to face Annie. Her voice was muffled

slightly in the pillow. "Funny, I don't feel that same need to talk to you. I'd like you to get out of my room."

Annie moved closer to the bed, ignoring the hate spewing out from Madison. She gently touched the bed with her hand. "Honey, you don't have to say anything. Okay? But will you just listen to me, just for a second?"

"Why the hell should I? You lied to me. You said I'd be okay. That this could go away."

Annie heard the tears that were being fought to remain inside.

"What kind of mother are you? To do that to me? Why didn't you just tell me the truth?"

Annie breathed as much as she could. She tried to be cool. But inside, she knew that she was on the verge of falling apart. "I didn't lie. I didn't, Maddie. You're going to be okay and this *will* go away soon. I just don't think Dr. Tanger knows you yet. He doesn't know how strong you are and he doesn't even know if the canc—" She caught her breath and continued. "He doesn't know if it has spread yet. I think until we know for sure, there is no reason to get upset. We just have to keep doing what we're doing, the vitamins and protein shakes and we'll keep your strength up and you'll see, Mad. We're going to be okay." Annie waited. She sat on the edge of the bed and rested her hand on the top side of Madison's body, praying her speech had worked. "Madison?"

The voice wasn't sad. Or even scared. It was flat, angry and deep. "What?"

Annie knew there was nothing more she could say right now. "I, uh...nothing. I just, nothing."

"I'm tired."

Annie nodded. She got it. It was going to take a lot more to fix this problem between the two of them than one lousy pep talk. Annie pushed her body off the bed and stood over Madison. "I'll be downstairs if you need anything, okay?" She paused as if she was going to get a response. Annie walked to the door and glanced to her daughter's back. "So you know, we're going to start the chemotherapy the day after tomorrow." Again, no words from Madison. In some sick way, Annie knew she brought up the chemotherapy to try to get some kind of rise out of Madison. They hadn't even talked with Tanger yet about when they were going to start the treatment, but she was hoping Madison would disagree. Fight with her about it. Refuse to go. *Something.* But Madison didn't move from her position. Annie ran through the things that might trigger Madison, letting her mind sift through her mental filing cabinet under 'things that piss Madison off.' Bingo. "Oh, and you should also know that Jack's been calling you. He's actually been calling a lot and I think you should tell him what's going on. He's your best friend and he could help out. Want me to talk to him for you?" Annie tried not to get angry. It was not her fault. This was the only way she could react right now and Annie needed to accept that.

"Madison? I said I could talk to Jackson if you would like me to. Explain everything to him."

"I heard you."

"What do you want me to do?" After a few tense seconds, Annie finally got her response from Madison.

"Leave."

CHAPTER 22

𝓐nnie ran around the kitchen on auto-pilot. A milkshake was being mixed loudly in the blender. She had eggs cooking on the stove and bread in the toaster. It had been like this for a few weeks. She had managed to keep things fairly light and easy with Madison. There had been days when Madison could keep nothing in her stomach. One of the side effects mentioned by Dr. Tanger. But no matter. Annie had an entire buffet of breakfasts, lunches and dinners always ready for her. And snacks. Just in case.

Madison hadn't acknowledged their big fight. Annie tried to talk to her a few more times about her situation to no avail. The day the chemotherapy started, Madison came out of her room and sat down at the kitchen table, as if today was normal, as if she was going to the rink. Like it was just another day. She didn't speak too many words to Annie, but Annie decided not to take it personally. She didn't speak much to David either. When Madison did address her, it was polite, cordial...and that was good enough for Annie.

Annie moved to the cabinet and took out an insane number of vitamins. She spilled out a few from each of the eleven or so bottles and placed them in specific groups on a napkin.

David stood in the hallway where Annie could not see him and watched her run around, wondering how she did it. He knew Annie wasn't sleeping more than a few hours each night. She got up with the roosters, just to be prepared, she had told him many times this week alone.

Annie placed the napkin full of vitamins on the table next to an empty plate. The toast popped up with smoke surrounding the bread. Before she sniffed it, she already knew she had burnt the toast.

"Shit."

She grabbed the blackened bread from the toaster and threw it in the sink. Immediately, two more pieces found their way down the ready and waiting open slots and Annie pushed the button down again. She glanced to the egg whites and noticed the huge bubbles rising in the middle of the pan. The edges now had a crusty brown look. She grabbed the spatula and in her speed, dropped it on the floor. "Shit!" She grabbed it and quickly wiped it on her shirt before sticking it in the pan.

David smiled compassionately as he entered the kitchen. "Want some help?"

"Nope. I got it." She hit the near-deafening blender off.

He walked over to Annie and made an effort to kiss her on the cheek. She abruptly switched directions and barely allowed his lips to skim her face. David disregarded it. He was getting used to this. He reminded himself of the probable reason behind it every time the subject popped up in his head. He leaned his body against the counter that by now was completely covered with every food item imaginable, ready for

Madison. *Just in case.* David looked over the choices and knew, most likely, none of it would be ingested. Not by Madison, and certainly not today. "Madison isn't going to try to go to school today, is she?"

"Of course she is." Annie dropped pans and pots she had already used this morning into the overflowing sink.

David's voice rose. One he rarely used. "You're kidding Annie, right?"

Her lack of response was all the answer he needed.

"She's going to school? How is she going to even get there without vomiting? I heard her last night, for your information. I know you were up with her, so you are fully aware of what the hell I'm talking about."

Annie let the hot water run down her arms as she scrubbed the dishes. Bubbles surrounded the items in clumps all over the sink. She turned the faucet higher and occupied herself with her task of the moment, completely and purposefully ignoring David.

And he knew it. He pushed himself away from the counter and moved around to the other side so Annie had no choice but to look at him. Or at the least, know he was there, watching out for his Maddie-girl. "Annie, what are you trying to do here? Huh? She was up most of the goddamn night. She hasn't slept more than a few hours in a row any night for the past week. She can't keep up like this. Who the hell could? Annie, she's only had two chemo treatments." David shook his head in frustration at the one-sided conversation he was having. He toned his voice down a few notches and tried it again. "What does Tanger say? I'm sure he wouldn't be sending her to school so soon, especially if she isn't sleeping through the night. What did he say about her going to school?"

Annie shut the water off and dried her hands on a nearby

towel. She turned away from David before she slowly answered him. "He didn't say anything about school."

David frowned. When Annie mumbled and turned away, there was usually more to the story than whatever he'd been told. "Ann, when was the last time you talked to Tanger?"

"David, I really don't want to get into this right now. Maddie will be up soon and I don't think it's a good idea if the first thing she hears is us talking about the fucking cancer treatments."

"Well that was polite of you."

"I'm just saying I would rather talk about this later."

David moved in front of Annie, blocking her from her non-important duties. He backed her into the counter with his words. "Did you tell Tanger you were getting Maddie back to school already? Even with the side effects? You heard Dr. Tanger loud and clear. There was one condition having her home before they add radiation treatments...she isn't supposed to do anything but rest."

Annie avoided looking at him.

David took another step closer to Annie. Without meaning to, his voice escalated throughout the house. "Does he even know about the *skating*? Does he know she's been trying to skate while she's getting chemotherapy treatments? Or did you just forget to mention that minor part to him? Because as far as I remember, he said she shouldn't be even trying to do anything! I was there too. I heard him say it, Annie! No school. No skating. You're supposed to give her time. Jesus! You're running her to the bone. Are you crazy? Look at what you're doing to her!"

Annie glared at David before she began to speak. "I know her better than anyone. No one knows her like I do. *I* do. Not some doctor, and certainly not you. No one but me knows what is best for her. The skating and getting to school for a few classes will only make her stronger, David. I don't give a *shit* what Tanger said. He doesn't *know* her." Annie's eyes filled with emotion. "She cannot stop pushing herself now. Because if she does, she will give up. She gives up everything we've worked for and I'm not about to stand by and watch that happen. And, yes, the skating helps her. She remembers what it's like to be healthy and that's what I want. For her to be healthy again."

"What the hell is that supposed to mean? I want her healthy and back to normal! I just don't want her to kill herself trying! Christ, Annie! Can you hear yourself?"

"Yes! I do!" Annie stormed away from David angrily. She was stopped abruptly by the small figure standing in the hallway, looking and listening to the two of them fight.

Madison eyed them, neither one getting more attention than another. They were equally at fault and she wanted them both to know it. She sluggishly stepped into the kitchen and looked at all the food Annie had prepared. For a moment her face took on a strange shade of green. Combining that with an exhausted appearance and a much-too-skinny frame, Madison wasn't looking very good. "Morning."

David walked over to her and gave her head a ruffle. "Morning, Maddie-girl." He walked to the table and sat down.

Annie changed the tone of the room immediately. A frozen smile appeared on her face like the kind of smile Mr. Rogers used to suddenly put on when his doorbell rang on cue. "Okay. I know how you feel about shakes for breakfast. I want you to know I heard what you were saying, about no milkshakes for breakfast, but Mad? *This* one is different. You are gonna love this one." Annie literally jogged over to the blender.

Madison glanced over to David. They shared a quick smile, and Maddie added an eye roll and a shoulder shrug for David's benefit.

Annie excitedly poured the dense liquid from the blender into a glass. "Ready?"

Maddie tried to look eager but it was not working. Her face said many things but not one of them was happy.

"Cookies and cream vanilla shake!" Annie grandly handed the glass to Madison. "With..." Annie grabbed the whipped cream can from the refrigerator and sprayed an atrocious amount on top. Swirling it up higher and higher.

Madison smiled. This was by far the grossest, yet one of the funniest things she had ever seen her mom do. "Mom!"

"Now that," Annie pointed to her work of art in Madison's hands. "That is a champion's breakfast!" Annie punched a straw in it and handed a spoon to Madison.

Madison took a small sip while walking carefully to the kitchen table.

"Well? How is it? Good?" Annie looked at her daughter expectantly. Who would've thought she'd ever feed her child milkshakes for breakfasts. *Whoever thought we'd be doing any of the things we now do that make up the better part of our days. And nights.* And who knows, Annie thought. What if the illogical combination of these ingredients somehow, *somehow* miraculously cured the evil that had invaded her daughter's body? Then, she smiled for her own benefit, it would all be worth it.

"It's good, Mom." Madison barely sat down before the prepared buffet started appearing in front of her. *There is enough food to feed a small town,* Madison thought. No one could eat all of this. Even if they felt one hundred percent. Forget the fact that she was in the under five percent category.

David eyed Annie as she brought plate after plate over to Madison. Annie ignored his leer and finally sat down next to her girl, bright-eyed. "So. Our plan, just to remind you. We're going to go to that Chinese herb doctor after school today. The one George's wife's sister told him about? She said they have something for the nausea. Also, I was doing some research last night and I have a couple more herbs that have been known to treat some rare forms of cancer. Can't hurt, right? Especially if I can find a way to blend it into a drink."

David picked at the food Annie had brought to Madison. If he didn't say something now, he would lose the chance. Or better yet, Annie wouldn't let him. He waited for a break in his wife's one-sided alternative treatment conversation and spoke. It probably came out slightly louder than necessary, but David wanted to err on the side of more safe than sorry. "If you're too tired, Mad, you don't have to go anywhere. Not to the herbalist guy, not to school and certainly not to the rink. They are just things to do when you're better. They aren't supposed to be a part of your treatment and if you are tired or you don't feel well in any way, there is no reason to push yourself."

Annie got up from the table and crossed to the sink. "Yes, there is, David. There is a reason and like I said, let's discuss it later."

Madison pretended to sip her shake and tried to overlook the tension between her parents. Neither one worked.

David stood up and kissed Madison on her forehead. "Call one of us, okay? When you get tired or you don't feel well and want to come home. It's okay to do that. You do know that, right?"

"Yeah." *Is it really?* She was not sure whether she did know that it was okay. But it was better than having a conversation about it that could potentially turn into another argument between Annie and David. She was not used to being the one in the middle and she knew after this short period of time, she didn't like it one bit.

"Bye, Maddie-girl." David exited without a word to Annie. Enough words were already said between them today.

CHAPTER 23

*M*adison hadn't talked to Jack in weeks. Had it been even more than that? She couldn't remember how long it had been and just the thought of trying to figure it out gave her a splitting headache. Obviously, she should've called him back after at least one of the countless calls he'd made. But wasn't that what friends were for? To understand when you blow them off or simply can't deal? She knew at least one of the hundred or so messages she had received from him should have been returned, but the last thing she wanted to do was tell Jackson what was going on with her. This was her battle, her sickness, and she was not about to be pitied by him or anyone for that matter. She had never once lied to him in all the years they'd been best friends. She had never had a reason to. Today, she had a reason.

Madison barely got one foot out of Annie's car before Jackson was in her face, blocking her body from further movement forward. She gave Annie a nod goodbye and shut the door.

Annie shot a look to Madison that clearly said 'tell him'. She waved a quick hello to Jackson lest he think something was wrong and drove away.

Madison darted around Jack's body and headed for the school entrance. She'd thought about what to say to him for endless nights and days...and how to tell him. But now that the time was actually here, "hey" was the only word that was vocalized.

Jack was right by her side, in step with her fast pace. "Hey? That's all you can say is *hey*? Where the hell have you been? You haven't called me back once."

"When?"

"When? How about when *didn't* I call? God, Madison. I called you last night and the night before and yeah, the night before that. I could keep going but I think you know what I'm saying. I've called you every day, on the average about three times a day. You never don't call back."

"Never *don't*? Double negative." She continued walking at the fastest pace she could without the fear of passing out cold. Or throwing up. That would be attractive. Maybe if she did either of those, he'd drop the subject and leave her alone. Then she would never have to deal with telling him. Or lying to him about it.

Jackson was getting more and more agitated. He grabbed her by the arm just before she entered the school and angrily whipped her around to face him. "Will you cut the shit? I have called you at least once a day for weeks. I have come over to your house only to be told you're not feeling well? I have emailed you..." He let his voice trail off, discouraged by the blank face staring back at him.

Madison occupied herself with the other kids entering the building, who they were with, what they were wearing.

Anything she could think of, besides what was really going on. "Sorry."

"What is it? Are you mad at me, or something? Cause we've never not talked for more than, I don't know…more than a few hours I think." Jackson smiled a little grin. "Sorry. Never not. Double negative." He waited for a quick response from Madison. He didn't know that no one got a Madison comeback nowadays. He brought his voice back down to normal and asked her seriously. "Did I do something? Or say something…to make you mad at me? Because if I did, you know I'm sorry. Whatever it is, I didn't mean to."

Tell him. He deserves to know. "You didn't do anything or…or say anything." *Tell him now, Maddie.* "It's me. I just had a lot of things to uh…to do. And some things I had to take care of last week." She finally got up the nerve to look in Jack's direction. "I'm sorry. You're totally right. I should've called you back."

Jackson shrugged it off. He couldn't be angry with Madison even if he tried. "Don't worry about it."

A pang of guilt hit Madison deep in her stomach. She hated lying to him. Or at the very least, keeping something important from him. "Listen, I do need to talk to you about something though. It's really not a big deal. But uh, soon…maybe tonight or…" *Or maybe I will somehow inexplicably be cured and never have to tell you what is really going on inside of my body.* "Anyway, I'll tell you—"

He interrupted her quickly. "Tell me now."

"Now's not good. It's just, not a good time at all. Really. Please believe me. But later, okay?" Madison put on a polite smile and started moving closer to the door that would separate them for a period. Right now, that seemed like an eternity to Madison and she'd take it.

Jack grabbed her arm again, this time with more caution, and stopped her. "Madison."

Madison averted her eyes from Jack's. If she could just get inside and do this later.

"Look at me."

Madison glanced back to Jackson like she hadn't a care in the whole world. "Huh?"

"What's going on?" His voice pleaded with her.

Madison lifted her head up and looked directly and deeply into Jack's eyes. "I have this...I have this..." She cleared her throat more than necessary. *Tell him now.*

"What? You have this what?"

Madison recovered quickly and put on her best face. "Last week? I had this *flu*. It literally took me weeks to get completely better. Guess all these years of never being sick caught up with me, huh? Between that and then um, training for the Olympic committee...anyway, that's where I've been."

Jackson did a double take. He laughed out loud. "The *flu*? Why didn't you just say that? What's the big deal?"

Madison smiled as much as she could, convincing herself that if she smiled big enough then she wouldn't physically be able to cry. "It was a big deal. It was a very bad flu. You know how I cannot stand to be sick. I loathe it. It's like this personal defeat or something."

"You should've called me back, loser. I could've come over and kept you company. Played some poker. Watched a movie. Something."

Madison looked at her best friend, who would absolutely without a doubt do anything for her and realized she just told the first lie in their ten-year friendship. She fought to keep her eyes from watering. "I didn't want you to come over. I didn't want you to catch it."

Jack didn't move his gaze from her face. "Mad, come on. I wouldn't care."

Madison choked back her tears and answered sweetly. "Yeah, but *I* would."

The bell rang loudly outside the building. They both started to finally move through the doors with the crowds of kids lingering until the last possible second, every one of them dreading the start of another school day. Madison couldn't wait. She secretly sighed a breath of relief to have this conversation come to an end, even if it meant sitting in a classroom, nauseous.

"Listen, you wanna hang out tonight?"

Madison was at a loss for words. She wasn't sick anymore, supposedly. So, there really wasn't any valid excuse not to hang out with Jack. She stalled for a second and when she finally spoke, she stuttered noticeably. "I, uh...I—I can't. Got the rink later."

Jack abruptly stopped walking.

Madison glanced back to him. "Come on. We're going to be late."

"What's with you? If you don't want to hang out, tell me. Because this is stupid. I don't know why you're acting the way you are. You're not calling me back, you're blowing me off." He paused, then... "Are you seeing someone?"

Madison couldn't help but laugh. Rudely. "Seeing someone? Are you joking? Jackson..." She took two steps back to where Jackson was still standing. She stopped her laughter and talked to him seriously. "I am not seeing anyone. You of all people should know that would be a miracle. I'd actually have to know someone other than you and my immediate family and well, that's not about to happen anytime soon. I explained why I didn't call you back and I am not blowing you off. I promise. Okay?" She looked away for fear of Jackson recognizing it was a lie. "We had to postpone my final skate for the Olympic committee. With that flu thing, I got behind. I'm in the rink tonight. For probably hours." She quickly remembered the upcoming new treatments over the next week. She would be back in the hospital tonight, tomorrow start the radiation along with chemotherapy, and she knew she'd be in the hospital for a few weeks. How was she supposed to cover that up? She had begged Annie and David to let her have one last day in school but she never considered all the questions Jack would have. Or how many lies she would have to tell to continue her ruse. "We have to work hard tonight because uh, because tomorrow we're…You know what? We should get going." Madison motioned for them to start making their way into school.

Jackson followed her closely. "Tomorrow, you're what?"

Madison thought for a second that maybe, Jackson would forget what they were talking about. Not a chance. "Oh, right. I was saying that…tomorrow…actually, I am, well, me and the parents, obviously…we're going out of town for a few days. Just for a quick break. You know, before we get any closer to the Olympics. Annie's idea. Which is probably one of her finer ones, huh? So, I'll just call you when I get back. From our trip. Okay?"

Jack held the door open for Madison and she walked through. "Thanks." There. Done. And after a few days, she would call Jack and tell him they've decided to extend their 'getaway'.

He was floored. He'd known Annie far too long and he was sure she was not the kind of person who would suddenly take her daughter out of school and away from training for a 'quick break'. The thought came back to him. *Madison is see-*

*ing someone, and maybe she's too embarrassed to say any-
thing.* "Since when have you ever had a break before a
competition?"

Madison turned to him before entering her classroom.
"There's a first time for everything, huh?"

"Yeah. Guess so." Jackson opened his mouth to say something to Madison. But he was too late. She was already inside
the room.

"I'll see you later," she called over her shoulder.

Jackson watched Madison sit down at her desk and take
out her books. She never once looked back at him. No wave
of her hand shooing him away, none of her infamous eye rolls.
He finally pulled himself away from her class and left.

⌘⌘⌘⌘⌘⌘

One thing could always be counted on to cheer her up,
Jack thought. No matter what was wrong or however stressed
she was, *or who she was seeing,* he had the remedy to fix it.
He had already stopped at her favorite coffee shop and
ordered her specialty. Hot milk chocolate, not dark, double
whipped cream, extra sugar. Didn't matter if it was in the
dead of summer and the humidity was at an all-time high.
Madison drank hot cocoa, any time, any place.

Jack stepped out of his car and closed the door. His mind
had been consumed all day with the possibility of Madison
seeing someone. *How could she?* Or better yet, *how could he
have let it happen?* He found himself running to the passenger
side of his car. He carefully took out a cardboard tray filled
with steaming paper cups. His foot closed the door for him
and he quickly scanned the dimly lit parking lot. Annie's car
wasn't anywhere around. Jack noticed George's truck off to

the side. Maybe David dropped off Annie and Madison earlier. That was probably it. Jackson neared the entry. He
balanced the flimsy tray in one hand, pushing it up against the
wall as he tried the door. It was locked. He knocked on the
glass and rang the buzzer. After a few moments of waiting and
knocking, Jackson saw George coming toward him and
smiled.

George looked puzzled when he saw Jack. He wasn't
expecting anyone at the rink tonight and certainly not Jack.

Jackson talked through the door. "Hey, George."

George grabbed the huge ring of keys from his pocket and
unlocked the door. He opened the door for Jack. "Jack?
What're you doing here, son?"

Jackson smiled broadly and raised his tray a few inches.
"Thought I'd surprise Madison. You know how she loves hot
chocolate. I even got a whole thing of extra whipped cream."
Jackson stepped through the doorway without waiting for an
invitation.

George didn't know what to say. A small frown began to
form on his forehead without time to stop it. "Listen, Jack,
she...Madison's not here." *How could he not know yet? Did
no one tell him what's going on?* He was not about to be the
one to break the news.

"Did I miss her? Did they come earlier?" Jack glanced into
the darkened rink. The lights had been turned off. "She said
they were going to be here until late tonight." Jack continued
talking, aiming to convince himself of the conversation he
knew for a fact truly took place today with Maddie. "She's
got to prepare for the Olympic committee. They're behind
because of that flu thing she had." He let the cold air fill his
lungs for a beat. Then in a small voice he invited the truth.
"George? Right?"

George looked away for a few seconds. *My God in heaven.* No one told Jack what was going on with Madison.

"George?" Even before Jack asked again, he knew in his heart Madison had lied to him. And he knew she wasn't seeing anyone.

George finally looked up to meet Jackson's eyes. "You should talk to Annie, son."

"Why? Talk to Annie about what?" His voice cracked noticeably.

The only sound Jackson heard was the air-conditioning unit clicking in the electrical closet a few feet away from them.

"George? Please. Tell me where she is."

⊙ CHAPTER 24 ⊙

*I*t was a thirty-five minute drive from the rink to the hospital. Jackson made it in seventeen minutes. He stopped counting the red lights he flew through after three of them had passed. There was only one thing on his mind. Only one thing that mattered.

He moved as fast as he could down the subdued hospital halls without disrupting any patients or calling too much attention to himself. He knew every short-cut, every little turn and every corner there was in the building. Madison and Jackson played there so often as children, especially during the hospital's renovation. Each wing would miraculously transform into a fantasyland for both of them. They would create worlds of their own, hour after hour, where no one and nothing else mattered. Now Madison was in one of those worlds, all by herself.

Jackson was completely out of breath when he reached the nurse's station on the third floor. He noticed a nurse sitting behind the counter, talking on the telephone. He changed his pace from a run to a fast walk and threw his body on the ledge in front of her. "Excuse me?"

The nurse eyed Jackson cautiously for a moment before talking into the phone again. "Hold on a sec."

Jackson wondered how he must look to the nurse right now. He could feel beads of sweat dripping down his face, even though it was wintertime. His clothes were disheveled and he was breathing far too heavily to be considered normal.

"Can I help you?"

"Madison Henry. Where is she?" He asked but more as a statement.

The nurse looked at the clock just above Jackson's head for effect. She knew what time it was. "I'm sorry. Visiting hours have ended. You'll have to come back tomorrow."

Jackson took a menacing lean forward, sending the nurse back a few inches. "I can't wait until tomorrow, okay? It's an emergency. Now either you tell me where she is, or I start yelling her name as loud as I can. And even if you should press that hidden security alert button to your right hand, just under the counter there? I'd say I still have approximately two minutes to make your life really miserable."

The nurse stared wide-eyed at Jackson. She looked down at the computer screen and hit a few keys. She lifted her head up to him and spoke quietly. "Down the hall on the left. Room 317."

"Thank you." Jack took off in a sprint, reading the room numbers to himself as he ran by each one. Then he saw it, 317. He pushed the door open angrily only to find a hospital orderly, changing the sheets on what appeared to be an empty bed. A curtain had been drawn blocking the other half of the room. Jackson caught his breath and double-checked the room number. "Sorry, I'm looking for Madison Henry."

The orderly nodded politely and pulled back the curtain. He gathered the used linens and exited the room.

Jackson stood in his position, frozen. He had spent the last half an hour thinking about what to say to her. Here he stood in Madison's room, and there was not one word that came to his mind of what to say to her now that he saw her. He looked at the small, frail girl in the bed a few feet away from him, looking terrible. Sick would be the word, if he had to describe what exactly he meant by terrible. An IV was attached to her arm. Fluid slowly and purposefully dripped into her body. Jackson tried to focus on Madison straightforwardly without giving his fear away. But she was so pale and so thin. And even though he had seen her hours before at school, suddenly she looked so different.

Suddenly, it all made perfect sense. *All of it.*

Madison lay in bed, flipping through an *US Weekly*. She heard Jackson come into her room, heard him ask the orderly where she was. She assumed he had heard what was going on, most likely from George, and here he was, angry, confused, hurt and ready to hate her. *Great*, she thought to herself. *Hate me. It'll make things much easier for the both of us.*

Jack took a step closer to Madison's bed and neither one uttered a word. With his second step coming closer to her, Madison lifted her magazine higher, pretending to be completely engrossed in the latest round of the Paris/Nicole publicity war.

"What the hell is wrong with you?" Jack shook his head, knowing that was truly the worst choice of words to put together in a sentence directed at Madison.

She refused to stop flipping pages in her magazine. As if she could read that fast. "Obviously, you know what the hell is wrong with me or you wouldn't be here, would you? I'm tired right now. Maybe we can talk tomorrow."

"I'm not leaving, Mad." He softened his voice. "Why didn't you say anything?"

"I did."

"What? That you're going out of town? Or that you had the flu? Is that what you call saying something? I mean, come on, Mad. What was that?"

Madison calmly closed her magazine and placed it on the night table next to her bed. She looked at the liquid saturating her blood stream, slowly, painfully. "How'd you find out?"

Jack moved closer to her bed, still keeping a safe distance. Safe for whom, he didn't really know. "I went to the rink to bring you hot chocolate. I figured with your long night of practicing, you could use…" His voice trailed off. *Some night of practice.*

Madison allowed herself to be mesmerized by the drip, drip, drip into her arm. *Focus on anything but Jackson's face.* "So, George told you?"

"Yeah. It…uh…it took me a few minutes to convince him to tell me what was going on with you, but…yeah. He told me. He told me everything." Jackson looked at Madison directly. "That was a pretty crappy thing to do, so you know. I have to hear you have *cancer* through George?"

Madison turned on Jackson crossly. "Oh, hey. Sorry. Didn't mean to hurt your feelings. Sorry I wasn't thinking about *you* more. Silly freaking *me* to have some things on my mind the last few weeks."

"You could've told me, Maddie. You could've said…"

She abruptly sat herself up in the bed. "Said *what*, Jackson?! What was I supposed to say? Hey, how was your game today? Oh, yippee-kay-eh. You won. Oh, yeah. Almost forgot, Jack. The thing is? I've got cancer. Come on over and join my victory party."

Jack looked away without responding.

Madison reached for a school book next to her magazine. If she ignored him long enough, maybe he'd leave. She was absolutely aware she should be dealing with the situation. Just, not now and preferably, not here in the hospital. Suddenly, Jack ripped her book right out of her hands and threw it hard against the wall. The thump of it hitting reverberated for a moment. Madison had never witnessed those kinds of actions from Jack and had absolutely no idea how to respond.

Jack took a deep breath and closed his eyes. When he spoke, his voice was back to normal, sweet and calm. "You should've told me the truth. It's me here."

Madison dropped her head in shame and when she finally responded, her voice was barely above a whisper. "You're right. I know I should've told you. It's just…I guess I thought if I didn't tell you, maybe it wouldn't be so…so real, you know? Maybe it would go away somehow."

"Yeah, I know." Jackson finally moved close to Madison's bedside and stood over her. "But it is, right? It is real? They're sure?"

Madison nodded a weak yes.

Jack quickly glanced away from her. The last thing he'd ever want was for her to see him cry.

"You wanna know what's going on? Cause you don't have to hear about it. If you don't want to. It's not like it's a great topic of conversation." Madison waited for his answer.

Jackson finally turned to her and didn't back off this time. "I want to know. I want to know everything." He carefully sat down on the edge of her bed, facing her. He was cautious not to put all his weight down on the mattress.

Madison smirked a little. "I won't break, Jack. You can sit on the bed all the way." She tried to make light of the situation as she explained it to Jack. Annie taught her to do that a long time ago. *Don't take things so seriously, especially about yourself. It's hard to get depressed if you make light of a bad situation.* Madison put on a reluctant smile. "So, it's uh…it's not exactly good, the cancer. Although, what cancer is good, right? The kind I have is called Ewing's Sarcoma. They ran some tests and apparently I won't be receiving a gold medal for the results. The doctor said it has spread and everything, which we were obviously hoping wouldn't be the case. This nice doctor is trying this trial thing: I have high doses of chemotherapy and radiation therapy. He was hoping it was just going to be the chemotherapy, but since he found out it spread, Dr. Tanger, the B.C.D.O.C., recommended a new two for the price of one combo treatment."

Jackson tried to digest it all. "Dr. Tanger is the B.C…?"

Madison rested her head back on the pillow. Even talking could tire her out rapidly. She grinned slightly to Jackson and hoped he noticed her attempt at moving her facial muscles. "Tanger is the Big Cancer Doctor on Campus. That's what I call him. The B.C.D.O.C. I don't think he's too fond of my nickname for him, but what the hell, huh? Madison grimaced a little at the drips invading her body and the severe stinging they caused going in.

"Are you okay? Should I get someone?"

Madison shook her head no and did her best to shrug it off. "Just burns sometimes." She glanced to the television in hopes of a distraction, knowing there would never be one big enough. "Look, I have to stay in here for a while, Jackson. I'm

not really sure how long that is, but…" Madison hesitated.

She didn't like hearing this part when Annie and Tanger tried to explain it to her earlier in the week. She was pretty sure she wouldn't like hearing it coming from her own mouth now, but Jackson deserved to know. She owed him that much after what she'd been putting him through. "These treatments? The chemotherapy and the radiation? The doctors don't know yet if they'll help me or not. Even with the high doses, they aren't sure what the outcome will be, I guess. But maybe, huh? Maybe they'll help." There was a long pause with no response from Jack. Madison hadn't looked in his direction since she started talking about her illness but now she forced herself to turn his way. He had turned his head away from her so she couldn't see his face. "Jack?"

Jack listlessly looked at Madison, visibly upset, his cheeks damp with recent and still-falling tears.

She had never seen Jack upset and it positively broke her heart in two knowing it was over her. "Jack. Say something."

"I'm sorry. I am so sor—" Jack couldn't finish his sentence. He dropped his head in her lap, burying it deeply as he cried.

"I know." Madison hesitated but soon let her hands rest gently on his head. "I know you are."

They stayed that way for a long time, Jackson lying in Madison's lap. *What should've been an uncomfortable time wasn't so bad*, she mused. Madison thought about the two of them, and how funny it might look if anyone, who didn't know their long history, walked into her room at this very moment. They might assume they had been boyfriend and girlfriend for years. *Or am I the only one who is thinking that?* She allowed her fingers to ever so gently touch Jackson's hair as he lay in her lap breathing softly. She found herself with a feeling of peace in her head, for the first time in a very long time. It was many minutes later when Jackson finally spoke.

He lifted his head up, startling Madison.

"What's wrong?"

"Nothing." Jack smiled to her and picked up the television remote off of the bedside table. And as if to make sure even he himself believed his words he repeated them. "Nothing is wrong." He shook the last bit of sadness away and smiled even bigger to Madison. "So, they got cable in here?"

Madison smiled. "DIRECTV. Why?"

"Cause we're gonna need some stuff to keep us busy in here, right?"

Madison barely nodded. "Right."

Jackson turned the volume up and flipped through channels as fast as he could until he found the Discovery channel. "Oh yeah, baby. Here we go. Sharks. This is so cool. Watch what they do here."

But Madison couldn't bring her eyes to watch sharks because she couldn't take her eyes away from Jack. She tried not to think about the burning sensation the medicine made as it found its way into every crevice of her body. She refused to think about the 'what ifs' that had plagued her every waking and sleepless hour.

"Don't think you're going to hog the bed just because you might be a tad under the weather." Jackson, smirking, motioned for her to move over in the bed.

She shimmied her body over until she was almost falling off the side of the bed. *Don't look at the pole standing at attention. Don't look at the bag of medicine hanging off the end. Look at Jack. Look at your best friend.*

Jack plopped down in the small empty space next to her. "Watch the shark, Mad. He's gonna eat that fish."

Madison smiled to herself as her drowsy eyes closed. But it wasn't the sharks she was entranced with.

It was Jackson.

CHAPTER 25

When something goes so horribly wrong with someone, it's often interesting to note how people who never knew the affected person even breathed before can suddenly become their true friends. Madison was painfully aware she wasn't the most popular girl. Or rather, even popular at all. Better yet, she knew she was like the last person anyone would be friends with. It was Jack who told her about Madison Henry Day at their high school. The cheerleading squad was big on lending a helping hand to special causes, especially ones that garnered them certain attention...from say, the local newspapers. More often than not, the squad would find their team photo, usually in some extraordinary pyramid, somewhere toward the front of the paper with a small caption that told the story of a person in dire straits. Madison just happened to fit the bill this quarter. The school had sent a large vase of flowers from all of the teachers and administrative workers. Along with it, they sent one of those "you're in our prayers and thoughts" cards with lilies all over it that can sometimes be detrimental to the sick person who's reading it. There were the flowers sent from the church Madison and Annie used to frequent before Sunday practices ultimately replaced Sunday sermons. Some of the floral arrangements had been sent from parents of the kids at her school. Quite obviously, Madison knew it wasn't the boy or girl that never said hi to her in the hallway who thought to send a get well floral fantasy worth well over a hundred dollars. Wouldn't that mean they would have been friends at some point? Even for a day? Maybe to sound cool, that kid went home and acted like he knew Madison, the Olympic skater that tragedy hit like a ton of bricks. How sad it was, how he wished he could have gotten to know her better. Or maybe it was a cheerleader that went home to her mother crying one afternoon...knowing it would buy her the night away from studying, being so distraught and all over her ailing friend. At any rate, the flowers came on a daily basis. Sometimes the token balloon bouquet would be brought in breaking up the monotony.

Jack only brought flowers to Madison once during her three-week stay at the lovely and well-decorated Harbor County Hospital. The first time he arrived after she told him, or rather, after George told him about her condition, he showed up with the largest bouquet of roses Madison had ever seen. Bigger than the bouquets they give to the newly crowned Miss America. Bigger than anything she had ever seen before. Madison couldn't even see who it was behind the arrangement until he put the flowers down and peeked out sheepishly from behind them. There wasn't just one color of roses wrapped in the sparkly tissue; that would have been too easy. Jackson had hand-picked every color available and even went so far as to have some dyed more exotic hues than the average red, white, pink or yellow. That's not to say Jack didn't show up with something for Madison after that day. He did. Every day he would show up after school. Every day there would be another little something for Madison in his backpack. Sometimes he would bring her silly putty just because she had never had it before, maybe a CD he burned the night before to help the treatments go by faster or a deck of cards and chips for a heads up poker game. There was a yo-yo to show off his skills, and Madison's personal favorites, coloring books and paint by number sets they would do together. Of course, just to aggravate Jackson as much as possible, she would never paint with the colors she was instructed to on the cardboard.

Madison smiled to herself as she put the finishing touches on her last page in the *Beauty and the Beast* coloring book, compliments of Jackson, of course. She autographed the bottom of the picture and wrote *"To Jackson, the beast. Thank you for everything"* on top of the page. Very carefully, she pulled the flimsy paper out of the book and folded it in half.

Annie entered slightly out of breath. "You wouldn't think it'd be this damn hard to find an envelope around here. But, lemme tell you something…"

Madison smiled to Annie as she interrupted her. "It was?"

She walked over to Madison and handed her an envelope. "It was." She collapsed on the bed, lying on her back, her arms thrown over her head in success. Or maybe exhaustion.

Madison turned the long white envelope over and noticed it had the hospital's return address pre-printed in the upper left hand corner and grimaced. "It says Harbor County on it."

Annie turned her head to Madison. "Well, it's all I could find, Mad. There was not a plain white envelope to be found anywhere on the premises. I would know, trust me. I looked everywhere. I told you I have one at home if you want to wait."

riley weston

"No. I want to give it to him today." She placed the folded colored picture in the envelope and sealed it.

After three attempts to lift her body into a sitting position, Annie finally succeeded. "Okay. What do you say we clean this place up a bit, huh?"

Madison shrugged a little. "I was thinking maybe I could wash my hair today. It's looking pretty nasty."

"Are you saying that because you want to wash your hair or because, maybe you don't want to help your old mother clean up your room?"

"Both?"

Annie smiled at her honesty. She was aware that Madison needed help washing her hair. She needed help with just about everything. With the IV in her arm, minimal tasks were not so minimal. Annie had learned to read between the lines, more than usual. Madison never used to ask for help. She never really did before this happened, and it had only gotten worse. She would simply mention she thought her hair needed washing. They both knew she couldn't do it alone. When she wanted a plain white envelope, they both knew she wasn't about to go walking around the hospital in search of one. If she wanted to call David, she would simply wonder, out loud, what he was doing right about then, and Annie would move to the phone and dial it for her. On the days Madison was in more pain than usual, Annie would sometimes stand over her, holding the phone up to her ear so she wouldn't have to lift her arm. She tried not to think about what her daughter was capable of doing, merely a few short weeks ago. The practices, the competitions, the jumps and leaps all on two thin blades. Every time she looked at Madison, she put those thoughts away. The ones where Madison would be skating around the rink, weightlessly throwing her body into the air at six in the

224

morning, or how she would be standing on the top riser, bending down to accept her gold medal. Any thought where Madison was healthy. It was simply too painful to think about right now.

"Mom?"

Annie snapped out of her daydream and looked over at Madison expectantly.

"What're you thinking about?"

She smiled politely and jumped off the bed. "I was thinking about washing your hair *and* cleaning up this messy room." Annie moved to the dresser and straightened out a picture of Madison and Jack. It was one of the many gifts Jack had brought to Madison. He had even found an antique frame to put it in.

Madison slowly moved her legs to the side of the bed, pushing the IV stand away to make room. She carefully stood and hesitated for a moment, grabbing the IV pole for support.

"Want me to help?"

"Nope. I got it." Madison stepped forward, IV pole in tow, with much trepidation to the bathroom, a long fifteen feet away.

Annie picked up magazines that had been thrown on the floor. She watched Madison closely out of the corner of her eye, organizing her pajamas and sweats, doing anything she could to keep busy. God help her if Madison should catch her staring, watching, waiting. They'd already been through that and Annie didn't care to have that incident repeated. She heard water running in the bathroom and knew Madison had made it to her destination safely. "God, Mad. This place is a mess."

"So leave!" Madison called out from the bathroom.

Annie didn't flinch. She even smiled at her attempt to be

snotty. "Not funny." Annie smelled some flower arrangements that appeared to be very dead. "Ugh, Mad, these flowers really have got to be thrown out today. Honestly. That's what the awful smell in the room is."

"Which ones?"

"The ones that smell like rotten eggs. The dead roses."

Her voice was somewhat muffled from the running water but Annie could hear her distinctly. "Jack gave those to me."

Annie carefully took the huge vase and quietly opened the hospital room door. "And that was nice of you to keep the flowers this long, but really, Madison, it's time. Pretty soon you'd start smelling like the muck that's sitting at the bottom of the vase and I have a strong feeling that would not be very attractive." She placed the vase on the floor outside in the hallway and reentered. She poked her head near the door to the bathroom. She continually had to remind herself of Madison's privacy. Knock first. Ask permission. But Madison had left the door somewhat ajar, which gave Annie at least the initiative to approach the door. "You okay in there?"

"Yeah. Fine."

With her curiosity getting the better of her, Annie gently pushed the door open to peek inside. Madison stood over the sink, trying not to get the arm with the IV attached wet. Water seemed to be everywhere but on Madison's head where it was supposed to be. Her pajamas were, from where Annie was looking, very damp at the least. Tiny bubbles from the shampoo were scattered over the tiled floor. Annie backed up out of the room before Madison knew she was being watched and brought the door back to its original position. She casually called to Madison through the door. "You want some help?"

There was a long silence, then Madison answered. "Yeah."

Annie pushed the door fully open and entered. She forgot about the amount of water on the floor and immediately slipped on the tiles. Before she could stop herself, she flew into the back of Madison, sending her upper body deeper into the sink.

And for the first time in a very long time, Annie heard Madison laugh. Not a huge, knee-slapping laugh, but a hearty laugh nonetheless.

"Mo-om! I could've cracked my head open on the sink or something."

"Don't go yelling at me. You're the one who dumped water all over the floor."

Annie straightened up and checked Madison's IV, making sure nothing detached itself. "Are you okay?" For some reason, maybe it was looking at both of their faces in the wet mirror, Annie burst out laughing again.

"Could you maybe ask me that without laughing? Hey, are you okay? Ha ha ha. There's something sinister in that, Mom."

Annie allowed one more little grunt of laughter to escape. "I know. I'm sorry." She took the glass out of Madison's hands and filled it up with water. "How about we start over, huh?" Very gently, she tipped Madison's head down into the sink and slowly poured the water over her long hair. "Is it too hot? Or cold?"

"It's good. Maybe a little hotter."

Annie adjusted the water and refilled the glass. She made sure no water dripped down Madison's back. "Okay?"

Madison's nose was stuffy when she answered. "Yeah."

Annie turned off the water and reached for the shampoo. She squeezed out a sizeable amount into her palm and rubbed her hands together before transferring the suds into Madison's hair. "Did I ever tell you about that competition when the toilet paper got caught on my skate?"

"No. You're kidding, right?"

Annie scrubbed Madison's hair with her fingernails and massaged her scalp as if she was in the best hair salon in the country. "I'm not kidding. I was so nervous, this one competition. I mean, I was always nervous, but this time, it was bad. And right before I was supposed to go on, I had to go to the bathroom. I leave Fred, my coach, and run like hell to the bathroom with my skates on. I didn't even have time to put on the guards. That's how close it was going to be. So, I run in there, go to the bathroom, and run out, hurrying back to Fred. They are literally announcing my name as I'm running to get back to the ice. Before Fred can stop me, I'm on the ice. People start to laugh out loud and I'm thinking, *What could be so funny that...?*"

Her voice slowly trailed off for no apparent reason to Madison.

"What happened then? They were laughing at you?" Annie didn't respond. "Mom?"

Annie looked down at her hands and little by little released her tightly clenched fingers. A huge clump of Madison's hair had fallen out into her hands. Annie couldn't speak, couldn't breathe and for sure, couldn't tell her daughter. She lifted her head up and peered at herself in the mirror over the sink. How was she supposed to tell Madison it had started? That from this moment on it was going to get even worse? It was nothing they weren't warned about; nothing they hadn't talked about. But now that the time was here, none of that seemed to matter. Annie looked down at the back of Madison's head, where the pieces of hair used to grow.

"Mom? You okay?"

Annie shook her head almost violently, trying to snap out of it. "I—I'm fine. I just...I forgot what I was saying for a moment. Hold still for a minute, okay? I just want to move this—this stupid garbage can. I keep bumping into it." Annie took the hair and wrapped it up in a wad of toilet paper. She quickly threw it away and moved the little wastebasket out of the bathroom, away from Madison's view. "Okay. Where was I?"

"The part where you skated onto the ice with the toilet paper. Everyone started laughing at you?"

Annie nodded to herself in the mirror, fighting back her tears. "Yep. The entire arena was laughing."

❦❦❦❦❦❦

Annie was ten years old when she was sent to the principal's office for fighting. It was something she had never done before, or ever engaged in again, for that matter. It was during recess and a group of the popular kids, The Swing Set Gang, as they called themselves, were hogging the swings. They weren't even using the swings but they wouldn't let anyone else on them. Annie watched them carry on from the blacktop area underneath the shredded basketball nets. She was not sure exactly what happened, why she felt the need to break through the circle. Before she realized it, she was standing in front of the swings, tapping the shoulder of the head jerk. "Excuse me?"

The boy turned to Annie with a frown. From that moment on, the order of events was rather fuzzy. The first thing Annie recalled for sure, though, was the boy, whose shoulder she tapped, went home with an enormous black eye and bloody nose. The second thing was Annie got herself expelled for five days. The third thing was not so much a thing, but still important to the history of Gertridale Grade School. Never again did the gang dictate where other kids could play. *Ever.*

Annie stormed into Dr. Tanger's office and without hesitating, she moved directly for Dr. Tanger's door. She knew it was discourteous to bypass his secretary, but at this moment, she really didn't care who felt insulted.

"Excuse me, Mrs. Henry, but..."

Without even a glance in her direction, Annie curtly answered, "I know where I'm going, thanks." She plowed through the door without a respectful knock warning Dr. Tanger a hurricane was about to enter his world. She slammed the door shut behind her.

Dr. Tanger was on the phone mid-conversation. He looked up to see Annie standing angrily in front of him, invading his space. He took a quick breath and spoke into the phone. "I'll have to call you back." He hung up the phone and hit his intercom button. "Please hold my calls." Then he lifted his head and looked at Annie, sympathetically. "You have to start making appointments, Annie. I do have other patients. And calls that are extremely important. I'm sure as a nurse, as well as a mother with an ailing child, you can understand that."

Annie paced in between his desk and the leather chairs she sat in weeks ago. Back and forth, she moved almost frantically, like a caged animal. "Those other patients aren't my daughter. No offense, but I don't give a shit about them."

Dr. Tanger took another deep breath. He knew there were certainly different ways to handle difficult situations. And when it was a parent who had to deal with this severe of a condition with a child, he tried to expect this kind of a reaction.

"I understand, Annie. But you still need to call my office before barging in here like this."

"There's got to be something else to do. Something you're not thinking of. Something? Because she—she's getting worse, I think. You of all people, you have to see that—that she's not getting any better. That clinical trial crap is done and she hasn't gotten any better, has she? You would've told us. You would've told us if it was working...if it worked. Right?"

"Annie..."

"What about higher doses? Huh? What if we increased her medication? Still using the suggested combination, but we just upped everything? All of it?"

"Annie. Please sit." He was afraid Annie would pass out if he didn't find some way to calm her down. He had watched her over the last few weeks. To his knowledge, he was fairly sure she never went home. Any one of the nights he checked in on Madison, there was Annie. Right there next to her daughter. She looked physically exhausted. Mentally, he knew she wasn't fairing well, but that was unfortunately out of his jurisdiction. He had given her a few phone numbers of doctors to talk to, but last he checked she had not called any of them. "Will you please sit? Just for a minute?"

Annie spun to him full of rage. "I don't want to sit down! For Christ's sake, she's lost all her hair! Since I washed it only a very short time ago...when it started falling out...since then she has lost all her goddamn hair! You tell me how the hell I'm supposed to sit down!?"

"I did warn you of all the side effects, Annie. We talked about it numerous times. So that everyone would know what was happening. I don't mean to sound insolent, I hope you know that, but Annie, you are a nurse. You do know what happens to patients who undergo chemo and radiation. I know that's not the ward you've been working in, but you have been made aware of what happens."

Annie stopped pacing and stared at the large bookcase in front of her. Book after book, on how to treat diseases. None of them, not one of them, were saving her daughter.

She breathed in deeply and spoke barely above a whisper, but in a voice that commanded attention. "I know what the side effects are. In case you've misunderstood my anger, I'll make it very clear. This is not about Madison's hair falling out. I don't care if she's bald. I don't. I care that my daughter is not getting better."

Dr. Tanger cleared his throat uneasily. "When's the last time you went home, took a hot bath, and spent the night with your husband?"

Annie continued looking at the wall. Her voice was quiet now, reserved. "I don't care about a hot bath. Or spending time at my house. I didn't come here to talk about my life. I just want you to get my daughter back to normal. Shouldn't be that hard, you know? I know what you're about to say, and please, don't say it. Just let me..." Her voice progressively glided down to nothing but a breath.

Tanger allowed his eyes to rest on his desk, on the many patient files in front of him waiting for his expertise. This was part of the job. He was never paid for these talks, never compensated in any way. And that was okay with him. He was aware that he was the only person beside this woman who understood all too well what was about to happen to her life, her daughter's life. Not the therapist he recommended, nor her acquaintances who brought over lasagnas and casseroles on a weekly basis could ever comprehend.

"I think of the most ridiculous things I want for her, you

know?" Annie turned around and sluggishly collapsed in one of the leather chairs behind her, finally giving in to her trembling legs. "Like I want her to be able to eat pizza again without throwing up her guts. I want her to be able to sleep for three hours straight without waking up crying because it hurts her to sleep. I want her to be able to go to Jack's soccer game and be able to cheer and jump up and down and yell to him as loud as she can." Annie finally allowed her eyes to meet the man in charge. "I want her to have her goddamn wispy hair back." She paused, never losing her eye contact with Tanger and finally spoke. "I want to see her skate again."

"Annie." His voice sounded like a father who was about to tell his daughter her pet dog was just run over by a car. Full of sympathy, dread, and pity.

She shook her head and stood up while she talked. Whatever stillness she'd had for those few seconds were clearly gone. "No, don't. I know, okay? I know what you're going to say and I've heard it. I've heard it all before. You're doing all you can. And—and that's just great. Really, it is, Dr. Tanger." Annie walked toward the door. "It's just not fucking good enough."

"You have to know we've done all we can."

Annie turned back to him. "What is that supposed to mean? *You did all you could*? Is this the part where you give up or something? Because that's the kind of crap you hear in a TV movie of the freaking week. 'We did all we could.'" Annie laughed sarcastically.

Dr. Tanger stood, somewhat reluctantly, and moved around the side of his desk. "I was supposed to check in on you later today with the last of the test results."

"And?"

Dr. Tanger took a moment and glanced away to get his next few words clear in his head before he spoke. He inhaled too deeply to be good and faced Annie again. "The cancer has spread further, Annie. There is nothing more…"

Annie cut him off immediately. She knew the ending. She'd heard it in her head, every night when she finally did sleep, in her nightmares. She heard the saying over and over. And she didn't care to hear it again, this time live and in person. "I'm sorry. I'll be sure to make that appointment next time I have a question about my daughter."

❧ CHAPTER 26 ❧

"I've been trying to call you. I tried the hospital and I paged you probably eight or nine times. The hospital paged you at least that many times. Where the hell have you been?"

David's wrath was the last thing Annie wanted to deal with at that moment. She knew she should've told someone, even if it was just a random nurse on call, to let them know she was going out, should her daughter need her. She should've gone back to Madison's room and explained to her what was going on inside her body. And yes, she owed David a phone call to give him the update about their child. But she couldn't. She couldn't let herself do any one of those things. She could not fathom saying those hideous words out loud: *cancer...spread...nothing more they could do.* She refused to link them into a sentence. For, if she did, it would mean facing the inevitable. And Annie was not prepared for that. Not now. Not ever.

David pushed his chair back away from the kitchen table, where he'd obviously been sitting for quite some time. Huge

piles of bills, statements, the checkbook and a small calculator overwhelmed the table big enough for four.

Annie couldn't help but notice the separate pile that had
been designated for Madison's hospital bills. It was by far the
largest of the mounds waiting to be paid. Madison's health, or
sickness, sat right there on the table, creating its own moun-
tain. Annie wanted to rip them all to shreds, getting rid of any
evidence this was really happening.

David stared at Annie, waiting for an answer from his
wife. "Ann?"

Annie looked up from the table. *Oh God. What did she
do?* "Is it Madison? She all right?"

"Yeah, she's all right. She's sleeping. At least, when I left
her, she was."

"I...I'm sorry. I just..." Annie shrugged her shoulders as
the rest of her answer.

He hated the constant tension between them. But he hated
the unknown even more. Most of the anger disappeared from
his voice, with concern replacing it. "Where have you been all
night?"

Annie pulled out one of the chairs from under the table
and sat down. "I was driving. Then I—I parked the car, somewhere. I don't remember exactly where. Near the school?
And—and then I walked. I don't know for how long. For
miles, I think. Then I found myself back at the car, where I
started, and I drove home."

David shook his head and looked away. "You should have
called someone. You had Madison scared half to death." He
clearly didn't mean for it to come out the way it did and the
comment did not go unnoticed by either of them. "I mean,
Christ, Ann. You leave her for a few minutes to talk to Tanger
about medication, as far as she knows, and you never come

back? What the hell is wrong with you? Thank God Jackson showed up not long after you left. He called me after a few hours and told me no one could find you."

"So you went? To the hospital?"

"Yes, I went. I always go. Almost every night. You know that. I just went down earlier tonight, that's all. I stayed with her until she fell asleep."

Annie lowered her head.

"I spoke with Tanger. I couldn't find you and that was the last place you were. I don't have to tell you he was pretty upset to hear you just left."

Annie kept her head down. "Did he tell you? About...about what's going on?"

David glanced to the enormous pile of papers with HARBOR COUNTY HOSPITAL written elegantly at the top. "We have to talk to Madison, Annie."

"I know that, David! Don't you think I know that?"

Their fights were different now. They weren't talking as much anymore, about anything except Madison. Tanger was right earlier. Annie hadn't been home for weeks, except for the quick change of clothes and a shower and only when David wasn't there. It was certainly not intentional or meant to hurt his feelings. But Annie also didn't want to have to deal with one more thing, even if that thing was her husband.

Annie's voice trembled slightly. "I'm sorry, I—I just didn't...I couldn't...

David looked at her, got out of his chair and moved over to where she sat. Almost as if in slow motion, he reached out to her face gently and caressed her cheek. He bent his body over and, closing his eyes, he kissed the top of her head.

Annie flinched. "Don't. I can't."

"Can't what?" David lifted himself to a standing position

over her. "Can't *what*!? You can't allow your husband to kiss you? Kiss your damn head? That it? Or you can't have sex? You can't talk to me? You can't spend more than three minutes with me? Which of these is it, Annie? Huh? Or is it all of the above?"

Annie didn't answer. She simply couldn't find a way to open her mouth and verbalize exactly what she felt.

David jerked away from her, disgusted, like he was physically slapped. His head shook back and forth in utter frustration. "You know what? You act like this is your problem and your problem alone. I'll let you in on a little secret. In case for some insane reason you've forgotten, Maddie is just as much a part of *me* as she is *you*, and I feel like shit, too. More than you could possibly know. But we don't talk about me and what I'm feeling. No. We don't even talk! About anything." David moved toward the hallway as if he was going to leave her there in the kitchen alone. Within a few steps, he stopped himself. "I'm trying to keep us above water here and let me tell you something. It ain't all that easy. I'm doing everything I can to keep us going. But it's just a little difficult when there is only one of us trying to work things out." David turned his body halfway around to face Annie. "Look. I know, okay? I know how you feel about everything that's happening, but we—"

"Do you? You think you know how I feel?" Annie interrupted David furiously. "Let me ask you a few questions. Do *you* feel guilty for making Madison skate every fucking day of her life, realizing only now she's never actually had the time to be a normal kid? Do you feel bad about that, David? Do *you* feel bad knowing she might not ever know anything else besides shivering on the ice at six o'clock in the fucking morning because her mother said they could get in an extra goddamn thirty minutes? Do you feel bad about any of that? Because I do! And if that means me spending every waking moment with her trying to make her well again, and trying to keep her happy, I'm going to do it. If that means I harass the doctor about her meds, I'm going to do it. If that means I don't shower, don't come home...And if that means you don't get sex for a while or quality time to talk to me, you know what? Tough shit." Annie pushed her chair back, sending it crashing to the floor loudly. Without even picking it up, she walked past David without even a glance in his direction. "I'm tired. I'm going to bed."

CHAPTER 27

Madison's grandfather used to tell her when the leaves on the trees turn over and show their backside, there's a storm headed, for sure. They'd sit inside the small cottage on the shore and watch the wind pick up in the late afternoon. The ocean waves would start to increase in height and power with each break. Madison would sit by the window, never taking her eyes away from the impending cloudburst. It fascinated her. It could be the brightest, sunniest of days, and her grandfather would take one look at the leaves on the nearby trees and announce the storm's fast approaching arrival.

From the hospital bed, Madison could see out her window clearly. It had been cloudy since early morning. A nurse had woken her at seven for her daily blood tests. Annie got up with her, as she always did. For the better part of the day, Madison stayed perfectly still, waiting to see what the weather god was deciding to do.

She counted up to five and waited for the tree branches to hit her window. She waited again, counting another five seconds, and the branches tapped the glass once more. The leaves began to turn themselves over. She lay in her bed, watching and waiting for the inevitable storm. She reached up to the top of her head and carefully scratched through the bandana that was tied tightly around her head. Since she lost the last of her hair the week before, she would not let anyone see her without something, usually this bandana, covering her head.

Annie talked quietly on the phone, assuming Madison was still sleeping. "No, Jack. I just don't think it'd be a good idea. She really is tired and honestly..." Annie glanced to the small figure in the bed in front of her. She turned her body around so their backs faced one another. She lowered her voice even more. "Look, she...uh...she doesn't want you to see her...like this. Not yet, anyway." Annie paused, listening to Jack on the other end. "No, I know you don't care, but the thing is, honey, she does. Just give her a few more days. Then we'll pick a day for you to come and visit, okay?" Annie hated to be the one to deal with Jack. And for too many days now, she'd done nothing but deal with Jack. There had been nothing she could say to get Madison to let him see her. "Okay. I promise, I'll tell her as soon as she wakes up. Bye." Annie softly put the phone back and sat down in her chair next to Madison's bed. She picked up the book she left turned over a few minutes before and began to read.

"Was it Jack?" Madison didn't turn over. She continued staring out the window, her back motionless to Annie.

Annie was somewhat startled. "Yeah. Yeah, it was Jack. I thought you were still sleeping. Did you have a good nap?"

There had been a definite change within Madison. The day the bandana went on her head, her conversations with everyone but Annie had been few and far between. She would only answer certain questions. Rarely would she be the one to start any dialogue. Unless it was about Jack not coming. Then she had an argument in her ready to go. "Did you tell him not to come?"

This was one of the daily talks Annie had gotten used to with her daughter. Without realizing it, her eyes rolled slightly. "Yes I did tell him not to come, but this is stupid, Madison. I don't get it. I don't understand why he can't visit you. You would think you'd want to take a break from me, if nothing else. Wouldn't you like to hang out with someone besides your mother for a little while? He won't stay long if you don't want him to."

"If you want a break, leave. I don't care."

Annie put her book back down. If it would be a quarrel and not a conversation, so be it. At least she was talking. Feeling. Something. "That's not what I'm saying and you know it. I don't need or want a break from you. All I'm saying is, Jack really wants to visit. He misses you, that's all. And I could run home quick and grab some clothes or something."

Madison shifted away from the window and changed her focus to the ceiling. "No."

One more try. "Madison. Jack is your best friend, honey. He doesn't care about what you look like or if you feel bad. He just wants to spend time with you."

"I just don't want him to see me, okay?"

"But he doesn't care." Annie placed her hand on Madison's leg closest to her.

"I care! *I* care about him seeing me like *this*." Madison pointed to her head. "God, Mom! It's bad enough I have to be sick." Madison tried to finish her sentence, but tears overwhelmed her unexpectedly. She turned abruptly back to the looming rainstorm and paused. Her words were quiet and soft. "I just don't...I don't want him to remember me this way."

The statement literally knocked Annie out of her chair and she instantly ran out of Madison's room. It wasn't like she hadn't thought about what could happen. And she was quite sure Madison had thought about it, too. But they had never talked about it out loud, except to tell her the cancer had, in fact, spread. They stopped the conversations about it there, respecting Madison's adamant demand. No one had given up on her. Except maybe Madison herself.

When she heard the door shut, Madison rolled over and reached for the remote on the bedside table. Maybe she said it to get Annie to leave. Maybe she said it because she really didn't want Jack to remember her that way. Whatever the reasoning behind it, she was alone, and she didn't mind that at all. A picture of Madison and Jack sat next to the remote. Madison stared at it for a moment and then looked away. It was taken just months ago, right before Nationals. Did she know then she was sick? She found her head turning back to the photo. Did Annie have any idea her daughter wasn't well? *There is promise in that picture,* Madison thought. *Promise of two young people, both talented and full of life.* Madison turned angrily away from the two people in the picture. *Pictures lie.*

She turned on the television braced on the wall in front of her. She lifted the remote, and aimed it high in the air toward the TV. As she flipped through the channels at a ridiculous pace, she wondered what kind of screw or nail could hold up a huge television like the one she was watching. If they could find a way to hang a TV on a wall with one little metal bracket, how could they not have a cure for her? It was not the same thing and she knew it. But still, there was nothing to make her stop wondering about it. Something on the screen flashed in front of her and caught her eye. She flipped back a few channels and slowly lowered the remote back onto the bed. Her face immediately paled. The long program skating portion of the Olympics was on the television. Madison watched as the skaters she'd competed against for years warmed up on the ice. *The ice I was supposed to be on. The music I was supposed to hear. The gold medal I was supposed to come home with, hanging down low around my neck.* Her eyes welled up with tears and she turned off the set with a click of the red button.

For many minutes, Madison stared at the blank screen on the wall, imagining her healthy body skating again. Then she lifted herself up to a straighter sitting position. With all her strength, she threw her legs off the side of the bed. It was an obvious struggle for her to stand on the cold tiles beneath her feet, but she managed to hold herself up for a few more minutes. Her eyes traveled to the IV attached to her body, a constant reminder of her illness. With her free hand, she let her fingers travel along the small thin tube, and down to the needle stuck in her hand. She closely eyed her veins protruding against the needle. Carefully, she took off the tape securing the tube and needle into her skin. She wrapped her fingers tightly around it and held on to the tube. *You can do this. You've seen it done plenty of times.* Then, with every bit of courage she had, Madison ripped the IV needle out. It was one quick pull, one big, sharp sting, and then it was gone. She was free from the reminder. No more medicine dripping into her blood. No more. Blood began to seep out from the tear in her skin. She grabbed a bunch of Kleenex off the small table and put them over the spot where a needle once was. For a second, she looked as if she was going to fall back onto the bed. Then somehow, she weakly moved her legs one step at a time, over to her closet and opened the door. She hadn't walked this far by herself in days. She looked at the clothes she was wearing when she walked into the hospital. A pair of baggy jeans, with cut off ragged bottoms, and a Nike sweatshirt, compliments from Nike to the Olympic skater she was supposed to be. Madison almost toppled over as she reached for her clothes but she caught herself before her legs gave out for good. She threw the sweatshirt over her huge T-shirt and very slowly slipped into her jeans. She frowned as she zipped them up. They had become far too big for her, even with the belt. She noticed a baseball cap of Jack's on the floor and carefully lowered her body down almost parallel to the ground to reach it. She put the cap on over her bandana, making sure it was on as low as she could get it, covering as much of her face as possible. She looked back at her room briefly and exited, completely unnoticed by anyone.

☙❦☙❦☙❦☙

Annie walked up to the nurse's station and stood in front of the counter for a second. Kathy and a few other nurses were hunched in a group in the far corner. She smiled knowingly to their backs. Only Annie knew this wasn't some tribal ritual. There was that same small television hidden under every counter on every floor. It was the slow part of the day and the TV was on. Kathy had been her friend for so long, always helping her out, always picking up shifts, and she continued to be Annie's support system throughout each day. Even on her days off, like today, she found a reason to stop by Madison's ward with magazines, snacks or books for Annie and Madison.

As Annie left to go check on Madison, Kathy, sensing someone was watching, turned around and yelled to Annie, "Hey!"

Annie allowed the corners of her mouth to turn up slightly. It didn't really classify as a smile, but it was at least a slight change from the usual. "Hey."

Kathy walked over to Annie and leaned over the counter. "You get something to eat?"

"Maybe later."

Kathy smiled. "No, I meant, didn't you just get something to eat?"

Annie frowned a little. "No. I uh, I needed some air." She glanced to Madison's room a few doors away. "Long day today. Listen, how's she doing? Have you checked in on her?"

"Madison?"

"Yeah. Who else?"

The strangest look appeared on Kathy's face. "I don't know how she is. I mean, I'm free all afternoon so I can check on her later when she gets back if—"

"Back from where? Where the hell did she go?" Annie didn't mean to yell at her friend. Her voice just lifted up without her realizing how loud she was.

"Annie, I thought..." Kathy looked back to the other nurses who were now listening in on their conversation. "She had treatment. You took her there, right?" Because of Annie's stunned expression, Kathy knew something had gone terribly wrong. "She's not with you?"

Annie's mouth dropped open. "What? No! No, she's not with me! I left her..." She took off running in the direction of Madison's room.

Kathy looked back at the other nurses, getting shrugs from both of them. Kathy ran after Annie. "Shit!"

Annie flew into the room yelling for her daughter. "Madison!" She opened the bathroom door to absolute emptiness. Her eyes reached the vacant bed, then the IV pole and she rushed over to it. She followed the tubing down with her fingers to the end. The needle hung in the air by itself. No longer an attachment to a frail girl. Annie stared at it for a few seconds, thinking about the little hand it was fastened to just a short time ago. *Why did I have to leave like that?* Madison couldn't have gone anywhere if she had stayed with her.

Kathy entered the room. "She's not here?"

Annie shook her head and held up the IV in her hand. "How could no one see her? Jesus!"

"Annie, I'm so sorry. I just got here a few minutes ago. When she wasn't here, everyone assumed you took her to get treatment."

Annie looked away, clearly distraught. She sat down on the bed, trying to remain calm. "I should call David."

Kathy quickly moved to the telephone and dialed the nurse's station. "Call security and give them Madison's description. I'm not sure how long she's been gone, but maybe she left recently and they can stop her." Kathy put the phone down and looked at her friend. "You want me to call David?"

Annie shook her head no. "Where could she go? She can't get far. She can't even make it to the damn bathroom by herself."

Annie heard a muffled voice coming from a neighboring room. It was a low volume but too many years in skating had given her a sixth sense when it came to the sport. And years of being Madison's coach, she would recognize her competitor's name anywhere. Victoria Jerkins was introduced onto the ice and even before she turned the screen on in front of her, she immediately knew. She hit the power button and waited for the screen to come up in full picture. Olympic Skating, the long program, appeared on the screen in front of her and Annie knew this was the last channel that was seen on the television. And she knew Madison saw it too.

༺༄༺༄༺༄༺༄

She knew where she was going. Not a doubt in her mind. But first she had to walk out of the hospital without passing out cold on the floor or getting caught trying to escape. *Escape.* As if she was in jail. The latter would prove to be the most difficult. Everyone knew Madison. Not just for her skating, but because Annie had worked at the hospital for so long. She had to be careful and avoid all the major walkways, elevators and floors where Annie was known the best. Madison traveled quickly down the back stairway, used mostly in an emergency, or for those who were too impatient to wait for the elevator, or for those too health conscious to use one. She remembered all of the secret places she and Jack discovered when the county renovated the hospital years ago. All the halls and rooms that would ultimately lead her to the outside and subsequently, to her freedom.

When she pushed the last door open, she had to quickly shield her eyes with her arm. The sun wasn't that bright, but Madison hadn't been outside for many weeks. She raised her head high into the sky and hoped that her much wished-for thunderstorm would hold off until she reached her destination. Maybe it was the fresh air, or the cloudy skies that made her walk a fraction faster than she thought she could. The wind began to pick up and Madison felt the first drop of rain on her hand. She lowered her head and threw her hands into her pockets. She felt something cold. Must be coins. From what? How long ago had it been when she had bought something and received change? Months ago, when she had gotten a can of Red Bull at school one afternoon. How far away it all seemed. School, classes and homework.

And Jackson.

She barely made it under the bus stop when the sky opened up and let the rain cascade down. She snuck into the center of a circle of people, no one paying any attention to the short, sick girl in the middle. Madison had never taken public transportation of any kind in her life. Today seemed as good a day as any to start.

She carefully stepped down off the bus, quietly counting the stairs to herself. Three, two, one. Then she felt her feet land on solid ground. The bus pulled away noisily but Madison was oblivious. She walked straight ahead, on a mission. She tried to calculate how many more steps she had to take before she arrived at the front door of the ice rink.

Years ago, George had showed Annie where he kept a spare set of keys hidden, in case of some emergency. Madison prayed the keys would still be in the same secret place, waiting for her to use. She had assumed George wouldn't be here. Not yet anyway. She moved quickly to the old tank around the left side of the arena and reached her arm as far back as she could between the tank and the building. She finally felt the tiny hide-a-key box and grabbed it tightly, and pulled it toward her body.

⊙⊙⊙⊙⊙⊙

Annie decided it would be much easier to keep most of Madison's skating gear in the arena. It seemed ridiculous to continually pack it up only to bring it all back five or six hours later. *Good idea*, Madison thought to herself as she laced up an old pair of her skates.

Slowly and carefully, she stepped onto the ice, one thin blade at a time. She lost her balance briefly and grabbed the top of the low wall. *Maybe this is a good time to check things over*, she reminded herself. Once satisfied the loss of balance wasn't due to a skate or blade problem, which she already knew, Madison lifted her body up as straight as she could, took a deep breath, and began to glide on the smooth surface. It was slow at first, then faster as she grew more confident in her strength. Every move was as if she was skating in slow motion, even when she skated faster. It wasn't necessarily bad; she was just feeling every action like it was her first time.

Then she heard it. The front door slammed shut. She skated to a stop and waited for whoever was there to show their face. She had locked the door; at least she was pretty sure she had. Yet the footsteps got closer and closer.

George plowed through the doors of the ice area, his hands on his hips, and stared at Madison, speechless. He hadn't seen her for a while, since his visit to the hospital weeks before. Since then, with Madison refusing visitors, George had only heard she lost all of her hair, and she had dropped a few more pounds. But nothing could have prepared him, no matter how descriptive the words were, nothing could have prepared him for the girl he saw in front of him right now. *What in God's name is she doing out of the hospital and where the hell is Annie?*

Leave it to Madison to ease the uncomfortable situation. "Hi, George. Surprise!"

Then she smiled, and George couldn't help but laugh out loud.

He shook his head and moved closer to where Madison stood on the ice. "What in the devil are you doing here, Maddie?"

Madison shrugged and took a difficult breath. It felt colder on the ice than she remembered. Had she always felt the chilly air in her bones like this?

"Your mom know where you are?" Madison remained silent, giving George the obvious answer. "Maddie, I can't let you skate. You know I can't. Come on, now. Off you go, peanut."

Madison didn't move. She didn't try the cute smile or a funny remark. She simply looked at George and then looked out at the vast space of perfect ice around her. Her own personal ice cube. Then in a very diminutive voice, she spoke. "George?" Her skates did not move an inch. "Please?"

George continued to shake his head back and forth. Only then did he move his hands away from his hips and raise them to cover his face. After a few moments, he rubbed his face roughly with his calloused fingers and then released them right back to his hips. He looked at Madison and spoke with the strongest parental tone he could muster. How could he say no to her? "Five minutes, Maddie. That's all I can give you." George walked out of the arena and when he was sure he was out of Madison's view, he reached for his cell phone in his pocket, and dialed as fast as he could.

She skated at a leisurely pace around the edges, recalling the feeling of the flawless glass underneath her feet, the cold air that rushed against her face, and the indescribable sense she was flying. Without any warning from George, she heard her music begin to echo throughout the arena. She felt the corners of her mouth turn into a smile she didn't know was inside of her. Her music. Her gold medal. Her life. Madison extended her hands out from her sides, as if to catch the space with her arms. She jumped into her routine, skating through only the parts of it she knew she could handle and changing it to better suit her energy as it was now. She attempted a jump and nearly fell to the ice. But she seized control of her body at the very last moment and carefully pulled herself back up.

She slowed down and leaned over in what appeared to George to be near exhaustion. George turned the volume down on her music and spoke into the microphone, sending his voice booming through the rink. "Maddie? Come on, now, peanut. That's enough."

Madison lifted the upper half of her body back up and yelled to George up above. "Five more minutes? I'm okay. I promise." She resumed skating around the rink, trying to prove her strength but clearly losing her energy at a rapid rate.

George was not about to stand by and witness her foreseeable demise. He was crossing through the entry on his way to physically bring Madison off the ice when Annie ran in the front door, scaring the crap out of him.

He quickly nodded. "I tried calling you at the house and your cell and the hospital. I've been watching her, but she's stubborn, that one. I can't get her to stop. Was on my way to carry her off myself."

Annie reassured George with a little smile. "It's okay. I know you tried. Thanks, George."

"Not a problem." He wanted to tell Annie how awful Madison looked. How she could barely keep herself up on the ice, how weak she was...but then, Annie surely knew that already. George watched Annie enter the rink section and he exited toward his office.

Annie walked step-by-step down the narrow aisle that led her into the rink. She saw Madison almost immediately and from that point on, she didn't take her eyes off her. She watched in silence as Madison skated.

She didn't hit each mark and she couldn't jump high, if at all. She couldn't keep up with her music. But to Annie, not the coach any longer, now just the mother, it didn't matter. She fought back the limitless tears that so desperately wanted to fall from her eyes. Annie stopped walking when she reached the opening to the ice and saw Madison as she never had before. She didn't yell out instructions or tell her to lift her head higher, or make her back straighter. She simply watched her daughter skate. At that moment, Annie knew she'd never see Madison skate like that again.

Every move Madison completed was graceful. She took a few noticeable deep breaths and urged her legs to skate faster and faster. She whipped her body around the ice and before Annie realized what she was doing, Madison prepared for a huge jump. *She's not strong enough for this*, Annie thought. A fearful gasp got stuck in Annie's throat and her hand moved toward her mouth to capture it.

But Madison soared through the air, like never before. *Dear God*, Annie thought, *it isn't possible*. One, two times around and on the third rotation she was still high in the air. Then somehow, miraculously, Madison circled her body again before she landed back on solid ice, completing a quadruple jump. How she did it, Annie will never know. Maybe it was like the parent who lifts a car effortlessly off the child pinned underneath it, or the smoke-filled firefighter who exits a burning building carrying two survivors over his shoulders. All Annie knew was she would never again in her lifetime witness such a spectacular feat.

Madison stumbled on the landing but caught herself before she went down. She tried to recapture that same smile she found earlier when she first heard her music play. She was all too aware of her unbelievable accomplishment, and pushed her body to continue skating more, but she soon realized every ounce of energy she had was just used up on the quadruple jump. Madison attempted to keep her body up off the ice, but to no avail. She reached her hand to the slippery surface, trying to get her balance back. She stood up straight briefly, but both her knees instantly gave out from under her body. She deliberately knelt on the ice as her body trembled. *Just for a moment, rest.* She strived to get up and placed one skate firmly on the ice. But as soon as she tried to stand, her blades went out from underneath her.

From the side of the ice, Annie watched her daughter shaking. She couldn't bring herself to speak, to tell Madison she was there, to tell her it was okay, they could fix this. She could not bring her voice to say anything. The tears she so wanted to hide from Madison's view now flowed freely down her cheeks and neck. Annie decided this time there was no good reason to stop them.

Madison gave herself a moment of respite before she tried to lift herself up once again. She couldn't bring her skates to a steady enough position to clear her body completely off the ice. She was like a child who had ventured out into the ocean too far and didn't have enough strength to get back to shore. When she lifted her head up heavily, she saw Annie standing at the side, staring at her.

The sight of Madison so weak and so sick shattered Annie's heart into a million pieces. She stepped onto the ice and walked directly over to Madison still kneeling in the middle.

Madison was now shaking almost violently, unable to lift

herself up. She looked up to Annie with tears in her eyes. "I did a quad!"

Annie's face was an oxymoron; sad tears glided down her pale cheeks, and at the same time she wore a smile that was so happy and proud. "I know! I saw you. It was perfect, Maddie. You were perfect."

They were silent for a few seconds, Annie standing over Madison crouched in a condensed ball.

"I saw Victoria. I saw the girls at the Olympics. It was on television."

All Annie could do was nod with a sympathetic look that said, 'I know.'

"I just wanted to...skate too. I wanted to be better. Even if it was for just a little while."

"I know, baby. I know." Annie knelt down to Madison and helped her stand up. She wrapped her arms around Madison as tightly as she could, trying to stop the convulsing inside her daughter. Annie's arms enclosed around Madison and she hugged her tightly, rocking her back and forth on the ice.

Madison's weakened voice finally uttered the question Annie had feared for weeks. "I'm not going to be, am I?" Then, as if to correct herself, she repeated the words, now forming a statement rather than a question. "I'm not going to get better."

Annie looked up to the highest point in the arena and took a deep breath. *How is a mother supposed to respond to that?* For the first time since she was diagnosed, Annie was completely honest with Madison. "I don't think so, Maddie." She paused, mustering up her courage to continue with the answer her daughter should hear in its entirety. "I don't think you're going to get better, baby."

They stood on the ice with their arms interlocked around each other as if they were one person. Annie finally led them both off the ice. "Come on. Let's go get you warm. How does some hot milk chocolate sound, huh?"

Maddie, through her chattering teeth, answered quietly, "Extra whipped cream."

CHAPTER 28

Annie moved a tray of untouched food away from Madison's bed. "You gotta eat something, Mad."

"The food sucks. How the hell do they expect you to eat this stuff? Look at it. You eat it."

Annie took a piece of something that resembled a green bean and ate it. Her face scrunched up at once into a foul mask. She grabbed Madison's unused napkin and spit out the pseudo-vegetable item. "How about a milkshake? Would you have some of that?"

"As long as you're not the one controlling the blender."

Annie smiled. "Funny. That was a good one. You're a laugh a minute, aren't you?" She took the tray with her to the door. "I'll be right back."

"Better hurry. Don't know how long I'm gonna last." The corners of Madison's mouth turned up ever so slightly.

Annie shot Madison a scolding look.

"What? You should be happy. I might have lost all my hair, but at least I haven't lost my unconventional sense of humor. Yet."

Annie gave Madison a shake of her head as she exited her room. She rarely did that nowadays. Leave the room. But it wasn't as if Madison was going anywhere. And both of them knew it. She had been back for five days now, and the end of her new and improved treatment was near. They had told her about the cancer spreading, but Madison had already known it in her heart. Maybe that was why she hardly flinched when they told her how serious it was. She knew it and somehow, without the help of anyone, had already prepared herself to hear it out loud. Something had shifted in her, and Annie had sensed it. Her smiles were few and far between. Her laughs came even less often. Worst of all, though, she still refused Jackson's visits, as hard as he tried. Annie couldn't figure out why she wouldn't see Jack, but the mere mention of it became an argument, so she kept her feelings about it to herself.

Madison flipped through the channels on the television in search of a game. The one thing she really looked forward to was watching her basketball games. There was something so magical when the team came together and started playing as one. She hit the jackpot when she found a Knicks/Lakers game tipping off and she lowered the remote to the bed, satisfied for at least the next two hours. She lifted the hand with the IV attached and carefully scratched her head. It was difficult with the bandana on her head, and her movements were jerky with the needle buried in her flesh. With one itch too many, the bandana fell to one side of her head, lopsided. Madison tried for a few moments to get it back on straight, but nothing she did worked. She finally gave up, knowing it was no use and reluctantly got out of bed. She carefully moved to the bathroom, pushing her IV stand alongside her body, still mastering the perfect way to live with an additional limb. She pushed the door open and entered, shutting the door slightly behind her to make enough room for the both of them.

Without any warning, without a hello or a knock, the door to Madison's room was shoved open and Jack walked in. His arms were filled with shopping bags from almost every store imaginable.

Madison was still fixing her bandana when she heard the door. "Mom? The bandana came off again. Can you...?" With that, she opened the bathroom door without her bandana on, without any preparation for who was going to be standing in front of her, and continued talking, "...help me with—?"

She stopped in her steps and looked precisely into Jack's eyes and immediately tried to cover her head with her hand. She quickly looked away from him, embarrassed and uncomfortable. This was not what she wanted. She had made sure up until this very second Jackson would never see her like this. Now it was as if she was naked in front of the person she cared so deeply for. She turned her body around, looking for the fastest way to get back into the bathroom.

Jack dropped his bags and reached his hand out to her free arm, halting her from walking away from him. He gently turned her around to face him, took her hand away from her head and held her hand close to his heart.

Madison reluctantly let her eyes rise to Jack's and hoped they told him what was going through her mind. That this was the last thing she wanted, him to witness her like this, that she was so scared of what might happen, and that all she wanted was to sit in bed with him and watch the lame Discovery channel shark show that he loved.

Jack looked at Madison and smiled genuinely. He knew

what she was trying to tell him, even if it was only her eyes that were speaking to him. He'd always known it. He refused to let go of Madison's hand, as hard as she tried to pull away from his unyielding grip. He took his other hand and very deliberately placed it on the top of Madison's bald head. "Those bald-ass NBA players got nothing on you." Then he rubbed Madison's head until she cracked a small but noticeable smile.

Annie entered the room in a hurry, a milkshake in each hand. "Vanilla shake and…" She literally bumped into Jack and Madison. "Oh my God!" She didn't want Madison to have to deal with this. Not now and not without her there to mediate. Annie immediately eyed Madison, ready to handle whatever her reaction might be. Her face asked the question, but all she got in response was a little grin from her daughter.

"Jackson says I look better than the NBA players. What'ya think? Is he lying to me just to make me feel better or do I have one up on the big guys?"

Annie tried not to overreact at the moment presented in front of her. The last few days had been full of simultaneous fits of crying and laughing, then laughing and crying. She was not about to ruin this for Maddie. "I think Jack's right. I think they all take a back seat to you, my friend."

Annie tried to usher Madison into the bathroom to fix the bandana, but Madison told her she could fix it right there. In front of Jack. Annie handed the milkshakes to Jack. "Hold these for a sec, will you?"

Jack nodded his head yes and shared a secret smile with Annie. *It worked.* His plan to see his best friend had worked.

Annie retied the material around Madison's head. "I got a vanilla shake and a chocolate shake. In case you felt like either

one...I forgot to ask you when I left what kind you wanted."
She finished tying and led Madison back to her bed. "That
too tight?"

Madison shook her head no and carefully lifted her body
onto the bed.

Jack watched her from across the room. He couldn't
believe how she looked, how she walked, how small she had
become. For some reason, he didn't notice it when they were
standing so close together mere seconds ago. He knew he was-
n't supposed to be reacting like this. At least not so Madison
would notice his freaked-out face. But it was too late.

Madison stared back at Jackson. This was why she didn't
want him there. She knew he couldn't handle it. She refocused
her eyes to the television set and hit the volume up. "You can
go, Jack. I don't care. It was nice to see you and thanks for
stopping by." She hoped she said all of the polite things you
were supposed to say to someone who came to visit a sick person in the hospital. Then she turned the television volume up
even higher to a very disrespectful level.

Annie grabbed the remote away from Madison and
returned the level back down to normal. "Honestly, Mad."

Jack sluggishly walked to the foot of the bed and stood in
front of her. "I don't want to go. I want to be here with you.
So, I gotta tell you. You can go ahead and be rude all you
want to, a downright bitch if you choose. I'm still not leaving." He held up the shakes in his hands. "You going to drink
one of these before they melt or am I to claim them as my
prize for putting up with your sarcastic bald ass?"

Madison tried with all her might not to grin. "I want the
vanilla. You can have the chocolate one...if you bring mine
over here."

Jackson shook his butt like a girl as he walked the shake over to Madison in bed. She took it from him with a snotty, but real, thank you.

Then he turned to the bags he dropped on the floor earlier, picked them up and walked them back to the foot of her bed. "Before I get started with my fashion show—"

Madison started giggling. "What'd you do without me around? Get all sally on me?"

Jackson pointed his finger at Madison and spoke surprisingly in one of the most feminine voices. "I will have no more interruptions, missy. Or else, I promise, your butt will be thrown out of my show before you can...before you can meow."

Annie and Madison laughed out loud. "Meow?" Madison laughed louder. "Oh my God. What has happened to you?"

Annie pulled the chair closer to Madison's bed and sat down with relief. Part of her daughter had returned, if only for a little while and she wasn't going to miss it for the world.

Jackson mimicked a drum roll. "I call this line...Wellington Wearables." He put his hand in the bag and removed various hats, some very weird, some almost normal and some totally in style. He placed them at the bottom of Madison's bed. Jack dug into another bag and pulled out a rainbow clown wig. "*Voila!*" He lifted it up to his own head and put it on. "Now, I know this one isn't exactly for your everyday use, but come on. It is so you, Mad!"

Annie cracked up, making Jack laugh at himself. He dug into the bag again, and this time he pulled out a red nose. He pulled the elastic band over the wig, but it was a tight fit. The wig got pushed to the side, making Jack look somewhat like a retarded circus jester. He snapped the nose into place and gave it a couple of squeezes. "I know that, you know, there's nothing necessarily wrong with your nose, but this was way too cool not to buy." He grabbed a helicopter hat from a bag resting on the floor and threw it to Annie.

"It's not going to fit on my head, Jack."

"So?" Jack smiled. "Are the helicopter hat police coming? I think not, lady."

Annie got up out of her chair. "Well, if you two don't mind amusing yourselves for a little bit, I am going to the nurse's lounge and grab a quick shower." She tapped Madison on the arm lightly. "You okay with that?"

"That's fine, Mom."

"You remember the extension? In case you need me?"

"4780."

Annie was satisfied and gave Jackson a look. "You planning on hanging out for a while?"

Jackson smiled broadly with his nose and wig still intact, and spoke to Madison. "Long as she'll have me. And then for another few hours after that."

"'Kay." Annie walked to the door and yelled to the kids, as only Arnold the terminator could, "I'll be back." Annie left with one quick glance back to make sure Madison was really okay with the situation.

Jack delved into another bag of his tricks. There were long stocking hats, some so long they would probably touch the floor if a standing Madison wore them. He had almost every color bandana one could hope for. Sailor caps, fisherman knit hats. You name it. They were all spread out on Madison's bed, creating an eclectic new comforter.

Madison looked at the boy in the clown nose and rainbow

wig, standing just a few feet away from her. She watched in silence as he continued to pull out more and more hats, one after another. She must not have been paying attention because suddenly, Jack was next to her, carefully taking off her bandana. Her reflexes took over and her hand shot up to cover her naked head.

Jack didn't get mad, or even look hurt. He sat down on the edge of the bed close to her body and showed her a base-ball cap. On it, he somehow had the words 'my champ' embroidered on the front. He lifted her hand away revealing her bald head and he fit the baseball cap on. "There. I thought you could give the bandana a break." Jackson pretended to sniff it and made a face. "And I really think maybe you could wash it every once and a while."

Madison smiled, more than anything to be polite.

"Look, I know I took some liberty in using champ, but the thing is? You have been one many times in lots of competi-tions. But more importantly? You've always been a champ to me." There was a moment suspended in time where neither one of them moved away, their faces so close Madison could-n't breathe. As she was about to pass out, Jack stood with a smile and a quick flick on the bill of her new hat.

Almost sensing Madison's thoughts, Jack removed his wig and nose and threw them in the pile with the rest of his pur-chases. He caught the TV out of the corner of his eye and frowned at Madison. "I don't know what you think you're doing, but I do think it's time you moved your big, fat butt out of the way and made room for me in that bed of yours. No wonder you haven't been paying attention to me. There's a game on."

Madison moved over as far as she could and Jackson

threw himself on the bed right next to her. She thought to herself how easy that was he assumed her quiet demeanor was about the game. And not about what him showing up at the hospital really meant to her.

⌒⌒⌒⌒⌒⌒

Annie and David waited in Dr. Tanger's office, facing his unoccupied chair. Annie sat frozen, her hands intertwined in her lap. The only sound in the office was the ticking of a clock on the far wall. David glanced over to her, but Annie's focus was somewhere else entirely. Out of this room.

She would do anything, anything at all to be out of this space she was in right now. Not necessarily because of David next to her, although that would be nice too. She knew she needed to talk to him, deal with important matters, at some point soon, but that time didn't seem to be in her foreseeable future.

As David was about to say something to Annie, Dr. Tanger entered and quickly walked behind his desk and sat down. "I apologize for the unavoidable delay."

"I guess having an appointment really doesn't pay off after all." Her eyes did not move until the end of her statement. Then they shot needles aimed directly at Dr. Tanger.

He ignored Annie's comment, except for a nod in her direction. Knowing they were all too aware why they were gathered in his office, Dr. Tanger got right to the point. "Madison will have to come back every four to five days for blood work-ups and treatments, which I'm sure you already know."

David responded politely. "We are. Aware of that...the

tests and such. That'll be fine." David looked at Annie and nudged her arm when the look alone didn't register.

"Yes. That uh...it's fine."

"I also want you both to know I will be available, if you should need me, or have any questions regarding Madison. I do not make it routine to do this, but I feel this case..." He stopped himself and wrote his home number on a white card. "Madison is an exception to my rule. And should you need anything, please call. Day or night." He extended his hand with his business card in it.

David took the card from him and stood up from his chair, opposite him.

Dr. Tanger shook David's hand with both his hands enclosing David's. "Well then. I expect Madison will feel much more comfortable in her own room at home."

"We appreciate all of your help, Dr. Tanger. Both of us do."

Tanger nodded to David in understanding.

David touched Annie's arm and she rose as if on cue. She shook Dr. Tanger's hand and blankly said, "Thank you."

CHAPTER 29

David had already taken most of Madison's things home from the hospital. There were a few vases of flowers that still looked pretty enough to risk the trip. David had spent a good part of his weekend fixing up Madison's room, cleaning every speck of dust, washing her favorite sheets, and rigging a phone line next to her bed. He had thought of the idea when he was cleaning and the phone rang more than a few times. Each time, he found himself out of breath, running into the master bedroom, or into the kitchen, his body flying into the counter to catch it on the last ring. He thought it would be good for Madison to be able to talk on the phone even if she was tired, in bed. And even if it was just to Jackson.

Annie and David had gone over the necessary adjustments for days. Who would take off which days to stay home with her, and what each of their duties would be. They both felt they had everything under control. At least, as much as they possibly could control. The only thing neither of them could predict was what was going to happen next. And more importantly, how Madison would feel about everything that was going on around her.

David entered first, carrying the remainder of Madison's suitcases. Annie paused behind him, balancing one large floral arrangement in her arms as she entered. She carefully flipped on a light switch and smiled when she saw the sign. It was actually David's idea and Annie agreed it would be a nice surprise for her. He had placed the order for it the same day they found out it was pointless for Madison to remain in the hospital any longer. It was huge, much bigger than they needed, but that was the way David wanted it. It read, WELCOME HOME, MADDIE-GIRL!

Madison entered the house last. Annie and David were waiting, one on each side of the doorframe. It took her a little longer to get inside, but she refused any help from either of them. She said she could walk in by herself and they were not about to argue with her. When they saw her getting closer, they both simultaneously put on what Annie recently referred to as their 'upbeat faces'. As Madison stepped further into the house, Annie spoke up excitedly. "You like the sign?"

"Yeah. It's nice." Madison looked around the kitchen, as if trying to recall what it was like b.t.c., or the extended version, before the cancer.

David pulled her suitcases out of the way. "We got a little something else for you." He glanced over to Annie who took her cue from him. She smiled broadly to Madison, trying to raise the level of excitement, as she walked over to the counter and uncovered a large square. With one more look over her shoulder to Madison, she lifted up a large sheet cake. As Annie walked it over to David and Madison, David mistakenly blurted it out. "Your favorite victory cake from Costco!" He realized the inappropriate word, *victory*, as soon as it resonated in his mouth. Annie glared at David as if that would somehow rewind his words back to his vocal chords. He attempted to rephrase the sentence with a quiet, more subdued one. "It's your favorite...cake...with the sugary white icing." But it was too late. The words were spoken and were clearly heard.

Madison tried to smile and blow it off. She knew he didn't mean it. She knew they both went to a lot of trouble. Her shoulders shrugged up to her ears before she even realized it. "Guess it's not exactly a victory cake this time, huh?"

David walked over to her and touched the palms of his hands on her shoulders, almost as if to push them back down. "Honey. I'm sorry. I didn't mean..."

Madison interrupted him and put her hands on top of his, giving him her best 'it's okay' look. She had pretty much mastered that look by now. In the hospital, when the nurse would bruise her arm trying to find a good vein to withdraw her blood, she gave them that look, even though there were tears in her eyes from the excruciating pain. And when Jackson talked about school or the dance just around the corner, or his upcoming summer tour with the International soccer team? He would suddenly stop himself and she would give him that same look. *It's okay that you're not sick. That you're going to school or hanging out at the diner. It's okay,* her face would say. Madison used the same practiced look on David. "Dad. It's fine. Really, I know what you meant. I did. It's just that I...uh...I'm not really hungry, right now. But maybe later. Okay? It looks really good."

Annie nodded. "Sure. That's okay. Of course it's okay." She casually walked the cake back to the counter. She'd already resumed her cheery attitude by the time she turned around to Madison. "Here's an idea. How about we rent a movie? We could go to the video store and pick out something to watch. The three of us. Or we could do that pay-per-view thing. I don't think we've ever even tried that, have we?" She shot David a glance.

"Nope. We haven't done that, the three of us."

Madison stepped away from David, not necessarily by choice. Her body shifted to one side and for a moment, she thought she might pass out in front of both her parents. It had been an extremely long day. That was what the dizziness was. That was why she felt faint. A long and trying day. She casually moved a few feet away and pulled out a chair that had been pushed neatly under the kitchen table. "It's kind of late, don't you think? To watch a movie?"

Annie shrugged it off. "Who cares if it's late? We'll watch a movie, right David?"

David jumped in with an agreeable yes.

Madison smiled at their enthusiasm, trying to make everything feel as if it was somewhat normal. She knew neither one of them wanted to watch a movie and also knew by looking at them they would most likely fall asleep within the first twenty minutes. "That would be good. A movie. Maybe tomorrow night though. I'm actually kind of tired. Probably from the big move home, huh? I think I'll just go up to bed. If that's okay with you guys?"

Annie, once again, nodded her head far too energetically. "Sure. Yeah. That's fine." She glanced to David.

He looked at Madison sincerely. "Whatever you want to do is okay with us. You know that." He picked up Madison's suitcases and started through the kitchen with them. "I'll take your stuff up to your room."

"Thanks, Dad." Madison rose slowly and kissed Annie on the cheek. "'Night, Mom."

"Yell for me. Okay? If you need something in the night. Anything."

Madison looked back at Annie. "I will."

Annie couldn't help but laugh a little. "Kind of funny, huh? We won't be roommates anymore." She paused for a moment. "I'm going to miss waking up with you."

"Mom. You're in the room across the hall. You will still be waking up with me."

Annie was fairly sure she noticed Madison's eyes roll in her old sarcastic way. And if she was wrong, she was going to pretend she saw it anyway.

⌘⌘⌘⌘⌘⌘

Nothing happened, exactly. There wasn't one specific moment where they knew there was suddenly an issue with Madison, more than the obvious one. It just started. Maybe the night she came home from the hospital. She went to her room with the idea of the following night's movie and cake fiesta and never came back. There were a few nights where she ventured out of her cave to pretend to eat something for dinner at the table. Those rare appearances came less and less often. It soon became quite apparent she would only leave the house on the days she had scheduled appointments with the doctor. Sometimes Annie would find out only as they were supposed to be leaving that the planned appointment had been canceled. It was on the third cancellation Annie decided to check with the doctor's office, only to find out the appointments were being cancelled by none other than Madison.

She was refusing to see Jackson again, refusing to eat properly, refusing to do any schoolwork. Her curt response was deeply engraved in Annie's memory. "What's the point?"

Honestly, Annie had trouble answering the question. What *was* the point? Was Madison ever going to need a good grade in chemistry? Or would it matter that she only wanted to eat a bag of white chocolate covered pretzels for dinner? As for Jackson...Annie knew this would be the only thing to maybe cheer her up and that was a fairly heavy maybe.

The shades in Madison's room were drawn down as far as they could go, making her room far more depressing than necessary. It was like this when she entered every morning. Madison was curled up on her side in a ball, the covers hiding her entire head.

Annie walked in without knocking, since Madison never let anyone into her world even if they did knock. She yanked up the shades as hard as she could, letting in the bright sunshine from the outside world. It filled every inch of Maddie's room, suddenly bringing it back to some form of life. 'For how long?' was the question Annie and David asked, and then waited to see the answer each day. Annie occupied herself, picking up dirty clothes, which for some reason, couldn't seem to make it to the hamper five feet from Madison's bed. That was the other thing that frustrated Annie. Madison would hardly change out of her clothes. Rethinking, clothes might possibly be too strong of a word. Pajamas fit the description of her wardrobe these days.

Madison sluggishly rolled over toward the light and like a vampire terrified of it, turned her back on it at once.

Annie continued moving about her room. Today was a new day. And today David and Annie had a plan. "Hey. You still sleeping? It's eleven o'clock in the morning."

Her voice was full of irritation. If she ever was even a little bit of a morning person, she no longer was. "So?"

"So, nothing. I'm just saying it's late in the morning." Annie looked over her shoulder to see if there was any sign of movement. There wasn't. "Eleven in the morning."

"And?" It was barely a grumble that emitted from under the sheets, the same sheets Annie hadn't been allowed to wash for two weeks.

Annie thought. "And…" She wasn't expecting this to be her response. She threw some of Madison's dirty clothes on the floor only to pick them up again. It at least bought her a few extra seconds that were obviously needed. "You haven't been out of your room, let alone out of bed for quite some time. It's beautiful outside. The perfect spring morning and Jack has one of his scrimmage games today with his fancy soccer team. So Dad and I thought maybe you'd want to go with us to watch him. We're going to leave in about an hour. You could have a nice hot shower and take your time getting ready. We went out and bought some stuff, drinks and snacks to munch on while we're there. Jack was really glad to hear we're coming. He'll be so happy to see you."

"Did you already tell him I'm coming?"

Annie hesitated. If she said yes, would Madison feel guilty and go? That would work for her. But it wasn't the truth. She hadn't said anything to Jack about Madison coming. As a matter of fact, Jack didn't even know David and Annie were coming. Part of her big plan. "I…uh…no, I haven't said anything to Jackson yet."

"Good. Cause I don't want to go."

As she scanned her eyes around the room for something else to pick up, she realized there was nothing more for her to do. Annie moved over to Madison and stood on the opposite side of the bed, facing her daughter's back. "What is it? Come on, Maddie, it's gorgeous out and it would just be for a few hours. We could even come home at half-time if you wanted." Not a peep from Madison. "Do you feel sick?"

Madison languidly turned to Annie and looked at her for a moment before she made a move to speak. "I don't feel like I'm sick. I feel like I'm dying. So if it's all right with you and Daddy, I'm not going to a soccer game today." With that remark, Madison turned her body back over on her side and faced the wall once again.

They had tried everything but anger to get her out of the house. It was, Annie thought, at the very least, worth a shot. Annie stormed around to Madison's side of the bed and interrupted her concentration on the blank wall. "No, Madison. It's not all right. How's that?"

It was as if Madison stared right through every organ in Annie's body. Her eyes were vacant, and for lack of a better word, dead.

"Jesus, Madison. What are you doing? Huh? Are you just gonna sit up here and feel sorry for yourself every day? Is that what you want?"

Her voice was flat and even. She wouldn't even give Annie the decency of eye contact. Her voice was barely audible. "I can't have what I want, can I? I think you know that. Maybe out of guilt, you feel like I should be enjoying these last few months. But guess what? I don't want to. It's too late. So why should I go outside and see what a great fucking day it is? So I can think about all the other days to come that'll be just like this one, and I won't be alive to see them? I can sit on the blanket and watch Jack run around the field and know that I can't play with him? I had my moment to live. It's gone." Then she allowed her eyes to drift up to Annie's. "Thank you for the kind offer, but the answer is no."

"Well, what am I supposed to say to Jack?"

"You said you never told him I was coming in the first place. What's the problem?"

So, okay. She wasn't going to lie, but now, maybe guilt would help the situation. She had nothing to lose at this point. "I did. I did tell him you were coming. I thought you'd want to see him play. So, now...*now* don't you think you should go?" It was a long shot but worth a try.

"Call Jack and tell him I'm not coming."

She had tried everything from being sympathetic, to being angry to now out-and-out lying to her daughter. She was at the end of her patience. "You call him." She purposefully left the shades wide open with the warm light pouring through the glass. She also purposefully slammed the door to Madison's room behind her as she stormed out.

David busily packed up a large cooler full of sodas and water bottles. There was a spring in his step, a small twinge of excitement on his face. *If this works*, he thought to himself, *if we can get her out of the house today and she sees Jack, maybe just maybe...*He threw bags of fruit, popcorn, pretzels, and candy into a separate bag with the dry food. Maybe this would be the one event that could snap her out of this funk. It wasn't like Annie and David were ignoring the issue. It wasn't like they were pretending there was nothing wrong with Madison. They knew. They understood. But they also wanted her last memories, if it came down to that, to be wonderful. Enjoyable. Fun. If not for Madison's sake, for their own.

He stopped his springy movements when he heard the door slam shut. David could tell immediately by the look on Annie's face what happened. He spoke his thought before Annie had to. "She won't go?" he asked.

Annie let her body rest on the wall behind her. "Nope."

He knew Annie did everything she could, said everything she could. He knew because she'd tried before. And so had he. Still though, out of his own desperation, he had to ask. "Did you try making her mad? I mean, not really *mad*, mad, but a tad angry? Sometimes that gets her going."

"I tried everything, David. Like I do every day. Like you do on the days I can't. She doesn't want to hear it. She doesn't care if I make her mad, or make her feel guilty, she doesn't give a shit." Annie shook her head. "I even lied to her and told her Jack thinks she's coming. Didn't matter. She says she doesn't want to think about all the days to come..." Annie couldn't finish her sentence. She wished at that moment she could have let herself drop down to the floor and have a good cry. But it wasn't three o'clock in the morning when everyone was asleep. The dishwasher wasn't running to cover up her sobs and she wasn't about to let anyone in on what she went through in the middle of the night after she got Madison back to sleep. She collected herself before she continued repeating the conversation to David, then thought better of it. What did it matter what Madison said? The bottom line was she was not going anywhere. "She doesn't want to go."

David glanced to the cooler full of drinks and to the bag of goodies on the counter he had packed so excitedly just a few minutes ago. He knew what he wanted to say to Annie, and he knew how she was going to react. He started to put the drinks back into the refrigerator. If he looked busy, and he avoided eye contact with Annie, maybe what he was about to say wouldn't sound so harsh to her ears. "I don't know if you've thought about this, but I have been giving this some consideration. I was thinking maybe if you went back to work, for just a few days a week, maybe she'd have some room to breathe. Think about things on her own, without one of us constantly at her to do something."

Annie pushed her body away from the needed support of the wall. "What the hell will that prove? We just leave her here to…to die? Great plan, David."

Just keep busy. Act like it's no big deal. "That's not what I said."

"Well, what else could that have meant? Go back to work and let her breathe? What the hell does it mean?"

David let the cans of soda fall through his hands and they went crashing to the floor. He could say it was due to the wetness on them and they slipped. He could say the cold from the ice was shocking. But the truth was he couldn't be in the same room with Annie anymore. He casually picked up the cans and put them on the counter.

Then he walked out of the room.

Chapter 30

David sat frozen in his chair at the kitchen table. It was as if a bolt of lightening had struck him directly between his eyes, paralyzing his entire body. It was so strange this person, this woman he had married, standing just a few inches away, had become someone he simply did not know.

He had spent the majority of the night trying to decide which of the mountainous piles of bills deserved top priority and which ones he could delay paying. Again. It had become a monthly ritual. A game, of sorts. Before that, he had played Scrabble with Madison in her room until she was too tired to continue. He was hoping this night in particular she would stay awake until midnight. Even eleven would have helped him out. Then he could have convinced himself it would be worthless to start the bill game that late in the night. But as it would turn out, Madison wanted him to leave her alone by nine-thirty. Hardly too late for him to begin his duties as husband and father.

David had started on the hospital bills first. They were always the most important. God forbid one of them wasn't paid. Not that they would refuse treatment, but he wasn't about to risk it. He was licking the convenient pre-addressed return envelope with the signed check and statement enclosed when he noticed Annie standing nearby. How long she had been standing there, David had no clue.

"I'm taking her away."

David stared in Annie's direction in utter disbelief. He could not have heard his wife correctly. And if he did, well then, she clearly must have meant something else. Taking her to the market or maybe to school. Not *away,* away. Not for any substantial period of time.

David put down the pen in his hand and turned off the calculator sitting on the table. Before he had a chance to respond to her, Annie continued. As David listened to her, he realized this was planned to the last detail. How long ago, he hadn't an idea. But this was a prepared speech being preached to him. One that took some time to write, to memorize, and to practice, so that it might come out matter-of-fact.

Madison had gone downhill. Rapidly. Was it because she never went anywhere? Or did anything? Or even tried to? Maybe it was due to the very real fact she had Ewing's Sarcoma, a cancer, and it had taken over her system. There was nothing anyone, especially Madison, could do about it. It really didn't matter what the reason was. She had given up all hope. And each day was longer than the one before. Sure, she'd play a game or two with Annie or David; sometimes she'd venture out of her room to watch a DVD. Sometimes, though seldom, she would have Jackson come over and visit. Both he and Annie had thought it was worth a try and had approached Jack about it. Just show up unannounced. Don't even tell them when the surprise might take place, lest either of them mistakenly release the news to Madison.

Madison was mad as hell at first, but she let Jack stay to watch a basketball game. For a small window of time after he would go home, they would see hints, tiny gestures of the Madison they remembered from long ago.

"I would like you to know, I...uh...I've been thinking about this a lot. It isn't some fly-by-night scheme I just now thought of. I actually started entertaining the idea a few weeks ago. That day she wouldn't go to the soccer game? And you walked out of the kitchen? That day I just...I watched her. Realized she wasn't getting any better here. I thought, if this could at least make her happy, as things get...as they get worse, I want it to be in a special place. I think it...that it's the best thing to do right now. For her."

To say he was stunned wouldn't describe his feelings entirely. Stunned, yes. But he was also angry, confused, and hurt. "When were you going to tell me about your plan? We've sat up late every night in bed for the last few weeks. Both of us, one hundred percent aware she hasn't been doing very well. Never once, never did you say a damn thing about your newfound traveling plans."

"First of all, I *am* telling you about it. I'm telling you right now. I just decided for sure it's time and I told you."

It was the first time he noticed her voice shaky. Not nervous, but definitely not comfortable. And that was fine with him. She should feel uncomfortable.

"Can I ask where you're going?"

Annie stared at David and purposefully looked at the tiles on the floor beneath her bare feet. Where did they always go? But it had been different in the past. It was a vacation much-needed, a retreat from the skating. It was the ocean. The beach. The beautiful shore. The place Madison loved to be more than anywhere. *Except in an ice rink.*

David knew where Annie was referring to the minute she looked away. Now it was going to be up to him to play the bad guy. As always. He was going to have to be the one to say no. "We can't afford the beach this year, Ann. You know we can't. God, I can barely cover the house bills. I've put off some of them for over two months trying to keep up with the hospital costs." He looked closely at her face for any signs of a reaction. Even a small nod, anything. But he got nothing. Silence. "Jesus. A week there is like, I don't know. It's gotta be at least over fifteen hundred by now. I mean, every year it goes up another five or ten percent. We can't afford it. Somewhere else maybe, or maybe just for the weekend there."

"No, David."

"You can't even get a rental now anyway. It's too late. The ones we go to get booked up during winter, if not the year before. It's too late." Annie met his irritated gaze and didn't look away. Slowly, David got it. "Oh, this is just great. Just freaking great. You booked one already. Didn't you?"

Whatever shakiness or quivering David previously heard in her voice was now gone. She was strong. Defiant was a better word. It became glaringly clear this topic was not up for any discussion between the two of them. He would hear the words echo in his head over and over again.

"Here's the thing, David. I am taking Madison to the beach. We're going for the summer or until...until she..." Annie chose her words with careful consideration. "Until it's time for me to come home." She was all too painfully aware what her statement insinuated. So was David. Madison would not be coming home.

"Just like that? Well, what do you want me to do, Annie? Huh? I own a company. I cannot just simply pack things up and take off for a goddamn sick holiday, or say goodbye to

Madison and—and not see her...not see her until..." The words would not form in his mouth. He knew where his tongue had to be, the correct placement behind his teeth, for the words to come out. Still, he could not say it. Annie interrupted him, or saved him. He was not sure which one but he didn't care.

"You could come up on the weekends."

"I have jobs every Saturday, Annie. You know I do. I had to take them because you decided to take a leave of absence from a job we once relied on, remember?"

"So, okay. You could drive up on Saturday nights and go back on Sunday. Even Monday mornings before work. You can start scheduling people in the late afternoons on Monday or something."

"Wow." The laugh that spurted out of his body wasn't necessarily a real one, or even a funny one. "It's really nice how you've got it all figured out for me. Yeah, I appreciate it. Thanks so much." There wasn't one tone in David's voice that was sincere. "How about this though, Ann? What if I don't want you to go? Or what if you can't get off work for an extended trip? Did you think about that?"

Annie took a deep breath. She knew at some point she'd have to tell him. But when she thought about it before, rehearsing it in her mind, it had always been a more pleasant conversation between the two of them. There was going to be no easy way to say this, however long she thought about it.

"I quit my job."

She carefully paused, giving David time to digest those four small words. She had done it a few days ago when she knew for sure she had the house rented for an indefinite amount of time. It was Kathy again, coming through for Annie at the last minute, who helped her secure the place on the beach. Yes, she knew it would take all the money they had saved and then some to be able to rent the house for this long a period but she didn't care. "I decided this was simply the only thing to do. For Madison. Maybe when you've had time to think about it for a little while, you'll see it as clearly as I do."

He was as surprised as Annie when he finally spoke. He thought for sure the bottom half of his mouth was still on the table. "*You quit your job?* Just like that? And you didn't tell me? Ask me if—if...?"

"If what." It was said as a statement. She was not looking for any kind of response and David knew it. Annie refocused her eyes back to the floor tiles and noticed they were rather dirty. *Got to clean before I leave with Maddie.*

Maybe she had gone temporarily insane. David was knowledgeable enough in the medical field to know that could possibly happen in a situation as tragic as theirs. And in this state of temporary insanity, Annie forgot important, crucial issues. All he needed to do was remind her of said issues, and the smart, sane Annie would magically return to him. David altered his tone of voice. It would be easier for the old Annie to come back if he was pleasant. "What about her treatments?"

Annie had thought of everything. She knew she had to, if she was to convince David this was the most logical plan of action for Madison. "Her last one is tomorrow." She took baby steps to where David was, his head already bowed down in defeat. She reminded herself to be gentle and understanding. She tried to remember how absolutely nuts she sounded when she practiced this same speech in front of the bathroom mirror for the past few nights when David was sound asleep. "They can't do anything for her, David. Not anymore. You know they can't." *Another small step, closer to his touch.* They had walked this path before; David not agreeing with a decision Annie had already concluded. "I went ahead and ordered everything I could possibly need for her. Kathy helped me. It'll be delivered as soon as I call, after we get there. I also talked to a doctor at the hospital in town. Tanger knows him and he gave me his number. He has already been prepped on Madison. I had the hospital send over copies of everything pertinent to her and her treatments. And I can handle all that needs to be done for her in the house." *Another baby step.* He'll reach out to her and hold her tightly against his chest. She will feel him breathing and know it will be all right. At least, that's what she's been envisioning in the mirror. "It'll be no different for her medically whether Madison is here or whether she's there. But it might help her emotionally, and that's probably the most important thing right now. Don't you agree?"

David refused to respond to Annie. He didn't agree. Not this time.

"David?"

Without so much as a look in her direction, David started for the door. Her voice stopped him only momentarily.

"You should know...we're leaving tomorrow."

He didn't yell or scream. He didn't even give her the satisfaction of an argument. Why bother? She was going and she was taking his daughter. He was out the door before Annie could stop him.

Annie stood by the table where David left her casually running her forefinger along the edge. She waited for time to pass, knowing any moment he'd return. She could count on one hand the amount of times he had angrily walked out on her. He always came back. He'd take a walk around the neighborhood and think about what she told him, think about how great this would be for Madison, for all of them.

In the quiet of the early evening, she heard the car door slam shut outside the house and she quickly moved to the kitchen window, peeking out from behind the ratty curtains. Before she had a chance to scold herself for not replacing them years ago, she saw David's car descend down the slight slope of the driveway. Then it disappeared, being driven at a speed too fast for their small side street.

Annie's two fingers unconsciously released the material between her and the window and the old curtains dropped back into place in front of the glass.

"I want to go with you."

Jack had entered unnoticed and unheard, and now stood behind Annie in the kitchen.

Anne spun around to the unexpected voice, temporarily startled. She immediately relaxed seeing it was Jack and turned back around to the window in search of David's return. "How did you get in? Madison didn't let you in, did she?"

Jack shook his head no. "I heard voices kind of yelling in here so I went around to the front door." He hesitated uncomfortably. "It was always okay to come in without knocking before the...before. I didn't think it would be any different now."

A car peeled out near her house and Annie's hand yanked the curtains back again. She looked out to the darkened sky. A teenage girl across the street was waving to a teenage boy showing off in his car. It wasn't David returning.

She looked at Jack. "I didn't mean it like that, Jack. Of course I don't want you to knock. You know that. I was asking because I was hoping maybe Madison got out of bed to answer the door. Or maybe, she asked you to come over?"

Again, all Jack could do was shake his head no. "The door was open. She doesn't even know I'm here."

Annie smiled apologetically. She knew this was probably not going to go over too well with Madison. "Listen, Jack. It's sweet you came over tonight, but the thing is…well, she goes to sleep pretty early nowadays. David left her about an hour ago and she said she was tired then. I can go check for you, if you want to hang out for a minute."

Jack stopped Annie before she left the kitchen and repeated himself. "I want to go with you."

"Go where? Upstairs? I don't think that's—"

"I want to go wherever you're taking Madison. I want to go with you. I overheard you and David talking about it."

Her head shook no before any words were verbalized. "You shouldn't have heard that, Jack."

"But I did. I did hear it and I want to go, too." He took a step into Annie, not in a threatening way by any means, but in a way that solidified his seriousness.

Annie rolled her eyes in frustration, not sarcasm. "Jack, come on. I know you think you do want to go. I know you probably think you're really one hundred percent sure. But I've had a few really long days and an even longer hour that just came to a shitty ending, and I don't want to deal with this right now, okay? So let me go check on Mad and see if she's still awake." Annie started her feet moving out of the room, trying to comprehend the conversation she just had with a seventeen-year-old boy.

Jack took a few hurried steps toward Annie and stalled her, blocking her exit. "Why couldn't I go? Give me a valid reason. I can't think of one."

"Because." *Okay, that was a lame answer.* It's what every

mother of a teenager learns to say. She was about to finish it with '*I'm your mother, that's why*' when she remembered Jack was not, in fact, her son. As much as he had always been there, so much at times, it did seem as if she was his mother. Annie tried to think of something that made even a little sense to the boy in front of her, so desperate for an answer. "Well, for one obvious reason...what about your soccer team? You've worked so hard for this. And you get to travel all over the world for the summer. You leave what? Tomorrow? Or Thursday?" *That should do it. A little reminder.*

"I don't want to go anymore."

Annie snapped. She probably would've snapped at anyone; it just happened to be Jack who was standing in front of her. The words spilled together before she could filter them through her brain into the right thing to say and the wrong thing to say categories. "Take your chance and get away from here. Go to Europe and play soccer, just like you're supposed to do. You cannot come with us, Jackson. Okay?"

"Why?" His question was so serious, yet the smallest word. *Why?* Jack's voice was barely audible, yet Annie heard it clearly.

"Why? Because! Because she isn't going on some kind of goddamn vacation, Jack! She's going to the beach to die, all right? I'm taking her there *to die!*"

Jack looked at Annie and composed himself as much as he could, which wasn't much, given the discussion. His eyes filled rapidly. He tried not to taste the salty water that slid down his face and seeped into his mouth. "I know that. I know why you're doing it, Annie. I still want to go."

"You couldn't handle that, Jack! You can't!" Annie took a quick breath. "*I* can't! And if *I* can't, Jackson, how the hell could you possibly handle it?"

Jack's chin dropped to the floor. How could he explain this to Annie? How could she understand what Madison has meant to him? To his life? Without any preconceived thought of what to say, Jack opened his heart to Annie, once and for all. "I don't want to play soccer. I don't want to go to Europe or travel or even get a college scholarship. My whole life, Annie...my whole life...all I've ever wanted to do was be with Madison. It never mattered how little we were, how young. It never mattered what we were doing. It could've been anything. Or nothing at all." Jack knew he couldn't turn back now, not after those words had been spoken aloud. "Did you know when we camped outside some nights, in my backyard? Sometimes we would just sit for hours and not say a word. You know what the funny part is? I knew exactly what she was saying, in her mind. The whole time. Every word." Jack stalled, realizing this conversation with Annie made the situation all too real. And like Annie, he had tried to pretend it wasn't. Until now. "I can't imagine what my life would've been like without Madison in it every day. And I don't want to imagine what it'll be like when she's gone. All I know is..." Jack looked intensely at Annie, making sure she heard what he was saying, every word of it. "All I know is I want to be with her for as long as I can. Every minute she's here. Please."

Annie let herself forget about David leaving her earlier. She let herself forget she wrongfully snapped at Jackson. She looked at him and let herself remember what love was all about. What it felt like, tasted like, breathed like. It was far too late for her to halt her tears now midway down her cheeks. Annie had no way of knowing how many seconds she stood frozen after he had stopped speaking. *This young man loved my daughter. Maybe even as much as I did.* Annie stopped her thoughts. *Oh, God. Does. Does love her as much as much as I do.* Madison was still here and suddenly it became painstakingly clear Jackson had to be with her just as much as Annie did. *How could he not?*

She allowed her gaze to drift to Jack's dampened eyes. Before she was even aware of what she was doing, Annie nodded her head to Jack. "Okay."

Madison entered the kitchen abruptly. Annie immediately turned away so Madison couldn't see her crying and prayed she wasn't listening in on the recent conversation regarding her future. They'd had this discussion before when Madison listened in on David and Annie talking about her. As if she wasn't there. As if the time had already passed. As if she was already gone.

Annie inhaled a sigh of relief when she heard Madison's sarcastic tone with Jack. *Thank God.* She's not yelling at her. She's talking to Jackson. She didn't hear a thing.

Annie casually moved to the sink and pulled back the curtains. Maybe during her time with Jackson, David had returned. He hadn't.

"When'd you get here?" Madison leaned against the counter, not even attempting to hoist herself up on it like she used to.

Jack stalled noticeably and looked down at his dirty white sneakers. He remembered when he got them. Eight months ago, with Madison assisting him. He tried not to think about that time before everything changed. He didn't want to have to tell Madison why he was crying.

Madison cleared her throat. "Hey. I don't have much time to wait here for an answer."

Jack lifted his chin up and looked at Madison. What was the question? He couldn't remember. All he could think about was shopping with Madison in the mall the night they got his sneakers. Then almost as if he felt Annie's voice guiding him in the right direction, he answered with a shrug. "Just now. A few minutes ago."

Annie smiled to herself. He had heard her thoughts.

Jack reached up to the bottom of Madison's pajama top and let his fingers hold onto it, almost like he was doing a blind test on the fabric, for he never looked at the shirt. "You're wearing my pajamas."

Madison grinned. "Jack. When you give someone a present, it sorta isn't yours anymore. It becomes the property of the girl you gave it to. Which, in this case is me. Making them my pajamas. Not yours." *Does he realize he is still touching my shirt? Do I realize I still don't mind?*

"Probably a good thing too, huh?"

"Unless you take to wearing this kind of sleepwear when I'm not around." Madison's grin segued into a laugh. "What're you doing here? It's late."

"I just...I came to see you. That's all." He casually released his grip on her pajama top.

"You came all the way over here to say goodbye?"

Annie flipped her body away from the sink and faced Madison furiously. She'd had it with Madison talking like this to them. It might have been meant as a joke but it was not funny anymore, if it ever was. "Madison, do you have to be rude to everyone? For God's sake. Jack came over here to hang out with you. It's not funny, this saying goodbye crap to people. Or telling me to hurry up when I run an errand for you because you aren't sure how long you're gonna last. It's not at all funny. You should be thankful someone besides me is putting up with your rudeness."

Madison stared at Annie in disbelief. *What the hell was she ranting about now?* When she responded to Annie's outburst, she spoke with a calculated, slow pattern. "I meant, goodbye because Jack leaves the country tomorrow for the summer to play soccer. You should learn not to jump to your own asinine conclusions. I didn't mean anything by what I said except he is here to say good bye. Right, Jack?"

After all these years, Jack was used to being caught in the middle. But lately it was different. Madison didn't let things go easily any longer. She wouldn't stop the conversation if it began to get heated. Not that she did before, but at least there were times when she knew better than to push the boundaries. Jack was all too aware there were no longer any boundaries with Madison, no limits. He shifted in his shoes unnervingly. "Uh, yeah. I mean, I was coming to say good-bye, but..."

Before he had a chance to continue, Madison jumped on his words and stared at Annie with an evil face. "See, Mom? I told you. Not everything is about me dying."

Annie turned away from Madison. She knew when her daughter got in this state it was no use even attempting a decent discussion.

"I, um...I've decided not to go. Play soccer." Jack's voice broke the awkward heavy air in the kitchen.

Annie closed her eyes and allowed her head to fall in what was sure to be an upcoming beating. She was hoping Jack would just leave them alone. Simply say goodbye and walk out the door. That he would go home and think about the things discussed between them and realize he could never put himself in that position. That he could never give up this opportunity he had worked for all of his life. That he could never go with Madison on her last trip.

But he didn't do any of that. He was facing Madison, challenging her. Only Annie knew this could not end up good.

"What are you talking about? What do you mean you're not going?" Madison frowned deeply to Jack.

"I'm just not, that's all." Another shrug that wouldn't stop her words from soon attacking.

"Are you kidding? Is this some sort of stupid joke?" Madison looked over to Annie's face, now turned toward her. Annie stayed neutral, giving Madison the answer she was looking for. This was not, by any means, a joke.

Madison waited for an explanation from him. "Why aren't you going, Jack?" She watched him look at Annie for some kind of sign and wondered what went on behind her back this time.

Annie smiled nervously to Madison. It took her more than a few seconds to finally start speaking without the fear of stuttering. "I thought it would be really nice...be really good, for both of us, to get away for awhile. You've been cooped up here everyday in your room for weeks, Mad, and I thought maybe this would be a good change. So, I went ahead and I, uh, I got us a house. Right on the beach, just how you like it. I haven't seen the place; there were no pictures available on the website. We've never been to this specific one but, I think...I think it will be really perfect. It has two bedrooms and a pretty good-sized bathroom and..." Annie stole a rapid glance to Jack. This was the part she was most apprehensive about and she prayed Jack would be all right, no matter what might come out of Madison's mouth, no matter how horrible it might be. "And, guess what? Jack wants to come with us. To the beach. What do you think?"

"What do I think?" Madison looked from one face to the other. She didn't care whose idea it was. Whoever was behind it, the whole thing was one more concocted plan without anyone discussing it with her. And neither one of them was about to get off easy. Annie received the first blow. A sarcastic laugh flew out of Madison. "That's funny. No, really funny. What do you care what I think? I mean, you obviously went ahead without asking me and made the plans. You have the house, and you probably have the doctors ready wherever you're taking me, don't you? Oh, but here's something to think about, Mom. How about this? Did you think about my last day? How it will end for me? Where I'll be? Or maybe I'll surprise you and die during the night. That would really screw up your little deal now wouldn't it."

"Madison. Please just stop for a minute and listen to what you're saying."

"No! I don't want to stop. I'm trying to think where you get off telling me to." Madison allowed another contemptuous laugh to echo in the kitchen on purpose. "God! I am so tired of everyone making decisions for me. You tell me when to eat, when I should go to bed, when to take a fucking shower." Madison's head shook back and forth slowly. "So, no, Mom. I'm not going to 'stop and listen.' If you had the decency to ask me, I would've told you what I wanted." She eyed Annie before she answered in a steady voice. "And I don't want to go anywhere."

Madison looked over in Jack's direction. She didn't hesitate this time either to think about what she was going to say to her one and only friend. Her very best friend. "So what is it? You think by not playing soccer you can understand what it is I'm going through? Cause I can't skate? Is that it? Because if that's what you think, it's a bunch of shit, Jack. You have no idea what I'm going through every day. You will never understand. You can't just go out and buy me a bunch of stupid bandanas and pajamas and think you get it. Sitting in the hospital with me a few times a week doesn't qualify you to be a fucking cancer patient. You know what else? I'm going to be honest, because it really doesn't matter anymore. And anyway, you should know." She breathed deeply, catching what little breath she could. "I wouldn't want you there with me, wherever it is my mother is taking me to die. I don't want you anywhere near me, from now on."

There was simply no way this was the same Madison he had known all of his life. That girl would never say these vicious words to him. *She wouldn't.* They were a team. They always had been. Jack met Madison's dark eyes. Maybe if he looked deep enough into them, he'd find the girl he once knew. "You don't mean that, Maddie. I know you don't."

Madison stared at Jack long and hard.

If Jack thought he saw slight dimness before in Madison's eyes, he now was seeing only black.

There was nothing in her voice that was even remotely warm. Her words were hideously cold. Cruel. And she wasn't done. "Please listen to what I'm saying. I don't want you there, Jack. I don't want you here either, any more." With a solid pause, she didn't break her glare into Jack's eyes. "So, good luck this summer with the soccer team. I'm sure you'll do really well. Probably even get to go to the Olympics someday. You should go now, Jackson." Madison turned her back on him as fast as she could. She knew what she had just said could potentially ruin their friendship. She also knew if Jack was to accompany her on this trip of theirs, it could most likely ruin his life forever and she was not about to let that happen. She would have to make it difficult for him to remember her the way she was. The way she used to be... and if she did that, maybe there would be a chance for him to move on with his world and forget their world ever existed, that she ever existed.

"Madison. Don't do this. Please don't be…"

"Get the hell out of my house, Jack!" If that's what it would take for him to forget her, so be it. She had no choice.

Jack stared at Madison tearfully, patiently waiting for her to apologize, say she was sorry, like she'd done so many times in these past few months. But this time, she said nothing to him. She turned her back on him rather than take a chance on having to look him in the eyes. Jack glanced to Annie. She would say something, wouldn't she? She wouldn't let Madison talk to him like that.

Annie opened her mouth to speak. Jack waited for some kind of statement, some sort of reprimand to Madison, but no words came out of Annie. She lifted her shoulders ever so slightly to Jackson without a clue what to say anymore.

Madison only turned back around to Annie when the door shut loudly behind her, signaling Jackson's exit. She stared at the closed door half-expecting Jack to come barging back in. A pin could have been heard dropping on the kitchen floor at that moment and for many moments after.

"How could you do that to him? You crushed him, you know that? You couldn't have been more heartless, Madison."

Madison refused to acknowledge her. She took the few steps it took her to cross the room and opened a large drawer. She took out a brand new cardboard box of garbage bags and without a word to Annie, she left.

⌘⌘⌘⌘⌘⌘⌘

No one could have prepared Annie for what she was about to walk in on. She knew when Madison left her in the kitchen that she was upset. She knew those words spoken to both her and Jack weren't meant literally. At least, she prayed they weren't. But here was Madison in the middle of her room, filling up garbage bag after garbage bag.

Annie chose not to knock. At this point, what did it matter? Not knocking was the least of their issues. Madison was too preoccupied to hear Annie push the door open. Annie watched in utter shock as she witnessed her only child throwing away every single memory they ever made.

Madison had taken down most of her medals and trophies before Annie decided to come up and talk to her. She had already discarded the certificates in matching wood frames and flimsy awards she had won at an early age into a plastic bag. Her mirror was empty of most of her photographs. As Annie let her eyes scan around the room, all she could think was there was nothing left in the room to say Madison ever spent any time on the planet.

"What are you doing?" Annie had entered into Madison's room and before she realized it, there she was, her hand tightly gripping Madison's thin upper arm.

Madison's eyes traveled down to her arm where Annie's hand was squeezing her. Her eyes wandered back to Annie's face and she stared at her mother. Not an angry stare. This time it was more of an acknowledgement and it clearly said let go of my arm this instant.

Annie quickly removed her severe grasp and wondered if she should have asked herself what she was doing. She had never laid a hand on Madison. Never. But here she was, grabbing her roughly at a time like now.

Madison casually rubbed the area on her arm where Annie had just released her hold. Whether she did it intentionally or not, the words Madison spoke stung Annie deeply.

"I'm throwing my stuff out. I obviously don't have any more use for these things and to be honest, it's hard to look at everything all the time. Besides, the way I see it is I'm simply saving you the trouble when I'm dead."

Annie had a new mantra. *Don't react. That's what Madison wants. A reaction, preferably a big one.* If Annie could stay calm and not go off on her, maybe they could figure things out together. Like they used to. "Jesus, Maddie. If you want to be pissed, be pissed at me. Not Jack. You've had one person in your life besides me and Daddy and you just sent him away for no other reason than to be a bitch. It was my idea, the house was, and Jack wanted to go. I'm the one who said it was all right. So if you want to be angry, be angry with me. Not him. He's never done anything but be by your side through everything. It was all me, okay?"

"Well, no offense, but that's really nothing new."

"What's that supposed to mean?"

"It's simple." Madison randomly grabbed one of the many full garbage bags and tipped it first to the side then upside down. One by one, all of the contents, the memories, spilled out on the floor, on top of Annie's feet. Madison shrugged nonchalantly to her mother. "What do you think all of this is? I mean, really what do you think? I'd like to know your opinion. What is it to you? Because to me, it's all about *you*. All of this crap. You." Madison kicked a few trophies to the side. "Think about it. They've always been your ideas, haven't they? Which competitions to be in, when I should practice. How many hours a day I should be in the rink." In her best impression of Annie, Madison continued her tirade in the most disrespectful way she could. *"Madison should wear this costume, the one with the sparkles. No, I don't want it to be blue, it should be pink. Can you make it in pink? Good. And this time it should be two inches longer than the last skirt.*" As much as Madison knew she had already cut too deep for repair, she couldn't stop herself from pushing the knife in even further. "Why do you think I started skating? Do you honestly think I wanted to skate when I was what? Five? Do you? You think I really understood what skating even meant? Here's a better question for you, Mom. Do you think I wanted to spend my entire fucking life skating every single morning? And again every single night? With *you*?"

Annie fought back all the tears she wanted desperately to cry. She unconsciously folded her arms across her chest in front of her, as if to protect her body from the pain being profoundly and purposefully inflicted.

"And hey, by the way...a lot of good it did me, huh? To skate every day? Good thing I *almost* went to the Olympics. Now that I'm not going to live to be seven-fucking-teen. I am so glad you thought it'd be a healthy thing for me to skate as much as I did. And I'm especially so glad we got to spend all that quality time together. I had a goddamn blast. How about you? Have fun with me? I mean, come on. Who wants to have friends their own age anyway, right? I'm sure every girl wants to spend day after goddamn day with her mother. But you...you must be pretty upset with me. At the fact I didn't go all the way to live out your dream for you."

Before Annie had the chance to stop herself, or even comprehend what she was about to do, the palm of her hand flew hard and deliberately across Madison's left cheek, leaving a huge red imprint of her five long fingers.

Neither one of them moved the slightest bit for quite some time.

Little by little, Madison pulled her stare away from Annie. Without a word, she knelt down on the floor and began to put the photos and trophies back into the bag.

Annie looked up to the ceiling and then back down to her daughter crouched on the floor. "Madison. I'm so sor—"

Madison didn't meet Annie's eyes when she interrupted her. She simply answered in her quiet voice. "Please leave." She picked up a fairly large trophy she won when she was thirteen years old and read the inscription to herself.

Annie's voice quivered as she begged for forgiveness. "Please, Maddie. I'm sorry. I didn't mean to...I'm so sorry."

Madison refused to look at her. She threw the trophy into the bag.

"Tell me you didn't mean those things you said. Please say you don't really think that about me. About skating."

Annie got her wish for an answer.

Madison looked up to Annie and in the most cold-blooded tone, she spoke evenly. "I meant every single fucking word. Now I'd like you to get out."

There was one picture left on Madison's mirror. It was taken at the Pacific Coast Championships, just before Madison went on the ice. At the time, they didn't even know it was being taken. David had snapped it without either of them realizing it. As a good luck present before Nationals, David surprised them with the picture one day when he came home from work. Annie and Madison had their heads together and hands interlocked. David said at the time, he had never seen anything sweeter in his entire life. What came across in this specific photograph was nothing but pure love and joy between a mother and daughter, not a skater and coach. A connection that was so apparent, it came shining through on film. David made copies for both of them. Annie had kept the photo in her locker at the hospital. Madison had kept hers on the mirror.

Madison made her way over to the glass and took the picture down. As she walked back to the untied garbage bag, now almost full, she crumpled the picture in her hands. Then, very specifically for Annie, Madison threw the picture in the trash.

Annie had tolerated Madison's wrath on a daily basis for the past few weeks. But this? This was too much for her to endure. Annie ran out of the room and ran as far away from her daughter as she could.

Madison listened to Annie's steps moving further and further away. Only then, when she was sure there would be no return visit from her mother, only then did she reach into the bag full of her life and her memories. She pulled out the bent and wrinkled picture of the two of them.

A deep crease ran down the photo in between their heads, seemingly dividing them forever.

Jack grew up on the privileged side of life, but he would never admit it. He'd only known one house, a beautiful, white, two-story Colonial. It was the grandest house on the street, if not in the entire town. There was never a week when the lawns weren't perfectly manicured, never a time when some sort of flowers weren't growing, no matter what time of the year it was, and never a day when Jack wasn't watched by Rosa, the maid/cook/sometimes doctor. There was almost never a night when Jackson ate dinner with his father. Madison and her parents were Jackson's family. They were the only family he had ever known.

Jack paced around his room aimlessly, then found himself staring out the window into the massive, lush, green back-yard. How many nights did they sleep out there in some tiny little pup tent? Or how many Summer and Fall and even Winter afternoons did they play soccer out there for hours? It didn't matter where he looked or what he was thinking. Anything around him, anything at all, reminded him of Madison.

Over the years, pictures of them growing up had found a place somewhere in Jack's room. His father once joked that he might need to move to a bigger bedroom if he continued to hang Madison's photos on every inch of wall space. Jack laughed politely to please his father and in the same minute, thought to himself if he did move to another bedroom, he would only find more and more pictures of Madison to display.

Jack was in such a daze when his phone rang that he forgot about the two open suitcases right behind him and tripped into them. "Shit!" His foot was tangled inside the elastic belt whose sole purpose was keeping folded clothes straight. He threw his body across the bed and reached his arm out to the nightstand that held his phone. "Hello?" His face fell and disappointment replaced what had just been hope, hope that this call would lead to Madison's voice on the other end of the line. "Hey, Tommy." Jackson dropped his forehead into his free hand. "No. I haven't seen that movie yet."

☙☙☙☙☙☙☙

Annie spent the entire night packing up everything she thought they would possibly need for the beach. The rental agency had told her the house came equipped with all of the cooking necessities, from cookie sheets to woks. At least that was a bit of help. She packed up all of Madison's favorite snacks in a separate bag, and threw it in the back of the car, still reachable from the front seat. Not that there were many, but she wanted to make sure Madison had a choice if she became hungry. A long shot, but just in case.

Then she cleaned the house like she had never cleaned it before. From top to bottom, side to side, nothing went overlooked. By the time she had finished, close to three in the morning, the entire house looked as if it had been remodeled. Well, almost.

After that, she waited. Then waited more. And David never came home.

By the time the bedroom clock hands waltzed over to six in the morning, Annie was zipping up her suitcases. The doctor's appointment was in three hours and then they'd stop by the house one more time before heading out.

She had packed four cardboard moving boxes sometime between the hours of three and four. Or was it four and five? What did it matter right now? They were taped up and ready to go. There was nothing more to do.

Madison's clothes wouldn't take much time to put together; she'd finish that after the doctor's. There were very few things that fit her anymore and Annie knew she mostly stayed in her pajamas, day and night. It had become, as Annie liked to refer to it, a 'heated discussion' when she gently mentioned to Madison it might possibly be time to wash whatever pajama of the week it was.

Annie pulled back the worn curtain to the kitchen window and tried not to think where David was all night. He probably stayed in his office on the old frayed couch he'd had since his father died. For some reason, that couch became David's most prominent tie to his father. Annie never discounted it; she just refused to keep it in their house. So, to the office it went and stayed, way beyond its years. Annie only recalled one other time it was used for this same sort of night. It was their six month wedding anniversary. Annie vaguely smiled as she remembered her irrational anger when David showed up empty-handed. No Hallmark card. No flowers. Not even a hand-written post-it. *Funny how priorities change through the years.*

She forced down her last swig of too cold, too-sugared-down coffee. She was aware how much she'd thank herself for the caffeine later in the morning. A blank piece of blue-lined white paper from Madison's old school notebook and a Papermate pen sat on the counter in front of her. She tipped the coffee cup up to her lips for the very last drop and finally put it in the sink. Anything to avoid the paper and ink waiting patiently nearby, she decided it was of the utmost importance to wash the cup and the spoon, too. Telling herself she was doing this for David's return. Of course he would return eventually. When he did, Annie wanted everything to look clean and perfect, didn't she?

But the unwritten letter still waited. With the pen firmly in her hand, she stood looking down at the paper and wrote two words: Dear David...

<hr/>

The treatment rooms were always the same, no matter which one you were thrown into. Some jerk, most probably on a hallucinogenic drug, decided lime green was the perfect color to surround you as they drip chemicals into your once-perfect blood stream. *Great choice on the lime green, moron,* Madison thought. *Matches the vomit that overrides my system as soon as I walk through the door of my house.*

She always had to wear the hospital gown, any arguing would be pointless. At least today, they let her wear the adult one. Last time she went in for treatments, a new nurse at the hospital gave her the gown the preteens were forced to wear. Madison stood in the room for twenty minutes, refusing to put on the gown with circus animals all over it.

The nurses were familiar with Madison by now. They all

knew her story. They knew today was the last time she would be in for treatments. They knew it was the last time she would ever have to stare up at the puke green ceiling.

So did Madison.

She carefully eased down on her back and readjusted the bandana on her head. This was the part she hated. The waiting. Waiting for the moment the technician would come in and insert the needle heavily into her arm. Then waiting further for the moment there was metal, cold metal, rushing into her veins. That moment she hated most of all.

There was a quick knock on the door and Annie stuck her head in. "Hey. All set?"

Madison only barely nodded, and not even in Annie's direction.

Annie entered the room cautiously, not knowing how Madison would react to her presence. She grabbed a chair from against the wall and pulled it closer to the bed. She reached into her bag and pulled out Madison's iPod. "I brought this. Just in case you wanted it."

Madison took it gently from Annie's hand and immediately put the earphones in. She closed her eyes and tried not to think about how she might feel in a few short hours.

There was another quick knock, this time unheard by Madison, who could only hear her favorite alternative rock band blaring in her ears.

Jamal, Madison's favorite technician, entered her room. He gave a smile to Annie and walked up to Madison in bed. He leaned down close to her and playfully pulled an earphone out of her right ear. "Excuse me. Am I disturbing you, Miss *Thang*?"

Madison's eyes opened and she smiled broadly. "What are you doing here? I thought you didn't work on Thursdays."

Annie suppressed a round of applause for herself. Madison was smiling. And it, in a roundabout way, was because of her. Madison had merely mentioned she wouldn't be able to say goodbye to Jamal. So Annie ran with it. He was the one and only person Madison never attacked verbally, even when he was jabbing her with needles. Annie knew it was a stretch, but after the night they had had, she would do anything to make it up to Madison. Or at least make an attempt to. Today was going to be extremely difficult for both of them, and if she could do anything to ease the pain for either of them, she would. She knew Jamal was Madison's favorite technician, hers too for that matter, and knew it would ease this last trip to the hospital with him in charge of her.

Jamal prepped Madison's arm as he talked to her, trying to create the biggest diversion possible from what was about to happen to her body. "I don't work on Thursdays. Usually." He glanced over to Annie with a grin. "But, a little birdie called me in the middle of the night, disturbed my needed beauty sleep too…and informed me this would be your last treatment today. I couldn't miss out on that now, could I?"

Madison shook her head no as the needle pierced her pale skin. She tried to smile, but Jamal knew there was nothing but pain behind it.

"You okay, kiddo?" Jamal squeezed her hand tightly and didn't let go.

Not that she cared, but she had to say something to take her thoughts off the pain. "Who's next?" No one reacted to the drops of tears running down the sides of Madison's cheeks and onto the pillow beneath her head.

Jamal checked Madison's IV bag and adjusted it slightly before he sat down on the edge of the bed. "What're you talking about, girl? Who's next? No one's next."

"I'm the only one getting treatments today?"

Jamal smiled genuinely and held up Madison's hand, putting his other hand over hers. "The only one getting treatments from *me*. I told you. I don't work on Thursdays." He casually wiped the drops of water from Madison's cheeks and continued on, without missing a beat. "So, now we need to talk about the important stuff. Did you see that playoff game last night?

Madison shook her head yes. No matter what she did, she couldn't seem to make her mouth smile. She only hoped Jamal could see the thank you in her eyes.

⌘⌘⌘⌘⌘⌘⌘⌘

Jackson hated to fly. Not as much when it was first-class with his father, but this was the soccer team. Although he could've been upgraded, thanks to his dad, he refused to be different from the rest of the guys. A few players were already at the airport with their matching shirts and jackets. A small number of them from the same area were flying out together. The rest of the team they would meet up with in England.

Jackson stood in front of the check-in counter by the departing gate and looked around at the people in the terminal. His eyes went back to the guys huddled in a circle wearing identical clothing with his team emblem.

He didn't finish packing until a few hours before. He couldn't. He knew he'd be fine once he was on the plane with Tommy, and once he was away from Madison. It was right then he felt the same lump in his throat that he had felt the entire night.

Once I'm away from Madison. What was he thinking?

How could he be okay away from her? He had gone over and over all of the possible things that would make it all right. All the things he would experience during the summer. All the reasons why he needed to go. None of the explanations he gave himself were working.

Jack watched a few more soccer players say goodbye to their parents and kiss their girlfriends. He nodded politely to them as they walked by him and boarded the plane.

"We will now be seating passengers in rows twenty to thirty-five. All passengers in rows twenty to thirty-five. Please step forward and have your tickets ready. Thank you."

Jackson looked up to the anonymous voice of the announcer that was still echoing in the condensed area and glanced down at the ticket that had become damp in his hand. He must have been in deep thought because Tommy shocked him when he nudged Jack with his elbow.

"Hey. We still sitting next to each other?"

"Yeah." Jack looked down again at the paper, even though he'd memorized it by now. "Twenty-seven. Twenty-seven E."

Tommy held his ticket up in front of Jack's face. "Yep. Twenty-seven D."

Jack was used to Tommy's aggressiveness. That was just the way he was. It never bothered Jack before today. But all he could think of at this moment was smacking Tommy's hand away. Hard.

Tommy must have sensed it because he quickly dropped his hand to his side. "Did you hear? They're boarding us now."

"Yeah, I know. Go on. I...uh...I'll be right there."

"What do you mean you'll be right there? They're boarding us. Now. They already called our rows."

"There're not going to take off for a while. Jesus, Tommy. I said I'll be there. I'm just waiting for someone."

Tommy's mouth was already open to say something, but the look on Jack's face made him think better of it. This wasn't a good time, quite obviously. "'Kay. See you in a few."

"Yeah." Jack peered over his shoulder and watched his friend hand his ticket to the flight attendant at the gate. He tried to quiet the constant voice inside his head, telling him repeatedly Madison would show up and just when he thought he succeeded...

He saw her. Or at least, he saw the back of her. A skinny girl, wearing a bandana securely over her head. It had to be Madison. Who else would be standing at this specific gate waiting, looking like that? His feet were moving before he even had a thought about what to say to her. It didn't matter. All that mattered was she had come. To see him. To send him off on his trip. Or maybe she was there to stop him from going at all.

"Madison!" A few people turned around to get a glimpse of where the yelling was coming from. Jack approached her from behind hastily and threw his hand on her shoulder, spinning her towards him in one quick move. "You came!"

But it wasn't Madison. The girl standing in front of Jack wore multiple piercings on her face and a long piece of bright purple hair hung down in her eyes. She didn't say a word to Jack. She simply stared hard.

Jack gradually released his grip from her shoulder and allowed it to drop heavily to his side. "I—I'm sorry. I thought that you were..." His voice trailed off into nothingness. His eyes searched around the area where he stood. He saw other couples saying goodbye. Old and young. All shapes, colors and all sizes. He looked back at the Goth girl still standing in front of him and thought he noticed a change in her face. Could it be that she was sympathetic? Did she get it? Did she know he would do anything to blink his eyes and transform her into a different skinny girl wearing a bandana? "I thought you were someone else. I'm sorry."

"I hope you find her. The someone else you're looking for." The girl smiled.

"Thanks." Jackson watched the girl walk away and slowly made his way back to the gate. All the while, his eyes searched for the someone else he so desperately wanted to see.

A flight attendant leaving the gate area caught his arm as he passed by her. "If you're with that soccer team, I suggest you board the plane now. It's about to take off."

"I know. I was just waiting until, uh, the last minute to get on."

She responded like any other polite flight attendant who had had a fairly good day. "It *is* the last minute."

Jack nodded in understanding. "Right." He glanced over his shoulder, just in case.

"Can I have your ticket?"

Jack scanned the crowd one last time. He unenthusiastically turned back to the patient woman in front of him and handed her his crumpled ticket.

"Thank you. Have a great flight."

"Yeah. Thanks." Jack entered the gate and reluctantly made his way to the airplane.

⌒⌒⌒⌒⌒⌒⌒

Annie carried the suitcases out of the house and packed them in the trunk of her car. There wasn't a whole lot of room left and she cursed herself when her fingers got crushed in between the bags. This wasn't her job. It never had been. It was the unspoken rule this job belonged to David.

But David had yet to come home.

She ended the letter she had written to him signed with love and she meant it. They had an argument, like numerous times before. But this time, he didn't even call. Madison and Annie had done everything they were supposed to do. Now it was time for them to go. Annie knew there were no more distractions or delays she could stall with anyway.

She left all the information for David. The address of where they were staying, along with the phone number. She had even gone so far as to write out directions for him. Whether or not he'd use them remained to be seen.

She closed the trunk with a big push and saw Madison standing a few feet away from her with one more bag. She should have thought better about starting up even a minor conversation with her. Madison was not a happy camper and there was nothing Annie could say to make it even tolerable. "What's that? I thought you had packed everything you wanted."

Madison looked at Annie with glassy eyes. "*You* packed everything you wanted me to take. This is stuff *I* wanted."

The trip was off to a wonderful start, Annie thought. "Just put it in the back seat on top of the food boxes. Carefully."

Madison opened the back door to the car and threw it in without even looking at where the bag was going to land.

"Madison! There are eggs in some of those boxes!"

She responded to Annie as she made her way to the passenger side of the car. "Yeah, I would say that's really important. A few eggs might be crushed. Sure, in your big picture, I can see how that would be crucial. Unfortunately for you though, in my big picture, a few crushed eggs don't really mean dick." With that, she was in the car, seat belt on and door slammed shut.

Oh, yeah. Off to a really wonderful start.

Annie stood alone on her front lawn for a moment, gathering all the strength she could to get through the next few minutes. That was what she found herself doing lately. Taking a break every twenty to thirty minutes just to get herself through the next twenty to thirty minutes. She was still sane enough to know it wasn't working too well. Annie took a deep breath and leaned in through the driver's side window, left open after the trip home from the hospital. "Look, Maddie, I know you're confused right now about a lot..."

Madison interrupted her with an obnoxious laugh. "Confused? I'm not confused. *I'm dying.* That's not exactly the same thing, for the record."

Annie pursed her lips tightly together, halting the obscene language that so wanted to spew forth from her mouth. "Well, *for the record*, I'm doing all of this for you. Whether or not you choose to believe that, I am."

She didn't look at Annie. She just stared straight ahead with the same blank look on her face that she'd been wearing for weeks. "What about Dad? You doing this for him too?"

She knew Madison would most likely bring this up. Obviously, Madison knew David didn't come home last night, and obviously something needed to be said. She just dreaded being the one saying it. "In a way, yes. I am doing this for all of us. So we can enjoy each other's company and spend quality time together."

"You mean, before I die?"

"Madison, please! Cut the shit okay? I'm really trying here."

"I'm so sure you are but you sound like a fucking Hallmark card gone really bad. Just admit it. You screwed things up with Dad and now he's not coming. Because once again, you went ahead without any concern for what other people might think, and you made all the arrangements and never included him. Or me, for that matter."

Madison was right. She hadn't included anyone else in this decision. She never did before this disease became a part of their daily vocabulary and she never stopped to think things should be different now. "You're right. I didn't ask you or Dad." Annie grabbed the handle roughly and opened her door. With a quick slam, she turned on the ignition. "But guess what? We're going anyway." Maybe it was because she wasn't paying attention. Or maybe it was because she was too upset with Madison.

Whatever the reason, she never saw David's car pulling into the driveway behind her. The horn that blasted from behind barely stopped her before she plowed into the front of his pick-up. Her abrupt halt sent both of them jerking forward into the dashboard. Annie closed her eyes, half in disbelief, and half in relief when she looked in the rearview mirror.

"It's Dad!" Madison was out the door before Annie could stop her. She ran up to David who was barely out of his car and she jumped into his arms.

David accepted her overzealous hug, knowing full well it was only meant to piss Annie off a little bit more. "Hey, Maddie-girl."

"Are you coming with us?"

He knew it was all for Annie's benefit still, but he smiled at Madison's excitement. Put on or not, it was still nice to see her smile. David shot a glance to Annie and quickly turned back to Madison. "Uh, no. Not now. I'm not coming right now…with you guys. But I'll visit soon, okay?"

"When?"

David grinned. "How does Sunday sound? You got any plans?"

Madison barely shook her head no. "Promise?"

"Promise." David embraced her one more time and walked her to the car. He put Madison back in her original starting place and shut the door. He leaned in through the window and kissed her on the forehead. "I'll see you in a few days."

"Bye, Daddy." Madison tried to stick her head as far out the window as possible to hear the discussion going on behind her.

David approached Annie cautiously, meeting her at the trunk, the halfway point for both of them. They instinctively bent their heads to the ground, as if it was their first date and they were both thirteen again.

Annie broke the uncomfortable silence. "I went ahead and wrote out the directions for you. I left a copy on the kitchen table. For whenever you can make it."

"Okay. Good. Thanks."

Annie glanced to Madison out of the corner of her eye and smiled. "She's either going to fall out of the window or she's going to pull a muscle in her neck from straining so hard." She forced her eyes to move to David's, to really see him. "I'm sorry."

David met her gaze. "I know. Me too."

Moments went by and neither one of them moved an inch. They simply looked at one another. Remembering what it was that was so important in the first place to make them separate, if only for a night. Neither one had the answer. But they did know the one thing that did matter, the only thing. Madison. It was all about her. It had to be for right now and they both understood that.

"You better get going. You probably want to get unpacked and everything before the sun goes down." He paused for a second and corrected himself before Annie could say anything. "*I'd* like you to get there before it gets dark. It'd make me feel better. How's that?"

"David…" Annie reached out to him and grabbed his hand, enclosing it in hers.

He pulled Annie close to him and hugged her tightly against his chest. He spoke softly in her ear, but he knew she heard every word spoken, crystal clear. "You're doing the right thing, Ann. I know you are. We'll make it work. I don't know how yet exactly but we will. Okay? Don't worry about anything. Just be with Maddie."

Annie backed away from David and tenderly rubbed her hands up and down his arms. "Thank you."

David walked Annie to the car and kissed her lovingly on the lips. "I'll call you later, after you've had time to get settled."

"Okay." She moved to the door and turned back to David just before she sat down. "I love you. You know that, right?"

David smiled at his wife. Some days he wasn't too sure of that answer. Today, he was.

༺༒༒༒༒༒༺

Annie and Madison drove in silence. Neither one of them felt like listening to the radio and they definitely didn't want to speak to each other.

Annie turned her car to the freeway and looked around for the directions under the piles that had somehow found their way onto the front seat.

Madison rolled her window down entirely, sending the wind gushing in. Annie barely snatched the directions before they flew out of the car. She accelerated and blended into the speed of the other cars, already heading to their own destinations.

Madison stuck her head out as far as she could through the open space and looked up in the sky, as high as her eyes would allow.

A plane was ascending above her head. She knew in her gut it was Jackson's plane. She refused to take her eyes off of it until it completely disappeared into the clouds, taking Jackson out of her life.

CHAPTER 32

The drive took longer than Annie had expected and it was already dusk when they arrived. They had stopped twice to use the thruway rest areas, where Annie stocked up on her caffeine and Madison stretched her cramped legs.

They hardly spoke the entire way.

As she dragged two more suitcases into the house, Annie noticed Madison and quietly paused. The sun was going down rapidly and the sky was a brilliant combination of pink, red, and orange hues. Annie could not remember a time when she had seen anything so beautiful.

Madison leaned her upper body far over the short balcony that immediately overlooked the sand and then further, the blue ocean. She was unaware Annie was glued to her every movement, her every blink. She watched wave after wave crash softly into the sand mere feet away from her, reached up to her bandana, and for once, purposefully removed it. She squished it up in her hands and then allowed it out of confinement. She did this a few times before she simply held onto it and let her body relax to the sound of the water. The breeze that came up from the ocean tingled against her bare head.

Without her daughter knowing, Annie included herself in the small, private smile Madison gave to the ocean before her.

⊚⊚⊚⊚⊚⊚⊚

The house was smaller than Annie imagined it would be. As she walked around the outside, familiarizing herself with every nook, she wondered why the rental agency never bothered telling her the house was long overdue for a fresh coat of paint. She shook her head as she thought about her conversation with the agent, a mere two weeks before. Beautiful and spacious, she had said. Annie smiled. Nice and cozy would have been a more appropriate description. At least they had separate bedrooms and that was all Annie was concerned about at this point.

The great room consisted of the kitchen, living area and dining alcove, all in one big she-bang. Of course, she was under the impression, again from the nice rental lady, that the rooms were all separate great rooms, but who was counting? On the south side of the house in the living area of the great room, the side facing the ocean, ceiling to floor French doors opened out onto the balcony. Actually, three out of four opened anyway. *That made this house perfect,* Annie thought to herself. The balcony even had a barbecue on it and four sun chairs to lounge in. There was a redwood table with two benches that had been pushed off to the side to make room. For what, Annie hadn't a clue. She made it a priority to move the table and chairs first thing in the morning. They might as well enjoy them.

The living area came with an updated television set. Annie would have bought a TV in a heartbeat if one didn't come with the house. That had been the one thing Madison did without fail and it was the only time Annie could guarantee they would not fight. The couch that Madison was already stretched out on had seen better days. *At least the cushions are down, or partially down; it'll be comfortable for Madison to relax on every day,* she thought. *Another note to self. Buy a sofa cover in town.* There had to be some kind of department store and it'd be worth the hundred dollars to not look at the dreadful frayed fabric. Two overstuffed chairs held court on either side of the couch, waiting for someone to sit down. The chairs were perfect. So shabby chic and Annie smiled. The dumb chairs were about the best thing in the house.

She gazed around the room, still full of packed boxes. It was going to take her most of tonight and possibly some of tomorrow, to get them situated in their new house. At least she got Madison's things unpacked. Of course, Madison chose not to do it herself. Even after Annie tried explaining she would have no idea where anything was put away. The answer was still no. Annie thought for a second about putting Madison's underwear in the lower drawers and heavy clothing in the small top ones. It was a mean and dirty thing to do and she knew it. Only when she reminded herself why they were here, that Madison wasn't just a rebellious teenager in a sour mood, only then did she put her underwear in the small top drawer.

There was a little four-top table in the dining area just off the kitchen. Glass tables were not Annie's favorite, but at least it was mostly clean. She made a promise to herself to eat outside on the balcony as much as the weather - or Madison - would allow. Whichever one was more cloudy on that specific day.

Annie took a long look at the hospital bed. It had been delivered the day before, compliments of Dr. Tanger. The delivery men, as directed, had placed it off to the side, and shoved it tightly against the wall in the living area. They had called Annie yesterday in a downright panic. She had gone through explicit directions with the medical assistance company about where to put the bed. Don't put it out in the open. Hide it. Make it as unnoticeable as possible. When the technicians arrived, they realized there was absolutely nowhere to put the bed, except in the extremely noticeable, very visible living space. Annie had already driven herself into a frenzy about whether to have the bed there waiting for them or order it when she felt it was becoming necessary. Dr. Tanger felt it might be better for both of them to get used to the idea of the bed from the get-go. As hard as it might be for Madison to walk into the house and see it, it would be far more difficult for her to watch it be unloaded off a medical-supply truck, knowing what stage it must mean she was in.

For once, Annie agreed with Tanger.

They had ordered numerous boxes of medicines too. Some of them were precautionary. Some were going to be used for sure. Some were already being administered to Madison. Annie went through them nonchalantly and placed them on top of the bed in order of importance. The 'just in case' boxes went to the far side of the bed against the wall. The daily doses went closest to edge of the bed. *Easy access.* Annie decided if the bed had to be in their direct line of vision everyday, she might as well try to cover it up as much as she could. The boxes seemed to be a good start. She jammed the IV stand behind the bed and the oxygen tanks went underneath.

Madison watched her mother as she prepared, cleaned and unpacked. She didn't even attempt to help. Why should she? Wasn't she brought here against her will? And wasn't she the one who was sick? She stretched her legs out as much as she could before the pain began to shoot up through her body. Annie had asked her if she was chilly earlier and offered her a blanket. Of course, Madison had ignored her at the time and refused to even give her the courtesy of eye contact. Still, she indeed was absolutely cold when Annie had originally asked her. That was twenty minutes ago. Now she was borderline freezing. She reached up for the blanket Annie had thrown on the top of the couch. For later, in case Madison changed her mind. Madison hoped Annie wasn't watching her shivering as she pulled it down over her trembling body.

But Annie did. She noticed Madison's every move. Anticipated it, actually. She casually walked into the modest kitchen, pretending she saw nothing. Annie glanced around at the boxes of food and miscellaneous materials that had yet to be unpacked, counting them to herself. Four of them and a few bags too. Estimated time of completion…twenty-six minutes, tops. Annie sighed and leaned her sore back over a closed box. The first thing she saw when she opened the box was pancake mix. God, she loved pancakes. It was only then she realized neither one of them had had anything to eat for hours. She stood up, holding the box up high and called over to Madison. She could pretty much guarantee Madison's response, but it was always worth a try. "Are you hungry? I have some food here. Not really enough for a three course meal. But guess what? We can make pancakes tonight for dinner if you want. I'll need to go into town tomorrow and grocery shop. Do you want to come?"

Madison didn't turn around. "No."

Too many questions at once, of course, she thought. Annie tried to think of a response. Something, anything, to lighten the thickness that swarmed around them like an over-popu-lated beehive. "No, what? No, you're not hungry or no, you don't want to grocery shop with me tomorrow?"

"No to both."

She tried to psych herself up. It was a really nice attempt at a conversation. And now it was apparently done. Annie took a deep breath. Something must be said. They could not continue to live in this constant state of agitation. At least she was sure that she couldn't. "I know you don't want to be here right now. Okay? I know you think you were better off at home. But, come on. Give this a chance. We've got this great little house. We're right on the beach. Could you just try, Madison? A little? It doesn't take that much to be civil. I'm trying here, really trying."

"Yeah, well. I didn't ask you to." She hit the volume up on the television.

Annie raised her voice to equal the television volume. "I know you didn't. Could you please turn the volume...?"

Then it happened.

Out of nowhere, the main door to the house swung open wide and slammed hard against the wall. Annie dropped the box of pancake mix on the floor and screamed.

Madison turned to the loud noise with pure panic written across her face.

There stood Jack in the doorway, a suitcase in each hand. His eyes were glued to Madison and his voice offered no com-passion whatsoever. "First of all, no one tells me what to do. If I want to come on your damn...whatever this is...sick vaca-tion, death trip, whatever you want to call it, I don't care what you say. If I want to be here, then I will. You hear me?"

Madison did everything in her power not to react. But the

smallest hint of a smile was in her eyes. She simply nodded ever so slightly.

"Second of all, you're a pain in my ass. You always have been, and you always will be. So you know." With that, Jack dropped his suitcases on the floor with a thud. "Third of all, no matter how big of a bitch you are, just know right now, I am not leaving. Ever."

Madison shrugged as if his unexpected arrival was no big deal. Only she was aware of how fast her heart was beating. *Pounding.* Only she was aware how much she wanted to smile at this very moment and how much she thanked God for Jackson Wellington III. But the only thing that came out of her wicked wee mouth was, "Will you shut the door already? What're you trying to do? Kill me?" Madison quickly turned away from Jack for fear he'd see the grin now apparent on her face.

Jack smiled and shut the door. He threw a wink in Annie's direction and moved his suitcases out of the way.

∞ ∞ ∞ ∞ ∞ ∞ ∞

Jack leaned over the balcony, the same spot Madison stood just hours before, and looked out at the ocean. He had been there for some time, watching the sky leisurely fill with stars, as if each shining dot knew when it was their cue to twinkle.

Funny how some eight hours ago he was on his way to Europe.

He tried to imagine how it must have looked to the flight attendants, to the soccer team, and to Tommy, when he stood up as the plane was about to take off. How it must have looked when he yelled, "Stop!" at the top of his lungs. How he must have looked with tears running down his cheeks.

He laughed to himself. *I don't give a shit how it looked.*

The only thing that mattered to him was finding Madison and getting to her as fast as he could.

The car company his dad employed on a regular basis had driven Jackson plenty of times. Before he had gotten his license, his father would use them to pick Jack up from soccer practice or from Madison's house. It became a joke that Jorge, the driver, was more of a father figure to Jackson than his own father. Soon Jorge would show up to the soccer games and practices earlier and earlier, cheering Jack on more and more frequently. So when Jack called Jorge to come get him, there was no explanation needed. And when Jack asked Jorge to drive him on a five-hour expedition, Jorge simply said, "Of course."

He had enough clothes with him. If he should need anything when he got there, he had a credit card with an unlimited amount of money available. He had gotten the directions from David. He had thought of everything.

Except Madison.

What if she really didn't want him there? Or refused to see him at all? He told himself he had to pull out all the stops. Worse-case scenario, he would turn around and Jorge would drive him home. He would work in his dad's office after all. No harm done.

He allowed his eyes to close as he listened to the sound of the waves approaching closer and closer to where he was standing and he said a prayer. A big one. When he finished and opened his eyes, he could no longer see the waves. Even the stars had gone to sleep.

The light bulb suddenly brightened over the balcony and

startled him for a moment. Footsteps behind him became louder and Jack spun around.

Annie shut the door to the house and walked up next to Jack. "Thought it'd be nice to see the water. You mind the light?"

Jackson shook his head no.

She leaned up against the balcony like Jack and watched the water flow in and out for a few minutes before she spoke. "You all right?"

Jack nodded yes. Not totally convincing Annie or even himself that he was. "Is she okay?"

"Yeah. For a while." Annie paused briefly, wanting to word this in the best possible way. "You uh...you should know, Jack, this isn't going to be easy. You staying here with us. I'm not saying I mind it, at all. I was the one who agreed to let you come in the first place. But what you just saw happen a few moments ago, that kind of stuff happens a lot. She has some good moments, and then some really, really bad ones. She wasn't yelling at you to be cruel. She just didn't want you to see her like that. It's probably good you came out here to give her some privacy for a bit." Annie gave Jack a few seconds to let it all sink in and clear his head for the next bout of conversation. "She wakes up sometimes twice a night."

Jackson faced Annie. He wanted to understand, to know everything there was to know. At least he thought he did. "Why? Because she can't sleep?"

Annie didn't smile, that wasn't it. It was a sad, almost sweet shake of her head she gave to Jack, trying to lessen the impact of her words. "Because the pain is so bad."

"I—I didn't know. She never said anything about being in pain. She never told me about..." He turned his focus back to the night air, where he did not have to finish his thought.

"Jack. Look. I know that you being here is probably really great for Madison. Maybe even the best thing. But this isn't going to be easy, for anyone involved and if you're unsure, the smallest bit unsure about being here…"

He turned to her directly. "I'm not."

"If you are, Jack, if you are, I have to ask you to leave now. Before things get…before things become more difficult. I don't want anything to bother her or hurt her feelings. Trust me, she will sense something is wrong with you if you start to freak out about this whole thing. I'm begging you, please be sure about this. Okay? You don't even have to answer me now if you want to think about it." Annie studied his face for some kind of response. As she turned her head back to the ocean, she heard Jackson. Loud and clear.

"I want to stay. I can handle it."

"Okay." Annie took a deep breath. "Okay."

Jack thought about his commitment, about the promise he'd just made to Annie. He smiled, knowing it was the absolute only thing he ever wanted to do. Stay by Madison. "It's beautiful here, huh?"

"Yeah. Yeah, it is, Jackson."

⌒ CHAPTER 33 ⌒

*I*t was probably too cold for her to be outside but really, what did it matter? It was also too beautiful of a morning to miss.

The sun was about to rise. Madison had rarely paid attention to the sky just before it became day, unless of course they were late leaving for the rink. On their once-a-year vacations, who got up at the crack of dawn when that was what you did every other day of your young life?

This morning in particular she couldn't sleep. There were lots of mornings like this nowadays. Madison would find herself staring at the clock, watching each second tick by, trying desperately to return to sleep with not much success.

She had gone to bed earlier than normal last night. Probably due to the medicine Annie gave her. She had had a spell. That's what they referred to it as, a spell. That meant Madison was having difficulty breathing. It had only happened twice before. *Another really fun thing to look forward to as the cancer gradually takes over my body,* she thought.

The minute she woke up, she knew there was no way she was going back to sleep. She could blame it on the medicine, or problems with her sleeping, but Madison knew why she wanted to get out of bed. Her thought was confirmed when she tip-toed by a still-sleeping Jackson sprawled out on the couch. She wasn't sure if he'd still be there after Annie spoke to him outside. She didn't hear them, but she did know her mother and was quite positive a talk would be a top priority after she was sound asleep, or at least, when they thought she was sleeping. As she passed by Jack, a smile hinted on her face as she quietly let herself out through the French doors and onto the balcony.

Madison lifted both her knees to her chest to try to stay as warm as possible on the chaise. She was still in her pajamas and when she got up, she had only thrown a sweatshirt over her top. She knew she wouldn't be lucky enough not to wake up Jack if she ventured near him again in search of a blanket.

Some days, she would be so cold it literally hurt her bones. It wasn't an ache. It was pain. But for some odd reason, today the chill in the air didn't bother her. The moist, cool breeze from the sea was refreshing on her cheeks, giving her that natural blush in the perfect spot.

She lifted her chin to the clouds and watched the events going on above her. It was still overcast and the sun was trying to somehow find its way through the clouds' thickness. Anyone else might not consider clouds breaking and the sun poking through events, but Madison did. She found herself thinking of everything she never had time to before. Maybe she did have the time. Maybe it was that she simply didn't care. As she stared into the puffy, grayish-white mounds looming over her, she couldn't help but wonder if she would feel just like that sun some day. Trying desperately to get out from behind the clouds. To look at all of the people below.

Madison closed her eyes and felt the ocean dampness flick sporadically over her face.

Jack exited the house unbeknownst to Madison, a blanket under his arm, and moved carefully and cautiously, trying not to disturb her peace. He gently dropped the blanket over her body and stepped back, his gaze never leaving her.

Madison's eyes opened and she turned her head to face Jack.

"Sorry. I didn't mean to wake you."

"So'kay. I wasn't sleeping." Madison checked out the clouds, making sure she didn't miss anything. Any events. "I just like that feeling, the wind on my face. It kinda feels like I could be floating somewhere, you know?"

"Yeah." Jack glanced up at the still dark sky. "Is it okay? To be out here if it's cold?"

Madison smiled a little. She couldn't resist. "What? You think I'll catch a cold or something? Get sick?"

"No. I just meant—"

"I know what you meant." Madison gave Jack a tiny grin and tucked the blanket under her legs. "Thanks for the blanket."

Jack stepped toward her and tucked the blanket in the places Madison missed, never really acknowledging what he was doing. "Hey, you hungry? I could make pancakes. I think your mom had the box out last night. Does that sound good?"

Madison giggled out loud. "You can't even make pancakes."

"Care to make a bet on that statement, Miss-You-Think-You-Know-Everything?"

She eyed Jack closely and they shared a smile. "Actually, yeah. I do care to make a bet on that. Because you forget one thing Jackson Wellington the Ass. You forget that I've known you most of your life. And I know if there's one thing you so completely suck at, it's cooking. Or, should I say…attempting to cook."

"Well, then. I suggest you get off your chair and walk your skinny, white butt inside. Because you, my friend, are about to eat the pancakes of your life." Jack, without thinking, jogged in two big steps to reach the door.

Madison swung her legs sluggishly over to one side and struggled to get up off the chair. She gently pushed her body up as hard as she could with her arms. She kept her head down with the same thought continuously going on inside her mind. *Don't turn around and see me like this, Jack. Keep walking inside.* Then she saw it in front of her face.

Jack's hand.

"I got it. Just a little stiff, that's all."

He knew it was more than that, but he wasn't about to contradict her. He simply found reasons to take as much time as Madison did to get inside the house. He moved the table and chairs into the middle; he remembered Annie talking about that late last night after they had had their talk about Madison. He picked up a shell someone left on the rail and showed it to Madison, making conversation about the unique designs on it. He grabbed the blanket from her and threw it over both of their heads. By then, Madison was inside the house. *Job well done.* Jack swung the door shut behind them.

Madison was sitting down at the glass table when Annie exited her bedroom, dressed for the day. For a moment, her heart skipped a beat, thinking something must be wrong because there was no reason for them to be up at this hour.

But the look on their faces said something completely different than her initial thought. "Hey. What're you both doing up so early?"

Madison answered her and Annie held her breath as she watched her daughter's mouth open to speak. She was only too familiar with the foul responses that had been known to pour out of her uncontrollably.

"Jack is making us pancakes for breakfast."

Annie was completely ecstatic. Maybe it was a bit of an overreaction, but she didn't care. She wasn't yelled at, ignored or eye-rolled, and she actually heard a complete sentence out of Madison. A noun, a verb and a preposition. *God Bless America.* "He is, huh? This ought to be good. Too bad we can't put this on tape." Annie grinned to Jack and then to her daughter. "Mad, remind me to ask Dad to bring the video camera here when he comes this weekend. Because something tells me Jack cooking anything could be worth a lot of money someday."

Jack turned his baseball cap around to the back and shook out his arms, as if he was preparing for an arm wrestling tournament. "Have you no faith, you two?"

Annie and Madison answered in unison with a beginning case of the giggles. "No."

"You know what? You're gonna be sorry. Both of you." Jack pointed his finger back and forth to each of them. He searched through the drawers looking for a spatula. "I'll have you know, I can cook. All those days I wasn't with you, Miss Ice Skater Chick…" His finger poked Madison lightly in the arm and with the other hand, he pulled out his cooking utensil.

"Jack, what do you mean, 'all those days'? I spent almost every day with you. Don't even tell me you had cooking lessons on the five days in your life I didn't hang out with you."

Jackson put on his best cocky look. "Maybe I did have them. How would you know anyway?"

Madison grinned devilishly. "For one, Wolfgang, that ain't a spatula."

Jack looked at the thingamabob in his hand. "Oh, *really?*"

She positively grinned now and even let a chuckle escape. "That's for cooking spaghetti, ya ass." That did it for Madison and Annie. They both broke into hysterical laughter.

⬤⬤⬤⬤⬤⬤

"Well, all I can say is...thank God for IHOP," Annie said and laughed as she got in her car.

Madison, wearing a lighter face, got in the front seat next to her and put her seat belt on.

Only when Jack made sure she was settled in did he shut the door for her and hop into the back seat. "So I had an off day. Big deal. I'll bet you a lot of world-renowned chefs have a bad day now and then."

Madison looked over the seat. "You think they get a twelve-inch pancake stuck to their ceilings?"

"You wait."

Madison poked her head in between the front seats. "Jack, you can't cook. Just admit it and we'll all be not only grateful, but healthy." She realized the second she said it that it was an ironic thing for her to say. *Healthy.*

Jack immediately jumped in, hearing her completely, yet ignoring the comment. "Tomorrow it's all about the French. As in toast, ladies."

Annie pulled her car out of the parking lot. "Like I said. Thank God for IHOP." As she glanced in Madison's direction,

332

their eyes met for a second as Madison turned back around to the front. It wasn't anything that would end world hunger or stop violence in schools, but for Annie, that tiny look, that small glimmer of hope in Madison's eyes, made all the difference.

They were barely through the door when Madison instantly moved to the couch and hit the television on. Within a split second, her legs were curled up underneath her and the blanket was covering her body.

Jack glanced to Annie with a frown. The only answer Annie gave him was a shrug. This was what she dealt with every day with Madison. They could be having a decent time for a short period, then boom. She was back to the couch in silence, back to her cave where only she existed.

Annie excused her herself and walked into her room. It was a good time to check in with David anyway. Quite frankly, she really didn't want to be anywhere around when Jack pissed Madison off in the next few seconds.

The sun was knocking on the doors and Madison squinted slightly to block the light from her eyes. "Can someone close the curtains?"

Jack stood behind the couch, listening to her request, hearing it just fine. But he refused to answer her.

Madison turned around and noticed Jack posing behind her. Her voice carried a hint of agitation. "Could you close the curtains? The sun is hitting the screen and I can't see the television."

Jack folded his arms firmly across his chest. "So? Get up and do it yourself."

"What?" She sat up ever so slightly.

"I said, get up and do it yourself. If it's bothering you that much, get off your ass and close the damn curtains. I see nothing wrong with your legs. There are no heavy plaster casts on them, no braces or crutches that I can see anyway."

Madison stared at Jack for a moment. *Did he just say what I think he said? Could he be more rude?* She threw the blanket off her legs and angrily stomped to the curtains, shutting them so tightly no sunlight could be seen. She shot Jack a look that would kill a rabid animal and plopped herself back down on the couch. She wiggled her feet under the blanket and nonchalantly raised the television volume to an all-time high.

Annie watched...spied...from her bedroom doorway. She was afraid to breathe, the tension was so high. *There she goes,* Annie thought. There goes the television volume up to a level that would disturb even the fish in the sea. Yep, this one ought to be a good episode of *Madison's World.* Past experience said her money should be on the lead actress, Madison Henry, but this morning, this day, her money was on the new star in town, Jack Wellington.

"What are you doing?" Jack casually walked to the front of the television set, completely blocking Madison's view.

"I think I could ask you the same question. What does it look like I'm doing? I'm trying to watch TV. And if you would remove yourself from the front of it, I would be successful." Madison jerked the blanket up higher over her body.

Jack calmly walked up to Madison and yanked the blanket off her. "Come on. Get up."

Annie watched nervously, knowing how Madison could snap. Maybe she should have warned Jack more. Maybe she should have told him about the boundaries. Then he would have known he just crossed one. Big time.

"I said, get up. I mean it. Get off the damn couch." Jack stared menacingly down to her.

"Jack. Give me back the blanket. I'm cold."

He shook his head no and threw the blanket on the hospital bed. It landed on top of the boxes, with the corner of it hanging off. "If you're so cold, go to your room and get a sweatshirt."

Madison sat still, avoiding Jack's intense face, reluctant to move.

"Let's go. Not kidding, Mad. Get off the couch."

She allowed her head to rest on the arm of the couch and answered Jack without looking in his direction. "I'm tired."

"That's because you've been lounging around on your butt every day. Now, get up."

Madison frowned. "Why? I don't want to get up. I'm rather comfortable. And I'd be even more comfortable if you'd move out of the way so I can watch my TV show!"

"Jesus. You're a pain in the ass, Madison." With that, Jack bent down to her level, scooped Madison up and threw her over his shoulder.

"What the hell is wrong with you? Put me down, Jack!"

Jackson walked them to the door in between the kitchen and living areas. "Shut up."

As Madison lifted her head, she noticed Annie standing in her doorway, watching the entire incident. "Mom! Do something!"

Annie smirked to Madison. "I don't know what to tell you. Except, I guess you better hang on tight." She could have rescued her. But the look on Madison's face suggested this might not be such a bad idea, after all.

Jackson shut the door to the house with his foot, and

started down the flight of old, wooden steps that led to the white sand below.

Madison closed her eyes to block the bright sun. "This isn't funny, you know. I mean, it just isn't. In case you think it is. It is *so* not."

Jack didn't move cautiously with Madison on his shoulder. As a matter of fact, he did the opposite, bouncing her along as he walked them both down to the bottom. Only she couldn't see the huge smile on Jack's face as she ranted and raved.

"Is that what you think, Jack? That this is funny?" Madison looked up and watched them get further and further away from her beloved couch. Her cave. Her comfort zone.

The sand restricted his fast pace and he hesitated, thinking about his next move. He wasn't exactly sure he would succeed in extracting her from the sofa. If he did, he wasn't sure how she'd react to him dragging her outside. Yet, here he was, with Madison over his shoulder. *Now what.*

Before he had time to devise a plan, he tripped and lost his balance, sending both of them crashing into the sand.

Madison screamed loudly on her way down to the ground. She landed on her back with a thud and Jack fell directly on top of her, face down.

Jack quickly estimated their faces were about six inches apart. He watched her catch her breath and wondered what one should do at a time like this. Normally he would say, kiss the girl. But this wasn't a normal situation. "Are you okay?"

Madison nodded her head yes. "I think so."

"Good." So, Madison was okay and he was okay. Why then, was he having so much difficulty moving off her? When it got to the point of near embarrassment, Jack jumped up. "Don't move."

Madison leaned up on her elbows. "What the hell am I supposed to do? Just sit here in the damn sand?"

Jack ran backward and yelled to her, a smile on his face. "Yep."

Madison watched him take off up the stairs two at a time and enter the house. God only knew what he was up to, but she wanted no part of it. She was cold. Okay, so maybe not that cold, but chilly. Madison sat up a little and crossed her legs. The sun did feel nice on her face, but still. She was very content to be inside in the dark. Watching television. She heard children playing in the water twenty or thirty feet away and she opened her eyes, looking at them building sandcastles, running in and out of the waves, having fun. Living.

Madison stood up abruptly. She couldn't have that. Why would Jack make her come outside and see all the things she couldn't have? She angrily dusted the sand off her clothes. As she turned to go back into her self-induced hibernation, Jack reappeared carrying a soccer ball.

"Where do you think you're going?"

Madison folded her arms across her chest. "I'm cold. I'm going inside." She tried to walk around Jack but he stopped her, whipping out a jacket previously hidden behind his back.

"I figured you'd say that. Here. Put this on. Then you won't be cold."

She gave him one of her best eye rolls.

"That's okay. You can thank me later." He extended the jacket out to her a bit further.

Madison ripped the jacket out of his hand and put it on. She zipped it up as far as it would go to make her point. Didn't matter that she looked like an idiot.

Jack started bouncing the soccer ball on his knees. "You wanna know what I'm thinking?" Before she had a chance to answer, Jack moved forward. "I'm thinking you've been relaxing a little too long. Hanging out on the couch or in your bed on your skinny ass all day can turn you into a crabby bitch. That's kind of how I see it anyway."

She tightened the jacket around her body, even though tiny beads of sweat were beginning to form on her lower back and stomach. "Who are you? Fucking Freud now?"

The soccer ball soared high in the air and Jack caught it with his hands. He ignored her rude statement and smiled politely to her. "How about a friendly game of soccer?"

"What if I don't want to play?"

"Maybe I didn't make it totally clear, so allow me to rephrase myself." Jack gave her his best cheeky grin. "You're playing, potty mouth."

Madison's eyes darted everywhere but to Jack's. She was sure there were many ways to handle this situation but only one way came to her mind. She turned her back on Jack and pretended to walk away, counting to three. Jack would follow her. She knew him too well.

Just as she thought, by the count of three, Jack was at her heels. "Hey, Maddie, come on. I didn't—"

Suddenly, she spun around to Jack and knocked the ball out of his hands with a vengeance. The ball flew away from both of them. Betting on Jack being too stunned to move, Madison took off as fast as she could for the still rolling ball. She hadn't lost her touch.

Jack called after her as he watched her chase the ball down. Slowly, but good enough for him. "That was dirty!"

Madison smiled victoriously as she grabbed the ball. "I won!"

"You only wish that was the end of the game, my friend.

I now have to destroy you." Jack took off running toward her in full force.

Madison screamed gleefully and ran, or her version of it, in the other direction. She felt her feet moving faster in the sand and realized she actually enjoyed it.

Annie peeked at Jack and Madison from the balcony above. She made sure she wasn't overly visible to them. Especially Madison. The last thing she wanted to do was ruin whatever was happening down below on the beach.

Jack kicked the ball away from Madison and moved the game a little closer to the water. Madison stopped for a moment and unzipped her jacket. In an instant decision, she took the jacket off and threw it over toward the stairs. So what if it meant she was admitting Jack was right. She was having too much fun. She stopped walking as she heard herself think that. *She was having too much fun.*

He noticed Madison standing very still deep in thought and assumed this meant she was hurt somehow, or maybe she was having trouble breathing. He kicked the ball in her direction and ran after it. "Hey! You okay?"

She looked up and decided it was time to play dirty again. *What the hell?* It was mean, yes, but she instantly calculated she owed him another hit for bringing her outside. Her hand moved across her stomach, then up to her forehead. What it was she was feigning, even she didn't know. But it sure looked good.

Annie was momentarily silenced and on alert, moving a bit closer to the edge of the patio.

Jack reached her and grabbed her by the arms. "What is it? What do you need?"

"I need...I need..." Madison took a deep breath and gathered every ounce of strength she had left. "I need to *win*!"

She kicked the ball away from Jack and ran after it, screaming playfully at the top of her lungs. With a quick glance over her shoulder, she saw him approaching at a ridiculous speed.

"I *cannot* believe you did that!"

Annie breathed a sigh of relief and felt herself chuckle. When her daughter was good, she was really, really good.

Madison reached the ball and just as she was about to kick it into oblivion, Jack grabbed her tightly from behind and hugged her. He placed his foot around her right ankle so she couldn't kick the ball. "Now who won the game?"

Madison screamed out loud. "Me!"

"You think?" Jack squeezed her tighter.

"You're not fair!" She tried desperately to unclench his uncompromising grasp on her body.

"Oh, really? You think you're playing fair? Pretending you're gonna throw up or pass out is not playing fair. Please!"

"I am allowed to play however I see fit. You're the stupid professional. I have to make due with anything I can." Madison could hardly control her giggles by this point.

Jackson gradually released Madison and they both fell to the sand, tired and sweaty. "See? I told you you've been lazy."

"Yeah, maybe just a little." Madison leaned forward and grabbed the soccer ball resting a foot away from where they were sitting. "I get the game ball, right?"

"For now, you do. Tomorrow is a whole new day though." She was smiling as they rested, but Jack noticed Madison suddenly looked paler and her breathing was somewhat different than it was before they started. "Maybe we should go inside. I must admit, you did exceed my goal for your first workout."

But Madison shook her head no. "In a few minutes." She

had her focus on a group of children playing near the ocean waves.

Jack followed her gaze and looked at the kids, then back to Madison. Her eyes hadn't moved a bit. "What're you thinking about?"

"Nothing, really." She took a few strained inhales and leaned back on her elbows, still glued to the children. "I was ...I was just wondering what those kids will grow up to be. You know? Like that one with the glasses and red hair." She pointed to a child wearing big bottle-cap glasses, about seven years old, building a brilliant sandcastle. His hair was bright red, and tight curls covered his entire head. "I think he might grow up to be a scientist. Maybe one that works for the CIA. Or FBI." Madison nodded in agreement with herself. "Do they have scientists? The FBI or CIA?"

Jack had no idea where this was coming from. "I don't know."

"Well, I'm gonna find out." She sat her body upright again.

He couldn't help but laugh a little. "Why do you want to find that out?"

Madison shrugged it off. "Because. Because I can right now."

He stared hard at Madison and glanced back to the kids making their fantasies in the sand. Jack was painfully reminded once again, this time, right now, was all Madison had.

∽ CHAPTER 34 ∽

*M*adison's bedroom was the smaller of the two. It only consisted of a double bed, an old dresser the rental agency called an antique, and a small table pushed up against the bed. Of course, none of the pieces even remotely matched. She had insisted on the smaller room, telling herself she'd be spending most of her time on the couch in front of the television anyway. What did it matter where she slept?

But tonight, as she lay in bed violently coughing, the walls in the tiny room seemed to close in on her. She tried to breathe but couldn't quite catch her breath with the rattling going on in her chest. She repeated the words in her head. *It's a side effect. It's going to be okay. Don't panic. Mom will hear me and come in to help.*

Like an alarm sounding off in her ear, Annie sat upright in her bed, and heard Madison. Within seconds, Annie was sitting next to her on the bed, just like Madison had imagined seconds before. She rubbed her back gently, round and round in circles, like she did when Madison was five and had bronchial pneumonia. "Okay. Shhh. It's okay. It's stopping, see? It's stopping."

Madison's cough began to subside and she took deep breaths again.

Annie grabbed the glass of water on the bedside table and held it up to Madison's mouth. "Small sips, right?"

Madison listened to Annie, taking only slight drinks of liquid. One more minor cough and the spell was over.

Annie tried to smile. "That was fun, huh?"

Madison nodded slightly and sipped more water.

"Want me to stay with you for a while? I don't mind." A little humor never hurt anyone. "I don't have any plans tonight."

"I'm okay." There was a hint of a tiny grin from her daughter.

"You sure?"

"Yeah." Madison laid her head back down on the pillow.

Annie touched her head lightly and confirmed Madison's eyes were closed for good before she left her.

※※※※※※※

David stood near the barbecue, flipping burgers in the fading sunlight.

Madison was resting on a lounge chair nearby with the now ever-present blanket covering her. She took deep breaths every twenty seconds. Deep breaths that would not be considered normal to an average sixteen-year-old girl. She giggled quietly as she caught David dropping a burger on the wood planks.

"Crap." David bent over and picked it up with the spatula.

He glanced over his shoulder inside the house to make sure Annie and Jack weren't watching. When he was convinced he was alone in his minor screw-up, he casually dusted the burger off and threw it back on the barbecue.

Madison's voice startled him. "I saw that."

"I thought you were sleeping." David flipped another patty, successfully this time.

"I guess I woke up. At the perfect time, no less." Madison grinned.

"Our secret?"

Madison nodded, still grinning. She remembered when she gave him the goofy apron he was wearing. He refused to ever barbecue without it. She was ten years old and it was Father's Day. They had been in the rink for way too many hours that week. There must have been a big competition coming up, although which one, Madison couldn't recall. That Sunday, they walked out of the rink and had totally forgotten about getting David a present or even a lame card. The only thing around them open so early was this cheesy little dollar store. Everything there was a buck or under, didn't matter what it was. So Annie and Madison ran in there and grabbed the apron and two cards, one from Madison and one from Annie. They bought cheap wrapping paper and a roll of ten-cent scotch tape that didn't really stick to anything. In the car, they put together David's gift. To this day, David had kept the dumb apron that read, 'THIS BUNNY'S COMING TO TOWN'. There was a picture of a white rabbit that looked borderline retarded. It obviously had been leftover reject stock from Easter earlier that year. Madison would never forget how hard David laughed when he opened it. His feelings probably should have been hurt or he should have been mad even, that no one had thought about his special day until eight o'clock that same morning. Clearly, they hadn't. Otherwise, he would've opened a nice tie. Or maybe a Hickory Farms beef stick with his favorite sweet honey mustard. Instead, he got the bunny apron. Annie must have packed it, hoping it would eventually come in handy. And here he was in front of Madison, wearing it with nothing but love and pride.

Madison tried to sit up in her chair. "Hey, Dad?"

David moved to her and helped Madison prop her upper body higher. "Good?"

She nodded thankfully. "Can I ask you something?"

"Shoot." David returned to the barbeque and gently pushed the hot dogs over to the uncooked sides.

"Is it okay we're staying here? Like, with the money and everything?" She had been aware the finances were an issue and hadn't bothered asking Annie about it. It wasn't her department, but it was David's, and it had been troubling Madison since they arrived at their new temporary home.

David stopped and looked honestly at his daughter. "It's more than okay."

"Are you sure? Because I don't want you to..."

"Maddie. I'm sure. It's really okay. We're fine." *That's all she needed to know,* David thought. *That everything surrounding her is fine. Normal. Good.*

"Do you think, after dinner, we could go for a walk? Like we used to when I was little?"

David smiled. "I was counting on it."

❧❧❧❧❧❧

Aside from Madison being a bit taller, it was the same exact picture she had seen so many times before. Annie smiled at the backs of Madison and David walking on the beach in the distance.

They walked in silence at a sluggish pace, their hands grasped tightly together. Just like they used to.

David stole a sideways peek at his daughter. He noticed every few breaths, one was considerably deeper than the others, one that she tried to make last until she could do it again. She'd gotten worse since he visited last weekend. Annie had told him this already, to prepare him, but he had refused to believe her. After all, she was with Madison day in and day out. She would notice ridiculously small things, and it would be easy for her to blow them out of proportion. But now he could see it clearly. "You all right? You wanna rest for a minute?"

"No. Not yet." Madison trudged on through the warm sand. She wiggled her toes as the grains sifted through them, tickling her feet with each new step.

David refocused his eyes on the ocean. "It's beautiful here, huh?"

"Yeah."

"This was the same beach I took your mom to, you know."

"Really?" It was a genuine response. She hadn't heard this story in particular before, after all these years.

David nodded a yes with a grin. "It was funny. We had been dating for a few months and it was this beautiful, unseasonably warm spring day. So I asked her to come to the beach, just for the day, mind you, because I couldn't afford a house, even for a weekend. So we got up real early, five in the morning, so we could have the whole day. We got here and found the ideal romantic spot, far away from everyone. Laid out the blanket and all. Unpacked snacks and drinks. You name it. Perfect day. Then your mother took off her clothes and she was wearing the ugliest, nastiest looking bathing suit I have ever seen on anyone. Ever."

Madison laughed at her father. She had thought she heard all of the stories about Annie and David. "What did you say?"

"Well, she starts looking at me with this...this face. Totally flirting with me. I thought to myself, get it together, and just remember how cute she looked in her sexy skating outfit or in her tight designer jeans. I kept trying to picture her without her grandmother's bathing suit on."

"How old was she?"

"I think maybe seventeen. But I tell ya. That was it. One look from her with her nasty bathing suit...I knew I would spend the rest of my life with her. I already knew I was in love. But that day..." He let his voice dissolve into thin air as he remembered.

Madison interrupted his daydream. "Was she in love too, you think?"

David smiled. "I hope so. She said yes when I asked her to marry me."

Madison's breathing became more labored and David noticed instantly. "Maybe she just figured she wouldn't ever get anybody else to like her with her ugly swimsuit."

"Thank you for your support." David stopped Madison and made her sit down in the sand with him. "I think it's time for a rest."

Madison didn't argue and sat down with silent relief.

They both gazed out to the ocean.

David kept his attention on the waves, but his words were directed to Madison. "Listen, Maddie. I know things have been really hard for you and Mom lately. I'm not saying it's anyone's fault because it's no one's fault. But your Mom is really trying honey, to make things...well, as easy as possible for you. All of this, this was all her idea. She was adamant about it." He hesitated, not really knowing whether he had Annie's consent to continue on. When Madison didn't stop him, David ventured forward. "She uh…she thinks you blame her for everything…even the things she had no control over." David waited for what seemed to be minutes.

"I don't blame her. I don't. It's just…I don't know." Madison shrugged her shoulders up to her ears and quickly released them back down. "She wanted me to do so well. To be this huge success and it's only because she wasn't. Because she didn't do it. And now…now none of it matters, I guess."

David nodded. Of course Madison would assume that. She had no idea otherwise. Annie had refused to tell her just how good she used to be. Or how close she came to being that huge success. Or why she stopped skating in the first place. She wanted Madison to know nothing about it. *It is all about Madison, and not me*, she would tell David at least once a year. When there would be an issue that would arise about the skating, and every time, Annie refused to bring up her own past. Even if it would have made things easier on her, Annie would not have it. As David sat on the beach with Madison, he decided it was pointless to keep anything from his daughter. And maybe, just maybe, it might help the dangerous strain between Annie and Madison. "She could've gone to the Olympics. She was a great skater, Maddie. The best I had ever seen, before you started to skate."

She turned to her father. "I don't get it. Why did she stop then if she really was that good? Did you make her quit or something?"

"No."

"Then why did she?"

David turned to Madison slowly. "Because, Madison. Because she had you."

Madison let his words sink deep into her brain. An uncontrollable frown appeared on her forehead. "She quit because of me?"

"No. She quit because she wanted to be a mom. Your mom. That was far more important to her than any Olympic gold medal."

They allowed the silence to fill the space between them. David thinking about the crucial information he'd just given. Madison thinking about receiving it.

David leaped to a kneeling position. "Let's go. Hop on."

He cannot be serious, Madison thought. He used to carry her on his back when they walked too far when she was six. She would jump on his back and he'd give her a piggy-back ride all the way back to their house. "I can walk, Daddy."

David met her eyes. "I know you can. I'm not doing this for you."

Madison lifted her body off the sand and hopped onto David's back.

He raised himself to a standing position carefully, fearful of tossing his daughter to the wayside.

"Dad?" She whispered in his ear.

David glanced over his shoulder to Madison.

"Thanks. For everything."

David smiled to her. "No thanks needed, Maddie-girl." But he was glad she said it anyway. "You better hold on." David trotted down the beach, with his daughter giggling happily on his back.

Madison found it hard to sleep. She wasn't in any more pain than usual and her breathing was fair. Which was to say things were okay with her for the moment.

A ceramic angel nightlight lit up the bedroom. She glanced around her room. Probably her last room. Annie had brought little knick-knacks from their home and placed them all around the beach house to make it more homey and familiar. Madison wondered what Annie did with the garbage bags full of her things. She had left them in her room, tied up tightly. She would've brought them down to the recycling bin had she been able to actually lift the plastic sacks off the floor.

She had taken one item out of a bag after Annie stormed out that night.

Madison's mind played her words over and over. The ones she had spoken to her mother the night before they left for the beach. Then she recalled the conversation she had with her father after dinner earlier that night. Why had Annie never told her how good of a skater she used to be? That she too could've gone to the Olympics?

That she gave it all up for her? To be her mom?

And then Madison repeatedly posed the last question to herself, through what was left of the night.

What have I done to my mother?

CHAPTER 35

She could hardly keep her eyes open at breakfast. Even Jack noticed she wasn't as energetic during their daily work out as she had been over the past few weeks. She blamed it on the simple fact that she hadn't slept well the night before and that was really the truth.

There just happened to be another truth.

She was not feeling well, aside from the obvious. She was having more and more difficulty breathing and began keeping it to herself as much as she possibly could. There was no need to prematurely alarm anyone. In all fairness, she had been overextending herself more than she should have with Jack there keeping her company.

And the last thing she was about to do was give up now.

Annie had convinced Madison to lie down, for just a little while, after lunch. She didn't need much convincing. It was a relief to go rest for even an hour. Before she realized it, an hour had turned into three.

"You had a nice nap for someone who wasn't even tired."

Annie dumped a cup and a half of flour into a huge glass mixing bowl.

Madison yawned as she exited her bedroom, dressed in sweats and the ever-present bandana on her head. "I guess I was tired. What're you making?"

"Cookies."

"Chocolate chip?"

"What do you think?" Annie smiled. They were Madison's favorite and they were the only cookies Annie thought she'd ever made in her lifetime.

Madison smiled and made her way closer to Annie and the cookie dough.

Annie pulled a chair over from the table and placed it next to where she was working. "Thanks, Mom." Madison held onto the chair for support.

Annie savored those two words in her head. *'Thanks, Mom.'* She hadn't heard Madison say that in a very long time and mean it.

Madison used the seat of the chair like a mini ladder and crawled up on the counter, watching Annie mix the sticky ingredients in the bowl. She stuck her finger in the dough and played with it.

Annie eyed her cautiously. She knew the cookie dough was Madison's favorite. She also knew too much of it, and maybe even a bit of it, could make her feel very sick. She couldn't digest most foods any more. That had started recently and had already gotten worse. Annie became the queen of finding new ways for Madison to eat applesauce, banana squash, and ice cream. And when all else failed, a jar of baby food usually did the trick.

Madison took a ball of cookie dough and lifted it to her mouth.

"Not too much, Maddie. It'll upset your stomach."

For a moment, Madison thought about the possible out-come and then threw the dough into her mouth with a smile. She closed her eyes, wanting desperately to remember exactly how it tasted. When she opened her eyes, she found Annie staring at her.

"Well? Did I do good?"

"You did great, Mom." Madison continued to pick small pieces of dough from the edges of the bowl. Almost as an afterthought, she turned around and looked in the living area. "Hey. Where's Jack?"

Annie knew this would come up. She had thought of all the possible answers to give Madison, and none of them sounded very good now. "He, uh, he had to go into town for this thing that he...um...something he wanted. Or some-thing." *Oh, that sounded really smart*, Annie mused to herself. *Something he wanted or something?* Annie busied herself with the recipe she knew by heart. "Here you go. Time for the chips. You want to put them in?"

Madison shook her head yes but with a growing frown on her face. "Well, what'd he want to get? The something. What was it?"

She handed Madison the bag of chips. Maddie dumped them in and then stirred with all her might.

Annie busied herself throwing measuring cups and tea-spoons already washed back into the sink. Anything to not give this conversation all the attention it deserved. "I just...I'm not really sure. Really. He didn't say."

"Well, when did he leave?" Madison barely moved the dough in the bowl.

Annie moved to the stove and checked the oven tempera-ture. "He...I think he left when you went in for a nap."

Madison carefully slid off the counter, using her chair again as a stepping stool. "That was over three hours ago. He left three hours ago?"

"I think so, Madison. Maybe, uh...no. I really don't remember." This definitely was not the talk she wanted to have, and it was going to be an extremely troubled conversation if it continued.

Madison paced back and forth a few times before stopping and directly asking Annie to her face. "Do you think he left for good?"

Annie stopped her pretend interest of cookie-baking and turned to Madison. "Do you honestly think he would do that to you? Leave you, without saying goodbye?"

"Maybe." Madison's head dropped along with her voice. "Maybe he got scared. You know...of being around me."

"I don't think so." Annie gave the cookie dough a good few turns before she plopped spoonfuls of it on the baking sheet and stuck it in the oven. Here it goes. She might as well try to change this subject to an even more sensitive one. "It looks like you two are...I don't know, you both look..."

Madison gave her mother one of those irritated faces. The one Annie was hoping she wouldn't get. "What? What do we look like?"

"You just look like you're getting closer. That's all."

"We can't be. We can't." Madison walked away from Annie. And on her way out, she snipped, "Something's burning."

Annie turned to the oven and noticed the potholder sticking out of it. She left it in there when she slid the cookie sheet in. "Shit."

Madison had taken her place on the couch watching television, her eyes on the screen but her mind on Jackson.

He had not returned that day. He hadn't even called and it was now well into the evening hours. *The O.C.* was about to start in a few minutes and they hadn't missed one episode since they'd been at the beach.

Annie approached her timidly with a gift bag in her hand. "I got you something."

The commercials were on so Madison concluded it wouldn't hurt to answer her mother. She wasn't sure what exactly Annie knew about the situation with Jack, but Madison knew her mother knew something. For that, for not telling her what was going on, Madison had been keeping her conversations with Annie to a minimum.

"What is it?"

Annie sat down on the edge of the couch next to Madison. "I guess you should open it." She handed the bag over to Madison.

Madison couldn't do this lying down and sat up languidly. She poked her head into the bag and saw only white.

"Take it out."

Madison stuck her hand in the bag and touched the softest of cotton. She slowly pulled out a long, flowing, white nightgown. She had never seen anything like it before.

Annie tried to smile. "I figured we wore out most of your pajamas in the hospital and since Jack is going to be here with us…Well, anyway, I thought this would look really pretty on you."

"What makes you so sure he is going to be here? He might have left."

Annie removed the blanket from Madison's legs. "Why don't you go try it on?"

Madison wearily rose from the couch and moved to the bathroom. She left the door slightly ajar and changed out of her sweats. She allowed the nightgown to slide gracefully over her shoulders and land in perfect position around her neck. Madison caught a glimpse of herself in the mirror and stared. Her hair had started to grow back slightly and her face resembled a porcelain doll. *It's a weird time to feel beautiful,* she thought quietly. But she did.

Annie's voice came from just outside the door. "Let me see."

Madison pushed the door open as wide as it would go and held the gown out for Annie with both her hands. Then she let the long material fall to the ground.

To Annie, Madison looked like an angel. The bottom of the nightgown dragged slightly on the ground, giving Madison the appearance that she was floating.

"Do I look stupid? It's more like a princess costume, not pajamas."

All Annie could do was shake her head no vehemently. She was aware she probably was making too big a deal out of this but she also knew this was the closest she would ever come to seeing her daughter in a prom dress, or a wedding gown. "You look so beautiful."

Madison let a small laugh escape. "Mom. It's just a nightgown."

"I know." She laughed through the tears she tried to keep away. Annie wiped her face with her hands and smiled broadly to Madison. "Okay. You ready?"

"For what?"

"Come here." Annie walked to the door leading to the beach and opened it.

Madison stopped walking. "I'm in my new nightgown. I can't go outside like this. "

"Yeah, you can. Why not?" Annie threw a smile in Madison's direction and exited.

Madison shrugged and followed Annie to the door. Her mother had done some strange things before this, but tonight took the cake.

Annie took Madison's hand and led her outside. She walked in front of Madison, making her stay directly behind her body. Annie shot a look to Madison. "Okay. Time to close your eyes."

"You've got to be kidding me."

Annie stopped walking and faced Madison. "Come on. Close them."

"They are closed." Madison lifted her chin and showed Annie her tightly shut eyes.

Annie carefully led her down the steps. "Almost there."

"I cannot believe I'm walking around outside, at night, in my pajamas."

Annie stopped at the bottom of the stairs with a smile Madison could not yet see.

"Can I look now?" Madison waited patiently, her eyes still shut.

Annie looked first at the sight below them. When she got the signal it was okay, Annie turned to Madison. "You can look now." She stepped aside to allow Madison the full view.

Madison gradually opened her eyes and focused in the semi-dark evening. Her mouth dropped open in slow motion. "Oh my God."

There on the beach in front of her was an enormous party tent. Tiny white lights covered the tent and extended out to huge areas on the beach. She could hear music playing softly from inside.

And then she saw him.

Jackson exited the tent, wearing a black tuxedo with long tails and a top hat to match.

Annie touched Madison's arm gently and took a few steps backward, making room for Jack to approach her.

Madison was astounded. Beyond astounded. Shocked, confused and completely blown away. All of those things, all combined, and all at once.

Little by little, Jackson walked to Madison. He smiled shyly and took off his hat. With his fingers tracing the rim of the hat, Jack looked at Madison seriously. "We, uh...we never did make it to that dance."

"What dance? The one you didn't even ask me to?" She couldn't resist.

"I would've taken you, for the record, and not because I had to as your only friend."

Annie started her walk back up the steps to the house. "I'll be inside if you guys need anything."

Jack waited until Annie was out of ear shot and smiled at Madison. "You look beautiful."

"You shouldn't have done this. I mean, if you did it to make me feel better like some sympathy thing or whatever..."

Jack interrupted her with a touch on her arm. He let his fingers gradually drag down her forearm and land in her hand. "Madison. I did this for one reason and you know it. I wanted us to have this chance. To be together."

Madison dropped her head low. There was only one thing that this meant; the tent, the tux, the nightgown...and Jack looking at her like he was.

It could only mean one thing.

"Mad? You know how I feel about you, don't you?"

She refused to lift her head to him and simply shook a no. "We shouldn't be doing this. You shouldn't. You can't."

Jack dropped his hat on the sand and gently placed his hands on her cheeks. Bit by bit, he lifted her reluctant face up to meet his. "Shouldn't be doing what? Can't what?"

It came out louder than she expected it to. With tears she never could have imagined. "*Be* like this! Be *us* like this!" She moved her hands to her face and tried with all her might to remove his hands. "It's only going to get worse, Jack. And I just don't want to..." She cut her own voice off from continuing.

"Madison. Tell me."

"I—I don't want to hate you for feeling the way I do about you." She said it. The words she had implanted in her head since she became ill.

"Why would that make you hate me?"

"Because." She stopped to catch her breath. This had to come out the perfect way, not only for her, but for Jack. "Because I don't want to feel this happy with you and know that it won't last. Because it can't, Jack. It can't last. And I don't want to look at you and wonder who you'll feel like this with some day when I...when I'm not here anymore."

Jack looked more deeply into Madison's eyes than he ever had before. "But that won't ever happen." Jack shook his head in frustration. If he could only make her see, make her understand. "God, Madison. Don't you know? After everything?" He took a deep breath. "It has always been you. Always."

Madison looked at the ground. Her hands fell to her sides, giving up on removing Jack's hands from her cheeks.

"Madison." He lifted her head back up once again, making her face his reality. "It has always been you." Then Jack did something he had waited all of his life to do.

He kissed Madison.

First on the forehead, then ever so gently he moved his lips down both sides of her face, catching all of the salty tears from her eyes before they had a chance to fall further down. "Now. Are you going to go to this damn dance with me or not." Jack extended his arm around Madison and helped her into the tent.

She was speechless when she went inside. Jack had strung the white lights all over the inside of the tent too. He had baskets of flowers placed in the sand every five feet. Next to the music, he set up a table with two chairs. There was another long table full of drinks and snacks, and applesauce, and a plate of Annie's chocolate chip cookies. It was the most beautiful place she had ever seen and Annie had known about it all along. "I don't know what to say."

"Say you'll dance with me." Jack held her hand tightly.

Madison smiled up at Jack. "I'll dance with you."

Jack quickly moved to the stereo, letting go of Madison only for a split second, and changed the CD currently playing to a slow song he had already picked out, praying he would get the chance to use it.

Madison looked down at her nightgown and smiled at the thought of what she was doing. What they were doing and what they could have been doing for years and years. She watched him walk back to her in the middle of their private sand dance floor and wondered if this sensation she was feeling was the same one she had fought off all of her life.

Jack cautiously wrapped his arms around Madison and they danced together for the first time. "Are you okay? I'm not hurting you, am I?"

Madison shook her head no into his chest and closed her eyes.

"Madison?"

She lifted her eyes to meet Jack's, already staring down at her.

There was the longest minute of silence before Jack's words were spoken out loud. He had rehearsed them every day of his life, knowing in his heart he would one day say them to Madison. "I love you."

He leaned down, temporarily stopping their dance, and kissed Madison on the lips. Without hurry at first, then it became more passionate, more intense. Jack and Madison finally pulled back from one another and looked at each other with that identical connection they had ten years ago, on the day they first met.

⁂

When Jack had come to Annie with the idea, she wasn't totally convinced this would be such a grand thing to do. Who knew how Madison would react to something like this? Did anyone have the right to put this kind of pressure on her? Annie had called David after Jack told her how deeply he felt about Madison and repeated exactly what Jack had said to her earlier. He was in love with Madison. Always had been. And he wanted to be able to tell her before it was too late.

Annie almost fell over. Not that she and David hadn't talked about it, even hoped for it, but *now*? David said to let Jack do whatever he wanted. If Madison didn't like it, they both knew Jack would be the first to know.

Annie walked out onto the balcony and looked down at the tent below. Inside there were two people destined to be soul mates. And one of them was dying. And that was just not fair.

She allowed her eyes to travel up above to the star-filled sky. Annie was never one to be at church regularly on Sundays. But lately she found herself talking to God, to the angels she hoped were above, watching over them. The same few statements, wishes, prayers were repeated in hopes the recurring ones were listened to more than the others. *Give me more time with Madison. Don't let her suffer. Take good care of her when she gets to you.* Then it hit Annie like a ton of bricks.

Why her? Why Madison?

Just as her thoughts turned into an argument with the sky, she heard Jack's frightened voice.

"Annie! Annie!! Come here quick!"

⌇⌇⌇⌇⌇⌇⌇

Jack stood in the doorframe, still dressed in his tuxedo shirt, a few top buttons undone.

Annie stood next to Madison's bed, administering a shot of morphine into her arm. "Almost done, baby. Okay? Shhh. Almost done."

Madison's eyes were barely open but she winced in pain as the needle pierced her skin. Her voice was hoarse and weak when she spoke. She turned her head slightly to Annie. "I couldn't stop coughing. I couldn't breathe."

Annie withdrew the needle and threw it into a garbage pail near the bed. She gently rubbed her arm. "I know. It's okay, honey. It's okay now. You want anything?"

Madison didn't notice Jack standing in the doorway. "It hurts, Mom."

"I know." Annie looked at Madison sadly. "Give it a few minutes, okay? It'll stop hurting pretty soon."

This was a bad one. The worst one yet, Annie thought. She quickly tried to calculate the severity of this episode compared to the past few and the time it took to stop it. How much morphine did it take, and how much did this spell take out of her little girl?

They were running out of time, and Annie knew it more than anyone. Maybe even more than Madison.

"You okay while I go call Dad?" Annie adjusted the covers over Madison.

Madison weakly nodded a yes. "Where's Jack?"

Jack took a step into her room. "I'm right here."

Annie walked to the door and touched Jack on the arm lightly. "I'll be right back."

"Mom?" Her voice was barely heard.

Annie turned back in Madison's direction.

Madison tried her hardest to make her lips smile. "Thanks for the pretty nightgown."

"You're welcome, baby." Annie exited, leaving Madison and Jack alone.

Jack moved closer to Madison, finally sitting down on the bed next to her. He lifted up Madison's hand and kissed it, then held it tight in both of his hands.

"I'm sorry." Her speech slowed down as the morphine kicked in.

"Why are you sorry? You didn't do anything."

"I did. I ruined your beautiful night, your beautiful dance." She inhaled quickly and then resumed her normal breathing. Then after a long pause, "I'm sorry for being sick."

"First of all, you could never ruin anything for me." Jack kissed her hand again and smiled. "And second of all, I said and did everything I wanted to do."

Madison tried to laugh. "So this was like, a planned thing? What did you do...make a list?"

Jack returned her laugh. "Yep. A long list."

"Really. And that kiss? How long have you been planning that kiss?"

Jackson's smile faded and he looked down briefly, slightly embarrassed. He answered Madison when he lifted his head back up and looked her in the eyes. "Since I was seven."

"That's a serious time to wait."

"I didn't mind."

"Neither did I." A slow and sincere smile crossed over Madison's face. Her eyes began to close and she fought her heavy lids with each blink. "Will you stay with me for a while?"

"I'll stay with you forever." Jackson kicked off his shoes and cuddled up next to Madison in her bed. He draped his arm behind her, cradling her head in his shoulder. "That was another thing on my list, by the way. To stay with you forever."

Madison was sure his voice was the most beautiful thing she had ever heard. Her eyes closed for the night but a smile remained on her face. He bent his head down and softly kissed her on the forehead. It came out more mumbling than talking, but Jack heard her all the same. "I love you too, Jackson."

Jack smiled and closed his eyes, completely content, finally hearing the words he'd waited his whole life to hear.

⌒⌒⌒⌒⌒⌒⌒

"Your dad says he loves you and he's—" Annie stopped talking abruptly and froze. She stared at the picture in front of her for what might have been minutes. Jack and Madison were sound asleep in bed. Jack's big arms wrapped so protectively around her Maddie, their Maddie.

Then she noiselessly moved to the comforter at the edge of the bed and put it carefully over Jack and Madison.

CHAPTER 36

Jack kicked the soccer ball between his feet, continually glancing up in Madison's direction and each time he did, he found her in the same position, looking back at him.

He knew before Annie even said anything to him. Things were getting worse.

No one acknowledged the difference in Madison's breathing out loud. No one mentioned she was getting so weak it was hard for her to take more than three steps in a row without pausing. Each of them knew what it meant. Every morning, though, he insisted she come outside with him. Even if it was just for an hour. Then even if it was for a few minutes. Each day, he would come down to the beach first and get things ready for her. He set out an enormous blanket for her to sit on, a few comfy pillows in the event she wanted to, or had to, lie down. He would bring water bottles and a jacket and books and whatever magazines were around the couch.

And he would also bring a syringe full of morphine. Just in case.

Annie had showed him how to give Madison a shot in the event she wasn't there or couldn't get to her in time. Jack thanked God he had yet to prove his newfound medical knowledge.

Madison smiled to Jack and gave him a playful wave from her blanket. Her voice was small but sarcastic just the same. Just the way he liked it. "You call that talent? Kicking the ball back and forth?"

Jack pushed the ball gently to her and followed it over. "You think you're cute, don't you?"

Madison caught the rolling ball with her hands and clutched it tightly to her chest. "No." She giggled. "I know I am."

"Give me the ball." They both knew he could care less about the soccer ball.

"Make me." She rolled over onto her stomach, with the ball lodged underneath her body.

"Little girl, you are in some serious trouble." Jackson knelt down on the blanket next to her, careful not to hurt her in any way.

"You only wish." More giggles from Madison.

God, he loved hearing that, her laughter. Jackson delicately rolled her over onto her back and grabbed the ball with both hands, creating a mild game of tug-of-war.

Madison suddenly let the ball go, sending Jack flying backward onto his butt, and sending more laughter into the air.

Jack knew it would make her giggle and he wasn't beyond embarrassing himself to do it. "You're laughing? Is that what I hear from you? You're laughing at me? I'll give you something to laugh about." Jack moved in close to Madison with as mean of a face as he could manage. Then he leaned in and kissed her lovingly on the mouth.

They separated slightly, allowing only a few inches between their mouths. Madison grinned. "And that was supposed to make me laugh?"

"No. I just couldn't resist."

"Good. Cause I was gonna say, you'd make a real shitty comedian."

"Okay. Now see? You shouldn't have gone there. Now you're really gonna get it."

Madison grabbed his shirt and pulled him on top of her. She kissed him this time. Jackson swore to himself right then and there, he would never forget that morning, or that kiss.

∞∞∞∞∞∞

Annie opened the box and looked inside. After checking off another mark on her list, she closed the flaps up and put the package on the floor by the hospital bed. She looked at the open box of morphine and put it in front of the other boxes. She double-checked the IV bags and the oxygen tanks that had been moved to the floor in front of the bed. The boxes sat in different, yet specific sections all around her. With the bed now clear of all cardboard, she grabbed the sheets neatly folded next to the pillow and began making the bed.

"Need any help?" Jack had been watching her from the doorway of Madison's bedroom. He had stayed with Madison until she had fallen asleep, and then he stayed some more. Just to watch her be at peace for a few minutes.

"Thanks. But, no. I was...I was just getting things organized. You know? In groups. So I can be sure I know where everything is and get everything off the bed in case Maddie should..." They both were aware her voice trailed off. They both understood what she was trying to say.

Jack approached her while he talked. "Do you think she will need it? I know she will eventually, but soon?"

Annie tucked in the sheet at the foot of the bed, hospital corners. "Yeah. I think she will, Jack." Annie paused and ironed the sheet out with her hands, straightening every possible wrinkle.

Jack moved up next to her and did the same tucking in at the head of the bed. No words needed. He had heard Annie say she didn't need the help, but he also knew Annie and how exceedingly hard this must be for her. They knew what this meant, getting things prepared. What words could possibly be said to make it any less difficult? Jack took a step back when the bed was completely made.

Annie moved to the boxes under the bed, this time setting them up in an organized fashion. Out of the corner of her eye, she saw Jack standing there, staring at the empty bed. "You wanna help me? I've got to organize these boxes." She didn't need any help but the look on Jack's face said he needed something to do.

"Sure."

She called off names of various medications and showed Jack where to find the name on the top of the boxes. Jack found the one she needed and slid it over to Annie. When they finished the task at hand, Annie looked at Jack. She needed to keep busy as much as he did. "I bought some cards in town today. You up for a game?"

"Okay."

Annie tried to let a small grin out. "You should know, I like to win."

"And you should know...so do I."

She could see it in his face, the pain, the fear and the sadness. She knew because she'd had it written all over her own face for weeks, for months.

Jack walked over to where Annie was standing and she caught him in her arms, just as he fell into her. She let Jack cry on her shoulder and then let him cry some more. She gave him a couple of squeezes and then with her arm around his shoulder for comfort, silently led him out to the balcony.

👁️👁️👁️👁️👁️👁️👁️

Annie threw her cards down on the table and looked over at Madison. "I swear to God, you've got to be cheating." She wrote down their scores in a notebook off to her right.

Rummy had become a great way to pass the time. Even Madison had tired of the reruns on television. They had gotten fairly inventive over the last week. Some nights, Annie would read to Madison from a book she loved or Jackson would sit with her and read a magazine out loud. Some nights, it was an all out war with Scrabble or Monopoly. Other nights, the three of them would simply sit on the balcony and watch the sun fade into the sea.

It was warm outside, but Madison wore flannel pajamas and a wool blanket over her legs. She touched the new addition to her wardrobe, her oxygen tank. The tube sat in her nose all of the time now. It took a few days to get used to and a lot of urging on Annie's part, but Madison finally agreed. She had been outside with Annie playing rummy for over an hour now, watching her mother more than the cards sitting in her hand.

The sun lit up Annie's face and Madison wondered if her

mother had ever or could ever look more beautiful than she did at that very moment.

Annie's concentration was on the cards in her hand. She shuffled them more than enough times and dealt them like she had spent years in Vegas. She picked up her new cards and looked at them excitedly. The smile was soon replaced by a frown. "Why do I get the shittiest hand when I play you? Can you answer me that?"

Madison laughed quietly. It had become a standing joke with them. Every time she played a game with Annie, Annie lost. Didn't matter if it was rummy or Scrabble, Madison won.

Annie noticed Madison's cards still sitting on the table in front of her. "Let's go. I got a game to win and dinner to cook."

Madison picked up her cards without taking her eyes off Annie. "Promise me something?"

Annie didn't look up from her cards. "Lay it on me."

"Promise me..." Madison tried to get as much air in her lungs as she could. What she had to say couldn't wait any longer and probably should've been said a very long time ago. "Promise me when I...when I'm..."

Annie lifted her head up, inch by inch, to meet Madison's already watery eyes.

"When I'm not here anymore, with you...promise me you won't feel bad. 'Cause you shouldn't, Mom. Ever. I—I said some really awful things to you that I—I never meant. All my life, all I wanted to be, was to be like you." Madison tried unsuccessfully not to cry in front of Annie. But the only thing that concerned her now was finishing. Before it was too late. "I want...I wanted to skate like you. I wanted so much to grow up to be..." Madison could not find a way to finish her sentence. "I wanted to skate. I did. I wanted to skate every day. With you there…with you there next to me. You have to believe I didn't miss out on anything, Mom. I didn't. I only wish…I wish I could've won. Not for me, for you." *Almost there, one more big breath.* "For us. So, promise me you'll never feel bad because I got to have something no other girl will ever have. I got to have you as my best friend." Madison looked down at her cards, tears streaming down her face. She did it. She had spoken every word she had rehearsed.

Never in a million years could Annie have been prepared for Madison to say those words to her.

"Oh. Rummy." Madison laughed while she cried and gently laid down three aces and a two, three, four and five of hearts.

⌒⌒⌒⌒⌒⌒⌒

Madison lay on the couch with Annie by her side. Annie turned the television volume down so it could barely be heard.

Annie massaged Madison's legs gently and watched her as she closed her eyes. She did it a few times a day, the massaging. "How's that. Better?"

"Yeah. Thanks."

Jack walked in carrying a large pizza box and a brown paper bag. "Anybody hungry?"

Annie laughed quietly. "As long as you're not the one that's cooking." She looked at Madison's face and caught the hint of a smirk.

Jack put the pizza down on the table and brought a flyer over to Annie. He stopped briefly to kiss Madison on the cheek and continued moving to the kitchen while talking, getting plates out for dinner. "I thought maybe we could go. It looks like fun, doesn't it?"

Madison's eyes opened when Jack kissed her, but she couldn't see what Annie was holding in her hands. "What is it?"

Annie read the flyer. "It's a parade. This weekend, in town."

Madison's face lit up. "Can we go?"

"We should see how you're feeling and..."

Madison looked at her mother. It didn't matter how she was feeling.

Annie put her best face forward and smiled at Madison. "Sure. Yeah. We can go."

Madison giggled as she readjusted the oxygen tube in her nose. "Even if you have to carry me?"

"Even if that."

She held on to Annie for support as she sat up a little on the couch. She peeked over the back and addressed Jack. "Hey, soccer jerk! Did you hear that? You better start working your lazy ass out to carry me."

Jack grinned to Madison as he opened the pizza box. "Who's calling who lazy?"

Madison smiled adoringly.

Annie got up first and bent down to help Madison. This time, Madison accepted her assistance without missing a beat. Annie wheeled the oxygen tank in one hand and practically carried Madison to the table with her other arm, sitting her down in the chair gently.

Madison took a deep breath and smelled the open box of pizza.

Jack carried over a bowl of applesauce and plate of dry lightly toasted bread and put them in front of Madison.

"Try this one. Old Mrs. Sally Ginter supposedly makes the best homemade applesauce in a three hundred mile radius. Some big secret about the ingredients she uses."

Madison picked up her spoon but her focus was on the pizza. "I really miss pizza."

"It's gonna make you sick, Mad. You can't digest it." Annie took a slice out of the box and dropped it on her plate. "Honey, I told you we don't have to get pizza if it's too hard for you."

"No, Mom. Really, I'm fine with it. I was just saying I miss it. That's all. Have some for me." Madison stuck her spoon in the bowl and tasted the applesauce. She made a big deal for Jack's benefit. "This is the best goddamn applesauce I have ever had. You think if you slept with old Mrs. Sally Ginter she'd give up her secret recipe to you?"

Jack smiled and sat down, moving his chair as close as he could to Madison without sitting on her lap. "I'm working on it, actually. I'm thinking she wants me."

Annie groaned. "You are both disgusting. Disgusting foul pigs." She took a bite out of her pizza slice. "Poor old Sally Ginter."

As the three of them cracked up in unison, Annie casually closed the pizza box and pushed it to the edge of the table, away from Madison.

CHAPTER 37

They had rarely been to town, minus the check-ups with the doctor. But they never stayed after the appointments to walk around. Madison was usually too exhausted from the trip to do much else afterward.

But today was all about the parade. The main road was filled with townspeople from miles around and tourists from neighboring states. The quaint shops lining the road had their windows and storefronts decorated for the town's one hundred-year-old birthday.

By the time they arrived, there were already lines of people waiting for the parade to start. Annie and Jack fought their way through the crowd to get a spot for Madison. Annie cursed herself for not thinking ahead. With the oxygen tube a definite necessity and no longer just for comfort, it took them twice as long to get anywhere.

Annie managed the tank through the crowd with Jack and Madison right by her side. Madison adjusted the oxygen tube in her nose. "I hate this thing."

"Yeah, but it's helping you breathe and that's always a good thing, right?" Annie gave Madison a quick smile before throwing a nasty look toward a staring couple.

. "I know what it does. I just…people are looking at me like I'm some kind of freak. They don't even know me." Madison lowered her head slightly.

Jack saw a larger group gathered up ahead. Annie looked over at Madison to make sure Jack had a tight grasp on her. Jack casually tightened the space between his arm and Madison, pulling her as close to his body as possible. He leaned into her. "Give 'em the finger. Those people who are looking at you weird. Just pop them one."

Madison looked up at Jack. "You cannot be serious."

Jack laughed out loud as they passed through one large cluster after another. "What? Why not? Just smile at them, give them a nice nod of the head, maybe even a, 'hey, how are you,' and then, give 'em the finger."

Madison sent a glance to Annie and rolled her eyes. "He's lost it. For real this time."

Annie smiled at Madison mischievously. "I think Jack's right. Give 'em the finger. They shouldn't be looking at you like that. So, I agree. It's a free country, isn't it?"

For the perfect trial run, an old man and woman approached Madison, Annie, and Jack. The woman gawked at Madison and rudely nudged the man she was walking next to. They both stared at Madison and the man looked away. The woman couldn't seem to peel her eyes off the odd three-some coming her way. Just as they were about to pass by Jackson, he gave her a big cheesy smile. "Hey. How are you?"

Then Jack promptly gave the old woman the finger.

The woman's mouth flew open, completely horrified. She pushed her husband quickly out of the way.

Annie and Madison laughed out loud hysterically.

Jack grinned. Again, it was all about the laugh he so desperately wanted to hear from Madison. "See? I told you. It works."

Annie spotted part of an empty bench a half a block away. "There's a seat up there. Can you make it?"

Madison nodded. She was exhausted already and they hadn't even watched the parade yet. But that really was fine with her. Her motive today wasn't the parade. She would hopefully accomplish something far greater than any parade ever would. And she didn't care how horrible she felt, or how sick she was. Nothing would have stopped her from coming to town today.

Jack sat Madison down on the bench carefully. "I'm gonna go move some people around so you can see. I'll be right back. You okay?"

Madison nodded again. Speaking at this point simply took up so much of her energy. Out of the corner of her eye, Madison noticed a large flower shop and her eyes lit up when she saw their huge bay windows full of balloons and gifts.

Madison watched Jack take off into the congested crowd. She looked over her shoulder to Annie, standing behind her, adjusting the oxygen tank.

"That feel right?"

"Yeah."

Annie sat down next to Madison and put her arm around her with a squeeze. "You glad we came?"

"Yeah, I am." Madison eyed the street across from them. She spotted a huge old-fashioned ice cream parlor. "You think they have milkshakes in there?"

"Where?" Annie's eyes darted from store to store.

"Over there. Across the street."

Annie frowned slightly. "Why? You want one?"

"Yeah. It sounds really good right now for some reason."

"You're kidding, right? Maddie, the parade is about to start any minute."

Madison took a few deep breaths. "Forget it. I don't need one. It's okay."

Annie got up off the bench. There could be the running of the bulls about to plow through town and she would still go to the ice cream store for her daughter. "I try to get you to drink a freaking shake everyday and the one time you want one, there's a damn parade coming and I can't cross the street. I'm probably going to get arrested, you know."

"Did I mention I want vanilla?"

Annie grinned. "You gonna be all right? Maybe I should wait for Jack to come back here before I go."

"Mom. I'm fine. Have oxygen, will travel." She patted her tank lightly for her mother's benefit.

"Okay. Just stay put." Annie exited in a hurry.

The moment Annie was out of sight, Madison took off her jacket and carefully removed her oxygen tube. She lifted it up over her head and placed it on the bench, then used her jacket to cover it. She slowly and painfully stood up and stepped a foot away from the bench. She did a quick scan of the nearby area.

An older man sat on the end of her bench by himself. Madison smiled politely to him. "Excuse me? Would you mind watching my things and possibly holding my seat on the bench? I'll be right back."

The man looked at her sympathetically, but without pity. He had watched her take off the tube. He watched in anxiety as she stood up and leaned into him without any help. He also saw her eyes and they told him she needed to do something crucial. That she needed his help to accomplish something very important.

He nodded to Madison and made sure he saw exactly where she was off to, in case she needed his help even further. All he could think when he saw her enter the floral shop was: *What in God's name is that girl doing?*

A ringing bell was set off when Madison entered, extremely shaky and out of breath. It had been a while since she'd gone without the tube helping her breathe. She took a few quick breaths, instead of the suggested slow and even ones and moved further inside the shop. She didn't have any time to waste.

There were flowers of all kinds inside the tiny shop, everything from the exotic to the carnation and so many in between. Huge balloons, little gifts and stuffed animals were fixed in some sort of display in every corner.

"Are you okay?"

Madison turned to a concerned young employee wearing one of those green flower shop aprons. She attempted to appear as normal as possible. But she knew more than anyone, how sick she looked to a healthy person. She smiled genuinely to the worker and estimated the girl was probably just two years older than she was. She couldn't help but wonder what the girl would be like twenty years from now, or what she did when she was off from her flower shop job, and if she was in love. Like Madison. "I—I need to talk to someone, a manager, if there's one here. About a special delivery I need to order."

The girl nodded sweetly and took Madison gently by the arm. "Why don't you sit here and I'll go get him for you."

Madison allowed the girl to lead her to a chair nearby. She sat quickly and tried to keep her heart rate as steady as possible.

"Just give me a minute to get him. I'll be right back." The girl disappeared behind the counter.

Madison closed her eyes and told herself once more: *Just a few minutes. That's all I need. Keep breathing, in and out. Almost there.* Suddenly, a hand was on her shoulder and Madison opened her eyes.

A tall and skinny bald man was kneeling on the floor by Madison's side, his hand resting on her shoulder. "I'm Michael, the owner. Grace tells me you need a special delivery."

Madison smiled a thank you to the girl named Grace and then turned her attention to the man kneeling on the floor.

He looked at Madison with the kindest eyes and a loving soul. And right at that moment, Madison thought, *he knows.* He knew everything about her.

Her breaths were shallow and she knew she must hurry. She gave a quick glance outside to make sure Annie and Jack weren't having hysterical fits because she wasn't where they left her. "I do. I need a special delivery." She stood wearily and dug into her pockets. She removed a large stack of bills from her jeans and she left them on the counter.

As she explained in great detail exactly what she wanted, what she needed to happen, Michael didn't lose eye contact with Madison, even for a second. When she asked if something like that was possible, he took her hands in his and without hesitation, said he would make it possible.

She knew by this time Jack or Annie or both of them would be searching for her. She just hoped for the lesser of two evils and hoped again it would be Jack and not her mother searching the crowd frantically, or harassing the nice old man sitting on their bench.

She saw him before he saw her and for a moment, she felt guilty about the fib she was about to tell and even more guilt for the concern she must have put him through. She tried to walk without showing any pain and waved nonchalantly to Jackson.

"What are you doing?" He was out of breath and near panic-stricken.

Maybe if she blew it off, he'd calm down. "Nothing. I just wanted to smell the flowers in there." She pointed back to the shop only to find Michael watching her from outside the storefront. She gave him a small wave.

It worked. Jack was already calmer. "Jesus, Maddie. You should've waited. I could've taken you." He put his arm around her and led her back to the bench. Jack listened to Madison breathing with difficulty and did a double take to her face. "Where's your oxygen?"

"I took it off. I needed to save our seats with it."

He shook his head at Madison. "You're so lucky Annie isn't back yet."

Madison grinned to herself. "I'm okay." She did what she came here to do. Everything was in place now.

Almost.

And now she could begin to let go.

Jack sat her back down on the bench. He handed her the oxygen tube and helped her put it back on.

Madison gave a peek to her side and mouthed, "Thank you," to the nice man still sitting a few inches away from her. When she turned her head around to the street, she noticed she could see the road perfectly. Jack somehow moved all the people in front of them, clearing a direct path for Madison. A few people turned around to get a glimpse of Madison and smiled politely to her.

Madison frowned to Jackson as he sat down next to her. "How'd you do that? How did you get everyone to move out of the way?"

"Easy. I just gave 'em the finger." Jack kissed Madison and put his arm around her shoulders.

Annie ran up to them, completely out of breath, holding the milkshake out to Madison. "There you go. You better drink this. All of it."

Madison smiled sheepishly. "Actually, I kinda don't feel like a shake anymore."

Annie stared at Madison. "Mad! You are not serious. I ran all the way there and waited in line for what...fifteen minutes and fought the crowd!"

"Kidding. Totally kidding." She took the shake from Annie and sipped it slowly. It was the least she could do.

The crowd began waving their flags and the sound of a small town marching band was heard in the distance.

Madison looked at Jack. "Hey. We finally got to see our parade."

"Yeah, we did."

めめめめめめめ

Jack carried a sleeping Madison into the house. Even as she slept, they could both hear her breathing had worsened over the last few hours.

Annie closed the door quietly after she entered with the oxygen tank, following Jack. As Jack turned for Madison's bedroom door, Annie stopped him. "Put her on the bed, Jack."

Jack stopped mid-step and faced Annie, knowing what this meant. Maybe he misunderstood. Maybe Annie meant the bed in her room. "Which bed?" He cursed himself for letting his voice crack emotionally, as if he had any control over it.

Annie understood. She walked the tank to the side of the hospital bed and turned to Jack. "This one."

Jack moved ever so cautiously toward the bed where Annie was waiting. He gently placed Madison down flat, removing his hands from under her body with the most care he could, so as not to wake her, his sleeping champion.

Madison groggily opened her eyes and sat up immediately when she realized where she had been laid. She shoved her body to a sitting position before Annie could stop her. "I don't want to be on here. I'm not ready to be here." Tears suddenly dampened Madison's eyes without concern to halt them. She knew what it meant to be on this bed. She was running out of time. She looked to Annie, her eyes pleading. "Mom?"

Annie sat down on the bed and somehow spoke to her with the most soothing voice, like silk, trying to ease her daughter's worst fears. "I know you don't, baby. But, it's all right. It'll be easier to give you the medicine here. Like we talked about, remember? I'm going to stay out here with you and Jack is going to be right in your bedroom. Okay?" Annie caught Madison's falling tears in her hands. She must be strong. Stronger than she ever had been and ever would be for the rest of her life. *The rest of her life. Without Madison.* She couldn't cry in front of her. Instead, she gave Madison a compassionate expression. She tried to ignore the sadness that was lodged in her throat like an over-sized golf ball. "We're gonna have to start the IV soon, Maddie."

Madison's big brown eyes overflowed with tears. She slowly shook her head back and forth. "I don't...I can't..."

Annie lowered her voice as she slowly moved Madison back to a flat position on the bed. She tucked the pillow perfectly under her neck and head, and caressed her face. "We're not going to start it now, okay? But you wanted me to tell you everything as it happens, right?"

Madison nodded slightly. "I still do."

"Okay, then. I'm going to call Daddy. I'll be right back with the phone so you can talk to him and say good night." Annie kissed Madison on the forehead and slid off the bed. She looked back at Madison. "You know what? That bed is a helluva lot more comfortable than the lumpy one in your room."

Jack passed Annie and walked over to the bed. "And you know what else?" He gave Annie a wink and looked back at Madison. "This bed is bigger. So you can share it with your boyfriend." Jack gently hopped on the bed and slid his body down next to Madison. "See? This is going to be great." He snuggled into Madison and did a pseudo-whisper so Annie could still hear. "We can watch TV all night and your mother doesn't ever have to know."

Madison's voice was strained. "I don't want to have to be here."

Jack stopped joking and looked at her seriously. "I know, Maddie. I don't want you to be here either. But it's all right. I'm not going anywhere." Jack wrapped both his arms around Madison as tightly as he could, as if his grasp on her would keep her there with him forever.

❦ CHAPTER 38 ❦

*A*nnie jumped off the couch in emergency mode. She heard Madison immediately and within seconds, was by her side. There was something about the nighttime that made everything far worse then it would've been in the daylight hours. Annie flicked on the lights as she ran to her daughter. "Right here, honey! I'm right here."

Madison couldn't breathe.

When Annie reached her, she was sitting up in her bed, grasping the oxygen tube in her hands as if she was trying to physically push more air into her body.

Annie, in one quick move, kicked the chair away from the bed. She grabbed the oxygen mask she had prepared earlier from the top of a nearby box. She hastily removed the tube from Madison's nose and dropped the large oxygen mask over her head. Annie turned up the amount of oxygen getting to Madison to the highest level on the tank. Then she noticed Jack standing a few feet away wearing a t-shirt and boxers on his body and a scared shitless expression on his face. She was not about to have Madison see him look like that. She yelled to Jack over her shoulder. "Come here and go in the box by my right foot. Take out one of the plastic bags that says morphine."

Jack snapped out of it and dived for the box on the floor.

Annie prepared a needle quickly, and tapped Madison's arm at the same time. She gave her daughter a reassuring face throughout the panicked few moments. "Almost there, baby. Okay? A few more seconds. Are you breathing? Nice and slow, in and out." She listened closely and realized her breathing was still not normal. "Come on, Madison. Nice and slow."

Jack jumped up with three plastic bags and shoved them under Annie's nose. "Here!"

Holding the syringe, she ripped one of the bags out of Jack's hand and tore it open with her mouth. She spit out the plastic on the floor, hastily tested the needle and shoved it into Madison's arm.

Madison whimpered softly through the mask on her face.

Annie took a few needed deep breaths of her own then bent down to her daughter's face. "Okay, baby. There you go. It's all done now. Keep breathing." She checked the line and made sure the needed medication was flowing into her daughter's body. She rubbed Madison's head gently. "You're okay now. See? It's getting better, right?"

Madison tried to nod her head. Little by little her breathing got back to normal.

Jack stood by the bed, still holding the two unused bags.

Annie didn't take her focus off of Madison. With the same soothing voice Annie had been using on Madison, she addressed Jack. "Can you put those bags back into the box for me?"

Jack nodded. "Sure. Yeah." He bent down and inhaled deeply. He put the bags back, closed the box up and slid it a few inches under the bed. He listened to Annie talk to Madison, and stayed hidden, kneeling on the floor to catch his own breath.

"There you go. Close your eyes, honey. We're not going anywhere, okay? Shhh. Let's get you some sleep."

Madison's eyes dropped down and shut.

Annie sat her body up on the bed, not wanting to disturb Madison's rest.

Jack finally stood and looked at Annie in silence.

"You okay here for a minute?" There really wasn't any reason to ask him if he was all right. She knew he wasn't, and there wasn't anything she could do about it.

Jack nodded his head and whispered. "Yeah."

Annie slid her body carefully off the bed and touched Jack's arm. She took a deep lungful of air, walked over to the phone and dialed. She calmly spoke in her head. *Don't get emotional. This could go on for a long time.* She heard David's voice on the other end. "Hey."

She turned her back to Jackson but he could hear her loud and clear.

"I think...I think it's..." She lost her battle with the golf ball in her throat as tears slid out of her eyes. "I think you should come. Tonight, David."

⊛⊛⊛⊛⊛⊛⊛

Madison lay in the bed, her eyes wide open. The wind blew the clouds to the west.

Five days before, Jackson had rearranged the living room

area so the hospital bed would sit alongside the French doors. If they wanted to get outside, which hadn't been lately, they could always wheel her bed out of the way. But now, Jack had thought, Madison would be able to look at the sky all day long...and all night.

She knew there wasn't much time left. She knew it the day of the parade. She had already said the things she wanted to say and did everything she needed to do.

Almost everything.

Jack brought her a bowl of ice and put it on the bed. He took a paper towel, carefully wrapped it around the ice cube, and handed it to Madison.

Madison smiled as much as she could and lifted the mask up over her head. She took the ice cube from Jack and sucked on it.

He sat down on the bed where Madison's knees were. "I made some lemonade ones for later."

Madison grinned and tried to complete the sentence without having to pause for a breath. She didn't succeed. "Variety is...good, right?"

"I kind of like the ice cube I have now." Jack kissed her free hand and held onto it with his fingers. He grabbed the TV remote and hit the power on.

"Where's my mom and dad?"

"They ran to get some groceries. Why? Do you need something? Want me to call them?"

"Not really." Madison slurped on the melting ice.

"So? What should we watch?" He flipped through the channels like only a guy can, a hundred miles an hour.

"Jack?"

He stopped flipping and looked at Madison. "Yeah?"

"Take me to the beach."

"You should stay in here. It's kinda windy today and it's colder than it has been." He flipped through several more channels before Madison got the strength to talk more.

"Jack, please? Just for a few minutes. Please?"

He stared into her pleading eyes. He knew this was the one thing not to do today. Annie was explicitly clear on this one. It was too windy and stormy today. One thing Annie didn't think of...Jack could not say no to Madison. "Hold on." He jumped off the bed and walked to Madison's old bedroom.

Madison listened to him opening and shutting drawers and the smallest of smiles began to form on her face. She won.

Jack returned with a sweatshirt and flannel pajama bottoms. He looked at Madison seriously and gently lowered the comforter that kept her body covered and warm. Down over her chest and past her underwear. Jack was relieved to see the t-shirt covered most of her. He was not about to enter into new territory at this point. Not that he hadn't thought about what could've been, might've been. He had. But he was a healthy teenager. *Healthy*. And Madison was clearly not. He carefully turned Madison's body around to the side so her legs dangled off the bed.

Madison pushed the oxygen mask off her face and left it on the bed. Another thing on Annie's 'not to do' list. "Jack?"

Jack prepared the sweatshirt and tenderly pulled it over Madison's head, fixing it for her as he continued pulling it down over her chest. "Yeah?"

"Thank you."

He nodded, unsure of what he was helping Madison do.

Most likely Annie was going to be mad, if Madison was thanking him. He placed his hands under her arms and lifted her off the bed in one easy motion.

Madison touched the side of the bed for support. This would be the last thing on her list.

Jack grabbed the pajama bottoms from the floor and one leg at a time, lifted them up over her body. He grabbed a jacket and then a large wool blanket from Madison's bed. He draped the blanket over her shoulders and wrapped her body into the wool. He lifted her up in one quick move and carried her in his arms to the beach below.

He spread the blanket out a little, but kept Madison wrapped up cocoon-like in most of it. He positioned himself behind her, enclosing her small frame in his, and rested her head back on his shoulder. They looked up and down the sand at the empty beach. The sky above them darkened by the minute, the sun no longer seen behind the growing set of incoming clouds.

Jack had gotten used to Madison's constant struggle for air, but as they sat there in silence, looking out at the vast body of water before them, he couldn't help but worry even more. "You want me to get the oxygen?"

He felt her head shake no. "I'm okay. I...I just want to sit...here for a few minutes. Just...just like this."

Jack allowed the silence to fill their thoughts before speaking. "I forgot to tell you. They do have scientists in the FBI." He could feel Madison laugh inside.

"What about the CIA?"

"Yep. There too. Both of them."

"Are you guessing? Or...do you know for sure?"

Jack didn't take his eyes off Madison as she continued her stare at the ocean. "I'm pretty sure."

She took a few quick breaths and answered Jack seriously. "Well, then that's what the boy is going to be. The one with the red hair and glasses. A scientist. With the CIA."

"You sure?"

"Positive."

Jack laughed out loud. "What else are you so positive about, champion of mine?"

Madison, still looking at the ocean, answered slowly. Carefully. Lovingly. "I'm positive I'm going to miss you."

He wasn't expecting an answer like that. It's not like he hadn't been preparing himself for a while now, he had, or at best, he had been trying to. But now. With Madison wrapped up in his arms...how could she be taken away from him? His only best friend, his true love, his soul mate? How would he ever be able to exist without her?

He turned his head into her neck, trying to capture that very smell, that very feeling of being lost in someone else.

Madison lifted her chin to him and looked at him. "Jack?"

He could only shake his head no.

"Jack. Look at me." Madison slowly brought her body to face him and touched her hands to his face, lifting his face up to hers. Just as he did to her, the night of their dance.

Tears fell from Jack's eyes. "I'm sorry. I didn't want to do this to you."

"Do what to me? Jack. Please. Look at me."

Jack's eyes finally met Madison's. Each of them with their own set of tears, neither one able to look away from the other. Like every other moment in their lives, they both knew what this one moment meant.

"I wish so many things, you know? But...but the only one I wish for every second...is the wish I could be with you for the rest of your life. More than anything. I wish for that. But you...you have to know I would've rather had this with you for only this short time than...than to have never had it at all. Cause you...you are the very best thing I have ever known."

"I'm so sorry, Mad. I am so sorry." Jack grabbed her and held her tightly against him.

"I know. But, you know what? It's okay." Madison tried to laugh. "It's okay because I did everything I had on my list."

Jack tried to laugh with her and moved her back gently. "You had a list too, huh? Since when?"

"Since I met you."

Jack leaned into Madison and kissed her softly.

Madison pulled away and stared at Jack. "There's one more thing. On my list." Madison deliberately lay down on her side and urged Jack down next to her.

Jack frowned slightly. She could not mean what was going through his mind.

"Please. Before I go."

He looked at the girl lying in front of him. The most beautiful girl he had ever seen and he knew with all his heart, the only one he would ever love truly, like this. He glanced up and down the deserted beach, shaking his head, unsure. "Mad, this isn't—I don't think..."

She lifted her body up on one arm and kissed him with more love than most will ever feel.

"Are you sure? Really sure?"

Madison nodded. "I've never been more sure about anything. Ever."

Jack lowered her back down onto the blanket, kissing her face in as many places as he could. And this time, wrapped both of them up in the blanket. Together.

CHAPTER 39

They say when the time has come to move on, that physically, mentally and spiritually one knows when to let go completely, with no regrets, no reservations.

Madison knew that time was here for her.

Looking over at her father on the couch, she caught his eye, and he gave her a wink. Looking at Annie on the chair close to her head, Annie gave her a smile and a rub on the cheek. She looked at Jackson. He sat on the bed at her feet, like he had been doing since that day on the beach. He hadn't left her side for more than a minute at a time.

And at this time, Madison knew she had no regrets. She reached her hand up to the oxygen mask over her face and tried to adjust it as she spoke. It came out so completely muffled even Annie couldn't translate.

"Wait a minute, Maddie. Here." Annie moved the mask away from Madison's face.

"I want...a piece...of pizza." Her voice was barely above a whisper. But each of them in the room heard her without a doubt.

Annie smiled as sweetly as she could to Madison and put the mask back over her mouth and nose. She shook her head yes as she turned to David with tears in her eyes. "She wants pizza."

David frowned slightly at Annie with a question on his face. "Is that...can she?"

Annie gave David a look he understood in a heartbeat and David nodded.

"Get a few different kinds, okay?" Annie looked at her sweet, precious child. "Get one of everything."

David stood up. "Okay." He moved to Annie and kissed her first. Then he leaned down to Madison's forehead, kissed her lovingly and gave her a wink. "Be right back with pizza, Maddie-girl."

"Thanks, Daddy." It was stifled, but heard by David.

Then Madison moved the mask again so she could be heard and understood clearly. "I want Jack to go too."

Annie exchanged looks with David and Jack and she looked back to Madison. She got it. *I know what she's doing.* "Go on, Jack. You're on a mission with David."

Jack crawled up to Madison and kissed her on the cheek. "Be right back, okay?"

"Love you always, Jackson."

Jackson eyed her face deeply. "Love you always."

Madison nodded to Jack. And in her heart, and in her eyes, she said goodbye.

◌◌◌◌◌◌◌

Madison's breathing was heavy and sporadic as she listened to Annie reading from *Catcher in the Rye*. It had been one of her favorite books of all time and Annie had read it three times already, never complaining about it when Madison begged her to start it all over again. She went over and over each section of Annie's face, memorizing her.

Annie looked at the clock ticking on the wall over the bed. "What do you think? You think they forgot about us or what?"

Madison weakly shook her head no.

"Should we keep reading?"

Madison shook her head no again and tried to take off the mask.

Annie put it back on. "Leave it on, Maddie. I know it's uncomfort—"

Madison's voice came out muffled and Annie lifted the mask up, away from Madison's face.

"I...can't. I can't, Mom."

"Okay. Okay, honey." Annie could no longer fight her tears. She bent down and reluctantly turned the oxygen tank off and ever so carefully, she removed the mask from her daughter's face. She caressed Madison's cheeks with both of her hands.

"I'm...so...so tired, Mommy."

Annie dropped her hands into Madison's and held them tightly. "I know, baby. I know you must be. But you know what? You have been so strong, Maddie. I don't know if I could ever be as strong as you."

"You...you've...always been...this strong." Madison smiled weakly. That's...how...I know...how...to do it. Because...of you."

Annie looked down at the book and let go of Madison's hands. She picked up the book and started to read again. If she read, if she pretended it wasn't happening...*God, don't let it happen. Not yet. Give us one more day.*

Madison's eyes filled with tears. She reached her hand out to Annie's and roughly grabbed her fingers. "Mommy?"

Annie dropped the book to the ground. "Right here."

"I'm scared." The tears, too big and too many for her eyes to hold, cascaded down Madison's cheeks.

"I know, baby. I'm right here with you. I'm right here." Annie cried openly with Madison, unable to make it better this time. The time most important.

"Can I...ask you something?"

"You can ask me anything, baby. Anything at all. What is it?" If keeping a conversation going would keep her Maddie there with her, Annie would never stop talking.

"Do...you think...do you think...they keep track...of time...in heaven?"

Except that question. *She can't go! She can't leave yet!* Her words came out scrambled through her sobs. "I—I don't... I don't know, Maddie."

"I hope they don't, Mommy. I don't want...to know...how long it will be...'til I see you again."

Then slowly, ever so slowly, Madison released Annie's hand, as her own hand dropped lifelessly to the side of the bed.

Then Madison closed her eyes.

And she let go.

Annie jumped up hysterically. "No! NO!!! Maddie! Please, God! No! Madison!" Annie shook her hard and waited for Madison to breathe again. "*Not yet!* Please!" She touched Madison's face with her hands and kissed her cheeks. "Oh God." She laid her body over Madison's as she sobbed.

David saw Annie first. "Oh my God." He ran over to Annie and pulled her off Madison. He hugged her as hard as he could and attempted to calm her down.

Annie collapsed hysterically in David's arms.

David bent down to Madison, and with Annie still in his arms, he kissed her on the cheek. He looked at Annie, with tears running down his cheeks and pulled her to him. "Oh, God. Oh, God." He moved Annie across the room and out the door as fast as he could.

Leaving Jack alone with Madison.

His little champion. His girlfriend. His love for all time.

Jackson dropped the boxes of pizza on the counter and stared at Madison. *It couldn't have happened.* Not without him by her side. Did Madison know? Did she not want him there?

Jack moved to her bedside and stared at this girl who forever changed his world. And now she was gone. He climbed into the bed with her and lay down next to her now pain-free body. They started off as small tears, and wanting to let all of the sorrow out somehow, all of the anger, his tears soon turned into uncontrollable sobs. He picked up Madison's little hand and brought it to his lips. He kissed it gently, over and over, and then held her fingers to his lips. Praying that somehow, some way, his lips, his touch, his undying love, would bring her back to him.

めめめめめめめ

Rain crashed down on the closed and locked windows. "What a screwed up way to say goodbye," Annie said out loud and only for her own ears to hear.

It was almost nine o'clock at night and it was time for her to go home.

Annie stood by the door alone, looking at the beach house that had become their home for a short time. Madison's last home. She sadly glanced around to the furniture she covered up with sheets that morning, leaving it just as she and Madison had found it. She traced her finger over the crisp white cotton as she walked around the space they jokingly referred to as the great room.

The hospital bed remained in the same place Jack had moved it, by the French doors. So Madison could see the sky, Annie thought to herself. *Madison would probably still be looking out at the sky, even on a shitty day like today.*

She knew David was waiting for her in the car. She had screamed for him to stop the car as they were backing out a few minutes earlier. She had to be here, even if only for a few more minutes, with Madison.

As she turned to the door to leave for the last time, something caught her eye.

The pillow. Madison's pillow.

Step by step, she made it over to the hospital bed, Madison's bed. *It's just a pillow,* Annie thought. But it was Maddie's and it would be the last time she could hold a piece of her. Just for one last moment.

Annie lifted up the pillow, held it close to her chest and suddenly gasped for air.

There under Madison's pillow was the wrinkled picture of Annie and Madison. The one Madison had crumbled up in front of Annie the night before they had left for the beach house.

Madison had it with her the whole time. Hidden under her pillow.

Annie set it on the bed and flattened it out as much as she could with her hand. She brought the picture to her heart, and said goodbye to the beach house.

And said goodbye to her Madison.

⚬⚬⚬⚬⚬⚬⚬

Jack walked down his back yard with a shovel in his hand. He didn't care it was sometime after one o'clock in the morning. Nothing mattered now.

Except the box.

He threw the shovel hard into the grass, digging huge holes over every square inch of the yard.

He had turned a few house lights on before he came outside, giving him the slightest ray of light to see.

He looked up at the black sky. And the lack of stars in it.

And he continued to dig.

When the sun began to rise, Jack was still digging. He was beyond physically and emotionally drained. He scanned the enormous holes all over his yard and couldn't help but laugh out loud. He couldn't help but think how Madison would be laughing too. What in God's name would his father say about the new gardening job Jack had executed? *Madison was the one who was supposed to remember where the damn thing was buried.* She had told him she would years ago, that night in his tent. The night they buried their treasure box.

Jack lifted his shovel higher and pounded it further into an already deep hole.

And then he felt it.

His shovel hit something. Jack threw the shovel to the side and abruptly dropped to his knees. He began digging furiously with both his callused hands. He tossed clumps of dirt out of the way and dug some more.

Then it came into plain view.

The box.

He carefully lifted it from the ground and opened it slowly.

And there on the top was the old yellow balloon he had given Madison the day he met her. Jack took it out and held it in his hands. He remembered her like it was yesterday and he remembered what she had said to him. "I'll be your best friend if you give me the balloon."

He remembered the connection they had, and he knew, at seven years of age, it was for his lifetime. He remembered exactly what he had said to her. "*You don't have to be my best friend. You can have it for nothing.*"

That yellow balloon.

He remembered what he had said to her the day they buried the box. "*Wait. Why are we doing this again?*" He remembered word for word what Madison said to him.

"*Cause then when we're, you know, older and stuff, we can dig up the treasure box and remember always being best friends.*"

He could remember every word, every sentence she had ever said to him. Every look she had given him. And he prayed he would never forget during his existence.

"Excuse me?"

Jack had no idea how long the tall bald man had been standing there in his driveway, watching him cry. Watching him pray. Watching him remember Madison. "Can I help you?"

"I hope so. I'm looking for a Jackson Wellington III." He

read the envelope in his hand and a small grin escaped. "Emphasis on the Third."

"I'm uh...that's me."

The man smiled and bowed slightly in Jack's direction. "Well, then. I've got a delivery for you." He disappeared up the driveway.

Jackson put the balloon piece back in the box and stood up.

A white van with MICHAEL'S FLOWERS written on the side, carefully backed down Jack's driveway.

Jack moved half the distance to the van and waited.

The bald man hopped out of his delivery truck and moved to the back. A girl Jackson hadn't noticed until now jumped out of the passenger side and Jack heard the man call the girl Grace.

The man opened both back doors as wide as they could go and bouquet after bouquet of balloons started floating out of the van.

Jack was so mesmerized by the bouquets the girl was removing from inside the van that he didn't notice the man walking toward him with a single yellow balloon.

"This was supposed to come with the special delivery." He handed the balloon to Jack like the piece of rubber was worth a winning million dollar lottery ticket. A note dangled in the air, attached to the bottom of the string.

With that, the man left Jack standing, alone.

Jack took the note in his hands, completely dazed, and slowly and carefully, opened it.

And this was what Madison wrote to Jackson.

"So, Jackson Wellington III....If you're reading this note, I think we both kinda know what must have happened."

Tears fell uncontrollably from Jackson's eyes.

"That was supposed to be a joke. A bad one, maybe, but still. Jackson, I don't know where to even start...so I'll start here. Please, please don't ever feel sad, when you remember me. I know I had the best life. I did. Because I had you with me. I don't know why things happen like they do. Why things don't work out like we plan. Like we want them to. I wish to God I did, you know? I'll ask God when I get settled, if that's in fact where I end up. Another bad joke. Sorry..."

"Remember when we met? And I wanted the yellow balloon? That day will forever be with me. Wherever I go. Wherever I am. You are and always will be my soul mate. My very best friend..."

"I love you, Jack. Love you always...So, I need you to do me a big favor before I go..."

"Take all the balloons, all of them and let every one of them go. And I promise, I promise Jackson, I will be waiting to catch them up above."

Jack watched a tear from his eye fall onto Madison's letter. He wiped his face with his dirty shirt and looked over to the driveway. The van was gone.

But now there were at least twenty-five different bouquets, all weighted down to the ground. Each one had at least twenty balloons in it, some of them had even more. He had never seen so many colors and shapes and sizes, big balloons, small ones. No matter where he looked, there was a different one, a funny one, a weird one. Every balloon, another memory of Madison.

Jack took off in a dead run before he even contemplated telling his feet to move. He ran faster than he had ever run in his entire life, somehow narrowly avoiding the holes. He grabbed the weights that had kept the balloons on the ground and tore them all away.

And one by one, the balloons lifted away from the ground.

And away from Jack.

He untied the last weight from the final bouquet of balloons and held it tightly. He raised his head high up to the sky.

The darkness had given way to crystal blue, and the sun had come out once again.

With the last bunch of balloons in his hand, he yelled as loud as he could into the sky, hoping somewhere, somehow, Madison could hear him.

"Here they come, Maddie! Here they come!"

And then he lifted his arm up as far as it would reach, and he released the very last balloon, the sole yellow balloon Madison had sent to him, her special delivery.

And he let it go.

Up.

Up to Madison.

THANK YOU to all who read my first draft! Mom, Dad, Carol, Kathi, Tamara Watson, J.P., and Charlene Gawronski. A big thank you to my publisher Brad Sexton at Campfire Press.

Thank you to Patti Feeney at the Ice Skating Institute in Dallas, Texas and Dr. Carole Hughes Hurvitz, Dir. of Pediatric Hematology/Oncology, for their expertise. A huge thank you to Dotti Albertine of Albertine Book Design for her amazing talent and Jessica Trussell for her great work. Big thanks to Tracy Herriott for her brilliant photography.

A special thank you to Michelle Kwan for her extraordinary skating. I am forever a fan. Thanks to Christine Peters and Kary McHoul for their wonderful praises.

I'd also like to thank the following people who have believed in me since day one...Uncle Bobby and Aunt Mary Ann, Sybil my BFF, Toni and Gene, Eric, and my two great nieces, Alexa and Makena, aka my Gooberface and Buddhabelly.

A colossal thank you to a few people I could not do without...
To my mom for her love, support and faith in me, for the "story consulting" and blonde hair! I could never thank you for all the extraordinary things you have done for me and continue to do.

To my dad for his continuous love, support and faith in me...for our talks which help me through the day, for your advice and for our mountains. Thank you so much for always knowing what to say. I'm so lucky to have you as my daddy.

To my sister Kathi who will always be "Renie" no matter how old we are! Thank you for being the best sister I've ever had...even if you are the only one! I'm so thankful you're also my true friend.

And B.P., my best friend and my soul mate. There is no one I would rather be on this journey with.